A WEDDING FOR
THE BISCUIT
FACTORY GIRLS

Elsie Mason was born and grew up in South Shields on the real-life Sixteen Streets. Living beside the Tyne Docks inspired her story of the Farley family in *The Biscuit Factory Girls* series. She now lives in Manchester with her partner and their cat and writes full time.

Elsie has always wanted to tell the dramatic story of her own extended family in the form of a multi-generational saga. After years as a writer, The Biscuit Factory Girls series is the most personal and heartfelt tale that she has ever embarked on.

A WEDDING FOR THE BISCUIT FACTORY GIRLS

Elsie Mason

ORION

First published in Great Britain in 2022 by Orion Fiction,
an imprint of The Orion Publishing Group Ltd.,
Carmelite House, 50 Victoria Embankment
London EC4Y 0DZ

An Hachette UK company

1 3 5 7 9 10 8 6 4 2

A CIP catalogue record for this book
is available from the British Library.

ISBN (Mass Market Paperback) 978 1 4091 9654 9
ISBN (eBook) 978 1 4091 9655 6

Typeset by Born Group
Printed and bound in Great Britain by Clays Ltd, Elcograf S.p.A.

MIX
Paper from
responsible sources
FSC® C104740
FSC www.fsc.org

www.orionbooks.co.uk

For Jeremy - with love

Chapter 1

So this was Mavis on the most wonderful day of her life, sobbing in the aisle of the church.

'You gave us away! You got rid of us because you decided you didn't want us anymore!'

She was screaming at the older woman in the fine, dressy outfit at the back of the congregation. She had one finger thrust out, pointing at the woman, her face a mask of fury.

The older woman at the back was shocked and stammering, rising to her feet. Everyone turned to look at her.

'Who asked you here?' Mavis screamed, and her voice echoed horribly inside St Jude's hallowed walls. 'I never invited you to my wedding! I never would have invited you in a million years! Get out!'

Everyone watched as the smart-looking lady started to make a hasty exit. Mavis's groom, Sam, had his arm around his sobbing bride and the priest shot down the aisle, looking annoyed at all the fuss. The organist stopped playing because she wanted to hear what was going on.

As Mavis buried her sobs in Sam's chest, all her wedding guests were chatting and whispering, watching the woman leave.

'I'm going after her,' Irene said impulsively.

'Good idea,' said her sister-in-law Beryl. 'Find out what all this fuss is about . . .'

Less than twenty minutes ago the women of Number Thirteen Frederick Street had all been wondering about the elegant lady at the back of the church and who she might be. The mystery woman had showed up and quietly taken her place and Irene, Beryl and Ma Ada kept glancing backwards and wondering.

'She looks snooty,' frowned Ma Ada, the matriarch of Number Thirteen. She was tiny and indomitable and mother-in-law to almost all the women in the front row of the groom's side of St Jude's. There was hardly anyone at all on the bride's side, which was one of the reasons the smart stranger had stood out so much.

'Who do you suppose she could be? She looks ever so haughty standing staring ahead like that. Look at that big hat on her! Don't look now! She'll see you staring!' This was Beryl, boldest in turning around in her seat to stare at the interloper.

'Don't let her see you being nosy,' muttered Ma Ada.

'Anyway, look!' put in Irene excitedly. 'They're about to start!'

Mrs Richards, the organist, struck up the wedding march and Beryl said to Irene, 'I do think Mavis might have asked you to be matron of honour or a bridesmaid. You've been such a good friend to her . . .'

Irene chuckled. She didn't mind. As far as she was concerned, Mavis could choose who she wanted. Irene didn't get envious like that and she didn't play favourites. Mavis had chosen Bella Franchino, who shared her house with her, to be her chief bridesmaid and, quite unusually, to give her away, too. The pair of them had suddenly appeared in the aisle as the wedding march began. The thing about poor Mavis was that she had no family really, apart from her brother, Arthur, who was currently abroad with ENSA, the Entertainment National Service Association. He was entertaining the troops in Burma, according to Mavis, and so she really had no close relations attending the wedding.

'Eeeh, what's the lass wearing?' whispered Beryl.

Everyone stared at the bride and her homemade gown. This place was packed out with friends and well-wishers from the Sixteen Streets and Wight's biscuit factory where most of the women worked. Mavis was well known for being a dab hand with her sewing machine, making alterations and rustling up new outfits out of outmoded remnants and with her wedding dress she had really excelled herself. Her tiny waiflike body was lost in a torrent of ivory silk.

'Where did she get all of that?' Beryl asked, knowing that Irene would have heard all about it in the weeks leading up to Mavis's big day.

'It's a parachute,' Irene said. 'How Mavis got her hands on it is a saga in itself.'

But it was too late to go into then, because the diminutive bride in her many ruffled layers of silk was advancing down the aisle, wreathed in smiles, and being helped along by her radiant and raven-haired best friend, Bella.

Mavis's big day! Irene Farley thought proudly. *And she's marrying our Sam! She's going to be part of our family now. Who would ever have thought it?*

Mavis Kendricks was the kind of girl people didn't usually notice. She was skinny, pale and dowdy. She was like a little sparrow. Even her beloved Sam said that about her, though he added that she was the kind of little bird that you wanted to take home to look after.

It wasn't that Mavis blended in with the crowd and no one noticed her. It wasn't that, exactly. Certainly, she could make herself stand out when she wanted to. She had a strange rasping, croaky voice and you could hear her squawking laughter across the room, even above the chuntering, grinding noise of all the machines on the biscuit factory floor. And she was known for going on daft. She was a bit loopy, people said, and so she often stood out in the crowd for all the wrong reasons. As far as Sam and her closest friends were concerned, all these things only made her more lovable. And mostly, they did, but sometimes she could get too carried away and someone – often it was Irene – would have to tell the orphan girl to pipe down. Especially now that her lovely brother and lifelong protector Arthur was abroad.

Eeeh, it was such a shame that Arthur couldn't be there! What a terrible thing it was, the war and all that distance between them, preventing him from being here to give his blessing and to celebrate his little sister's happy day. Still, life had to move on and Mavis and Sam were set on the April wedding. If the war had taught anything to the denizens of the much-bombed streets of South Shields, it was that you had to seize life and never delay. You really had no idea what tomorrow might bring.

All the women of the Farley household sat in the front rows of St Jude's as the drunk old bugger of a priest intoned the words and the handsome, smiling Sam clasped Mavis's hands and she stared up at him as if he was a radiant angel come down from the stained-glass windows. Everyone gave out a collective 'aah' as the priest declared them man and wife.

'Well, she's one of ours now,' Ma Ada said, with a little shrug. 'And that's all four of my lads I've seen married now.'

Irene squeezed the old woman's work-sore hand, knowing that she was thinking about the son of hers she had lost last year. Tony, Beryl's husband. She hadn't even seen him buried. Her eldest had been lost at sea, his ship torpedoed off the coast of North Africa. Ma Ada knew better than most that you had to celebrate life while you could, and welcome any new additions to your family when they came. Even slightly daft ones, like Mavis. Mavis Farley, as she now was.

The bride and groom made their way back down the aisle at a stately pace, and they were beaming at everyone they saw. Mavis looked happier than Irene had ever seen her in the whole two years of their friendship. She looked so happy, it was like she could have gone off with a bang. But then at that very moment, Mavis spied the rather grand old lady at the back of the church, conspicuous in her large feathered hat. And that was when Mavis had started screaming, squawking and pointing.

'Get out! Get away from me! You're not welcome at my wedding!!'

Chapter 2

'I'll go after her,' said Irene. Before she knew that's what she'd decided to do, she was hurrying through the grave-yard after the stranger. The April sunlight was bright and sparkling after the gloom of St Jude's and it took her a few moments to pick out the dejected figure in the big hat. There she was, stiff-backed, making her dignified way to the main road.

Whoever she was, Mavis had sent her away with a flea in her ear. It had been a very public, shameful drubbing.

Now Mavis and her wedding guests were clustered in the doorway of St Jude's and the bride was behaving as if nothing untoward had occurred at all. The photographer was getting the gaggle of guests to arrange themselves to his liking.

Irene knew that at any moment her absence would be noticed, but something was compelling her to chase after this mystery woman.

'Hello? Excuse me?' she called, with the soles of her painful shoes borrowed from Beryl scraping on flagstones. 'Are you all right?'

The older woman stopped in her tracks and turned to look at Irene. She was what Irene's mother would have called a refined, smart-looking person, in her tailored costume and that haughty look on her face. She had a rather pointed nose and her eyes, Irene now saw, were pink and watery like she could barely hold the tears back. 'Pardon me?' The woman blinked and stared at the new arrival.

'You seem so upset, and it was awful . . . It was really unlike her – Mavis – to shout like that. In a church and all! I'm sure she didn't really mean to . . .'

'Of course she meant to!' the woman said in a harsh voice. 'Don't talk to me like I'm silly. That girl meant every word she said to me in there. Every single word.'

Irene stood frozen, not knowing what to say next. She was dying to simply ask: Who are you? And what are you to our Mavis? And why did she scream at you like that, as if she really hates you? Irene could hardly believe that such passionate feelings could come pouring out of her funny little friend. Whatever lay behind those feelings must be very serious and dreadful indeed.

The unwelcome guest let out a long bitter breath and said, 'I was a foolish old woman for coming here today. I don't know what I was thinking of. I should have known she wouldn't be glad to see me. But when I saw the notice in the *Gazette* about the wedding, I thought, well . . . maybe I'll just slip in at the back. No one would mind . . .'

'But . . .' Irene said, 'who are you?'

'I thought it might be nice to see her married, the little girl. Just to see her again and to see that she's happy.' Now the lady took out an ironed linen handkerchief and pressed it to her damp eyes. Her eyes were an intense forget-me-not blue. She wasn't a bonny woman in the slightest, thought Irene, but she had the most beautiful eyes. 'I'm Elizabeth Kendricks,' the woman said. 'I imagine your friend Mavis will have told you all about me? About what a terrible person I am and how much she despises me.'

'No,' said Irene, 'she's never said anything. As far as I know, Mavis doesn't despise anyone at all. Apart from

7

Adolf Hitler, of course. She hasn't got a nasty bone in her body, has Mavis.'

The woman who had introduced herself as Elizabeth Kendricks blew her nose like a brief trumpet solo and shook her head. 'I think you'll find that she does despise me. Her and her brother, I imagine they both do. They must do. I've seen neither hide nor hair of them since . . . since . . .' Suddenly those keen eyes fixed on Irene again. 'Where is Arthur, by the way? I couldn't see him in the church. I expected the lad to be giving his sister away . . .'

Irene explained, 'He joined up. Right at the start of the year. He's entertaining. Singing for the troops. Out in Burma. We've had a few letters.'

A wintry smile touched Mrs Kendricks' thin lips. 'Ah, good. Doing his bit. He always had a beautiful voice. He's got a special talent. As does Mavis, in her own strange way. I encouraged him, you know. I was the one . . .' Her words dwindled away and her feelings seemed to threaten to overcome her once more. 'Please, just tell the girl I didn't come to cause a scene on her wedding day. If I'd known she was going to be upset like that, I would never have bothered . . .' Then she turned abruptly and started hurrying off again back towards the busy hurly-burly of Westoe Road.

Irene called out, 'Mrs Kendricks!' But the woman paid no heed.

Kendricks, Irene thought. That was Mavis and Arthur's surname. Of course it was! But what was this Elizabeth to them? Arthur and Mavis had both said they were alone in the world. They were orphans and didn't have connections to anyone else at all . . .

'Irene!' called Beryl, breathlessly running down the sloping path between stone monuments, her court heels clattering like mad. 'You're missing out on being in all the photos,

8

hinny! Ma Ada's shelled out a fortune for the photographer and she'll go berserk if you're missed out! It's a family photo, pet, and there's enough of us missing already . . .'

Beryl looked very ungainly, dashing about in her cream woollen suit. Somehow she looked all knees and elbows, jostling along like a newborn foal. Irene almost laughed at the sight of her, getting aerated over the photos.

'Am I holding them all up?' Irene asked, turning to follow her back to the church.

'Aye! They're holding their positions with fixed bloomin' grins and then they realised you'd whizzed off. Sam told them that you must have been caught short, but I knew you'd run after her, didn't I? I knew you'd want to know who she was.'

'Yes, you're right, Beryl.'

'And did you find out?' Beryl was just as concerned and as nosy as Irene was.

'Not quite. I'm not really any the wiser . . .'

'It was quite an upset!' Beryl said, shaking her head. 'I've never been at a wedding before where the bride started screaming at one of the guests. Not even our Megan did that!'

The mention of Megan reminded Irene that their other sister-in-law was back at Number Thirteen looking after the babies this afternoon. The thought sent a ripple of cold unease through Irene. Some part of her would always feel that she could never fully trust the most glamorous of the Farley girls. She hated leaving little Marlene in her care and it had taken some persuasion for her to leave the one-year-old at home.

'Ha'way, let's get on these pictures then,' Irene said, trying to push her misgivings aside. Beryl grinned at her and Irene felt a rush of affection for the girl who had come running to fetch her. Beryl felt like a proper sister to her.

She had been close to her almost from the start, right from her arrival here in South Shields, less than two years ago. Already they had been through such a lot together. She just knew they were going to be bonded closely for as long as they both lived.

The family group was still assembled rather awkwardly on the steps of St Jude's and Father Michael was bellowing at them about a funeral party that was about to turn up at any moment. Irene took her place, fixing her grin, standing between Sam and his mother. Sam gave her a swift, quizzical look and Ma Ada muttered something irritably, the words muffled under her ugly, crumpled, velvet hat.

'Now, smile, everyone!' Mavis Farley née Kendricks exhorted them all. 'Make it look like we're having the most wonderful time of our lives! *Smile!*'

Chapter 3

The Farley family and all their guests headed to the Robin Hood pub for a small reception. With their wedding outfits covered in homemade confetti, the party ambled up the steep hill from the docks to the top of the Sixteen Streets. They walked at the leisurely pace that was comfortable for Ma Ada and their route was lined by neighbours coming out onto their front door steps to shout greetings.

Mavis felt rather famous and flushed, leading this procession up Frederick Street, Sam's strong arm at her back. 'Everyone's come out to see you,' her new husband told her.

'Aah, get away,' she smiled bashfully, but she knew it was true. She also knew that it was more likely that the people here were stepping out to heap their blessings on the blond, handsome head of Sam, the youngest of the Farley boys. He was a well-known figure in the Sixteen Streets, with his endless energy and laughter, the youngest of a popular clan and, in more recent days, his being able to lay his hands on various rare foodstuffs and luxury goods . . .

Ma Ada was picking bits of homemade confetti off her costume and complaining about it. 'What's this stuff made out of?'

'It's just cut-up pages of the *South Shields Gazette*,' the blushing bride told her. 'It took two whole evenings of cutting out to get enough.'

'Aye, well I wish you'd never bothered,' grumped the old woman. 'What do we all look like, coming up the street covered in bits of old newspaper?'

Actually what Ma Ada thought was that the Farley clan and their closest friends made rather a splendid sight that Saturday afternoon. They were all decked out in their finest outfits and, for once, no one was making a show of themselves. The only hitch had been that strange moment of drama in the church when Mavis had screamed at that woman. Ma Ada was prepared to avoid further drama by not asking Mavis about that moment just yet, but the old matriarch was keen on having some answers soon. It was unheard of! A bride screeching in the aisle like that. And Father Michael! What must the priest have thought? But Father Michael had been three sheets to the wind anyway, so that was lucky.

Still, Ma Ada couldn't help wondering about the woman at the back of the church. Hadn't she seemed somehow familiar? Ada couldn't be sure . . . Anyhow, the whole story was bound to come out in the end. In Ma Ada's experience, she was always made privy to the whole story eventually.

Here in the Sixteen Streets, that's how it had been for many years. Ma Ada was like the old empress of this pocket kingdom. On the hill rising above the South Shields docks, everyone knew her name and gave her respect as the head of a clean, respectable, hard-working family that had roots set deep in this part of the world.

Generations of Farleys had lived in these little red-bricked houses in the narrow streets. A great many of the women had worked at the biscuit factory, whose tower loomed tall over the smoking rooftops, filling the cool breezy air with the lovely scent of baking biscuits. In fact, most of the procession from the church to the pub this afternoon was made up of biscuit factory girls. Mavis's sisters-in-law Irene and Beryl had both worked there, though Beryl had moved on to welding at the shipyard these days. Megan, who was indoors looking after the babies, had worked on the conveyor belt at Wight's biscuit factory too, along with the gaggle of friends who were bringing up the rear this afternoon, covered in newspaper confetti: Gladys, Effie, Plump Mary and the rest of that noisy, excitable crowd.

'It's all lasses,' Ma Ada said, as Irene drew level with her, once they neared the Robin Hood. 'That's why this wedding party's so noisy. It's all giggling and gabbling lasses.'

'That's true,' Irene smiled.

'I wish the lads could have been here, to see Sam wed,' his mother said. Ma Ada knew it was a forlorn hope, but with Bob away in the army and Irene's husband Tom in the air force, neither of them had been able to get leave in time for the wedding of their youngest brother. Both had expressed amazement as well as joy that their Sam had managed to find himself a bride, and that she had turned out to be that funny little Mavis from the biscuit factory. Bob had exclaimed, with his usual bluntness, 'What, that daft little lass who quacks like a duck?'

But there it was. It was true. Sam had seemingly fallen for that little lass who had been making eyes at him for a full year, who'd been carrying a blazing torch for him month after month, determined that she would one day turn his head. Mavis's friends had tried to warn her, don't pin your hopes on Sam. He's too flighty and young, he's in a world of his own, he's not ready for any kind of grown-up commitment yet.

Irene knew better than most that Sam wasn't likely to pay any heed to poor Mavis. Irene knew that he was embroiled in all kinds of entanglements of his own. She knew that young Sam's life was a very complicated thing indeed. But she had been as amazed as all the rest of them when he had suddenly declared his intention to wed Mavis Kendricks in April at St Jude's, in front of them all.

But maybe, Irene had thought . . . maybe he's actually fallen for Mavis's simplicity and open-heartedness. There were no ulterior motives to Mavis. When it came to Mavis, what you saw was what you got. No secrets and no surprises.

Except . . . that's how it had always seemed. After all the screaming in the church aisle today and that strange conversation in the churchyard with the weeping Mrs Kendricks, Irene wasn't so sure about that anymore. Maybe Mavis had some secrets after all.

Just then Irene noticed her widowed sister-in-law Beryl flagging slightly in the middle of the jolly crowd. She braced her up with a swift hug and said, 'I'm sure your Tony is watching all of this. Looking down on us from above and saying, "Eeeh, what a rabble of noisy women." He'd be ashamed of us if he was here!'

Beryl grinned at her, grateful that Irene had realised just what she had been thinking about, as Irene often did. And it was true; her poor, departed Tony would have been abashed at this noisy jamboree of celebrating women. All of them were waving at other women. They were hanging out of windows and crowding on doorsteps. He'd have been all stiff and dignified in his navy uniform, putting up with it all for the sake of the women in his life. But he'd have loved it, really, Beryl laughed. He always said he hated a fuss, but he'd have been so proud of Sam today.

Aye, Sam had never looked so handsome and grown up and manly as he did today. He was wearing an exceptionally smart blue blazer with shining buttons. His wedding outfit, like his bride's, had come from Mavis's extensive wardrobe of reclaimed and renovated costumes.

'He looks like a movie star,' Bella from the ice-cream parlour said. 'And so does Mavis, doesn't she?'

Irene and Beryl weren't quite so sure about that. The beautiful and warm-hearted Bella was being overgenerous in her appraisal, but that didn't matter really – so what if Mavis looked like a secondary character, a funny cousin or a silly friend of the lead character? Somehow she had managed to wind up marrying the romantic lead! It just went to show: real life didn't always follow the same storylines as simple-minded Hollywood movies. Mavis and Sam were in love with each other and now their stories were forever twined together.

Irene reached out for her friend Bella's hand. 'She'll always be daft Mavis to us. I don't suppose marriage will change her all that much.'

'I don't suppose it will,' Bella laughed.

'You're next, lady,' Beryl told the Italian girl. 'You're the only one of us who's not spoken for yet!'

Bella looked surprised at this. 'I've got enough on my plate,' she said. 'I've got a business to run and a new home to find for myself. I don't need to go mooning about after some fella.'

They were interrupted then by Ma Ada's raucous shout. She could raise her voice until it seemed impossible that so much noise could emerge from so tiny a body. Framed in the doorway of the Robin Hood's public lounge bar, she bellowed at the wedding guests: 'The first drink for everyone is on the Farley clan! After that, you can all buy your own! Ha'way! Where's Aunty Madge to play the piano? It's time we got this party going!'

Chapter 4

So many births, marriages and deaths had been celebrated at the Robin Hood pub at the top of Frederick Street; there had never been any question about where the reception would be held. All the Farleys had assumed it would be in the usual place and Mavis was only too happy to go along with those plans. For once in her life, she was feeling included at the centre of everything going on and it felt wonderful to her.

In her ivory silk parachute, she took up at least twice the space she usually did in the public bar. The landlady raised a glass to her and loudly congratulated her on becoming Sam's wife and then she offered her a drink. Mavis flushed with pleasure and accepted a large brandy, grinning at the landlady, Cathy Sturrock, as the room filled up around her and old Aunty Madge started bashing away at the yellowed keys of the piano.

Sam came to stand with her and everyone cheered as he pecked her glowing cheek. 'I'm starving,' he told her. 'Can you see any sandwiches out yet? Cathy promised us she'd have the buffet ready when we got back here.'

'Starving?' Mavis laughed. 'I couldn't eat a thing. My stomach's still churning with nerves.'

'You have nothing to be nervous about,' her new husband said. 'We've done it. It's all done now.'

She gave him a funny look and tipped the rest of her burning brandy down her throat. 'I'm talking about tonight. I'm talking about the start of our married lives together.' Her eyes went so wide and her expression was so earnest that Sam had to smile at her. He had always found the way she just burst out with whatever she was thinking very comical. Now, however, she was anticipating their wedding night, which they were due to spend under his mother's roof, in his usual room and he found himself growing embarrassed.

'Hush for now pet,' he told her. 'Otherwise you'll have everyone talking about it and they'll start talking mucky and you won't want that.'

Mavis set down her glass. 'Enough talking, then! Dance with me, Sam!'

Gladly he took her in his arms and whirled her into the middle of the bare wooden floor and the crowd of guests parted for them. They whooped and clapped at the sight of the newlyweds.

At the bar Irene was ordering a trayful of drinks for the Farleys and reassuring Cathy Sturrock that all had gone well in the church.

'I wish I could have got down for the service,' Cathy said. 'I love a good ceremony, but I wanted to do all the sandwiches for the spread myself, right before everyone arrived. Keep them fresh. I just couldn't get away.'

Irene found herself wishing that Cathy had been able to be there too. Cathy was in her fifties – though you'd never think it to look at her with her creamy, unlined complexion and her sensational figure – and she had been around in South Shields for a long time. Perhaps she would have recognised the smart older woman who shared a name with the bride and who had been the cause of such a fracas this afternoon.

'And I wish Bob could be here, too,' Cathy said, plonking the last two brimming glasses down on Irene's tray. 'He's devoted to his baby brother Sam. He will be so upset, wherever he is in the world.'

'I know,' Irene tried to smile reassuringly at Cathy. Not everyone approved of Cathy and Bob's fairly recent union – the fact that Bob had left his wife Megan and their then unborn child living at Number Thirteen in order to take up with this buxom landlady. But Irene knew that it was the right thing for all concerned. She had hardly seen a happier couple together than Cathy and her somewhat younger pot man, Bob. And he was better off with her than he'd ever been with Megan.

The thought of Megan gave Irene a sharp stab of guilt. She wondered if she could nip back home and see how her middle sister-in-law was getting on with the babies . . .

'Get them drinks passed round,' Beryl shouted in her ear, over all the hullabaloo from the piano. 'Come on, you're in a daydream, hinny.'

Irene smiled at her and gave Ma Ada her milk stout and Beryl her tot of sherry. It did feel like a proper celebration, standing around in the daytime holding fancy drinks like this. After the long, tense months they had endured in recent times it felt like it was about time they could let their hair down a little, push back all the tension and fear they felt for their missing boys and the threat of air raids and invasion and everything else, for perhaps just a few joyful hours.

It was enough that Irene didn't have to listen to the war reports on the radio for just a few hours. For today, the dreadful battles could rumble on across the world without her attention . . .

'Cheers!' Beryl cried and clinked her little glass to Irene's own glass of beer, and Bella's and Ma Ada's.

'Well, here we are,' Ma Ada said, relishing her first sip. 'I shall have to give a lovely speech soon, so I shan't want to get too tipsy.'

'I'm looking forward to the spread,' Beryl admitted. 'I'm sure Sam will have managed to get hold of something fancy through all his connections.'

'Oh, his connections,' Bella rolled her eyes. The ice-cream parlour owner didn't approve of Sam's black market activities. Not wholly.

'I've heard,' Beryl lowered her voice and they all leaned in, 'he might just have got hold of some tinned salmon. That's what Mavis was hinting at the other day.'

'Tinned salmon!' Irene gasped and felt her mouth watering almost at once. She glanced over at Cathy Sturrock, who had been labouring over the finger sandwiches that morning. She hadn't given any hint as to what might be in the sandwiches. Meat paste had been Irene's assumption. Salmon would be spectacular. She could already imagine the lovely crunch of those soft little bones between her teeth.

'Ooh, look who's come in,' Ma Ada said, rather caustically, and they looked to the saloon door to see a skinny, rather overdressed young woman in a bizarre, fluffy yellow hat, making her way into the smoky room. Irene's heart sank a little at the sight of Lily Johnson, but Beryl cried out with glee and waved her arm energetically to get her attention.

'You hoo! Lily!'

Irene was surprised to see Beryl waving the arm she had broken at work only a matter of weeks ago. She recalled how she had fallen on it, having tripped up while welding at the shipyard, and it being this very same Lily Johnson who had been with her at the time. Some had blamed Lily for Beryl's accident but the fact of the matter was that Lily had been the one to look after Beryl when she was rolling and writhing in pain on that cold, wet metal floor.

'Eeeh, it's good to see you, hinny,' Beryl said to her fellow welder warmly.

'When are you coming back to the shipyard?' Lily asked her. 'It's hopeless without you. Just me and all those rough fellas. They're no company at all.'

'Soon,' Beryl promised. 'Who have you brought with you? Who are these two fellas?'

Irene thought it was typical of the showy, gobby Lily Johnson to bring two men as her beaus to a wedding do. She felt herself pulling a disapproving face as the vivacious young woman introduced them to a mostly bald young fella with rather large ears she called Alan and then a very tall, strapping ginger-haired fella with a moustache who she reckoned was Lily's brother, Jonas.

'Oh, you're the young fella from the butcher's shop on Fowler Street,' Irene said, shaking Alan's hand and finding it cool and dry. There was a faint scent of mince about him, she thought, even in all the smoke and sweat and alcohol fumes of the bar. Then she looked up at the tall and handsome Jonas and she couldn't help staring at him for slightly too long. So this was one of the Mad Johnsons! From everything she'd heard about them they were all supposed to be like trolls and troglodytes. But this young lad was beautiful! An Adonis! She felt Beryl nudging an elbow into her side and whispering into her ear, 'Just take a look at her brother! Just look at him!'

Then the bride had spotted them. There came an excited squawking and Mavis was bustling into their midst, clutching her frothing ivory skirts up in both hands and offering her damp cheek for the newcomers to kiss. 'Aw, it's lovely to see you at my do,' Mavis told her. 'How would you like to give us a song, Lily?'

Irene winced and knocked back the rest of her ladylike half of warm beer in order to hide her expression of dismay. In her experience Lily Johnson had a godawful voice. The last thing they needed was to listen to her warbling on.

But Mavis looked eager and excited as Lily graciously agreed to sing. 'Of course I'll sing for your wedding!' Lily cried. 'But is it true there's tinned salmon sandwiches for tea?'

'Oh, yes,' Mavis nodded. 'Sam managed to lay his hands on some.'

Ma Ada tapped Irene on the shoulder to get her attention. 'Those Mad Johnsons. Who invited them? It was them posting death threats through our front door on Christmas Eve! We don't want to be giving the likes of them any invites to our family do's!'

Then Lily was making her determined way through the crowd towards the old upright piano and Auntie Madge.

It was time for Lily to entertain.

Chapter 5

Lily gave them 'You Made Me Love You' and 'Run, Rabbit' and the whole pub stopped to listen, entranced by the huge voice coming out of that slight frame. Even Irene had to admit that the girl's performance was better than it had been when she'd seen her sing at the Christmas dance. Why did she have to wear that jet black wig though, and make-up that made her look like a clown? It was as if Lily actually enjoyed drawing attention to herself, something Irene hated doing.

'Well, she can certainly carry a tune,' Beryl said admiringly as the whole room shook with applause and the dancing began once more.

'Ma Ada's right, though,' Irene mouthed. 'Those Johnsons were sending us awful threats not so long ago, and that Lily had a fight with our Megan in the street, remember? With everyone watching.'

'Aye,' said Beryl. 'But perhaps it's time everyone made peace with everyone else. There's enough conflict going on in the world, without people in our own town being at each other's' throats?'

Bella was clustered with them at the bar, but she wasn't listening. She was staring at the tall redhead who was apparently Lily's brother. 'I've seen him from a distance before,' she told the others. 'Since I've been living with Mavis and Arthur, I've got used to seeing them Mad Johnsons in the street. They go around like they own the place and they're a rough-looking lot. I think Jonas over there got all the looks in their family . . .'

'He certainly did,' said Beryl, smirking at Bella Franchino's frank admiration for the young man.

Then Cathy Sturrock was clanging the bell and announcing that the buffet was all laid out ready for them in the Select, and they must attend to it at once before the sandwiches went curly. Yes, it was true too that some of them were actually tinned salmon! But folk mustn't fight over them since there wasn't quite enough to go around and some would just have to make do with paste.

'I still don't feel like eating a thing,' Mavis was saying happily as the others dashed past her. 'My stomach's bubbling with all the excitement.'

'Aah,' Lily Johnson hugged her. 'You enjoy all the excitement while you can, hinny. Mind, it might only be a bit of trapped wind. That dress looks pretty tight.'

'I wanted to show off my figure,' Mavis said.

Lily tended to think that Mavis looked a bit like an ironing board but she refrained from commenting. Let the lass enjoy her day. Let her feel wonderful and like the belle of the ball. Lord knows Mavis had had little enough joy and fun in her short life so far.

Lily knew a little more about Mavis's past life than most people round here did. She knew that it had been mostly disappointments and disasters and so it was good to finally see her happy, even if it was one of those insufferably smug Farleys that she had married. That Sam! What a drip he was. Messing about in her own family's affairs. Nicking stuff from them, even! He'd had to be taught a lesson or two, that lad. Maybe now he was a married man, he'd be less hopeless and more dependable.

Mavis was saying, 'You should go and get one of the posh sandwiches, pet. You deserve it after singing so beautifully.'

'Oh, I couldn't manage a thing,' Lily said. 'I'm right off my food.' It was true, she looked skinnier than ever. Her face under all the make-up looked rather sickly and wan, now that Mavis had a good stare at her. 'I'm all right,' the Johnson girl said. 'It's Ma. Well, you know how badly she's been. She's not stirred from her sickbed for three months and she's only had the doctor in once. She hates him. She lives in fear that he'll drag her off to hospital and she'll never come out again.'

'So it's you looking after her morning, noon and night then?' Mavis asked, suddenly grasping why the girl looked so frazzled. Lily was still in her teens but she looked ten years older.

'My brothers can't do it, can they? They can't bathe her and whatnot. Of course they can't. It has to be me. Like she says, that's the whole point of having daughters, isn't it? So they can look after you when you're ailing.'

'You must be knackered though,' Mavis said. 'You're still working at the shipyard every day too, aren't you? Then running home to look after everyone there.'

'It has to be done,' Lily shrugged. 'What else can I do?'

'I think those brothers of yours should be helping more,' Mavis said firmly.

'Huh, men,' said Lily. 'You can't ask them to do anything. Tell you what though, when I get married I'll make my fella treat me like the Queen of Sheba. I'll make my husband run around after me like mad.'

Mavis grinned at her and nodded at Lily's beau from the butcher's shop. 'Is that him then? Will you marry Alan over there?'

24

'Not yet,' Lily shook her head. 'He's going off to sea, did I tell you? Like poor Beryl's man, Tony. Let's see if he comes back first and then we can think about the future.'

Lily's brother Jonas came loping back from the Select, standing a whole head taller than everyone else around him, his bright hair shining in the smoky light. He held a plate of sandwiches aloft. He had a pronounced limp, Mavis realised, as he made his way across the room. 'I've nabbed the salmon,' he laughed. 'Here, you've both got to eat one.'

'Oh, all right,' Lily said, and her eyes squinched up with pleasure as she bit into the soft stottie bread and the rare treat of the flaky pink salmon inside.

'Ooh, this is lovely,' Mavis mumbled through a mouthful, finding that her appetite was returning. 'Were there any sausage rolls as well?'

Ma Ada loved a good raucous do as much as the next woman but by nine o'clock that night her ears were ringing and her eyes were stinging from all the smoke and she was longing for a sit down on her usual comfy chair beside the dresser in her parlour. Also, there was Lucky the cat to feed. He'd be going crackers, not used to being left at home all day by himself. He was a good cat but could get fractious when his routines went awry.

Also, the head of the Farley clan became irritable when people got daft drunk and started going sentimental and sloppy. By nine o'clock that's how many of the party were starting to behave. That kind of silly drunkenness tended to remind her of her husband and she had an aversion to all that carry-on. She knew how people's moods could flip when they were as soused as that.

She caught hold of Irene's arm. Sensible Irene was only mildly tipsy, of course. 'I'm going home to see to Lucky.'

'Oh,' Irene said. 'I've been over three times to check on Megan and to see that the babies were all right. I could have fed the cat then if you'd reminded me.'

'Are the bairns okay?'

'Megan's looking after them fine,' said Irene, looking relieved. 'Why not stay for a while yet?'

'Nah, I'm glad of the excuse to slip away, to be honest,' said Ma Ada. 'Getting a bit of a headache and I'm dying for a decent cup of tea.'

Irene smiled. 'I won't be long after you,' she said, though the wedding party itself was showing no signs of letting up. The music was still pounding and the floorboards seemed to be shaking loose underfoot. 'Eeeh look, Mavis has split her dress under the arms while she's been dancing.'

'Daft lass,' said Ma Ada, tutting and shaking her head. 'I tried telling her she needed more give under the pits, but she wouldn't be told.'

That was Mavis's problem in a nutshell, Irene thought. She simply wouldn't be told, not when it came to something she had her mind fixed on. She might seem dopey to some but there was a fierce and dogmatic personality underneath all that flightiness of hers.

'Right, I'm off, before anyone notices me going,' said Ma Ada and nipped out of the saloon door.

She breathed in the cool air of dusk with relief and stared at the vista of the darkening skies over South Shields. The blackout curtains were down over the pub windows and no light could emerge onto the cobbled street. Only the muffled thumping of the festivities could be heard out here. Frederick Street was mostly silent. Almost all of its inhabitants were inside the pub.

Taking her time, wincing a little on her arthritic knee and hip, Ma Ada made her way down the hill to Number

Thirteen. Lucky would undoubtedly be in a sulk with her, coming back so late. He would turn his back and flick his tail imperiously. And oh, but she could taste that first sip of sweet tea already. How welcome it would be. It had been such a long day since setting out for St Jude's this morning.

As she approached Number Thirteen, she realised there was a man standing on the pavement right outside. Of course there was no street light and so she couldn't make out who it was standing there in a flat cap and shirt sleeves.

'Hello?' she said and her voice came out as quavering and nervous-sounding. Then her heart leapt up inside her. Maybe it was one of her lads, come back unexpectedly to surprise his ma? The figure was very tall. Could it be Tom, maybe?

But that thought was quickly squashed by what happened next. It all happened so quickly that Ma Ada could barely take it in. The figure of the man convulsed and twisted suddenly and raised something high above his head. He reminded her of a bowler in a cricketing match and sure enough he was throwing something as hard as he could manage.

A brick! He was chucking a bloody brick through her front parlour window!

The crash was deafening on the silent street. A horribly violent noise, muffled by the thick curtains on the other side.

'Hie!' she squawked. 'You bugger!' She was appalled that someone could be attacking her home. 'Come back! Come back here, you bloody bugger!'

But the tall man had turned away and was running down Frederick Street as fast as his long legs could manage, away from the scene of the crime. In the moonlight over the Sixteen Streets, Ma Ada could see that the hair under his cap was flaming red. Then he turned at the bottom of the street and was gone.

She stared at the jagged hole in her beautiful bay window and she cried out in sheer rage. Adolf Hitler and his bully boys of the Luftwaffe hadn't managed to smash her windows with all their bombs and planes! But now some bugger on the street had done just that!

And all on what should have been one of the happiest and proudest days of her life.

Chapter 6

It was Monday and all the girls were back at the biscuit factory.

It was a bright spring morning and quite warm in the packing room as soon as work begun. The supervisor, Mrs Clarke, was frowning as the girls donned their pinnies and hairnets. She was alert to a kind of festive atmosphere. She wasn't sure what it was to do with until the newlywed Mavis arrived in the room with Irene. As soon as she appeared, a raucous cheer went up from Plump Mary, Effie and the others.

Mavis went puce. 'Oh, shut up!' she laughed, hurrying to her station.

The whole roomful of two dozen ladies should have been standing calmly at their benches, ready to work, but some of them were crowding around Mavis, and the girl was hiding her face.

'Here, what's going on?' cried the supervisor, who hated any kind of fuss and nonsense on her watch.

Irene stood well back, looking on ruefully as Mavis giggled and protested at being centre of attention. It was only a kind of mock protest, though, Irene thought.

'Tell us about it!' Gladys yelled at her.

'What was it like?' Effie laughed.

'Was it everything you imagined?' squawked Plump Mary. 'Honestly, when it was me, I had no idea what was going to happen. I was that innocent!' There was a roar of protest from the others over this. 'No, it's true!' Mary cried. 'By the time it was all happening and he was . . . well, you know . . . I was just about hysterical. And then I laughed! His face was so serious and the whole thing was so ridiculous, I just started laughing and I couldn't stop. My fella was awfully upset . . .'

The other girls weren't really listening to Mary's tale. They were keen on hearing how Mavis had coped with her wedding night, and what she had to say about connubial bliss. To all her friends in the biscuit factory and elsewhere, Mavis was mostly a figure of fun. They were fond of her, and some of them were even close enough to have been invited to her wedding, but it was true to say that they never quite thought of it as a friendship between equals. They tended for the most part to think of Mavis as defective somehow, and inferior, and they patronised her something rotten. Mavis seemed oblivious to this, but Irene wasn't, and the Norfolk girl felt her strong, sisterly, defensive instincts start to kick in at these moments.

'Leave the lass alone,' Irene said to them all, sounding more fierce than she had intended. 'She doesn't have to tell you lot all her private business!'

'But she wants to tell us, don't you?' laughed Effie. 'Look at her little face. It's all lit up. Why, she's even got a bit of colour in her cheeks! I think we all want to hear about what's livened her up!'

'I reckon we know what's done that,' Gladys crowed. 'It's that Sam of hers! By, he's a bonny lad. I still don't understand how a skinny little article like Mavis managed to nab him . . .'

There was a ripple of unkind laughter at this and, just as Irene was preparing to shout at them again, there came a thunderous yell from the supervisor. 'Will you please stop talking smutty nonsense and get on with your work!' Mrs Clarke stormed into their midst like a tank, scattering them all back to their workspaces. As the sniggering died down, she turned to Mavis and asked her, 'Are you all right, my dear?'

Mavis nodded dumbly.

'If there is anything you need to ask a more experienced woman of the world, then do not hesitate to come to me in private, my dear. I am a fund of knowledge to do with everything you might be uncertain about.'

There were more sniggers at this, but Mavis looked grateful. 'Thank you, Mrs Clarke, but I think I . . . we . . . can manage all right, thank you.'

The supervisor nodded and turned to leave. 'Love is a mysterious business, but married life is something you must work at, my dear. And always remember that men are not like us ladies. They are all beasts.'

Then she swept out of the room and they were left to get on with their paste pots and the endless penny packets of custard creams.

Marital advice from Mrs Clarke, Irene thought to herself. She wondered what kind of married life the widow woman had had. She couldn't picture it exactly. Probably she had been married to some weak little man who she was able to boss around. Perhaps she had mithered him to death?

As the morning's work went on and the noise of the conveyor belts dulled their ears, Irene found herself growing drowsy with the repetitive task before her and the warm sunlight coming through the high windows. She was jolted out of a reverie when she realised that Mavis had crept closer to her side and was confiding in her. No one else could hear, but she was telling Irene things that all the other girls wanted to hear.

31

'The thing is,' Mavis said in her strange, raspy voice. 'It wasn't really exactly what I was expecting. That's why I was blushing and didn't know what to say to the lasses earlier . . .'

'Mavis, you don't have to tell the lasses anything about it at all,' Irene reassured her. 'It's not their bloomin' business, is it?'

'But I thought it would be different,' said Mavis, looking more cheesed off than Irene had seen her for a while. 'I thought I'd feel . . . well, like a proper woman now. Like all the rest of them. As good as the rest of them, and I could joke and make rude remarks back at them . . .'

'Eeeh, Mavis,' Irene said, her heart going out to her. 'You're already as good as any of that lot. As good as anyone at all!'

Her new sister-in-law looked so woebegone then that it was pitiful. Irene tried another tack, 'What do you mean, it wasn't exactly what you were expecting?'

'It was just . . .' Mavis stared down at her hands as they absently fiddled with the penny packets before her. Even without thinking about it, her fingers cleverly went about their business, dabbing just the right amount of glue onto the waxy paper. She sighed and said, 'I'm not sure we were even . . . doing it right. Sam didn't seem very sure. And then when I asked, he got a bit cross with me.'

'Oh, Mavis!' Irene said. 'Cross on your wedding night? You never had a row, the two of you?'

'No, nothing like that, exactly,' said her friend. 'We just . . . haven't found the way yet. I mean, they talk about doing what comes naturally, don't they?'

Irene nodded.

'Well, it didn't feel very natural yet, that's all.'

'I'm sure you'll work it out, the pair of you,' said Irene. She felt embarrassed, suddenly picturing their Sam in the middle of some dreadfully confusing, awkward scene with Mavis. It wasn't something Irene was keen to conjure up. 'Now, shall we get on with our work and we can chat again at break time?'

Mavis nodded wordlessly.

When break time came around they took their bread and dripping to a far corner of the yard, away from the other, prying lasses. They sat down by the fence and through a mouthful of stottie cake Mavis said, 'I think what put a shadow over the whole day for me was that woman.'

'Oh?' asked Irene. She was all bristling attention suddenly, hoping that Mavis was going to explain who Mrs Kendricks in the feathery hat actually was.

'Don't get me wrong. I had a lovely day. I was so grateful to everyone. To all the Farleys . . .'

'You don't have to feel grateful,' smiled Irene.

'Oh, but I do, pet,' rasped Mavis. 'You've all made me feel like I fit in and belong with you. You have no idea how that feels to a person like me.'

Irene took a bite of slightly stale bread and waited for Mavis to go on.

'That woman though, turning up uninvited like that. Giving me a shock like she did. That's what unsettled me on my wedding day. It was like she was there to put a hex on me . . .'

'A hex!' Irene scoffed. 'I'm sure that's not true.'

'You don't know anything about it,' Mavis shot back, more snappishly than she intended.

'Well, who is she?' Irene asked. 'You haven't explained about her yet . . .'

'I don't want to talk about her,' said Mavis, and then the hooter blew noisily, calling them back inside the biscuit factory.

When they were home early that evening they saw that Ma Ada had managed to procure some hardboard from somewhere, and Sam had nailed it into place as a makeshift repair to her front-room window.

'I'm still finding splinters and shards of glass lying about in there,' the old woman groused as she sat in her parlour, nursing her tea. 'The poor cat's lucky not to have his paws cut to ribbons, walking about the place.'

Irene commiserated. 'What a thing to do on the night of a wedding like that! Who could have done such a thing?'

Ma Ada's expression turned dark. 'I know. It's obvious. And if you'd seen the back of that fella hightailing it down Frederick Street, you'd agree with me, our Irene. I saw his hair in the moonlight and it was bright red. It was that fella! The Johnson brother who was at the reception with us.'

'Never in the world!' Irene shook her head. 'But he seemed so nice . . .'

'He must have slipped out of the pub just before I did,' Ada went on. 'And I disturbed him in the middle of his nasty business.'

'But why would he even do that? Put a brick through your window?' Irene asked.

'Same reason they put a nasty letter through our door on Christmas Eve. They're trying to frighten and intimidate us, that's what they're trying to do.' Ma Ada's face crumpled and she let out an uncharacteristic sob. She covered her face with both hands for a moment, and Irene moved towards her. 'Nay, I don't need your cuddles, lass,' the old woman growled. 'I just want an end to this bother.'

In the scullery, Mavis was attempting to make a start on tonight's supper, it being her turn on the rota that Beryl had drawn up. She was staring at the almost-empty pantry nervously. When Irene came to help her out, she said, 'I think Ma Ada is right, you know. About that Jonas fella, with the red hair. It may well have been him.'

'But why would he be at a party and accepting our hospitality one moment, and then doing something as awful as chucking a brick through the window the next?'

Mavis shrugged. 'It's how they carry on, those Mad Johnsons. I've told you before, I live down their way, and I've seen them at close quarters. If one of the older ones in the family gives one of the others a job to do, then they do it. No questions, no excuses.'

'Well,' said Irene, 'I think that's horrible.'

'They put their family first, above everything,' said Mavis. 'But then, so do the Farleys, don't they? That's what you're all like. You stick together.'

'Yes, but we don't do anything criminal or violent,' Irene protested. 'Now, look. I'll give you a hand with dinner tonight, if you need me. It's a kind of meat pudding with the few bits of scrag end left, and riced potato and suet . . .'

'Thanks, Irene – I'm not much cop at cooking, really. I've been lucky with Bella living in with us. She's cooked lovely things. But I reckon I'd better start learning, hadn't I? Now that I'm a married woman . . .'

Chapter 7

Ma Ada wasn't really scared of anything. Not even the Nazis. Well, not until recently anyway.

The Germans had been flying over Tynemouth for what felt like a hundred years in their droning, evil engines. They'd been dropping fiery death at random on homes and people she knew. She had listened to the radio each night through all the hostilities, paying heed to all the dreadful things they did. That man Hitler's shrieking gibberish made her feel sick with dread.

But Ma Ada of Number Thirteen, Frederick Street was indomitable. She had been through so much in her life. She had faced pain, poverty, mortality and ruin again and again. It took an awful lot to scare her.

Even having to leave her home in the middle of the night to sit in a dank bunker with all her neighbours hadn't really scared her. It was cold, clammy and inconvenient and she'd been irritable all night, but she wasn't frightened exactly. Even the night that she'd been stuck in the house during an air raid hadn't been terrifying because Irene had been there with her. The two of them had been distracted by Irene's sudden revelation that she was going to make Ma Ada a grandma. Some things, the women realised, were more important than the possibility of impending death.

But then, Tony had changed all of that.

He had been her firstborn son and in many ways her favourite, though she could never actually say that out loud. But, as he grew up tall and strong, it was Tony's independence of spirit and his own innate courage that allowed his mother to feel brave, too. She didn't have to fret over his safety. Even with a dad as feckless and drunken as his was, there was no need to worry about Tony. Even living in a rough and tumble, and sometimes perilous, place like the Sixteen Streets, he had looked life in the eye and squared his broad shoulders. He had proved to his ma that not only could he look after himself, but he could keep her safe, too.

For many years she had felt so secure, in her little house down by the docks. She was surrounded by her boys. Four of them. She had created them herself, out of her own body. Four thinking, reasoning adult men who were strong enough to defend the good name of the Farley clan and everyone who belonged to it.

But then three of them were called away to war. Bob went into the army, Tom into the air force and Tony into the navy. Only Sam with his irregular heart was allowed to stay with her.

Ma Ada had kept strong and brave for week after week, month after month. She listened and waited and prayed. She celebrated with them when they came home on leave when they could, overjoyed to welcome them home. But each time she waved them off again, fear was stealing into her heart. It was like her ageing heart was leaky and defective. Salt water was getting in. She could feel its chilliness sloshing around inside her when she tried to sleep at night.

Then Tony's ship went down somewhere off the coast of Tunisia towards the end of last year. His name was on the list of the dead. His beautiful body was at the bottom of an ocean neither she nor his widow Beryl were ever likely to see for themselves.

It was after this that Ma Ada started to feel real fear.

It can happen to us. To our family. It isn't just something happening to others.

And then she thought: we aren't special. We aren't immune. We aren't invulnerable bystanders in this great big human catastrophe.

She found herself wondering: what if they all get taken from me? What if I lose all of my boys through this?

That was when she really started to feel frightened.

She didn't care for herself. That was just pain and an end to a lifetime of struggle and besides, she knew she had a lovely spot in heaven all marked out for herself (or so she resolutely expected). It was her lads she was frightened for. Her remaining boys. If they all died too soon – like Tony – then there really was no point in anything, was there? All that arduous living hadn't been worth the bother, had it? It really would have been a colossal waste of time. To Ada, that was the most frightening thing of all: if it all added up to nothing.

'You can't fight it, Ada,' her best friend Winnie had always told her. 'It's all mapped out from beginning to end. It all means something, of course, but that's not for us to know about. It's a mystery.'

Winnie was gloomy, with her witchlike hair and her prognosticating with tea leaves and palms. Sometimes Ada didn't even know why she was friends with her.

'Do you want me to do you a reading?' Winnie asked her.

'Nah, hinny,' Ma Ada told her. 'I think I'll just take the future as it comes.'

'But we could find out about what these Mad Johnsons are up to,' Winnie said energetically. 'Maybe we could be ready for the next stunt they try to pull . . .'

Ada sighed heavily and wished Winnie would keep her voice down. The two of them were queueing in the butcher's shop on Fowler Street on Tuesday, and she knew that others would be listening in. Winnie always seemed to draw attention to herself, and mention of the Mad Johnsons always made people prick up their ears. People in this town were very nervous of them, Ada knew. And now, thanks to death threats and bricks through her window, Ada was feeling frightened, too. It was a horrible sensation. For the first time she felt unsettled in her very own home.

'Eeeh, hinny,' her friend said. 'I hate seeing you worried like this. If I saw one of them brutes in the flesh, I'd have a word with them. I'd put a hex on the buggers!' But Winnie was all talk, as Ada well knew. They both played along like she had special powers of enchantment but they knew it was all nonsense really. Then Winnie went on, 'Or you could get that new lass in your family to curse them. Her who married Sam. The one who was screaming in the church and dressed up in a parachute.'

'Mavis?' Ada asked. They moved forward in the queue, scuffling sawdust on the painted tiles. 'What do you mean, pet?'

'She's got the gift,' Winnie said. 'Have you never noticed? Can you not tell? I could see it a mile off. She's got the Romany gift, that one. She's got the power.'

'Oh, rubbish,' said Ada, more disparagingly than she meant to. She was embarrassed in case the people around them were earwigging.

'It's true, all right. She's gifted, that one, even if she doesn't know it.' Then Winnie added, with sudden candour, 'I only dabble in spiritual matters, really. I'm not really adept. But I know true power when I see it, and that girl . . . Well, she's something special.'

Ada nodded. 'That's what our Sam says about her. He says, there's something wonderful about Mavis. She might sound and look a bit funny. And she's had a rough time all her life. But there's something really special about her.'

'More than he realises,' Winnie smirked, and fiddled with her false teeth. 'These are giving me gyp. Sometimes I think I'd trade all my own psychic gifts for a decent pair of gnashers. Here, look, it's our turn. I'll go first.'

Winnie lived alone and her ration was pitifully meagre. Alan the butcher's lad laid out her portions on greaseproof paper and she showed him her book with a sigh. The lad winked at her and Winnie asked him, 'You're the one going out with that Lily Johnson, aren't you?'

The balding lad blushed immediately. 'I am, yes.'

'Well, you tell her bloody brothers to stop menacing Ada Farley and her family. We know it was her brother who smashed in that window. You tell those buggers to stop it. Poor Ada here is terrified for her life. Her Sam could well be moving out soon, and she'll have none of her lads left at home. How frightened do you think she's gonna be then, eh?'

Alan mumbled and stammered excuses, about how he didn't really know the Johnsons at all, and how he was sorry for all of Ma Ada's trouble. Ada was thoroughly embarrassed by Winnie's carrying on, and merely passed the lad her written-down order for chops and sausages. Then she scooted out of the shop as quickly as she could.

Winnie tagged along blithely. 'He seems like a nice lad, really. Too nice to go running around with that Lily Johnson.'

'Oh, put a bloomin' sock in it, Winnie.' Ada had had quite enough of her friend for one day.

But Winnie ignored her, suddenly bursting out: 'Ooh, let's have a frothy coffee at Franchino's. My treat!'

Chapter 8

'I've not been down here for a while,' Ma Ada said. 'I've not had a chance.'

Franchino's ice-cream parlour was wonderfully welcoming this tea time, as the two older ladies stepped through the glass door. Jazz music was playing and there was a lovely aroma of real coffee brewing.

Mavis was behind the chrome counter and she squealed at the sight of her mother-in-law. 'Eeeh, Ma Ada! Whatever you want – it's on the house!'

'That won't be necessariy,' Ada said with dignity, drawing up to the counter. 'I'll pay my own way, and so will Aunty Winnie here.'

'Hello, Aunty Winnie,' said Mavis. Lately she had adopted the habit of most dwellers in the Sixteen Streets, of calling all older women 'Aunty'.

Aunty Winnie was eyeing Mavis with a shrewd eye. Measuring up the girl carefully. As usual, Mavis looked slipshod in her work outfit, with her lank hair stuck up at the back and her tights laddered. To Winnie though, none of that mattered. She fancied she could sense a strange aura flickering around this new addition to the Farleys. 'Frothy coffee, please,' said Winnie.

'For two?' Mavis asked, and soon had the gleaming espresso machine chugging away, emitting jets of hot steam.

'Irene not on with you today?' Ma Ada asked.

'We're rarely on the same shift these days,' Mavis sighed as she fiddled with coffee grounds, making quite a mess on the counter. 'Profits are down and Bella's had to change the rota quite a lot. Irene's home today, getting the dinner on.'

'Ah,' said Ma Ada, with a small stab of irritation. These lasses knew more about the day-to-day running of her own home than she did. What with Beryl's timetable and this new regime to make sure everyone did their fair share, Ada sometimes felt herself growing unsure about where she should be and what she ought to be doing. Is this what it felt like when it came time to give way to the next generation?

'Go and find a nice seat, and I'll bring your coffee over,' said Mavis brightly.

That girl was getting cockier, too, Ada thought, as she turned to consider where to sit. She remembered meeting her before she and Sam were courting, and the little scrap of a thing wouldn't have said boo to a goose. She had been too nervous to utter the slightest word to Ada, and now here she was, ordering her about and telling her what the timetable was for her own kitchen at home!

Ma Ada stumped over to a banquette and shrugged off her heavy woollen coat. She threw it down and seated herself crossly at the table.

'What are you so irritable about?' Winnie frowned. 'And don't lie. I can read you like a saucerful of tea leaves, remember.'

Ada scowled and hissed, 'It's just those lasses at home. They're all very nice, but I'm used to a house of lads, who I can tell what to do. I never asked to live in a house of women! I'm not used to it.'

'I bet it's tidier, though?'

'Not at all!'

'And I bet it's more harmonious . . .'

'Are you kidding? They scrap and bicker all the time!'

'It'll all be down to that Megan,' said Winnie, pursing her lips. 'You always knew she was the bad apple in the barrel. What I don't understand is why she's still there at yours, when Bob has gone off with Cathy Sturrock!'

Ada glared at her for bringing up such tender family matters in a public place, even if only three of the other tables were occupied. 'It's the bairn, isn't it? She goes, then Johnny goes with her. I couldn't stand that. And Megan's not daft, either. She knows that if she stays at Number Thirteen with the babby, she'll get everything done for her . . .'

'She still got the baby blues?' Winnie asked. 'Hasn't it been nearly a year?'

'I just think she's always like that,' Ada sighed. 'Something's gone wrong with Megan. She's not a happy lass . . .'

'And her the bonniest of the lot!' Winnie cried. 'I reckon she's the bonniest lass in all the Sixteen Streets.'

'Well, it just shows,' said Ma Ada, just as Mavis appeared with a tray of glass coffee cups, including one for herself. Winnie raised an eyebrow at Ada as Mavis plonked herself down unbidden beside them.

'I'll take my break while you're here,' she rasped at them. 'Have you seen Sam today, Ma Ada?'

The older woman shook her head tetchily. 'He's here, there and everywhere at the moment. They've had a lot on at the docks.'

Winnie put in, 'He's not still running errands for them Mad Johnsons, is he? He can't still be working for them, after what they've done recently!'

Mavis shook her head quickly. 'No, he's cut off all ties with them, he says, and they're not very happy. They say he still owes them money . . .'

'Oh, great,' sighed Ma Ada.

'But he reckons they're lying.'

'You see?' Ada snapped. 'You get involved with people like that, and you can't get free again. They've got you for life.'

'It's true,' said Aunty Winnie, and was about to launch into the story of a distant cousin who had come to a nasty end on the cliffs above Marsden Bay, when Mavis interrupted her.

'Well, the Johnsons are all preoccupied at the moment with their old mother,' she said. 'That's what Lily Johnson was telling me at my wedding reception. The old lady who's ruled over their family for years is fading fast, and that's all they can think about just now.'

'Apart from smashing in my bay window,' growled Ma Ada. 'Anyway, how old is this old lady? She can't be any older than me. That's no age! Stop calling people old, Mavis Farley!'

A chill wind had gone right through Ada at this hint of mortality. If the Johnson mother was on her way out, who was to say how long Ma Ada had left?

Winnie patted her hand and said, 'You'll be all right, hinny. I've checked your lifeline, remember. You've got an extremely long life ahead of you. Such changes you'll see! You won't recognise this world by the time you're ready to leave it!'

'Hmf,' said Ada, liking the sound of this even less than the idea of a premature exit.

'Anyhow, that's all just to say that I think the Johnsons have their minds on other things than frightening people and violence,' said Mavis.

Ma Ada wasn't so sure.

'Drink your lovely coffee while it's still hot,' Mavis urged her, and again Ma Ada rankled at being told what to do.

While they were drinking their coffee, Bella came down from the storerooms upstairs. She was togged out like Mrs

Mop, with a hairnet and looking most unlike her usual glamorous self. There were cobwebs stuck to her as she greeted them, making them all laugh. 'I've been giving the rooms upstairs a proper spring clean,' she said. 'You'll never believe all the muck up there.'

She deposited a fat stack of faded paper folders on their table. It looked like old deeds, paperwork and letters.

'What's all that stuff?' Mavis asked; rather nosily, Ada thought.

'My papa's files,' Bella said. 'It's worth going through everything, just in case he had anything else precious hidden away. Like his prized recipe for Fior di Latte!'

All the women sighed and smiled at this. They all knew the tale of Tonio Franchino's secret, stolen recipe for the most marvellous ice cream in the world. The crumpled piece of paper on which it had been written had come to light after Bella's father's death, and she'd be making that heavenly ambrosia every day if she could. If only she could get her hands on enough sugar.

'Maybe you'll find old love letters or something romantic like that!' Mavis burst out. Since her wedding she had become the local expert on anything to do with love and romance. It was becoming a bit tiresome to her friends and relations, if truth be told.

Bella patted the heap of papers. 'It's more his financial records I'm hoping to find.'

'Bella wants to expand the business,' Mavis said knowingly.

'Shush,' Bella nudged her. 'Don't go telling everyone!'

'Mavis never knows when to shut up,' said Ma Ada. 'I've learned that much since she's moved in with us.'

For a second Mavis looked rather crumpled by this. 'Hey, well, never mind! Things are gonna change, aren't they, Bella? I won't be under your feet for ever, Ma Ada!'

45

'What does that mean?' asked her mother-in-law, frowning as she took a mouthful of coffee and got a whole load of gritty grounds.

'Well, as you can see, Bella is sorting out her rooms here, above Franchino's, and she's going to make them into a fancy little flat for herself.'

Ma Ada gasped. 'Are you, pet? Are you going to live above the ice-cream parlour?'

Bella shrugged. 'I don't see why I shouldn't. Those rooms up there are standing empty. They just need a good cleaning and sorting out.'

'But you'd be living all on your own, hinny!'

Bella Franchino gave a brave smile. 'Ah, but I am on my own, aren't I? Since my family were killed, that's exactly what I am. And I just have to get used to it. I have to be brave and make my own way. Ever since my home was bombed, I've been living with Mavis and her brother. That's gone on quite long enough. With Arthur abroad now, and Mavis married to your Sam, well I can't go on taking up room at their place . . .'

'I'm sure they don't mind,' said Ma Ada. Irene had told her that the place had been a proper midden before Bella had moved in, and she had improved it immeasurably.

'It's not right, though. Mavis and Sam are newlyweds, starting out on their lives. They don't want to be moving into their home and there's an old maiden aunt living there!'

Ma Ada felt her blood thrumming in her veins. 'What are you saying? You're moving in above the ice-cream parlour because Mavis and my Sam are moving to her house?'

Bella nodded. 'I thought you'd know all their plans, Mrs Farley?'

Ma Ada glared at Mavis. 'They don't keep me completely up to date. Why should they? I'm just the daft old woman who's always the last to know anything. So, when is it to be, Mavis Farley? When are you and my last son leaving me on my own, then? When are you running away? Or were you planning on doing it in the middle of the night and not telling me?'

Beside her, Winnie was wincing. Ada was working herself into a very bad temper, she could tell. Across the table, Mavis was looking terrified.

'Saturday,' Mavis said. 'If that's all right? W-we're planning to move out of yours on S-Saturday . . .'

Chapter 9

Irene had made them a very simple supper that night of ham and pease pudding, plus a few curly lettuce leaves from Arthur's little allotment. In the few months since he'd been mobilised abroad, that patch of land had turned unkempt and rather tangled, but Mavis had managed to salvage a bit of salad and, as Irene said, it was most welcome. It livened up their meagre plates and made up for the almost translucent slivers of ham they were having to share round.

'Maybe Sam could take over looking after Arthur's allotment,' Mavis said. 'When we move into my house.'

Irene, Beryl and Megan all looked up from their plates, alert at these words. 'When are you moving out, hinny?' Beryl asked.

'This Saturday,' Mavis said, crunching her salad energetically. 'You've all been very kind letting us live here. Making room for us, and all. But this house isn't big enough for the lot of us. It seems plain daft, when I've got a house standing ready and almost empty across town.'

Irene thought she heard Ma Ada make a strange noise and she glanced over at her. Could it have been a strangled sob she had heard? The matriarch was staring gloomily at her pease pudding with an expression like thunder. 'Whatever you two think best,' she said at last.

Megan suddenly said, 'If Sam's leaving home at last, then either me or Irene should take his room over. We've been sharing a bed, the two of us in the attic with the two babies. We deserve a bit of space at last. We're driving each other scatty . . .'

'I thought we were managing all right!' Irene protested, though now that she thought of it, a bit of privacy seemed like a good thing right now. Both Beryl and Ma Ada had rooms of their own – albeit tiny ones – and they had the luxury of hiding away on their own when they felt they needed to. Sharing with the sly, duplicitous Megan, Irene rather felt like she was always on show.

Ma Ada spoke up, 'We can sort out who sleeps where after they're gone.' She glanced up at them all and her pouchy eyes were damp. 'We're going to miss them being here.'

'I know, Ma,' Sam said, unable to meet her eye. 'I've never lived anywhere else, but I reckon it's time that I did.'

'What are we going to do, eh?' Beryl asked, with mock jauntiness. 'A household full of women and bairns? Who's gonna protect us now?'

'We don't need protecting,' growled the old woman. 'We'll carry on as always. And anyway, what use was Sam at protecting us? He was the one bringing trouble to our door. It was him who started the bother with the Mad Johnsons in the first place.' She sounded more critical than she meant to, and Sam looked even more guilty.

'It's been lovely living here for a while with Sam's family,' Mavis said. 'But now we have to make our own home together.' She brought the words out so carefully in her queer, husky voice that it sounded like a prepared speech. Irene thought that perhaps it was.

'Aye, maybe you're right,' Ma Ada said. 'I just come from a time when families tended to stick together under one roof. There's strength in numbers, especially in times of tribulation, like this is. But maybe that's not the modern way.'

49

Waves of guilt spread out across the tea table, and almost all of her family members could feel their impact, just as she intended. Mavis popped a peeled radish into her mouth and crunched down hard and gave a careless shrug. 'Yes, it's the modern way,' she agreed.

Irene marvelled at the pale girl. She was actually becoming immune to Ma Ada's emotional warfare! Good for her, Irene thought.

'If I had a house of my own across town, I'd be away there in a flash!' Megan said, with a cynical chuckle. 'It's funny, really. The fact that you own a house of your own, Mavis. How's that, then? We always thought you were some kind of foundling or street kid. You always looked like you had nothing of your own. How come you have your own house?'

Megan was prying and rude, but everyone round the table was terribly interested in the answer to that question. Just how on earth had Mavis and her brother come into possession of their own home? It was a tiny, tumbledown cottage in what had always been the very roughest part of town, but even so. It was a mystery that each of the Farleys had wondered about.

'Well,' said Mavis, looking evasive. 'That's our . . . um . . . inheritance, that. The little house on Watling Street belongs to me and my Arthur lock, stock and barrel. I mean, it's falling down really, and it's not worth much, but it's been our refuge since we were bairns, just about.'

Ma Ada fixed her with an implacable stare. 'But how did you come by it? That's what Megan's asking.'

Was it Irene's imagination or did Mavis's lip tremble just then? 'It was given to us. By the woman who gave us . . . our name.'

Megan frowned. 'Your mother?'

'No!' Mavis burst out furiously. 'No, she's not our mother! She never was our mother! She never even really tried to be our mother! She just thought she owned us. Like we were trinkets or toys . . . She . . . That woman . . . She . . .' By now Mavis was gasping and sobbing, rising to her feet. She tried to dash for the door but the room was so crowded she had to wait for Beryl and Irene to pull in their chairs, squashing up to the table to let her through.

'Now she's upset!' Megan sneered, as Mavis at last made her way out of the parlour.

'You kept on asking her questions,' Sam frowned, getting up to follow his wife.

'Hey now, they were reasonable questions,' Ma Ada said. 'We're just interested. Anyone would be . . .'

Sam slipped out of the room, saying, 'She doesn't like talking about the past.'

Ma Ada watched him go, a critical expression on her face. She dabbed her lips with a frayed napkin and tutted loudly. 'Doesn't like talking about the past! What else is there to talk about? There's no use talking about the future, is there? We don't know anything about it! What else have we got but the past?'

'Wise words, Ma,' said Beryl, and she wasn't even trying to be sarcastic.

'Oh, do be quiet, Beryl,' the old woman said crossly. 'Eat the rest of your ham.'

Up in the tiny bedroom that had belonged to Sam all his life, Mavis was sitting on the counterpane and trying not to be upset. She stared out of the window at Frederick Street and the cobbles gleaming under a twilight shower. In the past few weeks, she had come to quite like this room of Sam's. She had come to understand more about the boy he'd been – not so long ago, it seemed. The faded wallpaper had pictures of footballers on it, though he had explained that had really been because of Tony, who had once slept in the room.

His books from childhood were lined up on a single shelf. *Black Beauty*, *The Secret Garden*, *Heidi*. Examining them carefully on one of her first nights at Number Thirteen, Mavis had said, 'They're not what I would call proper boys' stories.' He showed her *Treasure Island* and *Kidnapped* to prove the contrary.

'I loved reading all sorts of things,' he shrugged. 'This house was always quite noisy when I was a kid. Three older brothers, almost men. I mean I was pretty boisterous and noisy myself, I suppose, but sometimes I liked to hide away with my books.'

Mavis had touched the spines like she was touching religious relics. 'I've never been one for reading. All the lines of letters used to dance about when I tried to get them to stay still and make sense.'

Sam had to admit that he hadn't actually read a whole book since the war started. He couldn't concentrate long enough.

'When we move into my house,' Mavis told him, 'you'll have a bookcase all to yourself and a quiet, cosy nook with a lamp. And that will be your corner for reading. And you'll be able to concentrate at last.'

Tonight, still a bit upset from Ma Ada's inevitable questions, Mavis was thinking over this exchange with Sam. She was picturing him in his reading nook, perhaps leafing through his treasured copy of *The Wind in the Willows* (the most battered volume on his shelf), and at the same time Mavis could picture herself in the kitchen, mopping the floor perhaps, or taking something delicious out of the oven.

They could play at houses together. And even if it felt like daft kids pretending and playing a game, then that was all right. It was a start, wasn't it?

Sam came into the room. 'You're not upset, are you, Mavis?'

Her eyes were brimming with tears. 'I'm so happy, Sam. That's what it is. Nothing can spoil it for us now. I'm just so happy.'

Chapter 10

Mavis spent the rest of the week until Saturday in a state of heightened tension. It was almost as exciting as the build-up to her wedding day itself. Everything else became secondary: the progress of the war, her day-to-day routine at the biscuit factory, and all the routine goings-on at Number Thirteen. All she could fixate on was the thought of being back inside her little house on Watling Street, and her new husband being there beside her, like a proper married couple.

Bella had been amazingly kind and sensitive. 'You and your brother Arthur were so good to me, in my time of direst need,' she told Mavis. (Mavis loved the way the Italian girl could turn out phrases like 'direst need'.) 'When I had nowhere, and no one to turn to, the two of you were so generous and welcoming. Now it's time that I moved on. I'll be out of there before Saturday.'

Mavis couldn't help looking pleased. She loved Bella to bits, but she wanted a clean, fresh start. But what would it mean for Arthur when he eventually came home from the war? He'd certainly want to live there again – it was his home as much as it was Mavis's . . . But she pushed that thought away. It wasn't the time to think about that. She didn't want to jinx anything. Everything was going Mavis's way, for once.

She had never felt like a lucky person. She wasn't the kind of person for whom life went right. She was the kind who simply had to muddle along, swimming about in the confusing rapids. Mavis had always felt at the mercy of circumstance, and the mercy of more powerful people around her. Now, for the first time, she felt she was taking control of her life.

'Is that all you've got to carry over there?' asked her new sister-in-law, the kindly Beryl, as she surveyed their boxes of belongings in the downstairs hall. Mavis only had a single case of belongings here in the Farley household, and the rest were Sam's things. Much of his stuff he was leaving here, at home, his mother was gratified to see. Ma Ada assumed he was leaving many of his things here just in case the business of living together didn't work out for the newlyweds and he had to move back.

Sam didn't own very much at all, Mavis was discovering. He had packed up his few shirts and things like that, and his shelfful of treasured books. All they needed on Saturday was to borrow the hand cart that he sometimes used working at the docks, in order to transport his worldly goods across town.

'Eeeh, carried off in a hand cart,' Ma Ada squawked, shaking her head. 'The neighbours will think we're bloomin' paupers!' The head of the Farley clan was thinking about her own arrival here, at Number Thirteen, all those years ago. She'd had a cart and horse bringing her belongings to the door. A great big shire horse pulling a cart heaped with heavy, glossy, beautiful Victorian furniture. Far too much furniture than could seemingly fit into a tiny, low dwelling like this one. But she had been proud and determined. All these beautiful antiques and heirlooms would find their place at Number Thirteen and, with a bit of ingenuity and grit, she had made sure that they had. She had turned this low dwelling into an absolute palace.

But all of that was a long time ago, and quite another story, she thought ruefully, as she watched her youngest son leaving home on Saturday morning. That was her own story, so long ago. It had nothing, really, to do with the tale of these two humble youngsters and their paltry possessions. And what did that matter? The pair of them were happy to be setting up together. Ma Ada was still astonished that Sam had seen anything in that pale little girl that made him want to spend his whole life with her, but overwhelmingly his mother's emotion was relief. Sam was settled. Sam, who had come so close – several times – to going right off the rails due to thieving or lust or general carrying on – was actually settling down and growing up. Thank God.

But she was still going to miss him.

As the hand cart was being secured and it was almost time for goodbyes, Megan came slinking down the stairs in her feather-trimmed dressing gown, clutching baby Johnny to her chest. The bairn was more alert now than he had been for the first few months of his life (when Ma Ada had worried he might turn out to be a bit gormless) and now he was twisting about to see what was going on.

Sam was drinking a last mug of tea on the doorstep, and saying his goodbyes to all the nosy parker aunties who'd come out to see him leave. He turned to see baby Johnny watching from his blonde mother's arms and he froze on the spot. Ma Ada froze too, seeing the strangely tender look on her son's face.

He was looking at his own secret child. Almost everyone in the family knew of this relationship, but no one ever talked about it. By mutual consent it was never referred to, the fact that Sam had given his slinky, trouble-making sister-in-law her child. Almost everyone in her family knew, except Mavis and Megan's husband, Bob. It was one of the heavy secrets that Ma Ada had to struggle with, every single day.

Now it seemed to her that anyone spying that look on her lad's face as he stared at the babby would undoubtedly spot that he was the father. There was no mistaking that anguish and thwarted pride on Sam's face. He was trying to swallow down his feelings with his final swigs of sweet milky tea.

'Baby Johnny has come to wave to his aunty and uncle,' Megan said, with a playful, taunting note in her voice.

Sam came over and took the child's chubby had and very solemnly shook it. 'See you soon, little man,' he said.

'Take him. Give him a cuddle,' Megan urged him, but Sam stepped away, shaking his head. He would never pick up Megan's child if he could help it. The joke in the house was that he was too clumsy to be trusted, but his mother knew that he lived in dread of becoming too attached. He was fearing falling in love with that bairn. Ma Ada could read those emotions from a mile off. Megan was cruel.

'Ooh, I'll give him a cuddle!' Mavis said, scooting over, and passing Ma Ada her empty teacup, like the old lady was just a maid waiting on her. 'I'll cuddle and squeeze him all up! Oh, we're going to miss the little fella. And little Marlene, too! Where is she?'

Beryl went off to fetch Irene and her daughter from the scullery. Marlene was over a year old now, and starting to look like a child rather than a toddler. Her pale hair was held back by a slide and she was immaculate in a white smock. When Irene brought her out into the sunny street, she scowled at all her relations and looked outraged at being made to hug them. She kicked Mavis in the shin for getting too close.

'Marlene's a feisty creature!' Ma Ada chuckled.

'She hates me!' Mavis laughed. 'She always looks at me funny, and tries to kick me!'

Megan said, 'Kid's got good sense, I'd say.'

'Now, Megan, be nice,' Beryl said. 'You can afford to be a little nicer today. You're inheriting their bedroom, remember?'

Megan gave a surly nod and a fake smile. She told the newlyweds, 'Well, I wish the pair of you all happiness in your new home.' Then, without waiting to see them go, she took her son back indoors to see about some breakfast.

'She'll never change,' Ma Ada sighed. 'Right! Now, you two! Off you go! Get yourselves home! Stop dragging out the agony!'

They all laughed, and Sam went off to manhandle the wooden cart, but Ma Ada had spoken the God's honest truth. It really was agony to stand there on the doorstep she had scrubbed this morning, and had scrubbed every week for the past thirty-five years, and to watch her youngest son leave home at last. He was the last one of four to fly the coop. There was a hollowness and a sickly ache in her heart as she waved and waved with all her might as they trundled off down the hill and eventually turned the corner into Westoe Road.

'So that's them gone,' Irene said, hugging Marlene to her, even as the child twisted impatiently in her arms.

'It won't be the same round here without Sam,' Beryl smiled sadly.

Ma Ada turned to them and didn't care which of the neighbours could see that her face was wet and shining with tears. 'You've got this coming to you, one day, you lasses. When all your bairns leave you and then you're alone. It's the worst feeling in the world, this is.'

'You've still got us,' said Beryl with mock-brightness. Her feelings were bruised, though. Ma Ada had forgotten that this moment would never be hers, bittersweet or not, for the simple fact that she had no bairns of her own. The bereft feeling Ada had right now was how Beryl felt all the time.

'Come inside and we'll have something to eat,' Irene said. 'And let's not make ourselves sad. It's a happy day really. There's nothing to be sad about.'

Ma Ada didn't look quite so sure. 'What did they look like, with everything strapped onto a hand cart! They were like a couple of bloomin' tramps!'

Chapter 11

Bella Franchino had grown up belonging to a large family. She had always been used to living in a house and being able to hear someone yelling, whether it was her dad, running out to work, or her grandmother in the kitchen, or her much younger brother tearing about the place. The Franchinos were a noisy, rambunctious lot and always had been. Bella was used to the noise and only ever pretended to be bothered by it.

'Your papa always wanted an even bigger family,' she remembered her mother telling her. 'He wanted a whole army! He wanted even more noise and confusion and for our house to be even more crammed full. But I put my foot down in the end. "Let's not go too far, Tonio. The ice-cream business can support us now, the size we are. Let's not go bananas."' Her mother had chuckled at this point in the tale. 'Your papa loved me saying that, "Let's not go bananas, Tonio." He said, "Wow, you're speaking the language like a native! Let's not go bananas!" And he'd use that phrase all the time after that, even in conversations where it wasn't needed.'

Bella could picture her mother telling her this, sitting in their sunny garden, one long, summery day just before the war. Their house had had a wonderful view of the distantly glittering sea, and there had been a soothing breeze coming inland to cool them as they lay there reminiscing.

She hadn't let herself think about her ma and papa this past year or so. It was only now, in the summer of 1943, more than a year since they were killed, that Bella let her thoughts rove back and dwell on the specifics of the things they had said and done. Until now it had been far too painful to let her imagination attempt to bring them back to life. For some reason tonight, as she lay awake in her new flat above the ice-cream parlour, she couldn't stop herself. She could hear her mother's voice and see her still-youthful face and limbs as she lay sunning herself in the garden.

Her family were coming back to her unbidden. Their noise was filling up her head as she lay in the dark, lonely in her tiny and silent new home.

'Let's not go bananas, Papa!' she had repeated to her bemused father when he came home early from work that afternoon to find them sunbathing. He frowned and barked at them, although he was well used to being sent up by the women in his family.

'Stop talking rubbish,' he said. 'Come and eat ice cream. I brought back just the thing for cooling down in this weather.'

His ice cream! Bella and the whole family had grown up nourished by the ice cream that he lovingly churned and froze. And yet all that time he'd had the special recipe that he'd smuggled out of Naples when he and his wife and mother-in-law had fled for their lives, all those years ago. He had only rarely made the exquisite fior-di-latte. Thinking about it now, Bella didn't know why he hadn't made it every day. Back before the war, supplies of sugar and milk hadn't been at all scarce. He could have made it every single day if he'd wanted, but he hadn't. He had made it only on very special occasions, and only for the family.

She supposed it was a mystery that she would never know the answer to now.

Realising she wasn't going to be able to sleep again tonight, she got up and felt around for her dressing gown, stumbling on boxes and various belongings that hadn't found their homes yet. These few ex-lumber rooms she had adopted were turning out to be less commodious and designed for living than she had expected. She had moved in quite confidently, happy to give Mavis and Sam their own space. Now she felt cramped and cross. She felt sleepless and haunted by her own family.

It wasn't even four in the morning yet. There was only the barest streak of dawn light when she peered from the tallest window in the place. The night was absolutely silent. No air raids, no warnings, no awful drone of approaching planes. Of course, she ought to be making the most of the quiet and getting some sleep, but she simply couldn't.

Bella wrapped her gown around herself and went downstairs to the ice-cream parlour. She checked the blinds were secure before turning on the lights, and then she brewed herself some tea.

The pale walls of Franchino's and all the empty tables and chairs made her feel even more lonely and bereft.

'I've been doing my best, Papa,' she whispered. She wanted to say it out loud. She wanted to address her beloved ghosts directly, and though she felt a bit foolish for doing so, her voice shook as she added, 'I'm keeping the business going. I'm going to make you proud. And, when I can, I'm going to make fior-di-latte in your honour.'

The silence stirred and grew deeper. Bella was superstitious and fancied she could feel their presence drawing close. She hoped they approved of everything she was doing.

'I'm sorry I wasn't there with you on the night that you died,' she told her family. 'I was across town, with Mavis and Arthur, drinking their brandy and staying out late, having fun, and ended up sleeping on their settee till dawn. It was a freak chance that I missed out being at home and dying with you all in that . . . in that . . .'

In that fireball. In that hellish inferno. In that cellar underneath their beautiful house when it was hit.

For months she hadn't let her mind stray to those images and those thoughts. She hadn't let herself dwell upon the guilt that she felt. I should have died with them. It was just a random chance . . .

All she knew now was that, for whatever reason, she had survived them. And now she must do her best to honour them and make them proud, wherever they were . . .

'No,' she said aloud suddenly. 'I *do* know where you are, don't I? You're all here. My beloved ghosts. You're all here at Franchino's, aren't you? You're haunting this place for ever now . . .'

She would catch glimpses in the tiled mirrors on the walls and in the burnished chrome of the coffee machine that her father had been so proud of. Her mother's green eyes. Green as mint. Her father's lavish moustaches. Her grandmother's proud wrinkles and her poor gnarled hands. And her dancing, darting quicksilver brother and his mop of jet-black hair. Yes, they were here and keeping an eye on her, every minute of the day.

Bella sipped her tea, feeling heartened by the thought that she was being watched over like this. It made her feel less lonely, living in this place, now she knew that all the shadows were her family.

She knew she wasn't going to go bananas, at least.

'I'm going to be all right,' she told her ghosts happily.

When Mavis arrived at work the next day in the late afternoon, she found her boss frazzled with lack of sleep, but happy enough.

'Are you not comfy upstairs, then?' Mavis asked, feeling vaguely guilty that Bella was cramped in the storeroom upstairs. She wondered if she should think about inviting her to move back into the house on Watling Street.

'No, I'm fine,' Bella said, busying at the counter. 'I'm just getting used to it. I was awake making peace with the ghosts in this place.'

'The ghosts!' Mavis said, with a tinge of alarm.

'Well,' said Bella, 'you know, this whole place goes right back in time. It was a tea room for years even before Papa took it over for the Franchino clan. Generations of people have sat here with their cups, watching the world pass by on Ocean Road . . .' Bella was being light-hearted and almost whimsical. 'I bet they were here, going right back to Roman times, when this was one of the most important ports in all the world. I bet the place back then was completely full of Italians like me and the rest of the Franchinos!' She laughed at herself for being fanciful.

'Aye,' said Mavis, who wasn't quite following what she was on about. 'Hey, what have you got there, hinny?'

Bella was taking out a dish of fior-di-latte she had made in the middle of the night. It was frozen enough by now and perfect to eat. 'Share this with me, Mavis,' she said. 'We'll commemorate my new home, and you being in yours with your Sam.'

'Ooh,' said Mavis, fetching spoons and dishes. The parlour was empty at this point in the day, so they gave themselves up to the luxury of sitting at their favourite banquette and devouring what they both knew was the best ice cream in all the world. 'It's just heaven,' said Mavis, tucking in.

'I know,' said Bella. 'I just wish we could get more sugar, so we could make it every day . . .'

It was at that very moment that the door opened and in walked the man who was going to bring more sugar than Bella even realised she needed. He was going to bring it whether she agreed to it or not.

He was a very tall, handsome man in blue shirtsleeves and braces. He had a shock of wavy, bright red hair.

'Now then,' he said, with an amiable grin. 'I'm looking for the owner. Are you her?'

Bella pressed a paper napkin to her lips and stood up. 'What do you want?' she asked him. Hardly a suitable or very polite greeting, she thought, with one part of her befuddled mind.

There was an awkward pause as Bella and Jonas Johnson stared at each other across the marble floor of Franchino's. They knew in that instant that there was going to be some kind of connection between them. It was like a shock that went through Bella, like freezing ice cream on a sensitive tooth. She could tell he felt it as well.

'I've come to make you an offer,' the handsome redhead said.

Recognising him as one of the dreaded Johnsons, Mavis let out a worried squeak and swallowed up what was left of the delicious fior-di-latte.

Chapter 12

Sam kept forgetting which way was home.

Some days he'd set off from the docks at the end of the day and find himself heading up the Sixteen Streets, his feet finding their way automatically, and often he was too exhausted to contradict them. In the early days of his marriage he was still labouring on the ships and he finished each shift completely shattered.

'What are you doing here?' his ma cried when he stepped into her parlour. 'You don't live here anymore, pet!'

Sam blinked and came out of his trance. Ma was talking to him like a stray cat who'd wandered in over the threshold.

'Oh!' he said the first time he made his daft mistake, and they all laughed at him.

'Well, stay for a cup of tea anyhow, hinny,' said Beryl.

'You did this back when you went up to the big school,' Ma Ada reminded him. 'You forgot where you were supposed to be going, so you just wandered home, back to your ma.' She laughed at this, glowing at the memory and staring fondly at her youngest son. 'You've got the same vague look on your face today, pet.'

He sat down heavily at the dining table. 'I'm just worn out, that's all.'

His ma frowned. 'It's tough work, all that lugging crates about. It wore your da out, too, you know. You'll have to watch out. You're not physically built for such a heavy job.

Your da couldn't do anything else because he didn't have the wits and he was drunk all the time. But you could do better for yourself, our Sam . . .'

He shot his mother a look, like now was not the time to discuss his career prospects. Mercifully Beryl was back with a swiftly poured cup of tea, strong and stewed – just how he liked it.

'Well, you've not been back this way since you moved out,' Beryl prompted him. 'What's life like over in Watling Street?'

He pulled a face. 'I haven't seen much of it yet. Haven't seen the neighbours. But Mavis's house is very nice inside. I think Bella was responsible for making it liveable.'

'According to Irene, it used to be quite messy when it was just Mavis and Arthur,' Beryl said.

'Aye, well,' said Sam. 'It's like a palace now. You'll all have to come over and visit. You haven't been to see us yet.'

'You're right, we haven't,' Beryl agreed. 'We'll come over for tea this weekend, shall we, Ma? Bring the babies with us. Make it a proper afternoon out.'

'Aye, if you like,' Ma nodded. 'It'll be a trip out. It'll fill the empty days.' Then she heaved a sigh.

'What's the matter, Ma?' Sam asked her. 'Since when did you ever have empty days?'

'Nay, son,' she said. 'Don't you worry about me. You shouldn't fret about your poor old ma. She'll be all right.'

She sounded so pitiful he felt alarmed. 'What is it? Are you unwell?'

'Nah, nothing like that, pet.' She took out her hanky and blew her nose extravagantly.

Beryl sipped her tea. 'She's all right, Sam. Don't let her worry you.'

'I've just been a bit . . . you know. Down in the dumps.'

'Oh, Ma,' he said.

'No, you can't fight nature, can't you?' she cried. 'It's true. Even the littlest and most dowdy of birds have to leave the nest some time. And when they do, that's the end for their poor old mothers. The mothers' work is done! She might as well just fade away and die then because nobody wants her anymore . . .'

Sam studied his mother carefully. She had an extra knitted shawl around her shoulders, even though it was June and rather stifling in the parlour. She was still wearing her hairnet in the early evening and there was an air of bleakness and hopelessness about her that he found disturbing. 'Oh, Ma. What's the matter?'

Even as he said it, he knew he was falling into her trap.

'When your useless da went and left us, I only had you four lads,' she said. 'You were all I had in the world and, by! I was so proud of you all. I mean, you were perfect in my eyes, despite everything, all four of you. I was the envy of the Sixteen Streets. Old Ma Ada and her four strong boys. I was protected and safe with my own little army of lads. And – well, rather stupidly – I thought that would last for ever. I thought we'd always be happy together, me and my wonderful family . . .' She shook her head sorrowfully again.

Sam was sitting there, stricken to hear his ma talk in such heartfelt tones.

'But I'll be all right, hinny,' she added. 'Don't you worry. You've got your own life to get on with. You and that Mavis of yours. Don't you spare a single thought for me.'

'We'll come and see you more,' he promised. He was suddenly crushingly aware that this accidental return of his was the first visit he'd made since moving out. 'I promise we'll come by more often . . .'

'Nay, nay,' said Ma Ada. 'You've got enough on your plate. With your work and keeping that house tidy, and looking after your lovely new wife . . .'

68

'I promise,' he said steadfastly. 'And firstly, you'll come to tea at ours on Saturday. Mavis will do a lovely spread with cakes and all that, and we'll treat you like a queen.'

'Can I come too?' Beryl asked.

'And Irene,' Ma Ada said. 'Irene will want to be there.'

'Aye, of course,' said Sam.

'Not Megan, though,' Ma Ada said darkly, for reasons that all present understood and that didn't need going into. 'Well! That's a lovely plan. That's cheered me right up, our Sam. See? It was clearly no accident, you coming here this afternoon. It was God or Providence directing your feet. Eeeh, you've made a poor, lonely old woman very happy!'

Feeling somewhat dazed, Sam caught the tram on Westoe Road, at the bottom of the Sixteen Streets. Normally he'd walk, but he'd taken up enough time with his accidental visit.

He sat squashed between two older ladies with his gas mask box on his knee. He felt grubby and even more tired than before. He also felt he'd had his feelings and his loyalties twisted round by an expert.

What was Mavis going to say about his rash Saturday teatime offer? She wasn't going to relish putting on a fancy spread and having his whole family come traipsing in. Despite what he'd said, the house on Watling Street wasn't quite the palace he'd described. It was a bit mucky and neglected, truth be told. His ma was going to be horrified at the conditions he was living in, Sam was sure. But what could he do? Both he and Mavis were working all the hours God could send. There'd barely been time to do anything yet, in the handful of days and weeks they'd been living together . . .

It was only just in the past couple of nights that the pair of them had finally got round to consummating their marriage.

Consummating? Was that the right word? It sounded strange as he said it aloud inside his head, sitting swaying on the tram, between two nannas.

He felt a bit ashamed, to be honest, though no one need ever know that the pair of them had been a bit hapless and unskilled at the crucial act. Their honeymooning nights had been clumsy and awkward. There had been tears and hurt feelings. Sometimes one or the other of them was prepared to just chuck it in. Forget about it. It was never going to work. They just didn't fit together. They would never be compatible.

Sam knew that he was letting her down. There was nothing wrong with Mavis, but she took it all upon herself. 'It's all because of me,' she said. 'I know I'm not much to look at. And I've got no figure at all. Why would anyone want to . . . you know, do any of that with me? Why would anyone ever want to take me to bed?'

'But I do!' Sam burst out, and believed he meant it. He gathered her up in his arms and kissed her passionately, until she got the giggles because she was ticklish, and that destroyed the mood.

Sometimes when she went on daft it got a little bit on Sam's nerves. Couldn't she be serious about anything?

The first time she'd seen him naked, she'd burst out laughing.

'You've never seen a man in the buff before? Not even your brother?'

Mavis gasped with horror. 'Arthur would never let himself be seen in the altogether! Not by anyone! Certainly not by me!'

Her horror even made Sam laugh a little bit, though he still felt stung that she'd laughed at him in all his glory.

'Will we ever get it right, Sam?' Mavis asked him, much

later that night, lying in his arms. A close, stuffy summer's evening. They lay there, crumpled and dissatisfied on top of the counterpane.

'Of course we will,' he promised her.

And, perhaps, by now, they had. The marriage had been consummated; technically, at least, though they weren't still quite sure about it.

'Oh! Was that it?' Mavis asked.

'Er, yes . . .' said Sam.

That had been the night before last. It had been much the same muted palaver last night, too.

'We might be getting the hang of this,' Mavis had said.

Drowsing on the tram, Sam almost missed his stop at the end of Watling Street. He picked up his bait box and gas mask and hurriedly disembarked.

Home again. His real home now. More than an hour late. What was Mavis going to say when he told her about his daft mistake?

As it turned out there wasn't any time to go into the tale of how he'd wandered in a daze back to Frederick Street. When he set foot through his door, he could hear loud, gulping sobs coming from the living room.

'Mavis?' he called out, alarmed.

'It's all right,' she yelled. 'It's not me. We've got a visitor. It's Lily Johnson. I met her in the street and she's having an awful time. She's absolutely distraught!'

True enough, when Sam stepped into their messy front room, there was Lily in the best armchair. Her black wig was awry and all her elaborate eye make-up had melted down her face in black streaks.

'What's wrong, pet?' asked Sam.

'She's had an awful shock,' said Mavis. 'Can you make some tea and put some of that brandy in it?'

Sam scooted through to the kitchen. He could see the girl was properly and genuinely upset. But he didn't like or trust her one single inch. All of the Mad Johnsons were bad news. He knew that better than anyone. And letting one of them into your house – no matter how needy they seemed to be – that struck him as a terrible idea.

Chapter 13

Sam managed to keep out of the way while Lily was round their house. He brought the girls their tea and left them to it. He used the excuse of his tiredness to escape upstairs and lie on the bed drowsing as Lily sobbed her heart out downstairs.

After she had gone, Mavis came to check on him. 'Are you asleep?'

'How can I be, with all that racket downstairs? What was wrong with her?'

'You could sound a bit more sympathetic, Sam! She was so upset.'

He sat up in bed, trying to look contrite. He found it hard to summon up fellow feeling for anyone in the Johnson clan. They worried him too much. 'Has she gone home?' he asked.

Mavis nodded. 'I've never seen Lily like that, and I've known her nearly all my life. She's the toughest in all her family. And she came round here and went to pieces.'

Sam nodded. 'I think she puts on that tough face when she's out and about, like nothing can hurt her. Evidently she trusts you enough to let that mask drop.'

Mavis looked pleased by this. The idea that someone thought of her as a good and dependable friend! 'Here, did you take your boots off before getting under that quilt?'

'What? Yes, of course.'

'You shouldn't have got in there in all your work clothes, either. That's the good sheets you're mucking up with your work togs. They're murder to wash and get through the mangle, them sheets . . .'

'I took them off,' he interrupted.

'Good,' she said. The early evening sun was coming through the drawn curtains and casting a dusky amber light in the room. Everything was golden and slow for a moment as the two of them looked at each other.

'In fact,' Sam said, 'I've nothing on under here, Mavis.'

'Oh!' she said, still staring at him.

'What do you think about that?'

'But I was in the middle of telling you about why Lily Johnson was so upset—'

'I don't care about that just now. Get your things off.'

'What?' she gasped. 'That's rude!'

He laughed at her serious expression. 'Of course it's rude! I'm being rude! Let's both be rude!'

'Sam!' she cried, as he reached over the thick counterpane to take hold of her. It was as if she thought things like this were illegal during the hours of sunlight. As Sam moved across the bed towards her, Mavis realised it was true – he had shucked off every stitch in order to take a nap.

'But I was going to put the supper on!' she protested.

'Come here,' he said, with a note in his voice that she had never heard before. Without thinking any more about it, Mavis let herself fall into his arms.

Supper was just a bit of toast, hastily eaten with the last precious bit of butter, much, much later that evening . . .

It was a couple of days later that Mavis's shift coincided with Irene's, and they could properly catch up with each other. After a morning at the biscuit factory they had a rare afternoon off, so they took a bag of broken oddments to South Marine Park and they sat in the glorious sun together.

The park was busy, and it would have been easy to forget there was a war on if it wasn't for the boarded bandstand and the uniforms on some of the men. Mostly though, people were out with their sweethearts and making the most of the lovely day.

As she finished her custard cream, Irene loosened her work blouse at the neck and wrists and lay down on the grass.

'So you don't mind telling them?' Mavis was asking. 'You see, Sam shouldn't have agreed without sorting it out with me, first . . .'

'I'll talk to Ma Ada,' Irene said. 'Don't worry.'

Mavis heaved a deep sigh. 'I mean, it's not that I don't want you, Beryl and Ma Ada coming to tea on Saturday. You know I'd love you to come round.'

'I know,' said Irene, though she supposed that Mavis could be excused for feeling nervous at such a prospect. Ada would be casting a critical eye at her youngest son's new home.

'Just, I think, the next Saturday would be better for all concerned,' Mavis fretted, picking at bourbon crumbs. 'There's so much going on right now. Another week will let me get the house straight, and for everything to be nicer. And also . . . well, I think Lily might need me. The end is getting very close, you see.'

Irene sat up and blinked at her. 'The end of what?'

Mavis realised that Irene was behind with all the developments. 'For her mother. Old Ma Johnson. She's been gravely ill for some time and it's been Lily doing everything for her. Anyway, they say she's on a kind of downward turn, and Lily's ever so upset.'

'Oh, I see,' Irene said, feeling natural sympathy for any young lass who was facing such a thing. How terrible to consider losing her mum at such an age! A shiver went through Irene at the very thought, even in the warm sunlight. However, she found it hard to picture Lily Johnson seeming so vulnerable or revealing her true feelings to anyone.

'We're very close these days,' Mavis said. 'And, what with the end being so nigh, I think I should be there in order to administer solace.'

Irene nodded, wondering which melodramatic movie Mavis was getting her vocabulary from. Her brother used to be an usher in the Savoy at the Nook and he would always let Mavis in for free. 'I don't suppose waiting a week for her afternoon tea is going to hurt Ma Ada's feelings too much,' said Irene, though she had an inkling that the old woman was going to be irked. Especially when she heard that she was making room for one of the Johnson family.

'Thanks for telling her,' Mavis told Irene. 'Ma Ada still scares the bejabbers out of me.'

'Oh, she's all right, really.' Irene was studying her youngest sister-in-law carefully, with one hand shading her eyes from the sun. 'Hey, something's different about you, Mavis. What is it?'

Mavis squeaked, like she'd been found out. Then she bit her lip and tried to look away at the passers-by as they strolled around the bronze boating lake. 'There's nothing changed about me . . .'

'I think there is, pet,' Irene said. 'You seem . . . I don't know. Relieved, somehow.'

Mavis beamed at her, and suddenly it all came out in a torrent of words. She could hold it back no longer. Gabbling a little too loudly in that public place, she launched into the saga of how she and her Sam had sorted out the 'little problems' that had been plaguing them from the beginning of their marriage. The difficulties that had kept her awake fretting at night, thinking there was something wrong with her, or him, or both of them, had simply melted away.

'What problems and difficulties?' Irene asked.

'Personal ones,' said Mavis. 'You know. Rude things.'

'Oh!' said Irene, suddenly dreading what candid revelation might be on its way.

'But it turns out everything is absolutely fine! Everything works!' Mavis burst out, wearing an incredulous expression, and looking like she was going to go into a song. 'In fact, it's more than absolutely fine, Irene. It was wonderful! It was . . . I don't even know how to say it. But I feel . . . I feel more like a real woman, you know, than I ever did before!'

Irene laughed. 'But of course you're a real woman!'

Mavis gave her an old-fashioned look. 'But you know what I mean.'

'Aha.' Irene felt herself reddening slightly. 'Well, I'm glad to hear you're happy, pet.'

'Why did none of you tell me?' Mavis went on. 'You never said it was like this! You never said that it was . . . you know.'

'Like what?!' Irene wanted to know.

'That it could go on for hours! That it could happen three, four times in a row!' Mavis looked delirious, reliving her joy.

'It can?!' Irene was appalled.

Mavis told her. 'Irene, it took a while for us to work out what to do. But now . . . it's bliss, I'm telling you. I had no idea. I've known shorter air raids . . .'

Irene gave a weak smile. Three, four times in a row, she thought! Surely Mavis was pulling her leg?

'What's the time?' she sat up. They were both due at Franchino's for the teatime shift. 'We can't be late, remember.'

'We'd best go now,' Mavis said, crumpling up the paper packets and looking pleased with herself. 'Bella's given herself the evening off. Can you believe it?'

'It's not like her at all,' agreed Irene, as they made for the park's exit and Ocean Road.

'She's got a date planned,' Mavis confided. 'And you'll never guess who it's with!'

Chapter 14

At first Irene was delighted to hear that Bella was going out on a date with a young man. After more than a year of mourning, perhaps she was returning to life at last. The Italian girl was so vivacious that it had been very hard seeing her so bowed down with guilt and grief over her family.

'Aye, but just wait till you see who she's planning on going out with,' Mavis said gloatingly, as the two girls bustled quickly down Ocean Road to the ice-cream parlour. Not for the first time Irene had the unkind thought that Mavis revelled in bother and upset for others. It was one of the few things that Irene was irked by when it came to her diminutive friend.

'Well, who?' Irene asked. She couldn't imagine who Mavis was referring to. Who would be that bad? 'Eh, it's not some German, is it?' she asked.

Mavis squealed with laughter. 'How would she be going out with a German?'

'Well, there's that one they picked up on the White Leas, who came down wearing your parachute silk,' Irene said darkly.

Mavis shot her a glance. 'The military polis came and took him away to the prison. How could she be seeing him?' Mavis didn't like talking about the night she and Sam had mysteriously come by the silk for her wedding dress.

'Well, who is it, then?' Irene kept asking until they were at Franchino's, and face to face with Bella herself. 'Oh, you look lovely!' Irene burst out, because she did. Bella was wearing the purple dress that she had once lent to Irene for a dance at the Alhambra. Because of Irene's delay in returning it, the frock was Bella's single surviving item of clothing from her bombed home.

'It's my good luck dress,' she said, twirling round on the shiny marble floor. 'Well, it's my only one.'

'Come on then,' Irene demanded, tying her pinny on. 'Mavis has been taunting me all the way from the park. Who is it you're walking out with tonight?'

Bella bit her lip. 'I wouldn't be doing it at all. I shouldn't be going out with him, I know that. But he's been persistent. He's been ruthless!'

Mavis added, 'He's been coming here every night and beseeching her to go out with him.'

'Who?!' Irene laughed. 'Tell me!'

'It's Jonas Johnson,' said Bella.

Irene gasped. She felt like all the air had been sucked out of her lungs. 'What?'

'Jonas. He's—'

'He's the ginger fella who was at my wedding reception with Lily. She's his sister,' supplied Mavis helpfully.

'He's the one who put a brick through our front parlour window!' cried Irene, and all the coffee drinkers glanced over, earwigging with interest. 'At least according to Ma Ada!'

Bella looked crestfallen in her one remaining beautiful dress. 'I know I should never had said yes to him . . .'

He had kept coming back to Franchino's, just as Mavis had said, night after night, to see Bella, to lay siege to her, as Mavis saw it, and Mavis had quietly noticed his stealthy progress.

He was definitely worth looking at. He was the bonniest of all the Johnson clan. Their ugly duckling, is what Arthur used to say about him. You'd never know he'd belonged to that gaggle of gangsters at all, but for his flaming red hair. All the Johnsons were bald as coots, but they'd been ginger as bairns, Arthur recalled. Under her beloved black wig, it was rumoured that Lily was ginger, and the ailing mother on her deathbed had been famed around the town for her lustrous auburn locks.

Luckily Irene hadn't been working at the ice-cream parlour on the nights that Jonas had turned up. Perhaps that was on purpose, Mavis wondered? Could he have been so subtle as to work out their every movement and did he know their work timetable? Perhaps he was avoiding Irene because she belonged to the family that his family had a vendetta against? But then, she thought, she herself belonged to the same family, too. In fact, Mavis was married to Sam, who, in his blundering way, was the root cause of the family fracas in the first place (he'd been on the fiddle and been caught out, Mavis had been told). But Mavis had known the Johnsons for years, from living on Watling Street, and Jonas treated her no differently to a friendly dog he'd see on the street.

'What's he coming round every night for?' Mavis kept asking Bella.

Bella had seemed very uncomfortable about the whole thing. 'Trying to sell me stuff. Black market, I suppose.'

'Oh,' said Mavis. It was a kind of sore point between them. For a while Mavis and Sam had been bringing sugar and various supplies to Franchino's. All at a bargain price. Those nights lugging sacks down the dark alleyways had been arduous, but they'd also been a lot of fun, as far as Mavis was concerned. Smuggling contraband sugar was how she and Sam had courted, in fact! But Bella hadn't been all that pleased to learn that she'd been accepting stolen goods. ('What did she expect?' Sam had cried, exasperated. 'What did she think it was, magicked up out of nowhere?')

Mavis couldn't see what Bella's problem was, either. She got the feeling there was family pride behind it somewhere. She wanted to do things exactly the way her father used to do them, and apparently he'd never have accepted nicked goods, either. Nor would he have had anything to do with the Johnson brothers . . .

Well, that was all fair enough, she supposed, and so Mavis had avoided the subject in the ensuing months.

But here was Bella now, fraternising with one of the Johnson boys herself. The only attractive Johnson in the whole clan.

'He's only after supplying us with some eggs and sugar,' Bella said with a careless shrug, wiping down the tables one night. 'It's nothing.'

Mavis cried, 'But you wouldn't have it when you found out Sam's sugar was nicked! Do you think the Johnsons' sugar will be any more on the level?'

'I don't know,' Bella had said, starting to look cross. 'But he's being persistent. And we could do with the sugar. And the eggs.' She slapped the wet rag down on the counter and let out a cry of frustration. 'And yes, he's flirting with me like mad, Mavis. And do you realise how that makes me feel?'

Mavis had stared at her in wonderment. She'd never heard Bella raise her voice like this. 'Frightened? Worried?'

'What? No!' Bella glared at her. 'It makes me feel . . . *nice*, Mavis. It makes me feel attractive. It makes me feel like I'm coming alive again at last!'

'Oh!' Mavis had said. 'So you don't think it matters that he's one of the Johnsons?'

Bella sagged slightly. 'I don't know. Probably it does. I'm probably letting myself in for a whole lot of bother even talking to him, let alone responding to him and flirting back. And agreeing to going out with him . . .'

Mavis squealed. 'You're going to go out with him?!'

Bella looked shamefaced. 'For a fish supper and a walk along the seafront. Am I mad, Mavis?'

'Why, no!' said the newly married girl, who still thought romance was the answer to everything.

'I don't want to get in too deep . . . Not with a bunch of villains,' Bella had sighed. 'Mostly I think he just wants to escape from home. It's like a house of death at the moment . . .'

'Oh yes,' nodded Mavis, who'd been hearing all about it from Lily, of course. 'Eeeh, but what's Irene gonna say? About you running around town with one of the Mad Johnsons?'

Irene wasn't impressed, it had to be said. She went a bit stiff and quiet as Bella explained about her planned fish supper and stroll with the enemy that night.

'Couldn't you have found a nicer lad?' she said as she took up position at Tonio Franchino's cappuccino machine. 'And what would your papa have said about this? You once told me that he had to beat off the Franchino boys with your grandmother's ebony cane when they came round here!'

'That was years ago. That was the old uncles. They were downright nasty. They were running a protection racket and my papa wouldn't play ball.'

'All the Johnsons are the same,' said Irene, parroting what she'd heard at Number Thirteen from the lips of Ma Ada.

'I think Jonas must be different,' said Bella. 'He's a gentleman.'

83

'Gentlemen don't put bricks through old ladies' parlour windows!' Irene cried, and then reined her temper in. She didn't want to be upsetting her friend. 'There. I've said my piece. Just think on it. And don't get in too deep.'

Bella smiled at her and patted her hand. 'Don't worry, love. I'll be careful. I'll be fine!'

In that moment, Irene thought, Bella had never looked more radiant. It seemed that she really was under this lad's spell.

Then the door opened and in walked Jonas Johnson himself. He moved with a loping swagger. He was looking smart in a double-breasted suit (nicked, probably) and his wavy hair all combed carefully down. He looked marvellous, in fact.

Both Irene and Mavis gave a little shiver at the sight of him. Irene repeated a mantra in her head: don't get caught between. Don't start interfering. Don't mention the front parlour window . . .

Jonas nodded hello at both Irene and Mavis, and then he turned to Bella and gave her the full force of his radiant smile. 'Are we ready, lady?' he asked.

'More than ready!' Bella laughed. 'Take me out!'

Chapter 15

'But we can't go down there! It's not allowed . . .'

It was a beautiful summer's evening and the seashore was deserted. At any other time, when there wasn't a war on, the pale golden sands would have been packed with locals and visitors, basking in the last rays of the day. Bella could remember days in her childhood when her family would be here till after the sun had set, turning back for home only when the night chill had set in.

'No one's gonna notice us down here . . .' Jonas Johnson laughed, striding unevenly ahead through the tangled marram grass.

Eeeh, what am I doing down here with a strange fella? Bella wondered wildly, struggling to keep up in her heels and long dress. This wasn't the gentle stroll that she'd anticipated, but there was just no stopping Jonas. It was like taking out a headstrong young dog on a long leash. He limped, but it didn't hold him back much. He went galloping on ahead and she had no choice but to follow, even here, where folk were forbidden to go during the hostilities. There was rusted barbed wire strung out along the sands to deter the unwary and, rumour had it, landmines had been planted in strategic positions to fend off possible invaders.

'What if we get blown to smithereens?' Bella called out to him.

'We won't, lass!' he laughed. 'I know where I'm going.'

He certainly seemed very cocksure and, despite herself, Bella found that an attractive trait in a man. She spent a lot of time with women who tended to think too much about things. She herself could sometimes overthink things and longed to become more impulsive and daring. Well, perhaps this first date with Jonas was her chance?

The salt seawater and the sand would ruin the fabric of her dress, she was sure. Her only decent frock! And besides the dangers of the rumoured bombs and the razor wire that could rip their flesh, and the bother they would get into if they were caught, there was also the more imminent danger from Jonas himself, of course. What did he think he was doing, dragging her down here to this secluded spot? Clearly he imagined he'd be getting his wicked way with her, right from the off.

I've been a fool! Bella suddenly thought, coming to a dead stop on the brow of a dune. Her feet were sliding in the sand and she whipped off her heels, feeling cross with herself. I've gone and got myself into a dangerous situation with a known criminal and a gangster! She thought: maybe I can defend myself with my heels? Clatter him one in the face if he gets too close?

She tutted and shook her head. It was her papa who'd taught her to always think about how best to defend herself. He had always been slightly paranoid about ending up in a fight.

'Erm . . . Jonas?' she called out to the young man she hoped she wouldn't have to fight off.

He was on the flat, damp, shining sand and staring at the shoreline now. They had reached the sea's edge at last and it was reflecting the flaring orange and gold of the wide, open skies. Jonas looked triumphant as he turned to smile at her. Her attention was caught by the sort of birthmark he had by the corner of his mouth. If anything, the imperfection made him look even more handsome to her. There was something so unabashed and lovely about the way he carried on. Now he unloosened his jacket and tie and spread out his arms. 'Isn't it wonderful? All this space! We can see for miles out here!'

She ploughed through the crumbling sand in her stockinged feet to join him. 'I have actually been here before, you know . . .'

'Yes, but not for ages, I bet,' he said. 'Not since before the war started. All that time, we've been cramped up inside our tiny little houses. And worse, we've had nights squashed up in cellars underground, waiting for them bombs to start dropping on us . . .'

Bella looked away quickly, startled by his tactlessness. Did he not realise what had become of her family?

He went on: 'I get so claustrophobic. My arms and legs feel like they're full of aches and pains, like an old person already! And it's just from being indoors most of the time. And being in our house, where everyone's so quiet and careful and scared all the time. We're waiting and wishing our lives away . . .'

Bella was listening to him so intently that it came as a surprise when he suddenly burst into action and bolted away from her. He started running at top speed across the sand, leaving deep footprints as he sprinted away from her. Even with that lurching, limping gait of his, he could go at quite a speed! And his legs were so long, she thought, as she watched his jacket flare out behind him.

Wasn't the story that he'd been invalided out of the army with a funny knee or a foot?

She didn't have time to think about it.

'Ha'way!' he yelled across the empty sands. 'Catch us up, man!'

87

'What?' Bella laughed. 'I can't run in this frock . . .' Even as she shouted this, she realised she couldn't even remember the last time she had run anywhere. The very idea of hitching up her dress slightly and pitching herself forward and kicking up the heavy sand with her bare feet . . . It seemed so alien and impossible!

'Come on, Bella!' he shouted again.

But there was no one here to see her, except him. But what did she care anyway if anyone had been looking?

So she ran. She kicked up her heels and ran with all her might, soon getting breathless and squealing with joy as she hurtled towards him.

'That's it, pet!' he shouted encouragement. 'Come and catch me!'

And he set off again, with that long, loping stride, his auburn hair catching the last of the day's sun. Bella pursued him, yelling out with pleasure and flailing her cast-off shoes in the air.

She hadn't felt like this in ages.

When she caught up with him, he swung an easy arm around her shoulders and planted a kiss on her lips. A quick, joyful smacker. Nothing lingering and not pressurising her for anything more. Just a celebratory kiss that she barely registered as she fought to regain her breath.

'That was amazing!' she gasped.

'Let's go and get those chips,' he said. 'Let's get the best chips in all of South Shields, eh?'

Ma Ada always said she wouldn't give Swetty Betty any of her hard-earned cash. There was a long-standing feud between the two women, the nature of which no one quite fully understood, but Ada generally said that she thought that Betty was dirty, and the poorly spelled name of her establishment was hardly conducive to making you want to eat her greasy fried food. Despite all of that, Swetty Betty's was the place that all the denizens of the Sixteen Streets flocked to when they had enough coins for a fish supper.

They weren't put off by the fact that some years ago, someone had defaced the signage that said 'Betty's' by adding a crudely scrawled and misspelled 'Swetty'.

'Well, they're the best chips in town,' Megan said. 'You're cutting off your nose to spite your face, Ma Ada.'

The old woman said huffily, 'It'd be cheaper to make our own chips. Give me that pail of old taters. I'll soon have them peeled . . .'

Megan pulled a face. Even Beryl looked dismayed at the thought of Ma Ada's pale and greasy chipped potatoes. They certainly weren't a patch on Swetty Betty's. Rumour had it, the quality of the hot oil was what made the large, red-faced woman's chips and batter so dark and delicious. Ma Ada always disputed that fact: 'It's because she never bloody changes it, that's what it is! It's years' worth of muck turning everything that colour!'

That night Megan wasn't to be deterred. It was too warm an evening to be labouring over the range for very long and just the talk of Betty's chips was making her stomach curdle with hunger. She counted up the coins in her purse and told her mother-in-law: 'I'm dashing out to Betty's, whatever you say. Now, can you force a few chips down you, and a scrap of fish?'

Ma Ada glared at her blonde bombshell daughter-in-law. The lass was much cheekier than she'd ever been before. Since Number Thirteen had become a houseful of women, it seemed that Megan was getting bossier and inching her way up the pecking order somehow. Ada wondered whether she'd have to do something to set the lass back down in her place again . . .

'Ooh, I'd love chips as well,' said Beryl, who looked knackered as usual after her stint at the shipyard. She was stretching out her aching limbs, standing there in her bra and slip with her hair up in a scarf. The poor lass worked ever so hard – harder than all of them – but, eeeh, she did look a state, dressed like that in the back parlour.

Ma Ada relented and reluctantly fetched her coin purse from its usual place under her cushioned seat. 'I'll share a supper with the two of you. And ask old Swetty for some fish scraps for Lucky.'

Lucky perked up at this and hopped into the old lady's lap in readiness.

Taking coins from Ada and Beryl, Megan hurried out of the house, clattering the front door after her. This is what my life is like now! she thought, hastening up the long, steep slope of Frederick Street. My life is so bloody boring nowadays that it comes as a highlight when I get permission to go to the fish shop! She could have laughed at how pathetic it was, but still her mouth was salivating at the very thought of those chips.

Swetty Betty's was just a couple of streets away, at the top of the hill. With dusk coming on, the shutters were down, but golden light still spilled onto the cobbled road through the open door. A queue had formed and was out on the street. Megan seethed with impatience, but actually it was just the right time: not too early, not too late – the fat would be hot and Betty would have palmed off yesterday's leftovers onto her earliest customers by now.

Megan joined the queue breathlessly, nodding hello to various familiar faces. 'Hello, pet,' said Aunty Martha, togged up in her headscarf and heavy coat, even in the sultry evening warmth. 'How's the bairn doing?'

'He's all right,' Megan shrugged, and didn't elaborate.

She couldn't see what else there was to say about babies. In her experience they were boring things.

Megan waited impatiently amidst the chatter of her neighbours and peered eagerly through the doors into the hot fragrant steam, feeling her stomach gurgling with hunger. She'd had nowt but a single ginger snap with her tea all day. She was just starting to curse Ma Ada's frugal habits when there came a great clattering of footsteps round the top corner of the street.

It was a lad with his lass, chasing each other down the street, laughing joyfully. Going on daft. Acting like kids, really, as they hurtled towards Betty's and the back of the queue. And, by the looks of them, they weren't kids. They weren't even all that young. Late twenties, probably, the pair of them . . .

Megan's breath caught in her throat as she recognised them.

That was Jonas Johnson, surely? She'd recognise that good-looking redhead anywhere. He had a kind of birthmark on his cheek that made your heart go out to him, somehow. And his green eyes were just dazzling, Megan thought. And his lass? The one he kissed as they stopped running and joined the back of the chip shop queue?

Aye, Megan recognised her, an' all.

It was Bella Franchino, Irene's friend and employer. Carrying on in public with one of the Mad Johnsons!

'Eeeh, hello, there!' Megan called out in a falsely bright voice from her place in the doorway.

Jonas looked at her, blinking, like he had no idea who she was. But Bella gasped and the smile dropped right off her face at the sight of Megan. 'Oh, er, hello,' said Bella.

The sight of the blonde girl instantly took all the fun out of the moment. I knew we shouldn't have ventured over this way, Bella thought. But Jonas had been insistent. Swetty Betty's was the best in all of Shields.

Now here was that Megan Farley, narrowing her green eyes at them like a spiteful cat. So interested to see the pair of them together. So keen to make trouble whenever and however she could . . .

What kind of trouble could Megan make out of this?

Chapter 16

Early the following week, old Ma Johnson died and word spread quickly throughout the streets.

She was well known by everyone, her family renowned and feared throughout the whole of South Shields. A murmuring of respectful gossip rippled through the lanes and over the backyard walls. The Mad Johnsons were in mourning for the old lady who had commanded them for so many years.

Some even set to wondering whether their reign of terror might be over now, without that matriarch masterminding their every move and telling them what to do. Would they founder and lose their grip over their tawdry empire on Tynemouth? Hardly anyone dare voice these thoughts out loud. It was a time for paying tribute and being seen to pay respects to a woman who almost everyone had been afraid of offending.

Mavis felt sympathy for her friend, Lily, but also understood that Lily's strongest feeling at this time was relief. Her months of tending to the ailing old woman were over now, and there were about to be changes in her life at home, as the family reconfigured itself into a new order.

'Families are so complicated,' Mavis said, as she listened to Lily going on.

'Ours definitely is,' said Lily. She was in a headscarf and without a scrap of make-up on. It was Tuesday afternoon and she had called round to fetch Mavis on her afternoon off. Mavis had rashly offered to help her friend wash and prepare the body for the undertaker. It was traditional, of course, for the family to tend to the dead like this, in their own home, and the job generally fell to the women. As Lily had pointed out, she was the only lass in the Johnson clan, and she could really do with a bit of help.

'Yes, of course,' Mavis had readily agreed, and almost immediately regretted it.

'You daft thing,' Sam had shaken his head at her, before setting off for the docks that morning. 'What do you want with clarting on with some old dead woman? Lily's got a nerve, asking for help . . .'

But Mavis felt like she had given her word, and she felt loyal. Also, there was a part of herself that felt keen to see the inside of the Mad Johnsons' family home. It was a kind of legendary place in the streets where Mavis had lived for most of her life. A three-up two-down, just like anyone else's house round here, but rumour had it that the place was opulently rigged out and furnished with the best of all the spoils from generations of criminal activity. Folk always said it was like a proper Aladdin's Cave inside.

This Tuesday afternoon, however, Mavis had lost her eagerness to explore that notorious realm. Lily in her head-scarf looked grim as she walked with her down Watling Street, towards the Johnson home on Tudor Road. Mavis knew a little bit about the kings and queens of England from an old book that Mrs Kendricks had once given her to read. In her mixed-up, naïve way, the younger Mavis had assumed that because the Johnsons lived on Tudor Road, it meant that they were somehow blessed with royal blood and connections. Surely that was the reason everyone treated them with such fear and respect? And not just because they were famous for breaking jaws and kneecapping people who got onto the wrong side of them?

'You'll miss your mam, I'm sure,' she said now, to make conversation with the briskly marching Lily.

'She wasn't really herself in the last few weeks,' Lily said. 'It was a cruel thing. It was horrible to see her suffer like she did. I just did what I could to keep her comfortable. Any daughter would do what I did.'

'Aye, you've been a good daughter,' Mavis said, and Lily looked pleased to be told that.

Then they arrived at Number Seventeen Tudor Road, and it was time to step inside Aladdin's Cave.

Mavis didn't think the place was as fancy as all that. It certainly didn't live up to the rumours and all the things that the local gossips had promised. Yes, the furniture inside was old-fashioned and had probably been expensive, years ago, and the paintings on the walls were in proper frames and were dark and oily like ones you'd see in a fancy museum. The overriding feeling that the quiet, empty house gave Mavis was one of desolation and dreariness. She had walked in expecting Buckingham Palace and found herself in the middle of somewhere much more dingy and neglected.

'It's gone to rack and ruin, I know,' Lily said. 'I've not had the time. With all those lads in and out all day, and me either working at the shipyard or tending to me mam, there's not been time to keep on top of all the housework . . .'

'You don't have to explain anything to me,' Mavis said. 'I can't say anything.' She was thinking of the three days' worth of dishes stacked messily in her own Belfast sink at home. Neither she nor Sam were keen housekeepers. Houses were for living in, they both felt. And living was generally a messy and dirty business.

Lily was assembling clean towels and filling the kettle for a bowl of water. Soon it hit Mavis that she was really going to have to help her friend rub down and pat dry an actual dead body, up in the bedroom above. She was really going to have to go through with this.

Because she hadn't grown up within the warmth and comfort of a proper family, Mavis had never been exposed to this kind of ritual before, though she knew it was the done thing, of course. She had never actually seen a dead body lying in state. The only bodies she'd ever glimpsed were the ones you sometimes saw poking out of smoking, smouldering ruins after an air raid. And then you looked quickly away and tried to forget the horrible things you'd seen. This would be very different.

'Ha'way, then,' Lily said, when the dish of water was ready, and she led them up the stairs into the sepulchral room where Ma Johnson was waiting for them.

How tiny the pale old lady looked! Her hooked nose protruded above the bed sheets and her eyes were tranquilly closed. The afternoon light was milky through the drawn curtains and, now that Mavis stood there facing the terrible scene, she actually felt that it all looked rather peaceful and nice.

Lily set busily to work with soap, flannel and towels, telling Mavis what to do. The younger girl complied and was quite efficient in her work. She was quite used to being set routine tasks and simply getting on with it. The poor old woman's waxen skin glowed by the time they had finished with her, and Lily felt that they were doing something good in preparing her like this, as if they were getting her ready to look nice when she arrived in the place she had to go to next. Mavis felt her throat choking up with tears when she watched the usually brash Lily gently combing out her mother's tangled, silvery locks.

'She looks like an angel,' Mavis said, as Lily stepped back to survey her handiwork.

'Some angel!' Lily laughed. 'She was a flamin' terror!'

Just at that moment there was a clattering at the front door downstairs. Lily pulled a face. 'That'll be the lads coming back. I better go down and explain what we've been doing. They'll be glad, I reckon. Will you wait here a second, Mavis pet?'

Mavis nodded dumbly, and her heart was beating faster, she realised, as she heard the noise of those notorious Johnson boys downstairs. They crashed about and their voices were guttural and deep.

Lily hurried downstairs to see them, and Mavis was left alone in that bedroom with the pale, clean, dead old woman.

She felt unnerved just then. A shiver went through her.

To take her mind off the dead body and the rough lads downstairs, she glanced around at the rest of the room. They'd been so busy she hadn't had a chance to take in her surroundings. There wasn't a great deal to see, but the thing that arrested her attention straight away was the beautiful and ornately carved dressing table in the far corner of the room. The large mirror reflected back the whole room, and Mavis caught a glimpse of herself looking terror-stricken.

Lily was talking downstairs with those rumbly-voiced boys. Was it all of them? Had all the Mad Johnsons come home at once? Would they come traipsing up here to see their mam? Shuffling in, all teary-eyed and awkward? And Mavis still standing here, like a servant or a handmaid. Wouldn't they demand to know what she was doing here? Or maybe Lily would explain?

Mavis felt trapped and scared, but there was something about the dressing table that drew her attention. Her own reflection wavered closer as she stepped across the room.

There were trinkets and jewellery boxes and all kinds of glittering things on display here. Clearly this was the old lady's holy of holies. This was the true Aladdin's Cave of Tudor Road. Mavis had never seen so many rings of precious metal and fancy, multi-coloured jewels. She simply stared, holding her breath.

She had no idea why she did what she did next.

Was she crazy? She knew all about the Mad Johnsons. She knew all about the things they were rumoured to have done to those who had crossed them.

But still Mavis couldn't help herself.

At any moment Lily was going to walk back in here, bringing her terrible brothers.

But still Mavis reached out to touch those precious things on the dressing table. Her fingers touched cool, precious metal. She brushed her fingertips against ropes of pearls. She picked up a locket on a slender gold chain. It was a plain locket, surely not very precious.

But it stirred something in her. A queer feeling. What if I opened this? What if I opened this tiny clasp and opened this locket and found . . . a secret? A tiny cameo. A photograph or a painting. She fiddled with the clasp and it wouldn't come free.

What did she think she was doing?

Now there were footsteps on the stairs. She could hear Lily's voice. She could hear her explaining and she could hear Lily mentioning Mavis's name, and saying what a help she had been.

Mavis's heart was hammering in her chest. Her vision reeled and she almost fainted with fear, there and then, right in front of the dead woman's hoard of treasure. But she rallied. Mavis seized control of herself and, before she knew it, she pocketed the locket on its slender chain. She stuffed it into her trouser pocket and smoothed her apron down, and turned away from the dressing table.

When Lily came back into the room bringing her two oldest brothers, Mavis was standing sentinel beside their immaculate mother. She stood with hands clasped respectfully, almost as if in an attitude of prayer. Lily gave her a little smile as the lads filled up the tiny room with their huge presences, and Mavis's heart was still beating like crazy inside her skinny chest. And that stolen locket and its chain were burning a hole in her pocket.

'Come on Mavis, let's leave the boys with their mam,' Lily told her, ushering her out of that place.

Lily wanted to say, 'Wait! I've made a mistake! This thing I don't even want somehow fell into my pocket!'

But it was too late. Lily was leading her downstairs.

The boys took no notice of her at all. She was negligible.

She wondered: was the locket precious? Was it an heirloom they were going to miss?

What kind of trouble had Mavis made for herself now?

Chapter 17

Ma Ada wasn't impressed to hear the news about who Bella Franchino had been queueing at the chip shop with.

'I thought she was a friend to our family,' the old lady thundered. 'And there she is, walking out with one of the enemy! With the very one who put my front window in!'

Irene sighed. Ada was getting herself worked up like this quite regularly these days. 'You know you can't take Megan's word as gospel. She'd say anything to stir up bother.'

'Others saw them too,' Ma Ada snapped. 'Aunty Madge was in that queue at Swetty Betty's and she said the two of them were brazen. They were canoodling in full view.'

It was Tuesday afternoon and Irene had popped home between her morning stint at the biscuit factory and her hours at Franchino's. She had only come back to check on the bairns and hadn't been expecting to find Ma Ada in a full-on temper.

'She's carrying on with that ginger bloke and everyone knows that he's the one who chucked that brick at our house!'

Irene bit her lip, unwilling to point out that that fact was still moot. Only Ada herself had witnessed that act of vandalism. She could easily have been mistaken, though it was true that Jonas was extremely distinctive, even from a distance. Truth was, Irene wasn't mad keen either, that Bella seemed to be courting with one of the infamous Johnsons, but neither did she think it was any of her business.

'Ask her what she thinks she's playing at,' Ma Ada said, her eyes bright and fierce. 'When you see her this afternoon. Ask her if she knows what she's doing!'

Irene smiled weakly, thinking that Ada would blow her top if she found out what her new daughter-in-law Mavis was up to this very afternoon. She was even more mixed up in the Johnson family than Bella was!

It was time to change the subject, Irene decided. 'Have the bairns been okay this morning?'

The old lady scowled. This morning – and all the afternoon to come – she was in sole charge of Irene's Marlene and Megan's slightly younger son, Johnny. The two were toddlers, one unruly and the other too placid. Marlene was too bright and alert for her own good, demanding attention and terrorising her wide-eyed cousin. 'She's a right handful these days,' Ada said.

Irene knew what she meant, but what could she do? There was only Ma Ada at home today. Beryl was at the shipyard all day and Megan had found herself a nice new job at the butcher's on Fowler Street. 'There's only you at home all day,' Irene said apologetically. 'I know we rely on you a little too much . . .'

Ma Ada waved her hands. 'Nay, it's all right, lass. I shouldn't be complaining. I should be glad to have the two little angels here with me. I'll get them in the pram this afternoon and take a walk to the park. Some fresh air will do us good. We've all been feeling cooped up indoors . . .'

Irene felt like asking if a jaunt to the park was such a good idea. It was tiring enough for any of them to go that far with two bairns in the pram, let alone Ma Ada attempting it, what with how much they'd all been hearing about her bunions. Also, Marlene was getting too big and boisterous to be wheeled around in that old thing . . .

Still, Irene didn't want to dampen her mother-in-law's improved mood. She went to kiss both babies and realised it was time for her to dash to Ocean Road. Before racing out, she told Ada: 'It's not definite yet, but it looks like Tom's going to get home next week for a few days.'

Ada brightened up immediately. 'That letter you got this morning! Is that what he said?'

Irene nodded. 'But you know how these things are. Nothing's ever set in stone.'

'Of course! Does he say which day? When does he think he'll be here?'

'Next Wednesday. Week tomorrow. And he's got three full days, if everything goes according to plan.'

'Oh, that's wonderful!' Ma Ada crooned, hugging both babies to her. 'Did you hear that, Marlene? Your dada's coming home again!'

Irene hurriedly made her way through the busy streets to work. People recognised her and would shout and wave, and this never failed to cheer her. Some called out and asked about the bairn, and she was glad to tell them that Marlene was thriving. She was bonny and robust and noisy. No wonder her grandmother became so frazzled and short-tempered when she was left alone at home with her.

It was warm and clammy this afternoon, and Irene could already feel her work blouse sticking to her. At least Franchino's always felt cool inside, even when she was working the coffee machine. Bella had installed a fan at the counter and it was blissful to be standing in its cool breeze.

As soon as she arrived at work, Irene pledged to herself that she was not going to say a single word about Jonas Johnson. If Bella was going to go out with him, then that was her business. It had nothing to do with Irene, or anyone else. It was just nice to see Bella looking happy.

She really did look happy, too! It was only when she greeted Irene brightly and went about her business singing that Irene appreciated how low Bella had been for such a long time. This was the Bella she had known when she first came to work at Franchino's. She skipped about lightly between the tables, making daft jokes with the coffee drinkers. She welcomed everyone warmly to her tiny little kingdom.

All this from one date with that Jonas fella? Irene thought wonderingly. He must really be something!

As they settled into the rhythm of the afternoon's working, Irene gradually felt herself relaxing. Things were okay. She didn't have to worry about the bairns in Ma Ada's care. Sam and Mavis were happily wed and sorted in their home. Tom was heading home for leave next week. And maybe, just maybe, this new romance between Bella and Jonas could even assuage the ructions between the Mad Johnsons and the Farleys? Was that even possible?

If her Tom could hear the workings of her mind this afternoon, she knew what he'd say. He'd laugh about the way that she somehow got herself involved in everything and knew secrets about everybody's business. 'Only because they come and tell me!' she would protest, and she thought about it as she ground a new batch of coffee beans. 'It's folk who come to me to tell me all their problems and woes! It's really not because I'm nosy . . .'

Turning back to the glass-topped counter, she was surprised to find a customer standing there. The rather smartly dressed lady was waiting patiently for service, wearing a tight, wary smile. It took Irene a moment to realise who she was, and where she had seen her before.

That hat with the brown feathers sprouting out of the top, and the fine quality of her light summer jacket. She was standing there ramrod straight and spoke with an accent that was, while still local, quite clipped. She enunciated every word very carefully.

'Is Mavis Kendricks at work today?'

'Mavis Farley, she is now,' Irene pointed out. And in that moment, she realised who the rather grand-looking woman was. She looked less upset and flustered than the first time Irene had spoken with her, in the churchyard of St Jude's.

'Oh, of course. Is she here?'

'It's her afternoon off. Er . . . you're the lady who came to her wedding, aren't you? Do you remember? I came running out after you, when you dashed off.'

'Oh yes.' Now the lady looked uncomfortable, and ready to dart off once more. 'How do you do?'

'I'm Mavis's sister-in-law, Irene Farley. Would you like to leave a message for her with me?'

'No, no, it's all right . . .' Mrs Kendricks was backing away. 'I simply popped in on the off-chance . . .'

Irene said, 'You want to make your peace with her, don't you? That's why you turned up at the wedding. That's why you're here today. But she won't listen, will she?'

The older woman stood staring at Irene, who wondered if perhaps she had overstepped the mark. Perhaps I am just nosy after all, Irene wondered.

Mrs Kendricks' upright posture seemed to sag slightly. 'If only she would listen to me . . . If she would just give me a few moments of her time . . .'

Irene couldn't help herself. 'Look, I'll brew us both a frothy coffee. It's my break coming up. We'll sit in that booth over there and you can tell me what this is all about.

It's hard to get through to Mavis sometimes. But she trusts me, I'm her best pal. Will you stay for a coffee?'

Mrs Kendricks relented and favoured Irene with a little, hesitant smile. 'All right. I shall. Thank you . . . Irene.'

Chapter 18

'Hey, lady, you're meant to be working today . . .' Bella reminded her when she went to fetch two more coffees.

'I'm sorry, Bella. It's just the woman I'm talking to, she's—'

'You've been sat there ten minutes, Irene! I've been seeing to all the others on my own.'

'I know, but it's important . . .'

'Your work's important, Irene! You're here to be a help!' There was something sharp in Bella's voice that Irene hadn't heard very many times before.

Irene kept her voice low as she poured two more coffees. 'It's the woman who came to Mavis's wedding and caused a scene. I think that I'm about to find out why . . .'

'Work comes before gossiping,' Bella reminded her sternly.

'This isn't just gossip. It seems important,' Irene insisted.

The two women looked at each other, and there was a tension there between them that had never been there before.

Bella nodded. 'All right. Take her coffee to her, but don't sit there all day. There's lots to do.'

What was Bella being so snappy about, Irene wondered, as she frothed the milk. She seemed happy before, with her new boyfriend and all. Why couldn't she cut Irene a bit more slack?

*

In the secluded booth, Mrs Kendricks took a sip of her second cup and relished the richness of the flavour. 'I had no idea the coffee would be so wonderful here. I've often seen this little place, but I'd rather dismissed it, I'm afraid . . .'

'You're local, then?' Irene asked, fishing for details.

'Oh yes, indeed. I've lived in this area for many years. I live in Whitburn, right by the sea.'

'Lovely!' Irene said, picturing what kind of place a lady like this must live in. There were fancy houses down that way, she knew, and she could just picture Mrs Kendricks living in one of them.

'You're being very good to me,' the older lady said. 'You were kind to me after the wedding, too, when I was so upset. I'm glad you're here today. You must think me a mad woman . . .'

'Not at all, Mrs Kendricks.'

'Please, call me Elizabeth. And I think I owe you an explanation as to why I seem to be following your friend and sister-in-law Mavis all around the town.'

Irene smiled awkwardly. 'It would be nice to know, yes. I feel like . . . like there's something here that I can help with. I don't know. I feel like there's something tragic here, a misunderstanding of some kind, maybe . . .'

Elizabeth Kendricks smiled sadly. 'There's no misunderstanding, my dear. Not really. Mavis and I understand each other only too well. We know what we are to each other.'

'I see . . .' But Irene didn't really see at all.

'The simple truth of the matter is that Mavis is my daughter.'

Irene almost choked on her coffee. 'So that *is* the reason after all! But . . . but . . .' She stared at Elizabeth. 'Forgive me, but you're so different! You've got the same name, but I thought maybe a more distant relative, perhaps, or . . .'

Elizabeth looked bemused at Irene's stammering confusion. 'I adopted her. When she was quite small. Both Mavis and Arthur were my adopted children.' She bit her lip nervously. 'Did neither of them ever tell you that? Did they never say anything about me?'

Racking her brains, Irene came to the conclusion that they never had. There was a fuzzy, dark cloud where their pasts should have been, and both siblings tended to avoid the subject of their childhood. They both referred to themselves as 'orphans' and a vague sense of tragedy hung over them both at such moments. They didn't like to linger on their darker days.

'I did everything I could for them. For both of them.' Elizabeth produced a neatly pressed handkerchief and delicately blew her nose. 'I really was a mother to them. I would have done anything for Arthur and Mavis. And I thought they knew that. I built my life around the two of them, and I gave them anything they wanted and needed . . .'

Something must have gone dreadfully wrong, Irene thought. The fact was, neither of this poor woman's children ever referred to her at all. They both carried on like she didn't even exist. Imagine if, one day in the future, Marlene was to turn around and behave like that towards Irene? She felt her throat constrict and her eyes prickle at the very thought. Imagine being disowned and shucked off by your own children!

'What happened, then?' Irene asked, keeping her voice low and leaning in. 'What went wrong?'

It looked like Elizabeth was going to break down in tears at any moment. Her hands were shaking as she set down her cup. 'Th-they turned on me, Irene. The pair of them. They decided that I wasn't their real mother after all. They threw everything back in my face.'

'But that's terrible!'

'Oh, they were still only bairns at that point. They weren't very old when they ran away. But they were old enough to know what they were saying, and what they were doing. They were grown up enough to know just how much it would hurt . . .'

Irene gasped. 'They ran away!'

'Yes. Imagine how that felt. After everything I'd done. To put me through that. All that terror and worry and anxiety. It was a wicked, wicked thing to do.'

Irene stared at her. 'I can hardly believe it!'

'Oh, it's true.' Elizabeth Kendricks flashed her eyes. 'Do you think I'd lie about such things?'

'No, I just mean . . . the Mavis and Arthur I know, I can't imagine them ever being so . . . so cruel . . .'

'Well, believe it,' said the smart woman stiffly. 'When they were nothing but kids they upped and left me. He was barely a teen and she was just eleven. And they decided they'd rather live like ragamuffins on the streets than be a part of my life any longer!'

Irene was profoundly shocked by what she'd heard, but had to admit that the tale was beginning to dovetail with the life story she'd already partially known about the brother and sister. Yes, they had lived rough on the streets and they'd barely made it safely into adulthood. That was a story she'd heard them both allude to; both with a certain amount of relish and pride.

Another thought struck Irene. 'The other mystery about the two of them is to do with their house on Watling Street. All their friends have wondered how they came by it? When the pair of them had nothing at all? They don't pay any rent. They seem to own the place outright and neither seems to think there's anything unusual about that!' Irene looked steadfastly at Elizabeth Kendricks. 'Is that down to you, then? Is that something to do with you?'

'You're quite astute, Irene,' the woman complimented her. 'And you're quite right. They wanted nothing to do with me. They never even wanted to see me again. But when I offered to buy them a house to live in, they were more than happy to accept. They almost bit my hand off. And so that's what I did. Quite a modest house, in a not very respectable part of town. That much they would accept from me. But nothing more. They wouldn't let me visit. They never wanted to see me . . . ever again . . .'

The older lady properly dissolved into tears and her dainty hanky was soon wet through. Irene clumsily offered her a paper napkin, but Elizabeth managed to regain her composure.

'That's a terrible story,' Irene told her. 'I'm so sorry.'

'I knew you would understand.'

'But why on earth would the pair of them turn against you like that? What made them so bitter and so ungrateful?' Irene was quickly going back through everything she knew of both Mavis and her brother. Wasn't there a shifty streak in them? Something untrustworthy? Something that, though she loved them both to bits, made her wonder about their strangeness? Sometimes she had no idea what was going on in their heads.

'They hate me,' Elizabeth said. 'That's all there is to it. The pair of them hate my guts. After everything I did. After all the sacrifices I made for them. I took them into my home and my heart when they were so small and helpless. I really tried to do my best . . .'

'I'm sure you did!'

'But at the end of it, all I got was hatred and scorn from them. It broke my heart, Irene. I've not been the same woman in all the years since.'

Irene nodded, quite understanding why. These past two years she had grown to know exactly how a mother's heart felt, and how it was vulnerable. To be a mother was to live with your heart and your feelings for your child forever exposed. The idea of having those feelings spurned . . .

Impulsively, she asked Elizabeth Kendricks: 'Is it too late? Is it hopeless?'

'I thought, maybe not. I thought, when I saw the notice of Mavis's wedding in the paper, I thought I could go. I could make my peace. If I could just see her face to face . . .'

Irene nodded. Yes, she had seen how badly that had gone. Then she found herself patting the smart lady's cold, thin hands. 'I will help you,' she said. 'Anything I can do to help, I will do it. I promise.'

Elizabeth smiled thinly. 'Why, thank you, my dear. That's just what I hoped you'd say.'

Chapter 19

She was like a little bairn organising a dollies' tea party. Mavis had been talking of nothing else for days and, if he was honest, it was starting to grate on Sam's nerves ever so slightly.

'Stop fretting, love,' he told her earnestly. 'You don't have to go to masses of effort. It's just Ma and the others coming round for a cuppa . . .'

'But it's important!' Mavis gasped. 'You don't understand, do you? They'll be looking at everything and judging everything. They'll be seeing how we live and what this place is like. It's all about them seeing what kind of home you're living in. You're Ma Ada's favourite, you know.'

He shook his head and flipped through the evening paper. 'Hardly. I was never that, to be fair. Tony was. Or maybe Tom is now. And she's always had a massive soft spot for Bob, of course. Nah, I'm like the black sheep nowadays. I let her down so badly.'

Mavis looked up from her sandwich-making, appalled. 'Because of me? Do you mean, because you married me?'

Sam winced, cursing himself for his words. Why had he said that? 'Nay, nay, of course not, love. They're all chuffed as muck that you're part of our family now. No, I meant because of all that black market stuff, when I got in too deep with that. Nothing to do with you, pet . . .'

Mollified slightly, Mavis went back to slicing and spreading the bread with a thin layer of fish paste from a jar. Sam decided against asking her why she was making the sandwiches a full day early. Didn't she realise they'd dry out and go rock hard in the pantry overnight? He knew that she took any questioning of her method of doing things as a massive criticism, so he just kept quiet and read his paper.

'So that funeral's going ahead tomorrow, then, I hear,' he said.

'Hm?' Mavis asked, and then realised what he meant. 'Yes, right at the same time as our tea. I know Lily would like me to go and support her, but I stood firm and said, no Lily, I can't. My mother-in-law and them are coming over and I'm playing hostess. I've already put them off once and changed the day, so I can't be doing it again, or they'll think I don't want them.'

Sam thought it was peculiar that Mavis and that rough Lily Johnson had become so thick with each other lately. He wasn't sure he liked it, having done his best to sever his own links with the Johnsons. 'Surely they won't be going ahead with all the usual palaver,' he said. 'Not when there's shortages and everything going on?'

Shrugging vaguely, Mavis was piling up her lopsided sandwiches and attempting to cut the crusts off. She remembered once seeing at a fancy do, when she was small, the tiniest triangular sandwiches that looked so elegant with no crusts. Each one of them was bite-sized and melt-in-your-mouth. That was the effect she was after today, but the bread was crumbling and going wrong. 'Last I heard the Johnsons were having a proper cortege for their mother. They wouldn't disappoint her, dead as she is. Six black horses pulling a glass-sided hearse and men in great big top hats. They're having all the works, Lily told me. Because they wouldn't want to let her down. More than that – they can't be *seen* to be letting her down. It's dead important to them.'

Sam shook his head and whistled. 'What a funny bunch. They're all addlepated. I wish I'd never crossed paths with them.'

A queer, panicky feeling rippled through Mavis then, as she thought about the Johnsons and of her dreadful moment of wrongdoing by the old mother's dressing table. That precious object had weighed heavily on her mind since she had purloined it the other day. All this clarting on with her tea party was a welcome distraction from thinking about her guilt and fear. 'I'm nipping upstairs,' she told Sam, wiping her hands on the tea cloth and leaving her dainty sandwiches lying in a heap on the dining table.

Up in their room she sat on the bed with her face in her hands for a moment. What if the Mad Johnsons discovered her theft and came after her? Surely one of them would realise a locket was gone? But there had been so much jewellery there. Far too much for one old woman to wear in a lifetime. Maybe none of them even knew everything she had on her dresser?

But Lily might know, she thought. Lily would have an itinerary, surely, of every piece of treasure that her mother had possessed.

Nervously Mavis reached into her bedside cabinet drawer and took the gold chain and locket out of an old silk hand-kerchief she'd had for many years. In the dusky bedroom light, the gold glittered softly and she thought, it's very precious and expensive, this. And I've been such a fool. What would Sam say if he knew I'd been as greedy and as idiotic as this?

Her fingers pried at the tiny clasp. She hadn't been able to open it before, but for some reason this time it sprang apart under her fingernails. Maybe there would be something inside that would let her know how precious and personal and important it really was. Fascination overtook her fear as she opened it up.

Squinting in the dim light, Mavis peered closely and saw that it was a tiny cameo photograph. So small, the face inside, that at first she could barely make it out. The hair was long and dark brown and the skin was creamy like the froth on coffee. High cheekbones and soft, warm eyes. A humorous quirk of a smile. Mavis thought, I know this face, don't I? I think I recognise her. And there's a voice that goes with this lovely face, a voice so familiar and close that I can barely catch hold of it with my mind. It eludes me . . . it . . .

'Mavis?' Sam was calling, coming up the staircase.

Swiftly she stowed the locket back in the old hanky inside her private drawer. Then he was standing in the door, looking at her.

'Are you having a cry?' he asked softly.

'Just a little one,' she nodded, finding that she was.

'Eeeh, surely not about all the fuss over Ma Ada coming to visit? I'd never have asked them at all if I knew it was going to put you to all this bother.'

'No, it's fine,' she rallied. 'They'll just have to take us as they find us. And it'll be fine because Irene will be there for moral support, and Bella . . .'

Sam raised both eyebrows at that. 'You've asked that Bella Franchino to come as well?'

'Aye, well, she's a friend as well as my employer. And she's not been back round here for a while.'

'I don't know what me mam will say about that, though. Bella's not in her good books lately, you know . . .'

'Oh no,' Mavis said, realising what she had done, and started to fret about her tea party all over again.

'Ah, they'll just have to get along together,' Sam laughed. 'And I'm sure Ma will perk up if Bella brings some nice dainties, like she normally does. You can't stay mad with Bella for long.'

That was true, Mavis thought, as she went back down to the scullery to wrap her finger sandwiches in greaseproof paper for the morrow. But it was true that now she was walking out with the bonniest of the Johnson lads, Bella had, in some indefinable way, become somewhat different. She and Irene had already discussed it in depth during their last shift together at the biscuit factory.

The two girls had come to the conclusion that courting and carrying on with a lad had made Bella strangely snappy and impatient, especially with her small staff at Franchino's. It was a curious phenomenon. Surely happiness ought to have made her nicer and more forbearing? Instead, Bella seemed intemperate and impatient.

I wonder why, Mavis thought, nibbling on a bread crust in the scullery. And then the thought occurred to her that maybe it all had to do with sex. She blushed. She knew it was true that you just didn't know how people would react, or what they'd do, or how they would change when it came to sex. Everyone was a mystery.

Mavis was just finding out herself how sex changed things. It was like living in a mysterious, private country that belonged only to you and your fellow. What went on there – on that deserted island – only you two would ever know. It was magical and, for the first time ever, Mavis was starting to comprehend what all the fuss was about.

So maybe it was all to do with what went on in private between herself and Jonas Johnson that was making Bella seem so altered to her friends?

And now Sam was calling Mavis back upstairs. It was time for an early night.

Chapter 20

There was an extra bit of excitement at the start of Saturday because a letter arrived with exotic stamps and franking. 'It's our Arthur!' cried Mavis, thrilled to be holding the first substantial communication from her brother since his arrival in Burma several months earlier.

His handwriting was appallingly spidery and wandering, and Mavis sat for ages at the breakfast table trying to decipher it. The hour was creeping later and there was a lot for her to do in preparation for her afternoon visitors.

'He says it's so hot that when he puts on make-up for a show, it just sweats right off him. He has to paint it on an inch thick.'

'Oh?' Sam was listening with interest as she read out her brother's words, trying to picture this unfathomably foreign country where he was singing and dancing and mixing with a whole world of new people. It sounded bizarre and utterly dangerous. Arthur was showing off in his letter, as they might have expected him to: telling them how many times he'd almost been killed, and how many hundreds of men flocked to see him and his company perform on their makeshift stage. He, of course, was the star of the show. 'Does he do it all dressed as a lass, then?' Sam wanted to know.

'I'm not sure,' Mavis said, running through the letter, both sides, once more, as if trying to glean all the details she could from every single line. 'But there's a lot of talk of eyelashes and falsies and how hot wigs are when you wear them in the jungle . . .'

'He sounds happy, though,' was Sam's considered opinion.

'Yes, you're right,' said Mavis. 'That's just how he sounds.'

'Like he's found the exact thing he should be doing,' added Sam.

Mavis wore a little wistful look as she folded the tissue-paper letter back into its envelope, and propped it, pride of place, on the mantelpiece.

'Before I start making this place shipshape, I have to pop round to the Johnsons' house for one last look at the mother before the funeral.'

Sam rolled his eyes. 'I hope you don't think I'm going too.'

The Johnsons' home was what everyone would call the 'corpse house' today, with the old lady laid out in her coffin in the best front parlour. It was traditional for well-wishers and locals to flock round there in the hours before the funeral to take a look at her. The sons – who would have sat up all the previous night, holding a boozy vigil by her side – would be carefully noting who did and didn't come to pay their respects.

'All we have to do is pop our heads round the door and show willing,' Mavis told him. 'Oh, please come, Sam. If you don't show your face, they'll think you're showing disrespect. You don't want to be doing that. Not to those lads.'

He muttered and sighed, but he knew she was right.

Mavis wasn't too keen on going round there herself, as it happened. She still expected to be halted in her tracks and asked about that missing locket.

As the newlyweds nipped out that morning to the home of the Johnsons, Mavis was wondering whether she oughtn't to have brought the stolen necklace with her. Maybe she could have slipped upstairs when no one was looking and returned the dratted thing to its rightful place on the dressing table?

But it was too late now, and besides, that was a ridiculous idea. Imagine if someone caught her!

Nervously the two of them slipped in at the back of a gaggle of mourners gathered outside the Johnson house. 'It's like queueing to get into the pictures,' Sam whispered to his wife.

They weren't there long. There were so many visitors shuffling through the house, under the watchful eyes of those Johnson boys in their stiff best suits, that Sam and Mavis weren't even particularly noticed by anyone. They were just two of many who were ushered into the candlelit sitting room and invited to stare at a cross-looking, tiny old lady who was lying there in a box, wearing her Sunday best.

Mavis stared at Jonas – the youngest of the Johnsons – who was standing guard over the coffin itself. They had probably been taking turns through the night and day to stand sentinel like that. He didn't flicker or give any indication that he recognised Mavis, or anyone else who popped in. He and his brothers were impassive: in a trance of ritualised mourning.

Mavis and Sam did their duty and scuttled out as quickly as they could. Up the street they went, back to their own home. Sam was shivering. 'Stuff like that gives me the creeps. I used to hate going round to see folk lying like that, when I was a bairn. All those old aunties. Mam always took us though. She made us go.'

'Aye, it's the proper way,' Mavis said. 'And this afternoon, when the cortege goes through the streets, everyone will have to get out of their houses and doff their hats and stuff. The Johnson boys will expect it. We'll all have to line the route.'

'Oh God, you're right,' Sam groaned. 'What time will that be? Not when Ma Ada and that lot are visiting, surely?'

*

As things turned out, it was exactly when Ma Ada and the other guests were visiting that the funeral cortege went by. They had hardly settled at the tea table with Mavis's curly dried sandwiches before Mavis was jumping up again.

'We only have to go out for a moment,' Mavis said.

'What?' Ma Ada barked. 'I've only just sat down!'

'But it's tradition,' Mavis said, looking nervously from her mother-in-law to her new sisters and Bella. 'You know that. When a figure of that kind of standing in the community leaves the corpse house for the churchyard, we all have to go out and pay proper respect . . .'

The visiting matriarch tossed her head. 'Not me. I had absolutely no respect for that old crow. She brought them boys of hers up to be little monsters. That family have terrorised everyone in this part of town for years! No, I'm staying here with my tea. It'll go cold otherwise.'

Ma Ada was sitting there in her best blouse with her ancient cloche hat set firmly on her head and it was clear to everyone that she wasn't budging an inch.

'Irene,' Mavis implored her most reliable sister-in-law, 'would you come out with me? It's just there'll be hell on if the Johnsons notice that no one from our house has come out to see her on her way. We don't want to stand out . . .'

Irene got up, 'Is that right?' she asked. 'Is it such a big deal if people don't go out?'

'Oh aye,' Beryl told her. 'Specially with a family like the Mad Johnsons. They're rotten for holding grudges, people like that.'

'Aye, and so am I,' Ma Ada growled. 'One of them buggers put my window in, are you forgetting that fact?' With that, she turned to glare at the startled Bella Franchino.

'It was your young man. He was the bugger tossing bricks around. I've still not been able to get a new pane put in. I lie there fearful in my bed each night, wondering what's coming next.'

Bella got to her feet, feeling uncomfortable. 'I'll come out with you, Mavis. It's only for a moment, isn't it? It's no bother.'

'Huh!' Ma Ada sipped her tea and watched them leaving the room. 'What if I stood there and I chucked a brick at them, eh? What if I waited till they went past and then I hoyed a brick at the coffin, eh? What would you say then?'

'Eeeh, Mam, you wouldn't!' Sam said.

'Of course I wouldn't, you dafty,' she sighed. 'People like that never get what's coming to them. They ride roughshod over everyone else and expect everyone to dance attendance upon them. Well, it's not fair.'

She watched all the youngsters get up from the table, abandoning Mavis's rather meagre and disappointing tea. As soon as she realised she was going to be left alone, Ma Ada got up painfully on her bunions and followed them out. 'But I'm doing it just to be nebby, not because I thought anything of the nasty old witch.'

Watling Street was lined on both sides with doleful-looking folk.

'It's coercion, this,' Ma Ada tutted, shaking her head. 'It doesn't mean anything if people are out on the street out of fear of reprisals.'

'Oh, please hush,' Mavis asked her. 'Others can hear you, going on like that.'

'I don't care!' Ma Ada spoke up. 'She was a nasty, vicious, horrible old woman and I don't care who knows I thought so!'

Even Ma Ada had to admit, though, it was nice to see the horses. They made a wonderful clatter, high-stepping on the cobbles, all the way along Watling Street. Six stallions, black as night, with headdresses and gleaming livery.

'Well, I want ten horses when it's my turn!' Ma Ada told the young'uns. 'And I want more flowers than that, too.'

It was true that the floral display wasn't all it should have been, but presumably it had been hard for even the Johnsons to get their hands on enough fresh blooms.

The old lady's sons were marching alongside the gleaming glass-sided carriage, all within sight of that tiny, gleaming box: the three older, thick-necked, bullet-headed boys and the youngest with his wavy auburn hair. As he strode past their little gang, Jonas Johnson caught sight of Bella and gave her a firm wink, which everyone saw, and which made Ma Ada gasp. 'The cheeky bugger! Fancy winking at ladies!'

Bella looked pleased, though.

'You should have taken your hat off,' Mavis told her mother-in-law as the cortege vanished round the top corner of the street.

'Like fun I should have,' the old lady said. 'I've not washed my hair this week.'

'Back inside, everyone,' Sam urged them. 'Show's over.'

'There's plenty more to eat!' Mavis said.

Just as all the inhabitants of Watling Street were turning to re-enter their front doors – relieved that the tense ordeal was over – they all heard the piercing noise that every one of them dreaded hearing the most.

'The siren!' gasped Irene, hugging her toddler to her chest. 'Where's your shelter round here, Mavis? Where do we have to go?'

Chapter 21

Ma Ada was disgusted to find that the air-raid shelter they took her down to was much worse than the one she was used to. The shelter beside the Sixteen Streets was clean and commodious compared to this damp, wormy, horrid hole. She muttered to herself as she was led into a dingy far corner and sat between Beryl and Irene, who was holding Marlene.

'Well, what a lovely finish to a tea party,' she glowered at her daughters-in-law. 'A funeral procession and a bombing raid!'

There seemed to be an awful lot of people down here with them, far more than the shelter was built for, surely. Again, the women of Frederick Street were used to having a little more comfort than this when they were sent underground. Here people were rowdy and shoving into each other, and it was a bit of a free-for-all when it came to getting sat down. Ma Ada was accustomed to receiving automatic respect from her neighbours, but no one here even spared her a glance.

'I don't like it much over this side of town,' she said, glaring at her youngest son.

'It's all right,' he smiled bravely, as they both tried to ignore all the tumultuous noise around them.

'She'll bring you down in the world, our Sam,' his mother warned bitterly. 'You'll see.'

Sam looked mortified by this but put his mother's spite-fulness down to fear of all the upheaval. Then, with a pang of dread, he realised that Mavis was nowhere to be seen.

'I thought she was here a moment ago!' Bella cried when he asked her. 'She was right behind us. I saw her just before we came down the stairwell, she was talking to Lily Johnson . . .'

Ma Ada tossed her head and tutted disapprovingly.

Sam had a strange feeling. He felt that Lily could lead Mavis into any old bother and his wife would gladly follow . . .

'I'll go back and look for her,' he said, making sure he had his gas mask.

'Oh, don't get lost in all those twisting tunnels,' Irene warned him.

'I won't.'

'She should be here with her family!' Ma Ada snapped. 'Not running after that rough lot!'

Sam had it quite right when he thought that Mavis would run anywhere after Lily Johnson. Her gratitude for the girl's friendship (compounded by secret guilt over the stolen locket, which even Sam didn't know about) made her susceptible to doing precisely what she was told. Mavis was also quite easily led sometimes, Sam thought, possibly because she had grown up with a bossy and charismatic brother like Arthur. She was doomed to simply trail along after others. It was as if she found herself dazzled by them . . .

He elbowed and jostled his way through the milling crowd. People were so disorderly round here. They were passing round bottles of brown ale and now they were singing songs like they were out on a works outing. He recognised many from the funeral procession of the old Johnson lady; they were in their best suits and hats and looked set to carry on the wake even here, in the mouldy passageways beneath the park.

He fought his way back through the press of agitated bodies, squirming through the confusing tunnels, and finding himself, at last, blinking in the brightness of daylight. The sirens were still blaring away, of course, and it felt shocking to be running in the wrong direction, towards the oncoming disaster . . .

Mavis was back above ground, in the street, in the midst of an air raid, and it was all because Lily Johnson was refusing to listen to sense.

'All them buggers! They've all abandoned her! They've left her out there to fend for herself!'

'But she's dead, Lily,' Mavis protested. 'There's nowt worse can happen to her, now . . .'

'I can't leave her there in the street!' Lily had half dragged Mavis along with her, back to the corner of Watling Street, where the undertaker's horses were whinnying and stamping. The men in their tall black hats were trying to calm them, but the horses were getting ready to bolt.

'See? The men are still with your ma,' Mavis shouted at her over the rising din. 'The funeral men are still there, seeing to the horses.'

'Aye, but what about me brothers?' Lily cried. 'Them buggers went running off and left her!'

As they hurried up the street, they saw that the undertaker's men were trying to unhitch the horses, in order to lead them away to safety. An ARP warden was shouting furiously at them from across the road, Mavis saw. And surely that was Jonas Johnson with his shock of red hair, standing by the carriage and his mother's tiny coffin?

'See, Lily? Jonas stayed with her! He's still here!'

'Jonas!' Lily shrieked, putting on a burst of extra speed and dashing full pelt towards him. 'They dragged me away.

They made me leave her. I should have known you'd stay here and look after our ma!'

Jonas was yelling at them both, his face twisted and his birthmark livid pink: 'Get back down that bloody shelter! I'll stay here with her. You get yourselves to safety!'

One of the horses, freed of the harnesses, panicked and reared up on its hind legs, kicking out against its pinions. Now the siren was louder and augmented by other, too-familiar noises. There came the awful droning of engines and the distant coughing of anti-aircraft guns.

'It's starting!' Jonas screamed at his sister. 'Get underground, you silly mare!'

Lily was beyond listening to his sensible advice. She was determined to be with her mother, who was lying helplessly there in the road. She had been abandoned in the middle of her own stately funeral, and Lily couldn't bear that thought.

'I'll stay with her, I promise!' Jonas cried, clinging to the side of the hearse as it was dragged sideways with a screech by the panicking horses. The undertakers – two older men and one young lad – were panicking too now, as their untethered charges started running rampant in the road. Mavis heard the ARP man cursing them loudly as he ran for cover. The droning engines were drowned out by the first of the bombs hitting targets somewhere across town. The huge eruptions of noise sounded louder than any Mavis had ever heard before.

'They're coming here!' Jonas bellowed at the girls. 'They're coming over this way!'

The horses were free. Great, surging mountains of glossy muscle wearing black plumes; they looked both absurd and wonderful as they took off down the street. Their hooves rang against the cobbles as the undertakers set off haplessly after them. Only one steed was left still partially attached to the hearse and it was this creature who wrenched the whole ornate vehicle onto its side. With a horrible rending crash the hearse went over and every gleaming pane of glass was smashed in an instant. The coffin slewed to one side and was buried under the weight of the cart. The wheels were sent spinning in the air and they looked futile and hopeless. Lily and Jonas were flung backwards onto the road.

The last horse reared up and, just before it went thundering after its stablemates, it struck out with its hooves and caught the hapless Mavis a glancing, ringing blow on the side of her head.

She pirouetted on the spot, with her tea party dress flaring out briefly around her. A curious kind of relief flooded through her stunned system, just before she was rocked by the pain. She felt relief because all the awful noise was gone. The bombs going off and the planes growing closer; all of it seemed to vanish. The horrible din of that hearse going over and the smashing glass and crunching of the coffin underneath – all gone. The satanic whinnying of the horses as they vanished up the lane. In one instant all that cacophonous hullabaloo was cancelled out and Mavis couldn't hear a single thing.

There was blissful, empty, calming silence and stillness. Absolutely everything was paused.

And then, inevitably, she crumpled to the ground beside the overturned hearse and she felt something like a bomb going off inside her head. Have we been hit? she wondered wildly. Has Watling Street taken a direct hit?

Near enough. The waste ground one street across was erupting in a huge fountain of earth and rock. Flames were leaping, bright orange, higher than the houses and the blast put out everyone's windows. Lily and Jonas were flung head over heels like dolls, back down the street. For a few minutes, until the Luftwaffe passed over and headed elsewhere, further along the coast, they felt like they had been sent tumbling through the gates of hell itself.

The noise went on in great buffeting waves, shattering everything in its wake.

Heaped on the cobbles, however, Mavis had stopped hearing it. She lay there motionless, covered in blood and shards of glass, a horrible cloven-hoofed imprint on the side of her head.

She would never hear anything else again.

Chapter 22

By Wednesday evening Tom was home, and that was a great relief for Irene. The days had been fraught and difficult, and just the sight of him ambling tiredly up the railway platform lugging his bag made her heart melt all over again.

'Hey, what are you crying for?' As he hugged her close, he reeked of stale cigarette smoke and bodies in overcrowded carriages. His journey north had been a tortuous one, with several frustrating delays. He'd been travelling for so long, he had dark stubble coming through on his cheeks.

'It's been just awful, Tom.'

'Let's get home and you can tell me the whole thing. Where's the bairn? Didn't you bring her to meet me?'

His train was so late it was past Marlene's bedtime. She'd have been grouchy if Irene had dragged her down here to wait for her dad on the platform. Marlene was growing up to be the kind of bairn who let the adults know exactly how she was feeling.

Their journey through the streets of South Shields to their home reminded both of them of that first time, almost two years ago, that Tom had brought Irene home, as a new bride, to meet his family. On that occasion, of course, they had arrived right in the midst of an air raid, and the town had been in flames all around them. They'd had to run to dodge the bombs, hoping against hope that Frederick Street hadn't been taken in a direct hit.

Luckily tonight's arrival was a much quieter and safer affair.

Nowadays Irene was so at home here, that it was she who led the way up Fowler Street towards the town hall and then the warren of streets by the docks. She carried her exhausted husband's kit bag for him and her feet hurried unerringly towards the Sixteen Streets.

It felt to them both as if she had always lived here and Tom was pleased to see her so settled. He had never been convinced that it was a good idea for her to move in with his family in the first place. He thought she would have been much safer back down in the obscure wilds of Norfolk, but Irene was determined to make a place for herself at the heart of his family, and indeed she had. It was impossible to imagine Number Thirteen now without her living there – and Marlene, too, of course.

It turned out he wanted a quick drink at the Robin Hood before going home, which wasn't really like him. Tom wasn't really a pub-type man, Irene thought. When she'd first met him at dances in Grantham, by the air base, back when she was a land girl, he'd always seemed less sure and cocky about himself than the others when it came to standing around in bars. Tom was shyer, moon-faced, slightly innocent-seeming. Not the beer-swigging rowdy type, like some of them she had seen.

'I'm just dying of thirst,' he shrugged, leading her into the gloom of the saloon.

Irene didn't mind. It was a few minutes extra that she and Tom would get to spend together, before he was back with Ma Ada and the others and she would have to share him.

The bar was very quiet, but Cathy Sturrock was dolled up to the nines, as ever, with her hair piled up in a great big chignon. She beamed at the sight of Tom. 'This one's on the house!' she declared, manhandling the beer pump with great aplomb.

'You can't go giving away free beer,' he laughed.

'Shush,' she said, patting his hand. 'Eeeh, they'll all be glad to see you at Number Thirteen, hinny. All the dramas round there lately. It's all gone crackers.'

Tom looked alarmed. 'How do you mean?' He darted Irene a look, as if she'd been holding back on him.

'Well, maybe not crackers exactly,' Cathy said, backpedalling slightly. 'But you've missed a lot. The wedding reception here, and your Sam moving out, and then that Johnson fella putting a brick through your ma's front window, and now how he's running about with Bella Franchino. And then this awful air raid on Saturday and what happened to poor Mavis!'

So this was how she gossiped about the regular drinkers in her pub, Irene thought. Cathy kept up to date with all their goings-on, and spread them about like this. She was better than the World Service.

Tom sank the first half of his pint of mild and sighed deeply. 'You don't get beer like that down south,' he said, and added, 'Mavis is all right, though, isn't she? She's not badly hurt?'

'She's looking better than she was, apparently,' Cathy said, wiping down the bar with a soggy cloth. 'It's bad concussion, so she's been out of it for a few days. And her hearing still hasn't come back.'

'Poor thing,' Tom said.

Irene was giving Cathy a hard stare. It wasn't her place to pass on all the family news! Irene had been waiting till they got home, in the privacy of Ma Ada's back parlour, to update Tom with all the details of their lives. Mavis's injuries – thankfully much less awful than they had seemed to everyone during the horrible confusion of last Saturday – had been top of her list of news items. But Cathy had jumped in and stolen a march, making it seem as if Irene had been unconcerned about her poor sister-in-law!

'Will her hearing ever come back?' Tom turned to ask her.

'No one knows for sure,' Irene said. 'And it's hard communicating with her at all. Sam's writing everything down and trying to get her to write down what she wants. He's put a little pad of paper beside the bed. But she can't even write her letters straight just yet. She's still quite shaky.'

'I'm not surprised,' Cathy tutted. 'Caught out in a raid like that, and with those Mad Johnsons, too. See how they always cause bother? They're proper bad luck. From what I heard, Mavis was trapped underneath the upturned hearse with the coffin on top of her! And the old woman's body had fallen out, as well!'

Irene shook her head. 'That's rubbish. That's just idle gossip.'

The landlady shrugged. 'By the time the tale turned up here in the Sixteen Streets on Saturday night, that's how people were telling it. Mavis had gone deaf and blind and all her hair turned white because the funeral cortege had been struck by a bomb and that old corpse was dancing out of its coffin in the middle of the road!'

'It wasn't like that at all,' Irene sighed. 'Aren't people awful gossips? Do you see how everything gets so distorted? Mavis got kicked in the head by a funeral director's horse. And the body didn't fall out of the coffin, though the coffin did fall out of the hearse. It was ghoulish enough, seeing all that, when the all-clear sounded . . . We thought Mavis was lying dead there on the cobbles . . .'

'Sam must have been out of his mind with worry,' said Tom.

'He was!' Irene said, remembering Sam's horror as he pelted up the street. 'There was Jonas Johnson, trying to revive her, kneeling in the wreckage of the hearse and all that. And Sam goes running up yelling, "Leave her alone, you ginger bastard!" Like he thought Jonas was trying to do further harm to her.'

'He wasn't though, was he?' asked Tom, looking shocked.

'Of course not! He was taking care of her while the air raid finished. He crouched there as the bombs went off, getting further and further away, and houses burned on streets nearby. He didn't want to move her because she was bleeding and he didn't know what her injuries were.'

Tom toyed with the end of his drink. 'Seems to me that we owe him a debt of gratitude then.' He looked like he had misgivings. Like a Farley who hated being beholden to a Johnson.

'I reckon we do,' Irene said.

'By, he's a good-looking lad, that Jonas Johnson,' grinned Cathy Sturrock, leaning on her pumps and unconsciously pushing out her chest. 'When he was here at that reception, having a dance around with the lasses, I almost abandoned my post at the bar and chucked myself under him. What a bobby-dazzler! No wonder Bella's mad about him. Even if he does limp a bit.'

Tom rolled his eyes at her. 'Aye, well thanks for the drink, pet. And all the news. I reckon it's time we got back to me mam's house, don't you, Irene? She'll be wanting to tell us all this stuff herself.'

'Make sure you come back in here before you go back down south,' Cathy told him. 'How long are you here for, hinny?'

'Just three days,' he said.

'Eeeh, not very long, then!'

Irene took hold of his arm as he slung his kit bag back over his shoulder. 'It'll have to do,' she smiled up at him. 'Come home now, Tom. Come and see the bairn, and your ma, and all the others . . .'

Chapter 23

All of the grown-ups had questions for Tom when he returned home that night. They gathered in the back parlour and fussed round him, bringing cups of tea. Beryl had made a pan of broth with a ham bone and pearl barley and he wolfed it down as they all watched.

Ma Ada stared in pride at her aviator son, but he did look shabby with his growth of dark stubble and his dingy travelling clothes! He looked exhausted, too, like he was about to keel over.

Something was said, in all the kerfuffle of welcome, about his having spent some time at an airbase in Scotland. It was the first time any of them had heard of this, and Tom looked shamefaced at letting it slip. Everything he did was completely hush-hush, of course. He was always careful not to let down his guard. Irene stared at her husband, wondering what kind of deadly dangerous mission he was involved in. She knew that she'd never really know all the details until, perhaps, long after the war was over.

Megan watched them from the corner of the room, flipping through her film magazine and listening to the wireless. She scowled as Tom made a big fuss of firstly his own daughter, and then little Johnny.

'Look how the baby's putting his arms up to be cuddled!' Ma Ada gasped with delight. She'd never seen little Johnny looking so animated and excited. When Tom picked him up, he kicked lustily with his chubby legs and even made excited gurgling noises.

'He's acting like he's chuffed to see Tom, just the same as the rest of us,' Beryl grinned. She watched her brother-in-law cuddle the family's youngest member, and Beryl experienced a strange, bittersweet rush of affection for them both. Tom was such a natural father. No wonder Johnny was delighted to be held by him, squirming in his arms like that. It was exactly the kind of tenderness that he missed when he was being held by his mother, Megan. She had never had very much time for the bairn.

Ooh, but families and bairns were complicated, thought Beryl. Because there was Marlene, looking peevishly left out. The emotion was clear on her face, an oddly sophisticated expression for a toddler. As she watched her dad hugging and giving some time to another bairn, Marlene was looking distinctly displeased.

'Look at her face!' Irene chuckled, drawing everyone's attention to it, like it was funny. Everyone laughed and Marlene looked even more irked by them all. Beryl didn't think it was funny at all. It wasn't nice, having your nose pushed out, even for the briefest moment. It looked to her like Marlene was storing up resentments already, even at her very young age.

'Ah, don't get huffy, baby,' Tom laughed, taking both bairns onto his knee. His daughter looked mollified slightly as he sang to them both in his rough, sweet voice. She clapped her fat palms to his song, knowing all the right moments to do the simple actions. Johnny merely stared up at the moon-faced Tom with an expression approaching awe. His utter devotion made the women laugh once again.

Megan wasn't laughing, though. 'If the kid likes you that much, Tom, you can have him. Why don't you and

Irene just take him off my bloody hands? You'd be doing me a favour.'

Ma Ada was scandalised. 'Our Megan! You can't mean that! You love your bairn!'

Megan pulled a face and turned the page in her magazine.

Both Irene and Beryl knew that their sister-in-law was being utterly candid. She would happily pass her child over for another woman to look after. There wasn't a shred of sentimentality about motherhood in her. When Tom had finished his song and Johnny was drifting into an exhausted sleep, she simply took him and put him to bed. She looked relieved she wouldn't have to be bothered by him for a few hours.

'Some people shouldn't even have kids,' Ma Ada frowned, when Megan was out of earshot.

Upstairs in the attic room a little later on, Irene managed to get Marlene to sleep in the antique cot, and then, in the silence, she turned her full attention onto Tom. He kissed her tenderly and told her she had lost weight. 'There's nothing to you! Are you eating right?'

She felt rather pleased at the idea of being more slender, but it was true that supplies were a bit more meagre without Sam at home supplementing their pantry with bits and pieces he'd come by at the docks.

'Well, you look a bit different too,' she told Tom.

'Leaner and tougher, eh?' he grinned, and his smile made her feel so happy. That grin was one of the reasons she had fallen for him in the first place. It was so open and unguarded. When he smiled his whole personality came flooding out, full force. When he turned that smile on Irene, she felt safe and happy. She knew exactly how he felt about her.

'Dirty and smelly,' she chuckled, wrinkling her nose.

'I should have had a bath when I got in,' he said. He held up his hands in the lamplight. 'This grease and engine oil on the skin and in the lines – it won't come out. It's tattooed into me now.'

They got ready for bed and slipped under the cool, fresh sheets.

'Are you sure everything's okay here?' he asked her, reaching for her hand. 'You all put on such a brave face all the time. It's hard to tell.'

'Well, I admit last Saturday was a bit hairy, when we were down in the shelter by Watling Street. We had to wrestle with your ma a bit because she wasn't happy going into an unfamiliar place. But she was just frightened. She gets cross when she's scared, but we managed her.'

'You're so good with her,' Tom whispered. 'You treat her so well. I was never sure, when I first brought you here, whether you and Ma would get on, but I should have known it would be fine. She trusts you completely. The way she looks at you! She can't imagine this place without you now.'

Irene glowed in the dark at this praise. Then her mind drifted off to Megan and her caustic words as she had sat there tonight. Flipping through her movie paper, staring at pictures of Joan Crawford in her Hollywood palace with her perfect bairns.

'How can she even joke about giving her baby away?' Irene gasped. 'She's got no heart. I think she's empty inside.'

'Maybe,' Tom said. 'I don't think she's a very happy lass. I don't know what will become of her. She's doesn't fit in with us, and she knows it, I think.'

'Baby Johnny is so lovely, as well,' whispered Irene. 'He's so placid and quiet. Almost to the point where you start thinking there's something wrong with him. But to see him tonight . . . and the way he reacted to you, Tom! That was wonderful to see!'

Tom laughed. 'I've got the knack! Bairns seem to like me.'

They drifted for a bit, dozing under the spill of moonlight that seeped through the blinds. Irene was half dreaming about the future. She was letting herself imagine the house of their own they would one day move into. When everything was over and there was peace and they could move away from Number Thirteen. Perhaps their family would be bigger by then, and she could rule the roost and have everything just the way she wanted it. No more poky rooms filled with ancient furniture. No more heavy curtains pulled against the daylight. No more Sixteen Streets.

Irene would have lovely, open windows and net curtains billowing in the spring breeze. Light and airy rooms. Modern furniture. Lots of space to dash around in. Beautiful colours. No more brown paint.

She started slipping towards sleep. 'One day soon . . .' she heard herself saying aloud.

'What's that, pet?' Tom asked her, blinking awake.

'Oh! I was just picturing when we get our own house. One day. I closed my eyes then and I could just about see it. I could see just what it's going to be like. And we were there, and Marlene . . . and the others! The other bairns we're going to have, after the war is over . . .'

He rolled over in the bed and she heard his stubble scratching on the pillow as he grinned at her. 'You saw all that when you closed your eyes, did you?'

'I see it every time I close my eyes,' she told him. 'Every single time.'

'You just keep those pictures in your head,' he said. 'Don't lose sight of them. Don't let them fade. And then one day

– I promise you – I'll make them all come true. We'll both make them all come true.'

Then it was time for them to sleep. He coughed a little as he turned over and made himself comfortable. His chest rumbled as he lay there and Irene didn't like the sound of it. He was wheezy and chesty and, at one point, it was like he couldn't even catch his breath.

'Ah, you know what it's like,' he said. 'We breathe in such horrible stuff when we're up there. Smoke and burning fuel and all kinds of noxious, nasty stuff. And it's so cold and misty, too. We're always coughing our guts up. The whole lot of us. That's just part of the life!'

He made it seem normal. He made it sound like an occupational hazard. But Irene lay there tensely in the night until his coughing eventually subsided and he fell into a deep sleep beside her.

Chapter 24

Early the next morning she left him still fast asleep, and took baby Marlene downstairs, where Grandma could look after her all day.

'It's a shame you couldn't take a couple of days off while Tom was home,' Ada said, hugging the sleepy baby close.

'It doesn't work like that!' Irene said brightly. 'Not at the biscuit factory. Anyhow, he'll be sleeping all morning, I should think. I've got time to get my shift in as usual.'

'You lasses are all so full of energy,' Ma Ada said admiringly, sipping what was already her second cup of tea of the morning.

Beryl was ready to set off for work too, looking bright and perky in her headscarf and overalls. Once they were on their way, however, marching down the hill towards the docks, she started confiding in Irene about wanting to leave her job.

'What?' Irene was shocked. 'But you were so determined to work on the ships. You went mad because folk told you it wasn't a job for a girl . . .'

'I know,' Beryl bit her lip and looked wistfully at the looming towers and cranes ahead of them, smudgy in the silvery morning mist. 'And I still hold by everything I said. But since I fell and smashed my arm . . . well, for one thing, it's a bit weaker, and another, I find I've lost my nerve a bit.'

'Your nerve?' Irene frowned, staring with concern at the sister-in-law she was closest to. The crowd of lasses was thickening around them and soon they would have to separate at the factory gates.

'Aye. And to think that I used to go swaggering in there. Thinking I would show them all; they'd find out that I was just as tough as any of the men.' She took a deep breath and squared her shoulders, wincing as her slightly wonky arm gave a twinge. 'It's since my Tony died and I had that fall. I don't feel as brave or as confident nowadays.'

'I think that's understandable,' Irene told her.

'They'll all say I'm hopeless, though,' Beryl sighed. 'If I tell them that I want to pack it all in . . .'

Irene couldn't help her with her decision. And besides, the hooter was going now, calling in all the girls through the factory gates. They had to part and Irene felt a pang of sorrow for Beryl. She wished they were both still working together at the factory. She had started there with Beryl, Megan and Mavis – and today she was missing all three of them.

The packing room was still full of familiar faces, however. The girls clustered around Irene as soon as she arrived: Plump Mary, Effie, Gladys and the others. They were all keen to know the latest about Mavis's health and state of mind.

'I haven't seen her since the last time you all asked,' Irene said, a little bad-temperedly, she realised.

'We're only showing our concern for the poor little mite,' said Plump Mary.

'I know,' Irene said, retying her pinny and pulling on her hairnet. It was time to get down to work, and she didn't really want to spend the whole morning chattering with the lasses. 'And when I see her, I'll pass on all your best wishes.'

'See that you do,' heckled Effie from her place at the work bench. 'We wouldn't want her thinking we don't care.'

'I'll be seeing her tonight,' Irene reassured her work colleagues. 'I'm taking Tom down to Watling Street to visit them in their new place. So I'll find out how Mavis is getting on then.'

This mollified them all, and the morning's work began in earnest. Irene's deft fingers expertly folded and packaged up the golden biscuits and by now she could work automatically, almost without concentrating at all.

Her mind wandered and she was thinking about how everyone at work usually treated Mavis. They were never that concerned about her well-being when she was just the butt of their jokes. Back when Irene had first started at the biscuit factory, Mavis had been a timid presence, scared of her own shadow. The other girls had barely even treated her like she was human. She was just the pale, skinny, raspy-voiced girl who people tended to pick on. At least things had been somewhat better for her recently . . .

Sometime around mid-morning, the double doors swung open and in came their supervisor, Mrs Clarke. There was nothing unusual in this, since she made her rounds as regular as clockwork, visiting each department and checking everyone's work. Today, however, she brought Mr Wight in with her. The factory owner looked much more frail than the last time Irene had clapped eyes on him, and his parlous state gave her a surprise. He seemed to cringe at all the noise on the factory floor, as if it was physically hurting him.

Mrs Clarke shouted at them all to pay no heed, and to carry on with their work and then she made a beeline for Irene.

'Mr Wight has heard all about your sister-in-law's dreadful ordeal.'

'Oh!' said Irene.

'It must have been awful for her,' the old man said. His voice was so quiet that Irene had to pause in her work and lean closer to hear him. 'A coffin falling on her and getting kicked in the head by a horse like that. My heart goes out to her. It does when anything bad happens to one of our girls.'

Irene nodded. 'I'll pass on your best wishes when I see her this evening.'

'Oh good,' said Mr Wight. 'And would you please give her this small presentation tin of Wights' teatime selection? It's just a very modest offering.'

Irene took the tin and thanked both the owner and Mrs Clarke profusely. 'Biscuits! Lovely!' And all she could think was, if the pair of them knew just how many biscuits Mavis ate each day as she stood there packing them up, they'd never be giving her presents like this, no matter what ordeal she'd suffered. 'Stop eating them all!' Irene had to keep telling her.

She was glad when her shift was over in the middle of the day and she could get out in the sun. Lugging her bag, coat, gas mask box and the presentation tin of biscuits, Irene hurried across town to Franchino's, where Tom was waiting for her.

He looked rested and smart, drinking coffee in a booth and chatting with his old friend Bella. She looked carefree and bonny, as ever, throwing back her head and laughing at some story of Tom's. By contrast Irene felt scruffy and mithered. Her skin felt gritty with biscuit crumbs. Even her eyes when she rubbed them felt like they were filled with tiny bits of custard creams.

'You look worn out, pet,' Tom told her.

She shrugged. 'Did you get caught up on your sleep?'

He beamed at her. 'Champion! And then I had some time to play with the bairns and have a bite to eat with Ma before coming out here. It's been a lovely day.'

Settling at their table with them, Irene noticed that Bella had her father's old papers out again. All the faded folders and envelopes she had found in his storerooms upstairs when she was cleaning up were laid out on the melamine surface, and she'd clearly been going through them with Tom. 'What do you think of the plans, then?' she asked him now.

'What plans?' Irene said brightly, nicking a sip of Tom's frothy coffee and feeling a little left out.

'I think they're terrific,' Tom said. 'I never knew your dad had been thinking of things like this.'

'Ages ago, ten years or more back, but he just never got time enough to see it through. Just running this place was enough for him, I think.'

'If anyone can see this whole scheme through, then you can, Bella,' Tom told her warmly.

'Maybe not for a while yet,' she smiled ruefully. 'I mean, obviously, it's the wrong time just now. But when it's all over. When things can get back to normal again . . .'

'Aye, you're right. When it's over. When things are better . . .'

Irene was getting frustrated. 'What's the plan? What are you planning to do?'

'It's the future of the Franchino ice-cream empire,' Bella beamed at her. 'I found these papers and notes amongst Papa's things. He was planning other branches, up and down the coast, Irene. And also, get this! Kiosks!'

'Kiosks?' she said the word like she had never heard it before. 'Like little huts?'

'No, fancy kiosks! All smart and glamorous, right on the seafront! What do you think of that?'

'Well . . .' said Irene, thinking of the razor wire and the landmines that currently occupied the beaches.

'When the world gets back to normal, people will want things like this,' Bella said. 'Everything will come back to life again and it'll be lovely. We have to think about the future like this!'

'I suppose so . . .' Irene thought it was all a bit pie in the sky, but didn't say so because it was nice to see Bella so enthusiastic.

'It all clicked into place the other night, when I was running along the beach with Jonas,' Bella said. 'I thought – what this place will need is a fancy little kiosk, selling Franchino's best ice cream and coffee. People will be flocking here when we get back to normal!'

Tom and Irene exchanged a glance. 'Running along the beach, were you?' Tom joshed her gently. 'With your new young man, eh?'

Bella blushed and started folding up her papa's precious papers. 'Jonas thinks it's all a smashing idea. He thinks I've got a smart head for business, actually.'

'I bet he does,' Tom twinkled at her.

Bella asked Irene, 'What do you think then? When we get Franchino's Empire up and running? Will you help out, Irene? How do you fancy being manageress of a little kiosk on the seafront, eh? What would you say to that?'

Tom's eyes widened as he looked across at his wife. 'Your own little empire, Irene!'

Chapter 25

'Hey, lad! This is where you're living, is it? Eeeh, look at you!'

Tom strode towards his youngest brother with his arms held open wide. Sam flushed and beamed, falling into his embrace, and Irene watched the two of them with her heart glowing. It was wonderful to see the two of them together again. Not for the first time it struck her that the four Farley brothers could never be united again.

'Tom, it's so good to see you here,' Sam said, standing in the middle of the front room of his Watling Street home. He looked properly at home here now, Irene thought. He looked like he'd never lived anywhere else. Probably a week of looking after his injured wife's every need had helped with that.

'How is she doing?' Irene asked. 'Is she not up and about?' She frowned, sure that the doctor had said that she'd be back on her feet before a full week was over.

'Ah, not yet, hinny,' Sam said. 'It's not quite a week yet. She still feels funny when she tries to stand up. Dizzy and that.'

'She'd better watch out for getting bedbound,' Irene warned. 'That can happen, you know.'

'Has she still not got her hearing back?' Tom asked.

'No . . .' Sam looked teary as he shook his head. 'Now we've been told there's no guarantee she'll ever get it back. That was quite some blow she took, apparently, and it dislodged something. I think that's what the doctor said.'

'Oh no!' Irene was appalled. 'If she never gets it back! That's awful!'

Sam said, 'We're just taking it day by day, thankful that she didn't get killed. She could've done, you know . . .' All at once his face crumpled and he sat down heavily on the ancient sofa. He mopped his face with a lace antimacassar and then set it back down on the arm of the chair. 'It's only just sunk in, this past day or so. I'm lucky to have her still alive . . .'

'Come on, let's get you a cup of tea,' Tom said. 'I'll do it. You look shattered, Sam.'

He did, too. To Irene's eyes it looked like her brother-in-law had aged five years in less than a week, simply out of shock and concern. While Tom went off cheerfully to find their kitchen and brew some tea, she asked Sam: 'She'll be all right with us going up there to see her, won't she?'

'Oh aye, of course,' said Sam eagerly. 'Well, you know you're one of her closest friends. Probably the best friend she's got. She'd love to see you, Irene. It's just . . . don't expect too much from the poor lass. She's finding it hard writing down what she wants to say, and her penmanship and her reading aren't all that great either, it turns out . . .'

'Aw, poor Mavis,' Irene sighed. 'Everything was going so well for her for just a while there. She was so happy! Married to you and settling into grown-up life at last . . . and now this!'

Sam's face darkened. 'I tell you, Irene, it's the curse of them Mad bloody Johnsons. It's like that old mother has cursed us from her deathbed.'

'Ah, don't be daft, man. There's no such thing as curses. It's just bad luck.'

'Is it?' He looked anguished and tearful again. 'Mavis was knocking around with that Lily Johnson. That lass was coming round here and crying on her shoulder. Well, you know how soft-hearted Mavis is. She even went round there and helped with laying out the old witch when she was dead. I reckon it's the same for anyone who comes into contact with that lot. They get a whole load of rotten bad luck coming to them . . .'

Sam sounded so certain that Irene was almost convinced by his words. But there was no such thing as curses or bad luck. It was just chance. That's all life consisted of, and you had to make the best of it. 'She'll be all right, love,' she told Sam. 'You'll see. Mavis is resilient.'

'Oh, I know! She's tough as old boots. Some of the things she's told me about growing up! About when she was a bairn, her and Arthur! They'd make your hair curl, her stories!'

Tom was back with a trayful of tea. 'Shall I carry it upstairs and we can sit and drink it with Mavis?'

'That's a good idea,' Sam said. 'She's bound to perk up at the sight of you two . . .'

She did indeed perk up when Irene and Tom put their heads round the door. The room smelled stale and unaired and the curtains needed pulling open to let the remaining daylight in. Blinking and smiling, Mavis looked dreadfully pale. Even worse than usual. Her unwashed hair was awry and she didn't have a clue what her visitors were saying to her, even though they shouted their greetings and enunciated very carefully.

'It's good to see you in one piece!' Irene told her, coming to sit close to her on the edge of the rumpled bed.

Mavis gabbled, all in a rush. Her words were too fast and running into each other. 'Eeeh! Irene! Tom! You're here! It's lovely to see the pair of you! Oh-hoh! Oh-hoh!'

The girl was trying her best to sound bright and cheerful for them, even though she still felt woozy and rather depressed. She sat up and kept alert throughout their visit, shoving the notepad at them and getting them to scribble down the things they wanted to say to her. She watched Irene and Tom take turns, screwing up their faces in concentration as they scrawled on the tiny pages, and then it was her turn to frown and stare at what they had written.

Only half of the words and the questions could she really make out. Plus, with the way she formed her own words without hearing them aloud, they could only really follow half of what she was trying to tell them.

'Slow down, Mavis man!' her lovely Sam interrupted her. 'You'll have to speak more clearly than that. You're just making noise.'

It was one lovely rush of noise, though. A sweet gabble of thwarted joy at being reunited with her dearest friends. 'Uh-hoh! Uh-hoh!' She kept nodding and smiling her agreement at everything they said. And then she elaborated on her tale from last Saturday: 'I was very nearly killed! The bloody horse kicked me in the head! And then the bloody coffin shot out of the hearse and that nearly killed me too. It was a bloody nightmare, it was! Uh-hoh! It was! Uh-hoh!'

Already, in her own mind, Mavis had jazzed up the story of her adventure with extra comic effects. Extra ghoulish, macabre effects. Part of her couldn't wait to be relating it to all the girls at the biscuit factory in person. Just wait till she told them that old Mother Johnson had fallen out of her own coffin and Mavis had felt her clammy hands on her flesh in the middle of the air raid. And with the flames and the bombs going off all around them it felt exactly like the old dame had been dragging her down into hell.

But at the moment, hampered by the ringing silence in her ears, she couldn't go into that level of detail with her friends. 'Uh-hoh! Uh-hoh! Nearly dead! Kicked in the head! Bloody hell! Uh-hoh!' That was about as far as her story went today.

They drank their tea and ate some of the biscuits that came in the commemorative tin Mr Wight had given Irene to pass along.

'Eeeh! Not broken! Uh-hoh!' Mavis laughed, nibbling a ginger snap. They all knew what she meant by this. Almost all the Wight biscuits they ever brought home were broken or misshapes, either bought cheap or hidden away in pinny pockets.

All too soon it was time to go home. Gently taking charge, Tom said, 'I think we should let the poor lass get some rest. And we have to get the tram home, Irene. You've work again in the morning.'

The invalid looked bereft at the thought of letting them go. When she cuddled Irene, she clung on to her, going: 'Uh-hoh! I'm so happy. I am! Uh-hoh, Irene!'

They left Mavis sitting alone in her bed, her hands stroking down her bedclothes and then going to the locket she was wearing round her neck. No one had mentioned it because she was careful to keep it hidden beneath her gown. She found the smooth locket reassured her and soothed her, and yet it still made her feel somewhat guilty. She shouldn't have it. Not at all. It was nicked. But it made her feel better. Especially now. For some reason she felt happier that she had that little stolen gold thing hanging round her neck . . .

But I'm just daft, Mavis thought. I'm overexcited and upset and having a daft time of it. And no one must know I stole this thing . . .

She kept it hidden safely away and tried to rest, even if it meant dreaming.

Going back downstairs Irene felt tears bubbling up. There had been something so desperate and sincere in her friend's voice. It was like she had felt she'd been right to the brink and was hopelessly grateful to have come back alive.

Down in the hallway, saying goodbye to Sam, Irene lowered her voice pointlessly as she added: 'Even if she never gets her hearing back, she'll soon be able to communicate more clearly. With practice. I'm sure she will, Sam.'

He shrugged. 'Of course. Of course she will.'

His brother rubbed his back. He ruffled his hair and said, 'See you, kidda.'

Then they were gone, dashing for the tram, and the youngest Farley boy was left alone with his cares.

He couldn't work while he was looking after Mavis. He had a feeling he was going to lose his job at the docks. The job was only a very loose arrangement, anyway. Perhaps it was time he sorted himself out with something more permanent and respectable?

He had meant to discuss the idea with Irene while she was here, but there hadn't seemed to be the time. Sam had come up with the idea of applying for work at the biscuit factory – they'd need heavy lifters, wouldn't they? There'd surely be something they could find for him to do there?

Upstairs Mavis had fallen into a doze.

As soon as her beloved friends had trooped out of the bedroom, closing the door gently on their heels, she had allowed herself a little cry. She was that frustrated. She was that annoyed with herself. She felt like banging her head against the wall, as if she had some kind of blockage in there and that might clear it. Oh, but her head ached and rang with that hollow, lonely sound.

I'm never gonna hear their voices again, she thought, and lay back on the warm, lumpy pillows. I'm going to be stuck, all alone, inside my own stupid head forever.

The wave of black depression that had been building up all week inside her was getting harder and harder to fight. As she lay there, she thought: Eeeh, come on, lass. You ought to be cheerier than this. That was your family. Your nearest and dearest, they came right across town to visit you. You should be glad of the sight of them!

To her shame, though, Mavis only felt worse, more miserable and alone than she had all week . . . and that was a wrong feeling, too. A selfish one. People had been killed last weekend in that air raid. People had had their homes blasted to pieces. Why should she be getting as upset as this?

But she couldn't help sobbing and giving in to that wave of blackness that was rising and rising inside of herself . . .

I've never had any bloody luck, she thought. I've had a rotten time, all my life. Uh-hoh. I have. Uh-hoh! It's been a rotten bloody life so far . . .

The thing about being forced to lie in bed all week is that you couldn't help your thoughts slipping back. You just couldn't help yourself being borne backwards by that dark tide into your own rotten past . . .

Chapter 26

They had nothing. Nothing in the world to their name. Just the rags they stood up in.

The little girl was tiny. She was like a mucky little doll, walking about the place and getting under everybody's feet. By rights she should have been at home. The quay was a rough and ready place. No place for bairns. Not bairns as little as she was, anyway.

But her mother had no choice. There was no one for her to leave the bairns with. There was no one to help her out. She had to take both her girl and her little boy with her to work all day, every day. As they got old enough, they learned to help her out.

The earliest memories Mavis had were of being in that fish-reeking, bum-freezing place, right on the water-front. In the bustle of everyone shouting and working and slinging their wares about. She grew up in the middle of all that stinking hullabaloo and she thought it was normal. She thought the whole world worked down there on the quay.

Before either bairn could read or write their own names, they could gut and clean out fish. The slicing and grasping and twisting to wrench out the messy innards became second nature to the pair of them. They didn't flinch from the job or think it strange or disgusting. Even the wriggling and flapping of still-living fish didn't disturb them. They just carried on stabbing and slicing and wrenching all day long. They did just as their mammy had taught them.

Their mammy was the most important person in their lives. In later years memories would grow a little vaguer and harder to grasp. Memories could be more slippery than fish guts in your hand. Mavis would have trouble recollecting the room where they had slept at night, and the building it was in. She had been so little that her surroundings from that time grew shrouded and vague. They left the place so early in the mornings and returned so late at night it seemed like home was always steeped in darkness.

But neither she nor her older brother ever forgot what their mammy was like. She was tall and rail-thin and the most beautiful woman either of them would ever see. Her complexion was creamy and pale and she had large, luminous green eyes and sumptuous dark hair that, when she let it down, fell to her waist. To her bairns she was more glamorous than all the women in the movies they would later love to see at the pictures. She was impossibly beautiful. Perhaps they even exaggerated that beauty in later years. Perhaps they even misremembered her, replacing her real face with a mishmash of beautiful faces they'd seen on the screen.

They believed that they remembered her correctly, and that was the main thing. They believed that nothing could ever take away the version of her they kept preserved in their heads.

Arthur was a couple of years older than Mavis, so he understood more. He looked after his younger sister fiercely. Their mammy had a lot to see to, so he had to do some of the looking after, making sure they were both clean and dressed, and watching over his baby sister when their mammy sometimes had to leave them alone. She had to go out to fetch things. Food. Money. She had a lot to do. She went off looking careworn, exhausted, sad. But when Mammy came back, her beautiful face always lit up at the sight of her bairns. She never failed to look delighted at the sight of them.

They had absolutely nothing, but they knew they were loved. Mavis and Arthur were never in any doubt about that.

Down on the fish quay they were known by all the other vendors and fisherman. Everyone kept an eye out for the young lass's bairns. Of course that rough and ready pier wasn't any kind of place for little'uns like that. Especially when the wintry winds came whipping in. It was harsh and bitter, working down there, exposed to all the elements. But what else could she do? Everyone understood that the lass had nowhere else to take her bairns while she worked.

It was a familiar sight: that beautiful pale girl with her hair tied up. And the two little ones tucked close in beside her, gutting fish and chucking the guts into a wooden bucket. A sight to warm the cockles of the heart.

All the men kept an eye out for that poor little family. All were concerned to see they didn't come to any harm.

And they didn't. Not for a long time. Even in that rough place and those harsh conditions. Nothing bad at all happened until . . .

Until the day she met the wrong'un.

Half the fisher folk knew that he was a wrong'un from the day they clapped eyes on him. He was much older than she was. He was nothing to look at. He was jowly and thickset. Had a bit of money. He was bellowing and bullying. He came round flashing thick wads of cash when he opened up his wallet. He was doing business, but his business was dirty. There was talk of him getting fellas down dark alleys and cracking heads. There was talk of all kinds of skulduggery.

They tried to warn the young lass to stay away from him. At first she kept her gaze averted when he came swaggering along the quay. He wore a rust-coloured suit and a bowler hat, looking a bit flashy in that dismal place. Everything down the quay was silvery grey: the sea, the cobbles and all the dead fish. Mr Alec stood out because he was florid of complexion, and had a ginger moustache like handlebars. Also, he was a dandy who favoured bright waistcoats and ties. He might have been a fat and ugly bloke to many people's eyes, but he stood out in the crowd. And soon the lass overcame her natural modesty and shyness and took a long, hard look at him.

Mr Alec stared back. He had noticed her a mile off. He asked around about that young beauty with the two mucky-looking bairns. But no one could or would tell him anything about them.

He was intrigued. And he was used to getting anything he wanted. They were like a ready-made family. He wasn't bothered about having kids. It was their mammy he wanted. Every day that he went back to the quay, ostensibly doing business and wringing the vendors dry of every bit of cash he could exploit from them, and yet really he was there to fill up his greedy eyes with more and more of that lass. At last Mr Alec decided that he simply needed to have her.

He presented it like a business proposition. 'You have nothing. I have lots. Let me have you. Let me take possession of you and everything you are. You'll always be comfy and safe. I'm nowt to look at, and I'm really not a good man. I probably won't even give you everything you deserve. But I will do my best by you.'

'And my bairns?' the lass asked him. She stared back bravely at him as he laid out his scheme. At first she had waved him away. She wasn't for sale. She was doing all right. She and her bairns could get along without anyone's help. But he came back again and again and put his offer to her day after day.

The two bairns stared solemnly up at this gruff, colourful man who said he wanted to take their mammy away with him and they were terrified she would go and leave them.

She was caving in, bit by bit. She was listening and taking him seriously.

'You need me. You don't have anything.'

'What about my bairns? Whoever takes me on will have to take them as well. We won't be separated. We'll never be separated.'

And Mr Alec had turned his fiercely avaricious eyes on the startled faces of the two bairns. Appraising them. Mavis and Arthur. Two encumberments he could well do without.

'Aye, well, of course,' he promised, in a wheedling tone. 'I understand that you all come as a package.'

Look at them there, he thought! The lass and her babies. The three of them were coated – every inch of their skin and hair and their ragged clothes – in shimmering fish scales. Every fish they ever gutted had shed bright little slivers and they were covered in briny silver buttons.

The lass and her bairns were glittering in the watery sunlight and Mr Alec had never wanted anything more in his whole greedy life. They were his ready-made family and his selfish heart leapt up with glee the day that she eventually said, 'All right. All right. We will come to you. You can take me, but you must look after my bairns as well. You must provide for the lot of us.'

'Why aye,' he said, feeling very pleased with himself. 'Of course, bonny lass.'

Chapter 27

It ought to have been easier every time. But it wasn't.

Irene set to work with a heavy heart, missing Tom more than ever.

Each leave was harder than the last. Him going back on the train. Setting off back for the war. It left a hollow ache inside her that felt as if her insides were mangled up.

Also, there was the strangeness this time, of his catching a train north to Scotland, where he was expected at a different airbase from usual. Naturally he couldn't tell her any more details. All she knew was that he was going north rather than south. More than that she didn't know but, on the day he set off, she was aware that there was something extra-nervous about the way he was carrying on. Not just nervous – he was excited. He was involved in something exciting, and she couldn't even ask him what it was.

One day, perhaps, she would find out. One day, when it was all over, Irene would hear the whole story of the war.

Living through things day after day felt to her like having only some of the pieces of the puzzle. Also, it felt like not having the lid of the puzzle box to show you how the full picture should turn out.

These were her philosophical thoughts during the week following Tom's visit home. It was a dull rainy week of getting back to normal. The summer had turned wet and town was dismal. At least there were no more air raids following the horrible one the previous week. Shields was left to count its dead and smooth away the rubble and debris as best it could, and to wait for the next one.

Sam came to the biscuit factory one day, dressed in his smartest clothes, hoping to get himself a job. Irene saw him from the yard while she was on her break, chattering with the girls.

'Aye, that's Sam, you're right,' she agreed with Plump Mary. 'It would be nice if he worked here, especially when Mavis gets back to work.'

'No sign of that yet then, hinny?' the large girl asked her, looking properly concerned.

'Not yet. She just lies there in her bed and she tries to look bright and cheerful, but you can tell it's mostly put on.'

'It's a shock she's had,' Plump Mary said dolefully. 'A shock can do terrible things. Did I tell you about our budgie?'

Irene blinked at her. 'What about your budgie?'

'It's been through air raids and all sorts and it managed fine. Then it was the sudden loud slamming of the parlour door that gave it a right shock, for some reason. Chippy went rigid and froze solid on his perch. Completely petrified.'

'Ah, what a shame,' Irene said, sounding sincere but wondering how Mary could compare Mavis with a budgie.

'Mam called the vet, even though he's pricey. And he came in, peered through bars at Chippy, who hadn't flickered for a whole day by then. "Aha," says the vet and he reaches in, oh-so-tenderly and takes hold of the little bird. He fetches him out and says, "I know what the problem is with this little chap." And he stares at the little mite in his palm for a moment. Then he turns round and chucks him on the open fire.'

'No!' Irene gasped.

'Aye, he did. And up went Chippy the Budgie in the flames. "That'll be a pound," says the vet, and we were all screaming with shock. "You've killed our bloody budgie!" And he was shaking his head, going: "His heart had burst with shock. He was never coming back! It was all I could do for him."' Plump Mary shuddered. 'Eeeh, I can still smell the burning feathers in the parlour. Horrible! Poor Chippy.' Then she squealed with laughter. 'Mind, that's an awful story to tell while you're worrying about Mavis, isn't it? Sorry, pet. I'm sure she's going to be grand again.'

Irene wasn't so sure, and she was wishing she hadn't got talking to Plump Mary, who never had anything sensible to say at the best of times.

Irene had to wait a few days to hear the outcome of Sam's interview with Mr Wight at the biscuit factory. She was busy working at Franchino's when he came dashing in, flushed and excited like a little lad. He was mad keen to tell someone his news. 'He said yes, Irene! He said I can start as soon as I possibly can!'

His sudden entrance into the ice-cream parlour took her by surprise. It was a quiet evening with Irene in sole charge. Bella was out with her handsome young man, and the jazz music was lower than usual because Irene was deep in conversation over coffee.

'Oh, sorry, pet,' Sam said. 'I didn't realise you were busy talking . . .' He looked abashed at coming running in like that.

'It's all right,' Irene tried to reassure him. 'I was just taking my break and chatting with . . . erm, Elizabeth, here.'

Sam stood staring at the older lady, and for a moment he was lost for words. It was partly being made shy by her rather grand appearance. She looked like what his ma would call a woman of quality. But there was something else. He recognised her, yes! 'Hey, you're that one from our wedding!' he burst out. 'You're the lady that Mavis was shouting at. When she had that funny turn in the aisle.'

Elizabeth Kendrick's smooth composure let her down for a moment or two and she lowered her eyes from his accusatory gaze. 'I'm afraid you're right, young man. And I believe I owe you an apology for inadvertently causing a scene at your wedding.'

Sam found he was simply staring at her. Here was a lady who used a word like 'inadvertently' as easily as any other word. The kind of word people only ever used in books! A grand lady with a fur coat around her shoulders. Real fur, that looked like. He groped for words, 'Well, who are you, hinny? Mavis would never even tell me . . .'

Irene stepped in, 'Sam, this is Elizabeth Kendricks.'

'So you're a relation, after all! I thought so. You see, Mavis so rarely talks about her family and the past and all that . . .'

The grand lady nodded graciously. 'Oh dear, perhaps my coming here to talk with Irene again will cause even more problems. I'm sorry, my dear.'

Sam stared at Irene. 'But how do you two know each other?'

'I've merely dropped in for a coffee, once or twice,' Elizabeth said. 'And luckily I have found a sympathetic ear in Irene.'

'Aye, she's that all right,' Sam said, and couldn't help sounding somewhat surly. Wasn't he the only one who confided his secrets to Irene? Clearly not!

'Sam,' Irene said tactfully, 'Elizabeth came here to ask after Mavis's health and recovery after that awful do on Watling Street. She heard what happened to her. She wants to know that she's all right.'

'Aye, well,' Sam said. He was studying Elizabeth carefully. 'Bit by bit. Day after day. The lass is getting there. She'll be back to normal before too long.'

'Good,' Elizabeth said.

'Can I ask why it is you should care?' Sam asked, with a note of defiance in his voice. 'Why should a woman like you be bothered about my Mavis, then?'

'Sam . . .' said Irene warningly. 'Elizabeth means no harm. She's . . .'

'I can speak up on my own account very well, thank you, Irene,' the older lady smiled. She took a deep breath and told Sam, 'Well, young man. The truth is that I am Mavis and Arthur's mother. I adopted them – legally and above board – when they were both quite small. They are both my children. And so you see, that's why I was so keen to be at her wedding and why I was so concerned when I heard about her accident.'

Sam simply gaped at her in surprise and dismay. 'You adopted them? But . . . but . . . she's never mentioned anything like that . . .'

'I don't suppose she has,' Elizabeth said, with a look passing across her face that made Irene pity her. It was a painful, desolate look that Elizabeth quickly smoothed away. 'Things happened, you see. There were problems. Everything I had planned . . . The lives we were going to live . . . They never quite worked out how I wanted.'

'I want to hear all of this,' Sam said, coming to sit down at the table with them. 'Will you explain it all to me? I want to understand.'

Elizabeth Kendricks smiled at him. Her whole face brightened at his words, like clouds had parted before the sun. 'Really? You really will listen?'

'Of course! It's about Mavis. It's about everything she'll never talk about.'

'Thank you,' said Elizabeth. 'I thought for a moment you were going to throw me out as well. I thought that I'd made a mistake again . . .'

'No, please, tell me,' said Sam. 'I want to understand her . . .'

Tactfully, Irene got to her feet and told them, 'I'll make some more coffee.'

As she was crossing to the coffee machine, however, she was interrupted by Bella hurtling in through the doors. 'I thought you were out with your fella?'

'I was,' Bella scowled furiously. 'And you were right, Irene. Do you know what? You were right the whole time about him. What the hell was I doing, running around with one of the Mad Johnsons? What was I even thinking of?'

Chapter 28

No more gutting. That was the biggest thing. No more fish!

Mr Alec was firm on that point. No lass of his was going down to that quay working all day. Hadn't he rescued her from that life of poverty? She didn't need that stinking job anymore.

'You can put all your previous life behind you,' the man in the orange tweed promised her. 'You and your bairns. You're all mine now.'

He had a little cottage near Jarrow. It was like being in another country, because it was further from the sea and the air tasted different. It tasted of soot and dirt. The skies were smoky and orange-dark. The landscape was littered with slag heaps. A greasy pall of smoke hung over everything and the lass and her bairns could feel it lining their throats. They coughed and choked and couldn't sleep at night in their new place.

'You'll soon get used to it,' laughed Mr Alec. He had a raucous, snorting laugh. It was the sound of a man used to getting his own way.

He didn't live with them all the time. 'I can't be tied down to one place. I've too much to do.'

He dashed about in a gleaming sports car. Oxblood red. A noisy engine that had all the neighbours coming out of their doors to see the hullabaloo. He loved the attention and would give a lordly wave.

Mavis and Arthur had never seen a car before, let alone been allowed to climb inside one. It made everything worthwhile, to get in the back of that monstrous machine, while Mr Alec took them on a spin along the coastal roads. Mammy was in the passenger seat, her long hair streaming out in the fresh breeze. She was shouting with delightful laughter as her new friend bowled them along the cliff-edge road. Faster and faster! Honking the horn and gobbling up the empty road!

'But what should we do all day if you won't let us work at the fish quay?' Mammy asked him earnestly. 'I'm used to working for my living. The bairns are used to being out all day.'

'Oh, you'll earn your money,' Mr Alec snickered.

But Mammy was distracted by an idea she'd suddenly had. What kind of work can I do from home if I'm to be staying here most of the time? Why, I can sew, can't I? I can take in sewing. I can teach the bairns needlecraft, too! That'll keep them quiet . . .

Not for a moment did she consider rebelling against Mr Alec's dictats. Not at first. She was too grateful. Also, she was too amazed by the novelty of living in this place.

A whole house! A whole beautiful house with rugs and curtains and polished sticks of furniture. A range and a hearth and a sideboard for setting out the knick-knacks and geegaws she could start collecting! And he had told her the whole place was in her name. It was all hers!

Such a change from tiny, dingy, smelly rooms with no ventilation and rags heaped upon a mattress. The young mammy felt like she'd died and gone up to heaven. Except heaven reeked of sulphur and smoke and the sky was dark most of the day . . .

'Sewing?' Mr Alec asked sneeringly. 'Whatever for? You don't need money. I can give you whatever you need.'

'Oh, I know, I know,' she said, in the wheedling voice she used with the new daddy. 'But I'll need something to occupy myself. My mind is too busy. Needlework soothes me . . .'

He shrugged and agreed and took a list of things she would be requiring. He made a muck of buying them and the next time she had to go along with him, taking the bairns round the grand old haberdashery shops. Up and down Fowler Street like a fancy lady with cash to spare. Bolts of fabric and needles and bobbins and bits of this and that. The kids helped out with carrying all her wonderful new wares and the mammy bustled along, looking delighted with herself. 'Is that enough now?' Mr Alec asked peevishly. 'Do you have everything you need?'

'For now!' she winked at him and the two kids laughed at the mischief in her voice. Why, at first they had been rather scared of Mr Alec. He seemed to bark and bellow and always get his own way. Now they could see that their mammy had him dancing to her tune. He was giving her everything she wanted.

But sometimes they would hear her crying, and sometimes she'd have cuts and bruises. Mr Alec would stay some nights and there'd be raised voices in Mammy's room. The sound of Mr Alec locked up in that room with their mammy was like a furious little bull, stampeding around inside four walls. The bairns were scared of him again those times.

Some days he didn't come by at all. Whole weeks would pass without a visit from Mr Alec.

It was strange to find themselves missing the fish quay. Those bone-cold mornings. The reek of it all! The slippery innards squishing in your fingers! Fancy missing all of that! But it was the company, as Mammy said. It was all the familiar faces that you knew on the harbour. It was like they were lost to you for ever.

They distracted themselves and put all their efforts into learning to sew. They had nimble, clever little fingers. 'Must have passed my talents on! You're both naturals!' Mammy gasped, watching her two bairns working away, heads down, stitching like mad.

They were just glad to please her. They'd have done anything for their mammy. The two of them glowed at her praise when she inspected the hemming and bordering she had given them to do.

'I could take in work,' she told Mr Alec. 'Alterations and mending. There's money in that. Everyone needs those things doing and not everyone has the skills or the time . . .'

'No way,' he growled at her. His face was flushed red and he was angry. In fact, he was a lot less jolly and carefree in recent days. If Mammy thought she could still wind him round her little finger, then she was wrong.

'Bugger him, if he thinks he can tell me what to do,' she said. 'I'm no one's prisoner.'

As soon as he was off again in his oxblood car, it was time to get out into the streets and knocking on doors. Mammy made herself up lovely and smart and respectable-looking. She took a basket with her, and made sure Mavis and Arthur were immaculate, carrying little baskets of their own. Then they went round all the streets of Boldon Colliery and asked at each door, very politely, if there was any mending needing doing, any alterations to make.

The area was poor and folk were used to doing their own repairs, of course. But one or two said, 'Eeeh, yes, as a matter of fact . . .' because they didn't have the time or they lacked the skills or their eyesight was fading in the smudgy gloom of their homes. Others were charmed by the bonny lass and her smart bairns standing on their doorstep.

Soon Mammy had a great long list of jobs and addresses scribbled down and all three had baskets filled with cloth. Happily they came back to their own little cottage, knocking on a few final doors close to home.

Some nasty old man with no teeth called her a gypsy and yelled at her. Mammy took hold of both bairns and scurried away. At another door, a horrible fat old woman called her 'the Johnson whore' and flicked a filthy dishrag to shoo her away. 'Get your mucky arse away from my door! You're just his latest piece, you are! He allus puts them in Number 36, he does. We've had your sort before! Spoiling the good name of our bloody street!'

The bairns were confused by this awful ending to their triumphant day of filling three baskets with sewing jobs. Why had those people been nasty to them? Mammy was tough, as they knew, but still she cried when she got back indoors that afternoon.

'Maybe I should never have brought us here,' she said, sitting in her armchair and staring at the parlour. Then she saw her Mavis and Arthur. They looked cleaner, better-fed. They looked less pasty and thin. No, she had done the right thing. What did she care what the old folk called her? Bugger them. It would be a fine thing to be high-minded. But others couldn't afford such fancy principles, could they? Others didn't have that luxury.

'Let's work,' she told her bairns, feigning happiness and brightness. 'Let's get on with all this sewing! We've got so much to do!'

So they set to work and the bairns learned skills that would never leave them, and that they would continue to use for the rest of their lives.

They filled up that dainty house with garments and sheets and all kinds of piecemeal jobs. Dresses and shirts hung from every doorway, banister and curtain rail like pale, fluttering ghosts. They were phantoms held together with almost invisible needlework.

'It's like a Chinese laundry round here!' roared Mr Alec, stomping and snorting through the place. The little bull was on a rampage, Mavis thought. He scared her. He seemed to get louder and more destructive each time he came back round. He smashed crockery and brought pictures down off the walls with his rages. The pot dog Mammy had bought off the little market was smashed in the fire grate one night and Mammy wore more and more bruises in the days that followed each noisy visit.

The bairns grew to dread his every appearance in their home. They started hating this strutting, boisterous little man.

Arthur said, 'My thumbs and fingers hurt each night when I go to bed. The needles are making my fingers bleed. The skin is cracked and it really hurts.'

'It'll get tougher,' Mammy promised him. 'The skin heals up and it gets tougher and tougher and then you can do your work and you won't feel anything. That's how it goes. That's what life is like, my pet.'

But for weeks on end both bairns went to bed and their fingers bled and stung from work. But that hurt was nowt compared with what they felt about Mr Alec. He was hurting their mammy.

'We have to stop him,' said Arthur, in the pitch dark of their bedroom one night. 'We have to make him stop hurting our mammy.'

Chapter 29

'Irene! What are you on about! Of course I haven't! What do you take me for?'

Bella Franchino looked absolutely scandalised as she stared at her friend and employee. The two had been chatting rather earnestly as they cleaned round the ice-cream parlour and shut up shop for the night. Their last few customers – including Sam and Mrs Kendricks – had been despatched, and Irene had set about finding out just why her boss was so cross following her date.

She hadn't expected to upset her like this.

'I-I'm sorry, Bella. I don't know why, but I just assumed . . .'

'Well, don't!' Bella was wiping down the coffee machine, looking more angry than embarrassed by now.

Clearly Irene had misjudged Bella badly. Look at the girl's reaction! Fancy blowing up at such a simple little question, and such an easily made assumption. 'But there's no shame in it, Bella, you know,' Irene said tentatively. 'Because of the war, it's a different world. It's not like it was before.'

Bella shot her a look as she polished the chrome of the coffee maker. 'It might be for some people, but not for me. I was brought up in a strict Catholic household. My mama's looking down from heaven and she can see everything I get up to. Do you think I'd shame her?'

'Of course not!'

'And my nonna, too. They're all looking. What would Papa say? He always knew I was a good girl.'

Irene was flabbergasted. She wanted to tell Bella, 'But you're nearly thirty! How can you have lasted out so long?' She stared at her vital, beautiful, sexy friend and marvelled at what Bella was claiming for the truth.

She had never been with a man in her entire life. Not in that way. Not in any of the ways that counted. She'd hardly been with one at all, in fact.

Irene tried to mollify her. 'Even the most devoutly religious folk are saying that, well, with the hostilities and life being like it is these days, the Lord won't mind so much, if . . . if . . . you know . . .' Irene felt the words melting uselessly on her tongue.

'Maybe for some,' snapped Bella. 'But he'd mind soon enough if I got up to anything before I was married.' She glared at Irene. 'I thought you understood! I thought you knew me, Irene. I thought you knew what it was like for me.'

'Why, no! Not like that! I thought you were . . . normal. Like everyone else.'

'What does that mean? Jumping into bed with men, any chance I can get?'

'No!' gasped Irene, clutching her floor mop to her chest. Now it was her turn to be offended. 'That's not what I'm like! Nor anyone else I know. Well, apart from Megan, maybe, but she's just dirty . . .'

'I'm saving myself,' Bella said, and somehow, in saying it, she didn't sound at all prim or superior. All she sounded was disappointed. Bella was disappointed in the prosaic and fallen world they were all living in. 'And you think I'm a fool for that. The whole world would think I'm a fool, apparently. And certainly Jonas Johnson does.'

'Oh pet,' Irene commiserated. 'I'm sorry your date went to the bad tonight.'

'We had words,' Bella admitted. She threw down the polishing rag and yanked off her pinny. 'He got a bit heavy and I thought at first . . . well, I thought he was going to pressure me. He was a gentleman though, but still he couldn't believe what I was saying. Just like you can't.' She tutted and shook her head. 'We were sitting in the park, Irene. Near where the bandstand used to be. I used to sit there with my nonna when I was a little girl. What did he think? I was going to jump into the bushes with him?'

Irene bit her lip. 'Apparently, plenty of folk do exactly that. Folk with nowhere else to go.'

Bella looked stricken. 'It was such a gorgeous evening. Golden light coming through the trees. Hardly anyone about. It was so peaceful and still. And I thought I was having a nice time. I thought we understood each other. Until he . . . he pounced! He thought I was going to be easy . . . As easy as anyone else!'

Irene walked home in the last of the sunlight, listening to the gulls screeching crazily. She still couldn't believe what Bella had been telling her.

And I had thought she was such a threat! I thought she had been Tom's girlfriend, way back before the war, and before I first knew him. When they were just kids and they were part of the same gang that stayed out all night on Marsden Bay . . .

Both of them had told her the stories, about the wonderful days when the young people stayed out all night. When it was warm enough and safe enough to lay out on the sands under the moon. It seemed incredible now, in these days of bombs going off and searchlights, to imagine such a thing, but both Bella and Tom had glowed at the memory. And Irene had – perhaps unworthily – assumed that they had been each other's lover back then.

At first she had felt envious. Bella had known Tom well before she ever had. Irene had even allowed herself to think that, deep down, Tom must still prefer the Italian girl to the one he had made his wife. And how could he not? Bella carried herself so confidently. She was so sexy and self-assured . . .

Well, it just went to show – you couldn't be certain about anyone, could you? And you shouldn't make assumptions about people. Why, look at Mavis. Mavis and Arthur! Irene had taken them at their words that they'd been poor all their lives. That they'd had nothing at all to their names and they'd been homeless and on the streets as bairns, living from hand to mouth. But now Irene knew for a fact – thanks to Elizabeth Kendricks – that that wasn't true at all. They had been adopted by her and the pair of them had shared a large house on the coast with her. The two of them had been brought up in the lap of luxury, by all accounts.

It just went to show that you might think that you knew the whole truth about someone, but sometimes you didn't know anything at all . . .

Home again at Number Thirteen, Irene found herself alone in the scullery with Ma Ada, putting the finishing touches to a hearty supper of stew and dumplings so heavy they had sunk down into the crockpot without a trace.

'My dumplings are usually perfect!' Ma Ada cried, and then hooted with laughter at how rude that sounded. 'Eeeh, listen to me!'

The old woman was in a good mood and so Irene found herself confiding in her and telling her all about the surprise she'd had tonight. She let her guard down and gossiped with Ada like they were friends.

Ada said, 'Aye, well, there you go. They were a devout Catholic family. Good for her! Good for Bella! I'm surprised, but I'm glad for her sake. Especially when her suitor is one of the Mad Johnsons. You know what I think about her getting involved with one of them. Especially the one who put a brick through my window!'

'So you're not surprised?' Irene asked. 'In this day and age? That she can get to thirty years of age and she's never ever . . . given in?'

Ma Ada was digging around in the stew pot with a slotted spoon, dredging her dumplings out. 'Let me tell you something, Irene Farley. There's no such thing as "this day and age". If you ask me, some young folk go using that as an excuse – and older folk too! Folk who should bally well know better. They go jumping into bed with all sorts of unsuitable people, just because they think they might be dead tomorrow. Well, that won't wash with me, I'm afraid. There's a proper way of doing things and you can't bend the rules, even if there's a war on.' She stared at Irene beadily. 'Aye, well you understand that, don't you, lass? You were good. Look at you and our Tom. You got married and everything, didn't you, before you gave into temptation?'

'Oh, yes,' Irene said, going off to fetch the dishes and cutlery. 'Aye, of course we did. All above board!' And her face was scalding hot with embarrassment as she turned away.

'That's just how it should be,' Ma Ada said haughtily. 'War or no war. I expect all my family to do the right thing.'

Irene smiled tightly, suddenly keen to change the subject. 'According to Bella, the right thing is exactly what Jonas Johnson is prepared to do. If she's that set on it, he says.'

'What do you mean?' Ada asked sharply.

'Apparently he's asked her to marry him! But she's still not happy. She doesn't think he means it. She thinks he's just saying it so she'll give in to him.'

'But she can't marry one of the Johnsons!' Ma Ada gasped. 'Not a lovely lass like that. She can't get any more mixed up with that awful lot. Doesn't she realise just how bad they are?'

Chapter 30

The little family in the house in Boldon Colliery all of a sudden found themselves quite happy. For a short while it hardly mattered that the skies were filled with soot and when it rained it dirtied all the washing in the yard. And Mr Alec came by so seldomly that they could almost forget that they were beholden to that stroppy little man. It was just the mammy and her kids in that small house, and that was just how they liked it.

They kept their days busy with taking in the mending. After an initially rocky start and the bother with some of the neighbours, the business soon took off. They had almost more work than they could handle, working late into the night until their eyes and fingers were sore. Mammy was right, though: the skin of their fingers toughened up with work, young as they were.

They could afford to go into town and visit those wonderful shops again, staring at the bolts of fabric that were stacked ceiling-high and getting the ladies to open drawerfuls of buttons and ribbons in every colour conceivable. They loved just to stare at it all. Sometimes their mammy had earned enough cash to buy a few yards of some lovely, rich stuff.

'We're keeping this for ourselves. I'm making new clothes for you two, as a treat.' And hey presto – between her commissioned jobs she would run them up matching outfits out of some wonderfully colourful remnant she had picked up at a bargain price.

In that dowdy, smoky corner of the world where they now lived, Mavis and Arthur became known as a pair of little dandies. They dashed about the place in Regency stripes or amber velveteen or faded purple damask trews and bloomers, chemises and knickerbockers. The pair of them looked adorable: as if they had been transported into the present from a previous century.

The local kids – not exactly welcoming in the first place – jeered and catcalled over the crumbling walls of the back ginnel and in the streets as the bairns went about their daily business. Mavis and Arthur carried their baskets from door to door, holding their heads up proudly, wearing their homemade couture.

'What have you got those bairns done up like that for?' Mr Alec cried, when he clapped eyes on them. He was aghast at the sight of the bairns he was responsible for. 'Why are you drawing attention to them like that? The lad looks like Little Lord Fauntleroy! And the little lass is done up like Little Bo Peep! What, do you want the kids round here to rough them up, or what?'

Their mammy was simply staring in dismay at their pretend dad. 'You don't even know their names! You can't even remember my bairns' names, can you?' She must have been really furious, since she never usually allowed herself to answer back or challenge her benefactor like this.

'Of course I do,' he flustered. 'Of course I remember their names! It's, er . . . little Mabel and . . .'

Mammy's eyes flashed. 'You don't! You don't even know their names!'

'But it's you I come here to see,' he growled. His face was growing a darker pink. It was a warning sign.

'Go up to your room and get dressed in your everyday clothes,' Mammy told the two of them, and they went up reluctantly to change. They were so proud of their fancy new outfits. They had never had anything new in their lives before and, though they were frightened of Mr Alec, and didn't really like him very much at all, they had been excited to show off their new clothes. Neither they nor Mammy had expected such an appalled reaction from him.

Arthur paused on the stairs and listened to the man down there, shouting at their mam: 'They'll get strung up! Living round here with the dregs of the earth! Strutting around like flamin' fairy tale princesses!'

Mammy was trying to calm him down. He was getting his dander up. Soon he'd start crashing around, smashing things up, lashing out at her.

'Arthur?' Mavis asked him, perched on the stairs beside her big brother. 'What's he saying to her?'

Arthur looked at his little sister and her face was screwed up with worry. 'Don't fret, love,' he said. The pair of them stayed there, halfway down the carpetless stairs, trying not to make the wood creak as they listened to what the adults were saying.

'And you!' Mr Alec was shouting now. 'You're all dolled up daft as well! What do you look like?'

There was a pause and the bairns could imagine how surprised their mammy was by his cruel words. She had been so proud of the summer dress she'd sewn from oddments and offcuts. It was unusual, perhaps, but it suited her perfectly. She looked like a gypsy dancer at a carnival, Arthur thought. When the three of them danced together in the living room, her skirts had flared out in a blaze of colour and they had danced themselves into a joyful frenzy, until they collapsed, worn out, on the sofa.

'I thought you'd like it, Alec,' they heard her saying. 'I made it myself, and the bairns' outfits, too . . .'

He laughed bitterly. 'Aye, anyone can see that. The three of you look like something off the bloody stage. A pantomime! No wonder all the neighbours are sniggering at you. Aye, I've heard what they say. Looking daft – that's bad enough. But they say you go round looking like a street walker! With your hair all undone and your legs bare and all your wares showing . . .'

'What? But, Alec, who says that? They're just being malicious and horrible . . .' Mammy sounded shocked by the things he was saying.

'You're my woman,' he grunted. His voice was lower now. 'Everything I've given you. Everything that you owe me. You belong to me. You will not make a show of me in the street, girl.'

'But I don't!' she gasped.

Was he hitting her? Arthur sat up straight, alarmed. There was something punctuating their speech. Their words were fragmented, distorted. What was he doing to her? Arthur itched to dash back down there and throw open the door . . .

'I can see what you're doing,' Mr Alec was raving. 'These new clothes. The radio. The bits of rubbish on the window sill. I never bought you those things. You're getting money from elsewhere, aren't you? From another man, is it? You're taking handouts from other blokes, are you? And you're giving all your favours to them as well – admit it!'

'Alec, man, nay! You're wrong. I'd never do that! You've got it all wrong. It's sewing! The bairns and me, we're making that money from—'

And then – crack. There was no mistaking that noise. He slapped her so hard she went silent for a few moments. Arthur and Mavis heard the thud of her crumpling to the floor.

'Get up,' Alec said. 'Come on, get up. Don't cry. It was only a tap.'

The bairns could hear their mammy saying something, but her voice was blurred and quiet.

'You'll behave yourself, won't you?' Mr Alec asked her. Then there came the sound of another slap. And another.

Arthur couldn't hold himself back anymore. Mavis shouted with terror as he suddenly leapt up and plunged down the staircase. He yanked open the parlour door and threw himself upon the burly figure of Mr Alec.

Arthur was slight and small for his age, but his appearance in the room was so sudden that he took the man by surprise as he leapt upon him. Looking absurd in his homemade fancy dress, the boy clung on tight to Mr Alec's bald, sweaty head and wrapped his spindly legs around his bulging waist. 'Get your hands off my mother!' he shrieked, squeezing with all his limbs as tight as he could.

'Get – him – off – me!' Mr Alec roared.

Arthur hated the fuzzy vibration of all the shouting. He liberated one hand and started hitting the horrible man about the head as hard as he could without losing his grip.

'Arthur!' his mam cried, but Arthur clung on, even as Mr Alec stormed around the place, crashing into furniture and then against the walls. He howled as Arthur dug his fingernails into his fat, sweating flesh.

'Get – your – flamin' – bastard – son – off – of – me!' Mr Alec bellowed.

'Say you'll leave her alone!' Arthur shouted in his ear. 'Say you'll never touch my mammy again!'

The man simply let out a great, frustrated roar, taking hold of the little lad and flinging him to the floor. Of course Arthur was no match for him, in the end. The boy lay there winded as Alec towered over him. The man's voice was shrill with fury. 'I will touch her when I want. You lot would be on the bloody street if it wasn't for my money. I pay to do exactly what I want, little man. So just you keep your neb out of it.'

Arthur stared up at him, fighting to catch his breath back. 'Leave her alone! Leave all of us alone!'

Mr Alec sneered. 'I can do what I want. I've earned that right. I wish I'd never bothered taking you lot on. That dirty little sister of yours. And you – you're a creepy little fairy. She's got you growing up wrong. I would have been better off steering clear of the whole bleedin' lot of you . . .'

He was interrupted by the mammy, then. She was standing up and rushing to Arthur's defence. She gave Mr Alec a flat-handed shove that unbalanced him. She sent him toppling back towards the door. 'Just get out, Alec. Get out of our house.'

'Your house!' he snarled. 'Your house, is it? Who paid for it? Who pays your bills every month? Who buys all your food? You don't get all that from running up a few lengths of tat and sewing new hems on the neighbours' rags!' He glared at them all, spittle flying out of his mouth. 'You get it from me. You get the money you need from me! And what respect do I get, eh? Just look how you flamin' well treat me!'

At this he flung open the parlour door again, and there stood Mavis. She was looking tiny and tear-stained in her Bo Peep outfit. She stared up at the raging man and there was terror in her face. But she didn't move from the spot. She simply stared up at his empurpled face.

'Get out of my way,' he grunted, and shoved her over sharply.

Mammy screamed at this. It was one step too far. This time she launched herself at the man, and it was only as she did so that she realised she was holding the pan shovel from the fireside.

She swung it hard through the air as Mr Alec scooted out of the house. He tumbled into the street, feeling the breeze at his back. 'You mad bloody bitch!' he screeched. 'If you'd hit me with that, you'd have brained me!'

'Good!' the mammy cried and slammed the door shut in his outraged face.

Then she fell to the hall floor, clutching the pan shovel and sobbing with fright. Her children clustered round her, holding her tightly until Mr Alec stopped banging at the door and yelling on the front step. It wasn't too long before embarrassment must have overcome him.

They heard the revving engine of his oxblood motor car. And then it departed very noisily.

'Did he hurt you?' she sobbed, hugging her bairns to her. 'Did he hurt either of you?'

They shook their heads and hugged her back. The three of them lay in the downstairs hall of the home they shared; all three of them dishevelled in their fancy dress.

'We'll have to get out of here,' Mammy said at last. 'We'll not be able to stay here now . . .'

Chapter 31

She woke up from an evening's dozing in bed feeling very out of sorts. It was like she'd been drowning without knowing it, and suddenly came bursting to the surface. Mavis sat there gasping in the silence, feeling her heart racing and her head pounding.

Her sleep patterns had gone all over the place while she was recuperating. She slept as and when she could. Sometimes this meant that she was awake when Sam wasn't. Their days were drifting upside down next to each other.

Mavis knew her irregular hours were doing her no good really. She needed to take back hold of her life and start feeling normal again. She had to get herself back to work at the biscuit factory too, before they gave her job away to someone else. When she really thought about dozing her days away, she started to feel guilty. Who was she to spend her days languishing like this when there was a war still going on?

Whenever she lay still, however, she found herself roving over the past. The sights and sounds of her childhood had been coming back to her unbidden. She couldn't have stopped that train of thought if she'd wanted. She had to lie there and relive it all, even though it made her weep each day. She thought she wept soundlessly, but her sobbing could be heard through the walls.

She kept lying there and listening to the voices from the past and it slowly dawned on Mavis that these might be the only voices she would ever be able to hear again. The ones inside her head.

I've got to face facts, she thought. I might never get my hearing back.

Then, all of a sudden, she received another shock, as Sam came bursting into the room, still wearing his outdoor coat and grinning like mad. 'Mavis! Mavis!' he went. It was the only word that Mavis could lip-read.

He came bounding to the bed like a puppy and she found it alarming in her drowsy, headachey state. He was excited and beaming with enthusiasm, and his wife found herself struggling not to be irritated with him. Now he was gabbling away silently, as if carried away. As if by talking more loudly and holding her face in his hands could somehow overcome her deafness.

'I don't know what you're saying!' she shouted out loud. It was like being inside a dream still, yelling and not being sure if you could be heard. Like those dreams when she was wading through treacle and never getting anywhere.

Sam nodded and went scrabbling at the bedside table for her pad and stub of a pencil. He scrawled something down quickly and held it up.

'I can start when I like! Mr Wight says I have a job any time I like!'

Mavis frowned and peered closely at the letters as they danced around. She would never admit it to anyone, but she found reading quite difficult, even though Sam made his letters blocky and separated out for her. Squinting, she gradually came to realise what his news consisted of.

'Oh, that's wonderful!' she cried out, and she felt a sudden burst of happiness. It came crashing down on her like a wave surging on the beach. Her moods often changed like this – all at once, washing each other away. Mostly, one look or smile from her Sam was enough to cheer her right up. Mavis would never stop thanking her lucky stars that she had ended up belonging to him.

Next thing she was up on her feet and tying her dressing gown around herself. She felt a little wobbly on her feet, but she was determined to get up.

'What are you doing?' he mouthed at her, laughing, as she quickly brushed her hair.

'We have to have a little drink to celebrate!' she shouted. 'Uh-hoh! Aye, yes! We have to have a drink to this! It's wonderful news, pet!'

Sam hugged her hard to his chest. Seeing her come back to life like this, after days of darkness and dozing and uncertainty, was wonderful.

They had sherry and wished it was champagne, and just saying that made them both laugh, because they suddenly remembered a moment last Christmas.

'Do you remember when we had fizzy sherry?' Sam asked her, hurriedly miming opening a bottle of fizz that failed to go pop, then pouring a glass that made him pull a face when he pretended to drink it.

'Oh, oh-hoh! I do!' Mavis squealed with laughter.

Last Christmas Eve, it was. When he asked her to marry him, standing in the frosty darkness of the backyard at his mother's house. It had been the night when they all thought Beryl had disappeared with the babies, while everyone was at church singing carols.

Well, poor Beryl hadn't gone doolally after all. She had just been taking the babies to see her mother in her house by the park, and the drama had all been over and sorted out before many hours had passed. Then, late on Christmas Eve, Mavis and Sam were in that icy backyard, taking the midnight air, and he had asked her, so sweetly, to be his wife.

She had never had a happier moment in all of her life.

Then they were indoors again, in Ma Ada's cosy back parlour, and the old woman and the others looked at them like they knew something was up. Sam broke the news and everyone cheered. Even Lucky, the hairless cat, perched on Ma Ada's lap, looked pleased. And Mavis felt relieved that the news was met with such enthusiasm. She had feared that maybe the Farleys would baulk at having her as a member of their family. She knew that she was different, somehow. She came from a rougher background and she knew that's what everyone thought about her.

Nevertheless her Sam had seen through all of that. He had seen the truth of her and had fallen in love with who she was on the inside.

He was the one who had reminded Ma Ada of the special bottle she was keeping right at the back of her sideboard.

'Eeeh, but that's really for the end of the war,' the old woman said. 'I'd thought to myself that I would only open that on the day the hostilities are over!'

Sam said, 'Oh, let's open it now. We've got good reason to celebrate right now. And how long's that dusty old bottle been lying at the back of the cupboard? Since before I was born, wasn't it?'

The bottle of champagne had always been there, behind the cards and the papers and the fancy glasses. Ma Ada knew exactly how and when it had arrived in the house, and she wasn't about to go into that tale right now. But the lad was right. The bottle had been lying there for twenty years at least.

'It must be a fine vintage!' she laughed. 'You're right. Fetch it out. I can't bend down to get it – would you do the honours, Sam?'

And so those still up out of their beds gathered round as Sam twisted the foil and metal off and wrestled with the cork. It felt dry and crumbly in his hand and let out a kind of anguished sigh rather than a bang.

When he poured it into Ma Ada's nicest glasses it was darker than champagne ought to be.

'And it tastes of warm, fizzy sherry!' Ma Ada had laughed. 'It's ruined! It's vile! It's a complete waste! What a dud!' She threw back her head and laughed. 'Typical! Typical us. You hang on to something for year upon year and by the time you get it out it's ruined!'

Mavis sipped at her spoiled champagne. Well, she had little idea what it was supposed to taste like anyway. This was quite nice, she thought. Yes, it really was like fizzy sherry.

'It's a bit like drinking pee,' said Sam, pulling a face, and they had all laughed again.

They could laugh about it if they wanted, but Mavis was glad to have that bit of a drink, and to toast her marriage proposal, even if it was like drinking pee (Sam always said something awful!). She loved it because they all raised their glasses and smiled at her and welcomed her to the Farley clan.

Mavis would never forget that moment. It was only six months ago and already it seemed like a lifetime. So much had happened already . . .

She knew, though, that she'd be glad to toast every happy event with warm, fizzy sherry. Now it was her favourite.

Tonight she downed her ordinary sherry and felt it warming her all the way through.

'Oh!' Sam burst out impulsively and raced for her notepad again. 'In all the excitement of telling you my news, I forgot – there's something else I had to tell you, pet.'

His writing flowed so fast on the small page that she had trouble following him. He turned over the page and carried on: 'I went to Franchino's on my way back, I popped in on the girls to see them. And they had a visitor. Now, I'm not sure you're going to be glad about this . . .'

Mavis frowned. What was he on about? What was she not going to be glad about? What visitor did he mean? 'What? Who?' she shouted at him, starting to feel dread building up inside.

He flipped the page and wrote very carefully: 'But I think it's important, Mavis. She seems nice.'

'Who?' Mavis cried.

Sam wrote: 'She says she's your mother!'

Mavis felt her mood crashing down and she stared at the page and then up at Sam. She felt anger and resentment starting to well up inside herself. She told him, spitting out the words very carefully: 'My mother is dead, Sam. She is dead.'

Chapter 32

Straight away, Mammy took them to an old woman who sat in a caravan on the cliffs right above the sea.

Mavis and Arthur stood staring mutely at the old woman because they had never seen her before, and also because, to them, she was utterly terrifying. Her caravan was smoky and dark and it smelled strongly of tallow and kippers. Some of her teeth were black or missing.

'Come closer, let me have a look at you,' the old woman said, and reached out with strong hands like pincers to squeeze their arms until they hurt. It was like she was seeing if they needed fattening up for the pot. And they had already seen her pot, bubbling away over a fitful fire outside her caravan. It was a cauldron! Both Mavis and Arthur thought it at once.

The old woman laughed and her eyes flashed darkly at their mammy. 'Oh, you're wanting my help now, are you?'

'Please, just for a little while. I need to find somewhere. I need to get back on my feet. Find somewhere safe . . .'

The old woman snickered and shuffled forward on her tiny bunk. Her hands went to her hair, which was braided and coiled and winched spitefully tight. There was cruelty and suspicion etched on her face, and it never softened once during this visit. 'You got yourself into trouble with a man again, I suppose.'

'Never mind that,' the mammy said, casting a glance at

her babies. They didn't need to hear the story of Mr Alec hashed over again.

The two bairns were wearing all the clothes they owned. It had seemed the easiest way to get away from the house with all their things. Outside the weather was sharp and chill and so layers of homemade clothes actually came in useful. The pair of them looked rather strange, though. Like refugees from a theatrical pageant.

'You never brought them here before,' the old woman said. 'Funny you bring them now. Look – they aren't babies now. You've had them so long. Why didn't you bring them before?'

Mammy hung her head with shame.

'I know why.' The old woman laughed nastily and jumped down from the bunk. 'But never mind. They're welcome here. For a little while.'

Arthur had hold of Mavis's hand and he could feel that she was quivering. He squeezed her tiny fingers in order to reassure her, but he knew that he was quaking with fear, too.

Outside the painted caravan the old woman was tending to her fire and poking a long-handled spoon into her witchy cauldron. 'We'll feed them and wash them and keep them safe from everyone. You should have come to us before, though.'

There were three other caravans spaced out on this vast stretch of scrubby grass at the top of the cliffs. They were painted in faded colours, just the same. There was a shaggy-haired man sitting in his shirtsleeves on the steps of the closest one. He grunted, got up and went off to tend to the horses, who looked bedraggled as they stood together in a clump, shivering in the wind.

Mammy took her kids in her arms and hugged them close as the wind rose up and plucked at the shawl she was wearing. 'Listen, this is your nanna. You've never met her before, and that's my fault. She loves you and so do both your uncles, and they'll keep you safe.'

'You can't leave us,' Arthur burst out. 'We're coming with you! Wherever you go!'

Mammy shook her head, putting both hands gently over his mouth to shush him. 'Nay, lad. Now, I know that you've grown up fast and you think you're a proper little man. And I know that you think you're the one who's done all the looking after me and Mavis in the past. But you're just a little boy, still. You have to do what your mammy tells you. And now you must do what your nanna says.'

Arthur felt abashed at being called a little boy. At that moment he wanted nothing more than to wish away his entire childhood. He felt much too young and helpless. He wanted to be old enough and strong enough to take charge of his little family. He wanted to be the one who was responsible for his mammy and his sister. That's all he wanted to do.

'Now listen, Arthur. I know you've got a strong mind of your own,' his mammy laughed, and hugged him close. 'But for now, just do as you're told, eh? Your mammy has to go off and do things. She has to sort out her life and make some money again. And then soon . . . I promise! Soon, I'll come back for you.'

Mavis was looking up at her with huge, frightened eyes. She looked at her mam and then Arthur and shied away from the frightening old woman with the braided hair piled on top of her head. 'Mammy, we want you to stay,' she said, and started to cry.

This almost started their mother off crying, too, but she bit her lip until her teeth drew blood. She knew she had to be tough in order to leave her kids behind, even temporarily. 'Here, love,' she told Mavis. She unwound her shawl. The most beautiful thing she owned. It was Irish wool, lilac and grey, patterned with bright red songbirds. 'Keep this for me. Keep it safe.'

The shawl went three times around the tiny bairn's shoulders. She stood there swaddled up against the wintry winds coming over the clifftops.

'The two of you be good for your nanna,' Mammy said. 'And I'll be back before you know it.'

Then she turned and hurried off across the grey-green expanse, through the long grass, away from them. She looked back, waving at them only once. Then she was gone.

Everything felt strange for quite some time, of course. Nothing was familiar about this new life in Nanna's caravan. The fold-down beds and sleeping in the same pokey space. It was like living on shelves in a tiny, unaired cupboard. The rough blankets were stinky and made Arthur sneeze.

'Hush up boy,' Nanna roared in the night. 'Be more like your little sister. She's a quiet mite! She knows how to carry on. You be more like her. You too loud, boy!'

In those early days and weeks with Nanna, that's exactly how Arthur felt. He was too noisy and big and clumsy. He broke crockery that he'd been sent to wash. He knocked over the cooking pot and spilled the broth. Nothing he did was right. He felt lonely and shamed the whole time he was awake and at night all he did was dream about being back with his mammy.

'I can see you hurt, boy,' Nanna told him. 'You feel things strong, don't you? Deep inside?'

This was one night when it was dry enough to sit outside by the fire. The sun was going down and a pale light shone on the smooth sea far below. It was beautiful to be sitting here, right at the edge of the world, though Arthur would never admit it. He and his sister were wrapped up warm and their bellies were full with the warming food Nanna cooked. But he still felt a pain like a knife thrust deep in his guts. The pain of missing his mam would never go away, no matter how many weeks went by.

'The little lass, here,' Nanna went on. 'Now, she'll have a different kind of life to you, I reckon. She's not as clever as you'll be. She feels things less keenly. She forgives easier and she has a simpler soul. And so Mavis will find it less difficult to be happy than you will. Because you, little fella – you've got all kinds of strange, funny things going on inside of you, haven't you? Such wild and peculiar fancies!' With this said, the old woman croaked with laughter like a horrible old crow. She sucked long and hard on her stinking pipe and sighed with satisfaction.

'You don't know anything about us,' Arthur said mutinously. 'You're just making this rubbish up out of your head.'

'Ha! Some folk pay for this rubbish! This is fortune-telling, this is. This is what some people swear by.'

'It's just a lot of daft words,' Arthur glowered.

'Oh, I don't think so,' laughed the old lady and snickered as she pulled on her pipe again. The smell drifting over was like nothing the bairns had ever smelled before. Like strange spices from faraway lands. But she was a witch! Arthur reminded himself. This woman who reckoned she was their nanna was a witchy old witch and they had to be careful not to trust her too much.

Arthur barely slept those nights in his fold-down bed. He slept with one eye open in case the old hag tried to stuff either one of them or both into her cooking pot.

Mavis, being younger, was much more accepting. She sat by the firelight and stroked the soft wool of their mammy's shawl.

The horses whickered peacefully in their nearby paddock. Their stolid presence made things easier for Mavis, too. Her shaggy-haired uncles (or so they claimed to be) let her feed them handfuls of meal and she adored getting that close to the creatures.

Day by day, playing in the long grass of the cliffs and dashing down the steps cut into the sandstone to the beach, Mavis was learning to enjoy her new life.

'You're forgetting Mammy!' Arthur accused her crossly one day. It was morning and they were down on the beach. They were supposed to be gathering seaweed for the old woman, who liked to dry it in the sun on washing lines. Goodness knows what for. Something nasty, obviously.

'I am not,' Mavis shot back. 'I don't forget Mammy.'

Weeks had gone by and they had heard nothing at all. Somewhere over the fields and hills and in the midst of all the smoking roofs and chimneys, somewhere in all that morass of busy life, their mammy was trying to get her own life back on course. She was looking for a way to make ends meet. She would find a new place for them all to live, and one day she would come calling for them. Arthur had every faith it would be soon.

'You mustn't forget her,' he warned his sister.

'I won't!' she called, tiptoeing around the morning's fresh rock pools, and peering intently into their tiny worlds. But already Mammy's face was growing vague in the little girl's thoughts. Her voice was clear as anything, still. Mavis could hear that voice, especially when she wore the woollen shawl over her shoulders.

'I dream about Mammy,' Mavis told her brother, 'and sometimes I can see what's going on.'

'What do you mean?' Arthur frowned.

Mavis shrugged and danced away, stooping to pick up festoons of dark seaweed and whipping them through the air. 'She has a new daddy now. I saw it in my dreams. But he's not a nice man. I think he's worse than Mr Alec.' Saying this, Mavis paused and looked worried.

'How could you know what's going on?' Arthur said, feeling cross. He dashed up to her and shook his little sister until she was on the verge of tears. 'You don't even know what you're talking about.'

'He's a nasty man,' Mavis said, pushing the words out, even though she didn't want to say them. 'I've seen him doing horrible things . . .'

'You're lying,' Arthur shouted at her.

'I'm not, Arthur, honest! I-I can see things! When I close my eyes at night, I see real things before I sleep!'

Chapter 33

'So what have they got you doing, then?' Irene asked him brightly. She was glad to see Sam at the biscuit factory that day. He looked enthusiastic and chuffed with himself, and he was wearing a pristine white work coat.

'Ah, I'm just fetching and carrying all the pallets and boxes in the loading bay and that. It's pretty monotonous.'

'You'll be doing a good job, I'm sure,' Irene reassured him. 'Plus, you'll get lots of attention from all the lasses, as well. You'll be one of the very few young men working at Wights!'

He pulled a face. 'You know I'm not bothered by that kind of thing. It embarrasses me when lasses shout after me.'

'Aye, I know!' she laughed, and wondered just how he was going to manage with the likes of Effie and Glad and Plump Mary from the packing room ragging on him. 'But won't it be lovely when your Mavis comes back to work, and you can come and go together? You'll see more of each other, working in the same place.'

'I reckon we will,' he nodded, but his expression gave away the anxiety he was feeling. 'Eeeh, but Irene, I've gone and said something that's upset the lass and knocked her right back. She was getting up and about and feeling better at last and then I went and said something daft . . .'

'Here, come and sit down here with me.' They were in the corner of the factory yard, away from all the rest of them. It was the place Irene often slipped away to, in the shadow of the tall brick chimney, when she wanted a moment's peace in the working day. 'What are you saying? What could you possibly have said to knock her back?'

He sighed and fetched out a cigarette, lighting it in his cupped hands and drawing a disapproving stare from Irene. 'It was just this. I let slip to her about your visitor at Franchino's.'

'You what?' Irene blinked.

'Mrs Kendricks. I told her . . . that I'd met her.'

Irene saw trouble coming. 'Oh, Sam, you didn't . . .'

'I just sort of blurted it out. And I made it worse, too. I called her Mavis's mam. I said – I've met your mam! And she's been going to the ice-cream parlour regularly and talking with Irene . . .'

'Oh, Sam! That makes it sound like I've been talking about her behind her back . . .' But that was true, wasn't it? Irene thought to herself. That was exactly what she *had* been doing. But not maliciously. Just trying to get to the bottom of things, to learn about the past, and only with the hope of bringing people back together. If Irene had been sneaky or interfering, it was simply with that hope in mind. 'How did she react?'

He inhaled deeply. 'She went a bit funny, to be honest. I've never seen her upset like that. Ranting and raging at me. "My mam's dead!" she kept shouting. Like I was torturing her. Like I'd set out to dredge up her feelings and make her feel awful. I tried to tell her, "No, I mean Mrs Kendricks. It was her who I met. The woman at the wedding. The woman who says she adopted you and Arthur . . ." And Mavis just took on this wild, furious look. She stared at me like she didn't even know who I was. It was frightening, Irene.'

'Oh, how awful . . .' Irene whispered. She hated the thought of two of her favourite people going through the scene he was describing.

'And then she just hissed at me, "That woman is nothing to me. Do you hear, me, Sam? She's just nothing."' Sam shook his head. 'All this at the top of our voices, and me scribbling down scraps of sentences. Mavis bellowing and trying to make herself understood. It was awful, Irene.'

She hugged him and rubbed his back for a moment, until a thought struck her. 'Did you tell her that Mrs Kendricks has been coming back a number of times to talk to me, then?'

He nodded unhappily. 'Yeah, I'm afraid I did.'

Irene nodded. 'So now Mavis really will think I've gone behind her back. She'll start thinking she can't trust me. No wonder she's had a setback . . .'

'She won't come downstairs. She's taken to her bed again.'

'I'll come over. I'll explain . . .' Irene promised.

Then the hooter was blowing for the start of the afternoon shift. Irene sent Sam back off to his loading bay, keen that he should seem eager and punctual on what was still his first day, after all. She returned to her work room and got on with her customary tasks in a fug of silence for the rest of the afternoon.

Arthur. She would write to Arthur. That was the thing to do. He needed updating about the accident Mavis had suffered. She didn't think anyone had actually informed him about it. It would be best if he heard the facts directly from her, and she could tell him the way Mavis was reacting to her injury. Also, she could tell him about this business with the adoptive mother coming back onto the scene, and how Mavis was taking it rather badly. She could ask for Arthur's advice, perhaps.

But Irene had to be honest with herself. She also longed to ask Arthur for his side of the story as well. She wanted to know if it really was all true, all the things that Mrs Kendricks was telling her whenever they met. Had Arthur and Mavis really shared a childhood like the one that Irene was slowly developing a picture of?

Ma Ada knew the address to send Arthur's letters to. They had to go to this certain office or department, and then they winged their flimsy way across the oceans to the other side of the world. He probably had his own worries, there in the midst of a war zone, trying to keep everyone's spirits up. But he really ought to know what was happening at home . . . That's what Irene thought, at any rate.

Sam came home with Irene at the end of the day. It was ingrained in him to report back to his ma about his first day in a new job. In some ways he seemed like a little lad, coming home up the steep hill, after his first day at a new school.

On the way up the cobbled lane, Irene told him about her idea to write to Arthur.

'Make sure you tell him that she's all right, though,' Sam said. 'Don't panic him unduly. Her hearing might never recover, we know that, but physically she's still in one piece . . . It's just knocked her for six, that's all.'

'Of course I'll put it carefully,' said Irene, who prided herself on her letters and the way she expressed herself. She was very careful and exact in the way she passed on news, knowing how things could go awry when people got the wrong end of the stick.

Number Thirteen was in uproar when they stepped indoors. Both babies had got the colic and Beryl and Ma Ada were dashing about with medicinal concoctions and warm clean clothes. 'It's all hands to the pumps,' Beryl announced. 'How was your first day, Sam?'

'Champion!' he smiled, wincing at the keening cries coming from Marlene. 'It's so much better than the dirty docks. I don't know why I never applied before to Wight's.'

'You better watch yourself around all them women!' Ma Ada cackled. 'Lasses are terrible when they get together in a gang. They'll have your life, our Sam.'

'I can handle that lot,' he grinned.

'Eeeh, listen him!' Ma Ada passed the grizzling Marlene over to her mam for a cuddle. The toddler wriggled and shrieked even louder, pounding her irate fists against Irene's shoulder.

'And how's Mavis doing?' Ma Ada asked. 'Still stone deaf?'

'Aye, and she's down in the dumps too, worse than before,' Sam sighed. 'I stupidly told her about that woman sniffing round. The woman who adopted her and Arthur when they were bairns.'

Ma Ada glowered at him for being daft. 'Why did you tell her that? And what's all this about, anyway?' She darted a look at Irene. 'You know more about this than you're saying, as well, lady. What's going on?'

Irene jogged baby Marlene against her hip. 'I don't know. But I'm trying to find out. I just think this old lady is maybe trying to make peace . . . and also trying to make amends for something that went on between them all in the past.'

Ma Ada pursed her mouth and hugged the tiny, passively quiet Johnny to her bosom. 'You know what I think about meddling in other people's business.'

Covertly Sam, Beryl and Irene exchanged a swift glance at these words. Since when did Ma Ada keep her neb out of other people's business?

'Irene just wants to help,' Sam defended her. 'She's the best friend that Mavis has ever had.'

'Well,' said the Farley matriarch, 'then I think you should go round there. Go straight to where she lives. Ask her straight out: "Mrs Kendricks, just what is all this about?" It's all very well, her nipping into Franchino's now and then, looking all wistful and forlorn about the past. I think you've got to have it out with her. "Look here, just why is it you want to go raking up the past anyway? What is it that you want with our Mavis?"'

Irene and Sam both stared at Ma Ada. 'Go round to her house?' said Irene.

'Aye! You said she lives in a big place by the sea, didn't you? Well, go and find it! Go and see where she lives. Get a good look at this fancy place of hers. And ask her straight out: "What is it the likes of you want with us lot, eh?"'

Chapter 34

The two bairns went all over town, asking after their mammy. They went everywhere they could think of, sneaking off, just the two of them, every time Nanna's back was turned.

'You'll come back one day from all your creeping around, you two, and you'll find out that we've gone!' the old woman warned them. She gurgled with laughter at the thought of that: of their dismay at the sight of the empty field and the scrubby grass left by the horses and caravans. 'That's what'll happen to you two, if you don't watch out!'

Arthur muttered under his breath that they wouldn't care anyway. He hated living in her foul caravan and sitting round that fire every night. He thought he and his sister would be much better on their own.

'We could run away,' he told Mavis, and his sister looked alarmed.

'No, Arthur! What about Nanna? She'd be upset.'

He doubted that. The old woman didn't seem all that attached to her charges. She fed them but she didn't really seem to like them at all. 'She just puts up with us,' Arthur said.

As the weeks went by, the two of them were looking less pristine in their fancy dress. Their clothes were dirty and starting to fray. When they hurried about the streets of their town, they looked shabbier by the day.

The streets of Boldon were the first place where they knocked at doors and asked after their mam. The people she had mended clothes for: sometimes they expressed sadness and regret. Others were angry because she hadn't returned their garments. Others had simply forgotten about her and shooed these ragamuffin bairns away. No one knew anything about where she might be now.

They stood across the road from the house where they had lived, and they saw a new woman going in and out. She was unfamiliar and she didn't seem to have any kids of her own. They didn't feel brave enough to knock on that front door. What if Mr Alec himself had answered?

But somewhere at the back of Arthur's mind he knew he should be brave enough. He also knew that Mr Alec might know where their mammy had gone.

They left Boldon and traipsed all the streets of South Shields, returning to the drapers' shops where they had all had such a lovely time when their mammy bought her supplies of cloth and thread. But the people there just shook their heads and looked cross at the dirty-looking bairns coming into their stores.

The streets were dark, dirty, unfriendly places for two bairns alone like they were. The two of them had to scoot out of the way as folk went about their business and the light turned dingy as wet snow started to fall. Mavis complained about being soaked to the skin and exhausted. They had spent several days on the trot walking the streets of town to no avail. Her brother gripped her hand reassuringly and told her: 'We're going down to the quay. Remember when we used to work there with her?'

'All those fish,' Mavis pulled a face.

'Yes, and all those people who knew her, and knew us,' he smiled. 'I don't know why we didn't go there first of all. Someone at the fish market will have heard from her or seen her! They're bound to have done! You'll see!'

The fish quay was just as freezing cold and inhospitable as ever they'd known it. By the time they arrived, stalls were closing up for the day, and the stallholders were packing up their wares and sluicing the slime of blood and guts from the cobbles. The bairns were recognised by a woman in a tattered headscarf, who called out to them.

'Have you seen our mammy?' Arthur cried, hurrying over to her and dragging his sister along.

'You what, pet?' asked the woman. She was a huge, craggy-faced person with wispy hair. Arthur remembered her salty tongue and huge laughter, from when his mam held the stall next to her. Beattie, that was her name. 'Eeeh, what are you saying? Have you lost her?' Hands on hips, she stared down at the two dirty-looking bairns.

'She left us with our nanna and then she went off to find money and a new place,' Arthur said. 'We had to run away from Nanna.'

Slowly the fish woman wiped her meaty hands on her filthy apron. 'She ran away, eh? I remember now. She went off with that flashy ginger fella, didn't she? She was going on about the wonderful new life she was gonna have with him. Aye, an' I tried to warn her about him. I never liked the look of him, that ginger git.'

'Have you seen her?' Arthur asked urgently. 'I thought she might have come back here, to her old work . . .'

'Nah, pet, I've seen neither sight nor sound for ages.'

One of the others who worked at the quay thought he might have clapped eyes on her, though. An unfriendly old man with a lumpy, warty nose who Arthur had always found quite frightening in the past. He lurched past carrying empty crates and told them: 'I've seen her, I think. She was hanging around Ocean Road. I saw her with a foreign sailor, I think. Arab-looking fella. Well,

I think it was her. She was in and out of the pubs down there . . .'

'Eeeh, don't go sending bairns to go looking round the pubs on Ocean Road!' the large woman in the apron gasped. 'You two want to get home to your nanna! It's getting dark now!'

But Arthur had already turned away and was dragging his little sister after him, hurrying up the cobbled lane from the quays. 'Thanks for your help!' he called back, and was glad to get away from the fetid stink of the quay once more.

'Where are we going, Arthur?' Mavis asked, hurrying after him. She looked exhausted by now.

He kept ploughing on, even with the wind against them and the snow coating their homemade clothes. Ocean Road wasn't too far. And though they'd never get inside the pubs, they could hang about outside and maybe see her if she went into one . . .

Arthur made himself feel brave, but those dark smoky windows of the pubs made him scared. They spoke of a strange adult world and all the awful things that might happen there. Somehow his mam was caught up in that world, behind those smudgy windows. What could he really do to bring her back out again?

Suddenly he was aware of his sister dragging on his arm and crying out. She was just tired and complaining. 'Mavis, ha'way,' he told her. 'I can't go carrying you about, pet. You have to walk on your own two feet. Come on, now . . .'

But Mavis wasn't complaining and kicking up a fuss. When he turned round, he saw that her face was red and excited. She was pointing at the brightly lit windows of the place they were passing. 'Arthur! I just looked in and guess what!'

He didn't have much faith in his little sister's powers of observation really. He paused to look where she was pointing. 'What is it?'

Through the misted windows of the ice-cream parlour it was hard to make out the faces of the people seated within. Yes, there was a woman with long, chestnut brown hair and the same complexion as their mammy, perhaps. But it was hard to see her face. She was sitting right at the back with a couple of others. With men. She was animated and laughing, it seemed like.

'It's her! Is it her? I think it's her!' Mavis was rabbiting on.

Arthur thought she was clutching at straws. It was just someone with similar hair. But still, this person looked more like their mam than anyone they'd seen in all the days they'd been looking.

'We'll go in and see,' he said determinedly.

But as soon as they eased open the heavy glass doors, Mr Franchino himself was hurrying up to them. The old, bald gent who owned the place didn't seem so pleased to see them in his brightly lit parlour. 'No, no, no, no! You kids! You can't afford nothing! You got no money. You're just here to rob! You'll rob an old man blind!'

'Hey, get off!' Arthur yelled at him, as the old fella grabbed him by the scruff of his neck. 'You can't hit us. We've done nothing wrong!'

'You got no place here,' Tonio Franchino told him. 'You just scruffy kids, I can see that. Get out of here!' He was old but his wiry strength was too much for Arthur, and soon they were back through the art-deco doors. The old man snatched two wafer biscuits from the counter and thrust them into the bairns' hands. 'You can have these for nothin'. Now, go away and don't cause a fuss.'

'But, mister!' Mavis wailed. 'Our mammy's in there!'

'What? What's that?' Tonio Franchino frowned. He looked down at the mucky-faced Mavis as she held her wafer and cautiously nibbled a corner of it.

'It's true,' Arthur said. 'We've lost her, and we think she's in your place. At the back there, with those blokes.'

'What?' Tonio Franchino felt his heart melting, even in the freezing cold of Ocean Road. 'You've lost your mama?'

'She left us,' Mavis said, still gnawing her wafer. 'We want her back.'

'And you think that's her?' Tonio peered through the steamy windows of his busy café. 'The pretty lady at the back?'

Arthur nodded firmly.

'Well, come inside and see,' the ice-cream parlour owner said. His whole mood had changed. He welcomed the two of them in like they were long-lost bairns of his own.

In they trooped, between the tables and chairs and the potted plants. Arthur felt his heart beating loudly in his chest. It had to be her! It had to be her!

'Mam! Mammy!' Mavis cried out, dashing down the length of the parlour.

The woman with the chestnut hair turned round. She swirled around in her chair to look who was coming her way.

She was a stranger. A complete and utter stranger.

'Mam?' Mavis asked, as if she wasn't quite sure. As if her mammy's face might have changed. Or maybe she just couldn't remember exactly how she looked.

Arthur had stopped in his tracks, a few steps away. A desolate feeling came over him. He felt like he'd been robbed of all hope. A giant fist was closing itself around him and he hung his head.

'Hey, I'm no one's mammy!' the young woman said.

'Forgive them, lady,' Tonio Franchino told her. 'They just mistook you for their mama. She is a beautiful lady too, they say.'

He led the two bairns back to the front of the shop. Mavis was quiet now and Arthur didn't know what to say. He looked at the old man. 'We're sorry for causing a fuss.'

Tonio Franchino looked solemn. 'This is a very serious thing. You say your mamma is lost?'

Arthur nodded. 'We'd best be on our way. It's dark now.' He bundled his sister to the door.

'Hey now! Wait! Wait!' Tonio gabbled. 'You can't go out and about by yourselves. You're just two kids. You're just two babies. You can't go round this town alone!'

But Arthur and Mavis were already gone.

Chapter 35

Mavis couldn't hear Bella banging on the front door and it was lucky that Bella still had a key in her purse for the house on Watling Street.

Letting herself into the front hall reminded her of all the months she had spent here and the very depths of her mourning for her family: that's when she had been here, plying all her strength and focus into making the dilapidated and messy house liveable. By rights she should hate the sight of the place, but instead it filled her with a strange warmth, as she thought back fondly on her time as Mavis and Arthur's lodger.

Mind, in just a short time, Mavis and Sam had let the place become quite dirty and untidy again. But she wasn't here to inspect or judge the place. She was here to visit her friend.

'Hello? Mavis?' She went up the stairs, calling as she did, knowing that Mavis wouldn't hear her. 'Yoo hoo?'

The bedroom door on the top landing flew open, much to Bella's surprise, and there stood Lily Johnson in her bright yellow wig. She was glaring suspiciously at Bella. 'Who's this letting herself in without a by-your-leave?' she asked belligerently.

'I'm . . .' Bella began.

'You're the ice-cream girl,' Lily snapped. 'I know who you are. You've given Mavis quite a turn letting yourself in. What if she'd been here by herself?'

'She couldn't hear my knocking . . .' Bella said.

'Of course she couldn't! She's stone deaf! It's a good job I'm here!' Lily was more prickly than ever, it seemed.

'Who is it, Lily?' came Mavis's quavering, uncertain voice from inside the room. 'Oh, Bella!' Her face brightened as Bella hurried to her bedside. Lily scowled at her all the way. Clearly the Johnson girl wanted to be Mavis's only visitor today.

'I suppose I'll go and make us a fresh pot of tea,' Lily said. 'Will you be all right?'

Mavis smiled and waved her away. 'Uh-hoh. Thanks pet!' she shouted.

Bella wrote on her pad: 'You're still not up out of bed?'

Mavis shook her head firmly. 'Still feeling funny,' she mouthed.

Bella nodded, thinking that this had surely gone on long enough. Was Mavis even milking this situation and malingering in her room up here? The deafness was a bind, but surely it didn't prevent her from still taking part in her normal life?

Bella sighed and tried to smile brightly at her friend. Really, what she could have done with was a good, honest chat. Bella didn't have that many girlfriends at all besides the ones she employed at Franchino's, and she needed to talk to someone about her relationship with Jonas. Much as she loved Irene, she was out of the picture because Irene was one of the Farleys who were so dead set against all of the Johnsons. Plus, she was convinced that Jonas had put that brick through their parlour window. Bella had tried talking with Irene, the other night at the ice-cream parlour, but it had been hard. Irene had been incredulous that Bella was still a virgin. She had laughed nervously, in fact! Bella had been disappointed in her lack of tact.

Mavis was the only other friend she could talk to, really. And Mavis was a bit dippy even when she wasn't stone deaf. There was Beryl, of course, but Bella had seen little of her lately, between Beryl's exhausting job at the shipyard and then babysitting at home.

Bella was starting to feel a bit alone with the decision she had to make. She longed to tell Mavis about her marriage proposal from Jonas. But was it even real? Had he even meant a word of it? Or was it actually just a ploy to get his own selfish and wicked way with her?

When it came to moments like this, she felt the loss of her mother acutely – she and Mama had been able to discuss anything at all.

Bella realised that she and Mavis were simply staring at each other and smiling without trying to communicate at all. 'How's Franchino's?' Mavis asked at last, in her loud, blurry voice.

'Great!' Bella wrote on her pad.

'Have you seen this woman that Irene has apparently been talking to?' Mavis yelled.

Bella pulled a face and hunched her shoulders in a shrug. 'What woman?'

'That woman who I chucked out of my wedding!' Mavis roared.

'Oh her,' mimed Bella, knowing full well who she meant.

'She's going round saying she's my mam!' Mavis said. The words ran into each other, making her somehow sound even more resentful and cross.

'Who is she?' Bella wrote.

'She's a horrible posh old wifey. I want nothing to do with her! Arthur would be bloody furious if he knew she was hanging around!'

They were interrupted then by Lily returning with a tray of tea things, clinking her way into the room. She'd used all the best cups and saucers from a cabinet Bella could remember dusting in the living room. So Lily was properly making herself at home, then!

'Is she on about that woman who adopted her again?' Lily said.

'Do you know about all of this?' asked Bella.

'I know the story,' Lily said. 'It's really upset Mavis, her coming sniffing round lately. I wonder what she's after? It can't be money. Mavis has got nowt, and Mrs Kendricks is worth a fortune anyway.' Lily set the tray on top of the bed and started being mother, fussing with the teapot and the milk jug.

'What's that?' Mavis asked, feeling left out. 'You have to speak up!'

As Mavis strained to listen and catch up with Lily, Bella was wondering about the woman who'd graced Franchino's several times, as far as she knew. Irene really did seem to be in thrall to the old donna, without thinking how that might seem or how it might affect Mavis.

Sometimes Irene would get an idea into her head and simply assume she was doing the right thing, even though it was way off the mark. Her real failing, Bella knew, was that she loved it when people confided in her. It made her feel trusted, and as if she had been brought into a secret circle. Sometimes when Irene thought she was being discreet and subtle, she was being anything but. Right now she was letting her fascination with Mrs Kendricks overpower her good sense.

'I don't want the past going into,' Mavis said loudly. 'I don't want everything digging up.' The pain was all too clear in her voice.

'Never you mind, hinny,' Lily screeched at her. 'Drink your tea!'

And the three of them sat having a convivial cuppa.

'When are you getting up out of your bed?' Bella wrote on the pad.

'Not yet!' Mavis shouted. 'I'll get up when I'm ready! Not just yet!'

They didn't stay too long at Mavis's bedside. The shouted conversation and periodic scribblings became easier and smoother as time went on, but it was obvious pretty soon that Mavis was tired. Her two visitors left together and exchanged a few words of concern about their friend as Bella locked the front door behind her.

'My ma got bed-bound,' Lily said. 'That's what happened to her. She wasn't that old when she took to her bed, but that was it for her. I'd hate the same thing to happen to Mavis.'

'It won't,' said Bella, feeling disconcerted.

Both women were walking the same way. They were both heading towards the Johnson household on Tudor Road.

Lily said, 'Aye, but people can get scared of the world outside. It's easily done. Especially in times like these. It's just easier never to leave your bed. I had to wait on me ma all those years. I know what it's like.'

Bella studied the brash young girl walking beside her. She strutted along the road like she was a starlet of some kind, her wig plopped absurdly on her head with pins showing round the edges. Bella could picture her tending to an aggressive old woman all through her childhood. Dashing up and down the stairs and doing all the chores because everyone else in the house was a bloke. It would have hardened the little girl up, making her tough and snappy. Suddenly Bella felt touched by the fact that this fierce little Lily clearly felt protective of Mavis.

'You've been a good friend to Maeve,' Bella said.

Lily shrugged. 'Not sure about that. If it wasn't for me, she'd never have ended up underneath the hearse, getting kicked in the head by that bloody horse.'

That was true enough.

'Will your Jonas be in?' Bella asked.

Lily chortled. 'That lazy bugger! Of course he will. There's another one who loves his bed. But that's just because he's idle.' She shook her head, sighing. 'Aye, I've heard that you two are being all serious and that. You're properly courtin', aren't you?'

Bella felt herself blushing. 'I suppose we are.' What did Lily mean about him being idle? This was the first Bella had heard of it.

'And you don't mind running about with one of the Mad Johnsons, then?' Lily laughed, boggling her eyes queerly at Bella. 'Aye, I know what everyone calls us, hinny. It doesn't bother me. I guess some of my family have been completely crackers. Me older brothers, for example! And me mam's brothers! They were all a funny lot . . .'

'And Jonas? Is he crackers too?' Bella asked.

Lily smiled at her and Bella was surprised because it was a smile with no complications to it. No mixed feelings. Lily simply said: 'To be honest, pet, I think Jonas is the best one of all of us. He's a good brother. Whatever anyone else might say, you've got yourself a good lad there.'

Chapter 36

'No, we can't leave! We can't go away with you!'

Mavis was inconsolable when she heard the news. She grabbed at Nanna's woollen sweater.

'Hey, you're pulling holes in it, my girl,' the old woman growled, swatting her away. She went about her business remorselessly, stacking up her belongings and making sure everything was secure inside her caravan. She fed the horses steaming mash and whispered lovingly in their ears. She seemed to break the news more carefully to her steeds than to the kids she was looking after.

Arthur felt himself standing stoically by, watching all of this going on. He had retreated inside himself. He felt like he was watching from a hundred miles away, somewhere far over the churning sea. Then as he saw his little sister sobbing her heart out, he realised he felt sick to his stomach.

'Tell her, Arthur! Tell her we can't go anywhere. Not without our mammy. We're gonna find her, aren't we?'

Arthur held Mavis tightly and began to repeat her words to the old woman, but he found they dried in his throat. Their nanna was staring at the pair of them, glaring with hard, flinty eyes. 'Time to grow up, boy. You're the older one. You understand. You need to accept things as they are. You know your mother left you with me because she'd had enough of the pair of you.'

'No!' shrieked Mavis, appalled by what she was hearing.

'She gave you both to me because she wanted to go off and live her own life. She didn't want two bratty, needy kids hanging around her skirts anymore.'

With a surprising burst of strength, Mavis launched herself at her nanna, fists flying and feet lashing out. Arthur caught hold of her wiry arms just in time to prevent a bloody assault on the old woman. Where would they be then?

Nanna chuckled gruffly at the wriggling, furious girl. 'Some temper you've got on you. But you so much as lay a finger on me, girl, after all I've done for you, and I'll tan your hide. I'll rip all that golden hair out of your head and stuff cushions with it. You just watch.'

Arthur held his sister even harder, appalled at the venom in his grandmother's voice, and the dreadful things she was saying.

'I never had to take the pair of you in. It was out of the goodness of my heart! I only let you stay here cos I thought you might be useful. But all you do is whinge! You whimper and fret over that slut of a daughter of mine.'

For a second Arthur almost let go of his sister, to set her upon the nasty old woman. It would serve her right to have Mavis clouting her one. But he was sure Nanna would use her pan-shovel hands with impunity and hurt Mavis much more in return. Now he could see that their grandmother had no feelings for them at all, beyond what use she could make of them.

He was aware of the two uncles – Nat and Brock – standing closely by, watching with great amusement as this drama unfolded.

'Now, come on. Stop being stupid, you bairns,' the old woman said. 'Either help us get everything ready for the off, or else.'

'Where are we going?' Arthur wanted to know. 'How far are you taking us?'

'Long way,' she hawked and spat a wad of phlegm into the grass. 'Over the hills and far away. It's the gathering of the clans over in Yorkshire way. The winter horse fair in Appleby. It's a good long trip and we have to set off tonight.'

'Tonight!' Arthur gasped.

She shrugged. 'This is what we do. This is our life. Nothing, no war or any of that carry-on, nor dratted kids – none of these things can ever spoil our ways.'

With a violent shove, Mavis wrenched herself at last out of her brother's tight grip. For a second he feared that she was going to go for Nanna's throat, and he was sure he even saw the old woman flinch slightly. But Mavis turned on her heel and ran sobbing in the other direction, across the damp grass of the clifftop. Her mammy's shawl flared out behind her.

'Go after her, boy,' the old woman said. 'Make her see sense. She's only a little lass. She needs to do as she's told.'

'She's missing her mam,' Arthur said.

'She'll have to get used to it,' Nanna sighed, and her voice suddenly betrayed a deep, bone-weary sadness of her own. Arthur knew that he'd never get to know the truth that underlay that sigh and the expression on her crumpled face. 'We all have to get used to missing things,' she said. 'We just haven't gotta let it hurt us, or to give our feelings away. Now get after her, boy. Bid her see sense.'

Arthur turned and hurried off across the grass. 'Mavis!' he called, still feeling sick to his stomach. The wind blew freshly off the North Sea, ridding his head of that noxious fug of smells from his grandmother's caravan. 'Mavis?'

His sister had hurried away on fleet, sure feet, hardly thinking about where she was heading. She took their customary route down the tall, zig-zagging staircase chiselled into the sandy cliff face. She clutched the metal rail, and flew more quickly than was safe, running heedlessly down to the beach in her eagerness to be away from Nanna and the rest. She even wanted to be away from Arthur. How dare he hold her back, protecting that foul old woman like he had?

Mavis hurtled down to the beach, where she could be alone with her thoughts in all the noise of waves crashing down on the sand and the rocks. By rights, she shouldn't be down here. There were signs and rusted razor wire all too clearly on show. But she was little and nimble, and wasn't about to be told by anyone where she could go. She wanted to get right down to the waves as they broke on the slabs of broken yellow rock and to stand in the cold spume as it rose in a fine mist all about her. The violence of the water would calm her down, and its noise would drown out all of her frustrated sobbing.

She hugged her mother's fine woollen shawl around her thin shoulders. She closed her eyes, the better to focus her senses on picking up the still-lingering scent of her mother on the wool. Yes, she could still smell her and fool herself that her mammy was close. If she screwed her eyes really tightly and blocked out her surging thoughts, she could even imagine that her mam was standing there with her. Holding her in her arms.

Today it was different, though. That lingering presence came back to her only briefly. Mavis felt her mammy's slender, warm arms about her body, enfolding her in a lovely cuddle. But then something strange happened. Mammy relinquished her grip on Mavis. Her arms slipped away. The sense of Mammy melted away in an instant, like the sea spray from the waves.

Mavis opened her eyes in shock.

She could see Arthur running across the rocks towards her. He looked terrified, as if his sister was about to throw herself into the sea. 'Mavis!' he called.

She watched him come running at full pelt, his face full of fury and concern. He must have flown down those cliff-edge steps as fast as she had.

'Mavis!'

Arthur came pounding up the sand and grasped hold of her. She felt lifeless, unresisting in his arms. She shouted over the noise of the surf. She told him straight out what she had learned, closing her eyes so tightly and holding their mammy's shawl. 'She's dead, Arthur. I th-think she's dead! She's gone and left us behind!'

Her brother was shocked by the brutal matter-of-factness of her words. He squashed her in a hug, as if by smothering her in his love he could stop her talking. Stop her saying such terrible things. 'Stop it. You don't know. You can't know that. What are you talking about, Mavis?'

'I d-don't know,' she cried. 'I just know it. She's in the water. They killed her and threw her in the water. She's in the black mud. They weighed her body down. Sh-she's dead, Arthur!'

'No,' he murmured into her wispy, damp hair. 'You can't know that. You can't know anything like that.'

But something in his sister's words profoundly shocked and moved the boy. Her words crept coldly into his heart.

They couldn't have been down on the beach all that long. He had to stand there a while holding her tightly until she calmed down. He was aware that the light was shifting and the gloom was settling down over the sea.

'Come on,' he told her, and coaxed her back across the beach to the steps. The tide was coming in. It was idiotic, really, being down here at this time. The tide could come sweeping in faster than a man could run. They'd watched it from the clifftops and marvelled at the sheer force of it. A terrible and majestic thing and wonderful to watch. One of the only good things about living with their dirty, brutish Nanna this past while was that they'd been so close to the magical sea.

But it didn't do to get *too* close.

Arthur led the way back up to the top of the cliff, and realised the girl was shaking, frozen in her damp clothes and that heavy shawl. She'd stood for too long at the water's edge. It was winter, for God's sake! What was he thinking of, letting her get so close to the freezing water!

Maybe the old woman would still have a fire going, for an hour or so at least before it was time to set off? Maybe he could persuade her to keep it burning for a while, until Mavis dried off at least? The little lass needed to get warmed through again, or she'd catch her death . . .

At the top of the cliff steps the two bairns received an awful shock.

The grasslands extended flatly for miles all along the clifftops. Nanna's caravans and horses hadn't been all that far away. But now they were nowhere to be seen.

Arthur stared, dumbfounded at the empty field. Mavis gave a shout of demented laughter. 'They've gone! Arthur, they've *gone!*'

He couldn't believe it. Nanna had waited till the two kids were down on the beach, and then she'd scarpered.

She'd left them, all alone, with nothing.

Chapter 37

'It's even grander than I imagined it would be. Are you sure this is right, Sam?' Irene looked worriedly at her brother-in-law as they stood in the shadow of a tall box hedge surrounding the biggest and most lovely house Irene had seen in ages.

'Aye, this is where we'll find her,' Sam nodded. South Shields wasn't so big a town that you couldn't find out where anyone lived with a bit of asking around. Just a few enquiries round people he knew in the dockside pubs had brought him the address of Mrs Elizabeth Kendricks.

'I think I'm losing my nerve,' Irene said quietly. It was one thing talking to the woman when she turned up at Franchino's, and Irene was on safe, home ground, but turning up unannounced on her doorstep, that was another matter altogether.

'Eeeh, look at how some people live!' Sam shook his head at the size of the house on the cliffs. Imagine having somewhere with all this space, with miles of garden between you and the next house along! Her house had four chimneys and three floors and it looked like there were bedrooms up in the attic too, with patterned curtains. To Sam it looked like an impossibly fancy place. He and his brothers had grown up in a tiny house compared with this, one where there was never any room for privacy or quiet time alone. He was used to rooms filled with people all talking at the top of their voices. What kind of person might he have grown up to be, living in a place like this instead?

'I hope she doesn't mind us calling on her,' Irene said worriedly as they unlatched the gate and traipsed up the garden path. Clearly the gardens had once been very beautiful, with many kinds of shrubs and fruit trees and flower beds. But now everything was pruned right back, and lawns had been turned over to growing various vegetables for the war effort. However, the allotment seemed to have been neglected. The rows were littered with spiralling tendrils and woody stalks and huge yellowing leaves.

Taking a deep breath, Irene stepped up to the front door and rang the bell. 'What's the worst she can do? Send us off with a flea in our ears?' she shrugged.

But as it happened Elizabeth Kendricks was delighted to see her visitors. 'Irene!' she beamed. 'And . . .'

'Sam,' Sam reminded her.

'What a delightful surprise! Do come in. You must excuse me, answering the door in my rags . . . I was spending the afternoon at my desk, catching up on some correspondence . . .' She led them into a hallway shot through with coloured light from the stained glass in the front door. Irene reflected that, far from wearing rags, the older lady looked just as glamorous as she always did. Even home alone, sitting at a desk, she obviously still dressed for the occasion, and Irene admired that. Mrs Kendricks was wearing a rather beautiful housecoat in muted shades of orange and pink. From some distant corner of her mind, Irene plucked the word 'kimono'. Probably from reading one of Megan's picture magazines.

'We were just passing by . . .' Sam said, in a blatant lie. This exclusive enclave was so far from the beaten track and their own part of town it was almost laughable. To get here they'd had to take a trolley bus along the coastal road, and then they'd still had a lengthy walk in the afternoon heat.

'Come through to the conservatory,' Elizabeth told them. 'It's the nicest place to sit at this time in the afternoon.'

Soon they were installed in a glass-walled room teeming with overgrown fruit trees and rubber plants. They perched on heavy iron garden furniture and waited while their hostess floated off to fetch them some tea.

Lowering his voice, Sam asked Irene: 'Can you picture Mavis and Arthur running about in here when they were bairns?'

Irene shook her head. Never in a million years! Put into a place like this, the two siblings would have been just as overawed and gobsmacked as Irene and Sam were. And yet, they were both Kendricks' siblings, weren't they? That was indeed their surname. And Elizabeth had laid claim to them both unequivocally, even if Mavis had hotly denied it.

'Here we are,' smiled the owner of the house. She set down a tray with tea things and the most beautiful china Irene had ever seen, so fragile that Irene was nervous to pick it up. Colourful dainties were set out on a tea plate for them, and the napkins were quality linen, you could tell.

Sam kept shooting Irene glances, prompting her to start off on that hard line of questioning Ma Ada had suggested. Look here, what do you want with Mavis anyway? Sam had clearly lost his nerve, sitting there with wide eyes, drinking in the grandeur of the place, as Elizabeth poured golden amber tea into their cups.

Irene didn't feel cowed, though. She felt awkward and slightly nervous, but she took hold of herself – what did she have to feel nervous about? Elizabeth was just another person, and she had been friendly, too, so far. With a little cough, Irene spoke up at last. 'This house is so lovely, Elizabeth. It's like being in a dream!'

'Oh, hardly,' the older woman smiled gently. 'It's going to rack and ruin, I'm afraid. I've not been able to maintain things as I'd like to . . .'

A memory popped strangely into Irene's thoughts then. 'I remember going to a great big garden party at the big house near us when I was about ten,' she smiled. 'It was a huge country mansion, with servants. The old newspaper magnate's family owned it, and every year he held a party for all the local villagers, and we all trooped up there, in our fanciest clothes . . .'

'How lovely,' Elizabeth smiled. 'And this was down in Norfolk, was it?'

'Aye, it was,' said Irene. 'And there'd be all tables laid out with fancy baked goods and jellies and vats of lemonade for the bairns. And I remember this big silver salver thing, with cigarettes! There were cigarettes all arranged, fanned out, hundreds of them, for people to help themselves. Well, all the men and the young lads were filling their pockets with the bloomin' things!' She laughed, covering up her mouth and her crooked front teeth, rocking forward in her seat as she remembered. 'Eeeh, I'd forgotten all about that until now.'

Elizabeth chuckled politely and asked, 'Would either of you like a cigarette?'

Irene shook her head. 'I hate the smell of the things. I try to get my Tom to stop, but he'll never listen. And his coughing is awful these days. He's up in the night, doubled over with it.'

'Have you heard from him lately?'

'Oh, not since he went back. But he's been caught up in this mission. This thing he won't even talk to me about . . .' Irene shrugged. She knew she shouldn't even have been saying that much. Loose talk, and all of that. But she relished the chance to talk about Tom even for a moment, and was glad that the posh woman had asked after him. It showed that she did listen after all, and had taken an interest during their previous conversations. She wasn't solely interested in her own affairs, as most grander folk usually seemed to be.

Oh Tom, she thought, as she sipped her dark tea. With a slice of fresh lemon, too! What a treat that was. What was her fella up to, she wondered. Right this very minute? What kind of awful danger might he be in right now? He'd said something about flying very low. That was the most he had let slip when he'd talked to her during his most recent leave. They were carrying out endless practice flights in the huge, thunderous Lancasters, flying low along the lengths of the biggest lakes in Cumbria and Scotland. It was thrilling and dangerous, he said, seeing the water like a vast silver sheet rippling below.

She shook her head quickly, and came back to the moment. Now the afternoon sun was slanting into the glass room. You could see there was dust on the panes and the thick leaves of the plants. If you looked close enough you could see that the place was becoming dowdy.

Irene said, 'So this is really where Mavis and Arthur grew up, was it?'

Elizabeth Kendricks set down her teacup and fixed her visitors with a grave gaze. 'They were here for a number of years. Not that many, I suppose, in the grand scheme of things. Certainly not their whole childhoods. They came to me when Arthur was about twelve, I believe, and Mavis was almost eight. Where they had been and whose care they had fallen into before that – it was all a bit of a closed book at first. Those children were almost feral. They couldn't or wouldn't tell me anything at all. They clung to each other so protectively. As if they were ready to scratch your eyes out if you got too close to them. It took me some time to win their trust, and to show that I meant them no harm . . .'

'How did you . . .' Irene began, wrestling over how to phrase her next question. She almost asked 'how did you come by them?', which made them sound like they were acquisitions of some kind. 'How did you find them in the first place?'

'Well,' Elizabeth said carefully, 'you must understand that I was younger then, and foolish, perhaps. And I was desperate, too. I longed for a child of my own. I was half out of my mind with that need to look after a little one of my very own. What was the point of my life? What use was I at all, if I wasn't devoting my life to bringing up children? Do you understand what I mean?'

Irene nodded. 'Well, yes . . . of course . . .'

'Ah, you're a mother yourself, and a very good one, I'm sure.'

'I'm not so sure about that,' Irene chuckled, thinking of her own occasional clumsiness and naivete in looking after Marlene, and how she relied upon the vast experience of Ma Ada, and the easy good sense of Beryl to help her.

'You had no difficulties though,' Elizabeth said, with a strange fervency in her tone. 'You had it rather easy, in many ways. You wanted a child and you had one, in the first year of your marriage. How wonderful for you. How natural and perfect. It's just how things should be.'

Was that a touch of resentment in her voice, Irene wondered? She cast a glance at Sam, who sat there looking like he felt a million miles out of his depth. Women discussing childbirth! He looked like he wanted the ground to open up beneath him. Impulsively he reached forward, seized a handful of petits-fours and crammed them into his mouth. Irene almost laughed.

'Can you imagine not being blessed in that way?' Elizabeth asked her.

'Sometimes Marlene doesn't feel like such a blessing,' Irene admitted. 'Honestly, sometimes I think she's going to grow up to be a monster. She's got such a temper on her. And it's like she's picking up the conniving, manipulative ways of her Aunty Megan, somehow. Some days I think our Megan's put a curse on her . . .' What am I even saying? Irene wondered at herself. I'm gabbling on with ridiculous, half-formed thoughts while this nice woman is trying to open up her heart to me . . . She stopped talking abruptly and smiled apologetically. 'I'd never be without her, though.'

'Precisely,' Elizabeth said. 'She is yours. Yours and Tom's. I never had that kind of blessing. I was never as lucky as you. My beloved man was taken from me in the last war. No, please. It was such a long time ago. Don't fuss over me, I can't stand it. Many women lost their men. I've had time to bury my ghosts and yet . . . yet it's only human for me to regret what never was, isn't it? And I longed for a child. It's such a ferocious, awful longing. When nature denies you. When it seems as if you are fated never to have a baby of your very own. It can make you feel crazy, you know. It can make you feel like you're going out of your mind . . .'

'Oh, I'm sure it can,' Irene said. She thought about the fierceness and thwartedness locked up inside the body of her mild, kind sister-in-law Beryl. Yes, that fierceness and upset was something Beryl knew well. She had described it all to Irene, and she had sobbed and wailed and wept in her arms.

'I went on for years on my own,' Elizabeth Kendricks said. 'Living in this house of my father's. Keeping it beautiful. Making everything perfect. But what for? What's the point? What's the use in any of it, without children? Without having someone to pass it all on to?'

Sam was looking alarmed now. He widened his eyes at Irene and she shook her head at him. Elizabeth was spilling out her heart. She was showing her true feelings. It was nothing to be scared of, Irene thought.

At least, she hoped it was nothing to be scared of.

'So perhaps you might understand me and my desperation,' Elizabeth said. 'I hope you will. And that you'll forgive me.'

'I don't understand,' said Irene. 'Forgive you? What for?'

The grand lady sighed. 'When you're desperate you can resort to measures that aren't, perhaps, the orthodox ones. You can turn to somewhat unusual solutions. Or . . . illegal ones. And I'm afraid . . . that's what I did . . .' She looked desolate and much older than her years, sitting in the bright sunlight of her conservatory. 'You see, I bought them, Irene. I *bought* my babies.'

Chapter 38

For several days they wandered around the town. They had nowhere to go. No one was looking out for them. It was amazing, in fact, how little notice people took of you when you were free of everyone and everything.

A polis man shook his fist at them and gave chase at one point. It was down the market and Arthur had been trying to nick stuff from a stall. Pies. The warm gravy smell and the wafting scent of pastry had been too much for him and so he squeezed through the crowd, all grabby fingers, and attracted the attention of the stall holder.

'Run, Mavis!' With a pie in each hand he scarpered, urging his tiny sister ahead of him. The polis, alerted by the pie man's shouts, gave chase, but it was hopeless. He stood no chance beside two little kids who knew all the back ways and ginnels. They were soon off down the cramped gaps between the narrow buildings and away to safety.

It snowed that week. They were close to Christmas and there was a festive spirit abroad in the town. Everyone looked so well dressed and pleased with themselves. Even those who had nowt. But no one was as poor as Arthur and Mavis, the boy thought. Everyone had it easy compared with them. They were proper orphans now, out on the streets and probably they'd have starved to death by Christmas Day. Frozen in one of these snowy alleyways amongst the heaped rubbish and the rats' nests.

'You didn't mean it, did you, Mavis?' he asked his little sister, more than once during those hopeless days. 'You didn't really see our mammy lying in the dark water and dead?'

Mavis was evasive. She didn't want to talk about it anymore. Whenever she closed her eyes, she was plagued with those images again. She couldn't stop seeing them. She squinched up her eyes and Arthur knew she was sincere.

She had a gift. A strange kind of gift. He'd suspected it in the past, and so had their mammy. Even when she was tiny, Mavis had experienced strange dreams. More vivid than anyone else's dreams. She wasn't just fanciful, Arthur thought. She was gifted. And sometimes gifts like that could be a curse.

'Maybe we could go back to the nice man in the ice-cream parlour?' Mavis asked, as they sat in another filthy alley in the snow, chewing on pastry and relishing the savoury meat and jelly and gravy. 'He was kind to us. He gave me one of those fancy biscuits. The type that melt in your mouth.'

'He won't help us,' Arthur shrugged. 'Just because he was kind that one time, doesn't mean he wants the likes of us hanging round his door.'

But Mavis didn't understand that. She thought, quite straightforwardly, that if people were nice and kind, then that was the end of the matter. They would be good to you and look after you. Nothing in her short life had deterred her from that opinion yet. Not even her experiences of Mr Alec or their nanna.

They hung around Ocean Road for several days. They slept in doorways and kept moving during daylight hours. They stood by the entrance of the theatre on the nights when crowds went surging in to see the Christmas pantomime. Arthur stood there in ragged fancy dress, boldly holding out his cap for coins. Out came a man in a uniform with buttons and braid, furiously shooing them away. 'Hie, you little beggars!'

Because that's what they were now. Beggars on the street.

During pub hours they hung around the saloon doors, with the thought of picking up coins from unwary or generous drinkers. Still there was the hopeful idea that their mam would be there. Somehow still alive, despite what Mavis had seen in her vision. Gadding about with the rough men of the noisy taverns, trying to keep body and soul together. She'd appear one day on the doorstep of one of these old boozers. She'd emerge from the warm glow of the smoky interior and stand blinking at the cold and dark and then suddenly she'd clap eyes on her bairns again. Her Arthur and her Mavis, standing there in the gaslight, waiting for her.

Night after night they were up and down Ocean Road with this forlorn, unspoken hope in their hearts.

Arthur knew they couldn't last many nights out in the cold. After two he thought: We're going to die out here. They're going to find us in the snow, frozen blue and dead. It was up to him to take action. He was the oldest and the most responsible one.

The only thing for it was to return to somewhere that people knew them. Maybe someone would feel pity for them and take them in. They were only two little bairns, after all.

Arthur was admitting defeat. He couldn't take care of them both after all. He had thought he could. He had thought he was enough. He could be a little man, a small grown-up. He could keep them together and well and fed and safe. But he couldn't – it was too much for him. He wept silently all the way down to the fish quay and the tears were frozen on his face by the time they got there. Back by the docks, where the stones underfoot were frozen hard with fish slime and guts. Mavis, realising where they were going, clenched his fingers hard.

They longed to be younger. A year younger, maybe. When their mammy was still here, working long days at her ramshackle stall. They would be here with her, putting jagged slits in the wriggling herring and pulling all their doings out.

'We're going to look for that big wifey who allus talked to us,' Arthur told his sister. 'That huge wife with the craggy face. Old Beattie. I'm sure she'll help us. She'll be kind.'

But Beattie didn't look too pleased to see them. She sat in her usual place, against the backdrop of the grey, unwelcoming harbour and stared at the two frozen souls before her. 'You never found your mam, then?' she sighed.

Arthur shook his head. Suddenly all his words dried up inside him at the sight of that mountainous fish wife. Something inside him resisted against throwing themselves on her mercy. She didn't look as if she had much to spare.

'I didn't think you would,' Beattie grunted. 'She's gone without a trace. I thought it was funny, no one seeing her at all. I reckon she's come to a bad end.'

Arthur clenched his fists and tamped down his fury at her words. What good would it do, shouting and arguing with the one person who might show them some mercy? The one person in all of town who knew who they were?

'And you've been going from pillar to post since the last time I saw you?' the fish wife glared at them both. 'All these days?'

'We went back to our nanna,' Mavis said. 'But she's gone now. She left us as well.'

'And there's been no sign of that red-haired bastard who took you in? He who made all those promises to your poor mam?' Beattie asked. Her fingers moved unconsciously, toying with her gutting knife, as if she was picturing what she'd like to do to their mammy's ginger beau.

The two bairns hung their heads and said nothing. There was nothing more to say. Shame hung over them, though none of this was their doing. They both felt like it truly was their fault, however, that they'd ended up like this. There was something wrong with them. They were faulty somehow. They were damaged goods. They were unlovable children that nobody wanted.

'You'd better come home with me then,' said Beattie. She grunted and stood up with an effort. 'Mind, it's no palace, my place. You'll have to fight for room. And there's bugger all extra food, so it'll just be scraps.'

'Thank you,' Arthur told her. 'Anything. We just need to get indoors. Well, I'm all right. But it's my sister. She's still only little. She needs to be warm and indoors . . .'

'Aye,' Beattie said. 'The two of you look frozen solid. Come on. It's not far. It's crowded, but it's safe. But I reckon it's better than nothing for yer . . .'

She packed her few belongings into her basket. The filthy tools of her trade. Her stall was already empty and scrubbed down. The last of her wares – fish heads and scraps – she bundled into newspaper and explained how they'd do fine for the pot tonight. Arthur's stomach roiled at the thought of eating that stinking fish, even as it gurgled in ferocious anticipation.

'Come on, come on, you bairns,' old Beattie told them. 'It won't be much of a Christmas for you out on the streets. Better at my place. We'll see you're all right.'

'Thank you, Beattie,' Arthur made himself speak politely to her. Like a proper little gentleman, just as his mammy had taught him.

'Thank you,' Mavis said, after he nudged her.

'Eeeh, she allus had you two bairns talking so nicely and putting on airs,' Beattie tutted. 'I always thought she was special, somehow. A cut above the rest of us. Just goes to show, doesn't it? None of us are all that special in the end . . .'

Hurrying to keep up with her ambling, rolling gait, the bairns weren't really listening to her mithering on. The stars were out over the harbour and it was snowing fitfully again. They were imagining being indoors and feeling warm, and gratefully eating fish stew for supper. The whole thing seemed wonderful, just then.

Chapter 39

Irene and Sam were mostly quiet on the way home from Elizabeth Kendricks' house. They stepped onto their trolley bus in the lee of the cliffs and it trundled along with the late afternoon sun flashing against its panes of glass. The two of them sat with gas mask boxes on their knees and both were digesting everything they had learned that afternoon.

'Poor Mavis,' Irene said at last, after the conductor had been by, cranking out their tickets from his machine. ('Cheer up, folks!' he had said brightly, earning himself a scowl from Sam.)

'Aye, poor lass,' Sam muttered, more to himself than to Irene. Now he realised he knew things about his bride than she would never willingly tell him. Or worse still, perhaps she didn't even know these things about herself? Perhaps it would be news to her as well that she had, in fact, been sold to her adoptive mother?

'Who on earth would go about selling bairns?' Irene hissed. 'It's a wicked business. It's inhuman.'

The bus was quite full, and Sam was conscious that others might hear her, even though she covered her mouth with her hand as she spoke. 'Well, we know who'd do it, don't we? Elizabeth told us exactly who she bought her kids from. And wouldn't you just believe it of them?' He looked bitter as he thought it all through. 'What's Mavis gonna say about this? Are we going to tell her?'

'Oh, I don't think we can keep secrets from her, Sam. We can't know things like this about her, and then not tell her what we know.'

He gulped and nodded, and then pictured himself trying to explain to his wife the conversation they had been having this afternoon. He imagined painstakingly striving to spell it all out on her small pad. Sentence by sentence. Mavis squinting impatiently, scrying his words. She would feel betrayed by him, wouldn't she? She might well feel betrayed by the pair of them. 'She trusts us two more than anyone in the world, besides her precious brother,' Sam said heavily. 'Only we've gone behind her back today, haven't we?'

Irene gasped. 'But that makes it sound horrible. We were only trying to help. To understand . . .'

'Sometimes understanding doesn't help at all,' Sam said unhappily. 'And now we know things that maybe should have stayed hidden.'

Irene wasn't so sure about that. She knew that buried secrets tended to fester and infect everything around them. It was far better to learn the truth of things, she believed.

Surely there was nothing wrong about the time they had spent with Elizabeth today? They weren't intending to do harm. But then she thought about the shattered look on the face of the older woman by the time they had left her just now. They'd had time for two pots of tea and a plate of little biscuits. Time enough to hear just a small portion of her tale, but Elizabeth had looked wrung out with sorrow by the time they announced they'd have to go. She had stood up shakily to see them out the door. Just an hour or so earlier she had been her usual indomitable, smart self, and now she looked reduced, humbled.

Irene would never forget the sight of her, straight-backed on her iron chair in that conservatory, explaining how, in

236

her desperation, she had procured herself two children. 'I only wanted one. That's all I wanted. But then the chance came. The opportunity. The people I was dealing with . . . the ones whom I had come into contact with, they had told me that two children had become available at the same time. I must take both. I couldn't split them up. It was Christmas. A bitterly cold Christmas that year and these poor children had been living on the streets, in the midst of terrible conditions. They had gone from pillar to post. They were half-dead from their experiences, by all accounts.' Elizabeth looked upset as she relived all of this. 'Well, you tell me. What could I do? Was it so immoral for me to let them into my life? To take the pair of them on? No one else was going to. No one else could have cared less about them. Those children would have died on the streets during that winter if I hadn't taken an interest and let them into my home, and my heart . . .'

'But you gave money for them . . .' Irene said, and she couldn't keep that tinge of accusation out of her voice.

The woman shrugged helplessly, unashamed. 'That was the type of people I was dealing with. How far I had sunk. So mad and desperate I'd become by then. And when you deal with folk like that, you end up having to follow their rules. They loved money and cared little for human life. It was just a transaction to them. They had something I wanted, and I was fortunate enough to be able to pay for it. What else was my money good for? It never did me any good. Oh, I've been comfortable all my life; I've lived in luxury compared with most. But I'd never known true happiness. I just knew that happiness was within my grasp for the very first time that Christmas.'

Both Irene and Sam had been dying to know how much. How many guineas had passed hands that Christmas? What had two seemingly valueless lives been worth in cash that year? But there seemed no decent way of asking.

'Of course I did everything they said. And, to give them credit, the people I was dealing with were as good as their word. They never tried to swindle me, as I supposed they might have done. They could have taken the money and scarpered. They could have left me with nothing. But they had a bit of honour, after all. And so, Christmas Eve, they brought my new babies to me. It . . . it was magical.'

'They weren't babies, though?' Irene prompted.

'Oh no. They were grown. Arthur at twelve was almost the height of a fully grown man. Mavis was eight. But a young eight. There was barely a squeak out of her. They both looked terrified when they arrived here. They stared around at their surroundings with these huge eyes. They were awestruck, I suppose . . .'

On the trolley bus Irene was thinking about Elizabeth's words again, and thinking about the relish with which the woman had relayed this scene to them. Yes, upset as she was, she had enjoyed telling the tale of how these children had shuffled uncertainly into her comfortable, luxurious life. She still looked back and enjoyed the thought of surprising them with a new and much better world to live in. When Elizabeth was telling the tale, it seemed like she vanished into that past. She could almost, even, fool herself that the future was still going to work out fine . . .

Sam caught Irene's eye and smiled ruefully. 'Those Mad Johnsons, eh? They've got a lot to answer for, that bloody lot.'

Irene nodded grimly. It was queer, when she thought about it, the ways in which those two families – the Johnsons and the Farleys, and all the people connected between them – always seemed so tangled up together.

Irene left the bus first, hopping off on Ocean Road to begin her shift at Franchino's. She was rather late and hoped Bella wouldn't yell at her. That curious tension between the two friends was still there of late, and Irene being tardy for work wasn't going to help matters.

Sam looked nervous as she waved him goodbye. 'Don't say anything to Mavis about this afternoon,' she told him. 'Not yet. We have to think about how to go about this . . .'

Nodding, Sam had waved her goodbye and watched her skip off the bus before it had even stopped fully. She was nimble and sure-footed, dashing across the road to the glowing pastel hues of the ice-cream parlour.

What are we going to do? Sam wondered. What can we do about the old woman's final demand? The thing she'd asked of them, as they had finally left her grand house this afternoon?

'Could you possibly? Do you think? Would you please try your best for me?'

Soft-hearted as ever, Irene had jumped in with both feet and agreed on the spot. Sam didn't think it was such a good idea. It was the one bit of the visit they hadn't discussed on their journey back along the coastal road.

'Could you convince her to come back and see me again?' Mrs Kendricks had implored them both on her doorstep, in the moments before they left her. 'Would you please ask her to come and visit me here? In this place that was once her home?'

No way, Sam thought to himself now, as the trolley bus shunted him home. There's no way Mavis would agree to that, and what's more I'm not going to be asking her . . .

After a few hours spent somewhere unfamiliar and rather intimidating, it was a relief to be back within the warm, cream and coffee-painted walls of Franchino's again. There was jazz playing and the hiss of fragrant steam, and Bella smiling at her from behind the shining chrome of the counter. 'Hey, madam,' her boss smiled as Irene hurtled in, and thankfully didn't take her to task for being late.

'I'm sorry! Urgent business . . .' Irene started gabbling.

'We're hardly very busy,' Bella shrugged. 'Place has been dead all day.' Curiously, whereas this would usually have spoiled her mood, today she was bright and breezy, humming along with the music as she worked.

Irene went to change into her smart work clothes and her comfier shoes. When she returned to the front of the café, Bella slid a coffee towards her. 'Look, I'm sorry if I've been snappy lately.'

'Oh! You've haven't really . . .' Irene began.

'I have, and you know it,' Bella smiled. 'There's been a bit of edginess between us, at work and elsewhere, and I'm sorry for it, Irene. You're a good friend to me, and I should never take you for granted.'

'That's all right . . .'

'It was just . . . well, you and the Farleys. You're all so blind when it comes to the Johnsons. Lily and . . . Jonas. The whole clan of them. You can't see any good in them at all . . .'

Maybe that's because there isn't any good in them at all! Irene bit her lip and kept her thoughts to herself.

'And I suppose I've been a bit strange, too, over the question of . . .' Bella smiled wryly. 'Intimacy, and all of that business. I think my feelings have all been mixed up and stirred around.'

'That can happen,' Irene conceded. 'But I'm glad that we're still friends, Bella. You mean an awful lot to me, you know.'

'And you to me, too!' Bella burst out impulsively. 'So that's why I'm going to ask you, and I hope you'll say yes . . .'

'What?' Irene grinned, caught up in the Italian girl's enthusiasm. She sipped her hot coffee. 'What do you want me to say yes to?'

'Being my matron of honour. When I marry Jonas in September. When I become Mrs Jonas Johnson. Will you be there for me, Irene?'

Chapter 40

They never understood just how it happened to them. Later, Mavis said that it had probably been down to magic. Arthur went along with that for his little sister's sake, though he was far too cynical and grown up ever to believe in such a thing. And there was no Father Christmas or Tinkerbell the fairy involved, that was for sure. But if Mavis wanted to believe it was a Christmas miracle happening, then he was happy to let her.

The fact was, they didn't stay at old Beattie's place for very long at all. This came as a relief, because her two tiny rooms were overcrowded and not very clean. Beattie seemed to have a lot of children and relations of her own, and they clustered and squabbled in that tiny space as Beattie stewed up their supper. At first Arthur and Mavis were content simply to thaw out, and to have a little corner that was theirs.

There were no curtains at the single window, and after darkness fell the snow kept coming down in one continuous flurry. Mavis went over and stared out at the opaque view and Arthur wondered what she was thinking. He was always amused by the fact that Mavis had her own thoughts going on inside her head. When she told him about them, he was often surprised and amazed. His sister was growing up to be a whole person of her own, and their mother was missing it all.

Wherever she was. Wherever their mother had got to.

Arthur didn't believe that horrible vision that Mavis had shared, down on the cold beach. Their mother wasn't dead. She couldn't be. The fierce psychic, spiritual, instinctive link he had felt with her all his life was still there. If anything terrible had happened to his mam, he would know all about it. He was sure about that.

Then, some hours after they had first sat down in that smoky den of Beattie's and eaten her porridge stew, a man came calling at the flimsy door. For a moment Arthur's heart leapt up in fear because he thought it was Mr Alec. What a thought! If that horrible man had come here to find them again! But this man was older, and he had a younger one with him. It was their dark red hair that put Arthur in mind of his pretend stepfather, of course.

'This them?' the older man asked Beattie.

She had called these men here. When she had briefly slipped out after supper. She was nodding earnestly, standing in the doorway. Staring at the ground, not meeting Arthur's eyes. He wasn't sure what was going on, but he knew it couldn't be anything good.

'Arthur?' Mavis asked, framed in the milky light of the window as the men came over. They were dressed in dark clothes, snowflakes still on their heavy coats. Arthur flew to his sister as the men approached.

Beattie was all of a flap. The huge fish woman dithered and waved her arms. 'It's for the best! You'll see. You'll understand, boy. It's all for the best!'

'What? What are you talking about?' Arthur shouted, aware that all the other dwellers in Beattie's hovel were staring with interest and muttering amongst themselves. Something was happening and they were glad they weren't part of it. The two newcomers were being seized by their skinny arms and dragged away. It was only a couple of hours since their arrival, and now they were leaving, and no one knew why or where they were going. 'Get off us! Leave us alone!' Arthur kicked and spat and lashed out and earned himself a clout round the ear. 'What are you gonna do with us?'

Mavis was very quiet. That was the worst thing for Arthur. His little sister didn't resist or cry out. She simply went limp in the arms of the men who had come to take them away. She was like a little ghost. Light as air. Insubstantial. Her spirit had fled on Christmas Eve.

Arthur had a filthy palm over his mouth and his arms were clenched together behind his back so hard he felt his shoulders popping and cracking in their sockets. He tried to bite the sour flesh of the man's palms as he was dragged out of the room.

In one wild instant he was aware of seeing Beattie taking a handful of coins and a single note from the older man. Her large, scarred hands were cupped, gratefully receiving. She's sold us, Arthur found himself thinking. She's sold us for loose change and we were never even hers to sell . . .

The two bairns were in the dark for a while then. It felt just like they'd been popped into a poacher's sack and now they were being bundled along with no idea where their journey would take them.

They were in the back of some kind of van. There was the reek of engine oil and the aggressive roar of a motor and wheels revving against the icy roads.

As ever, Mavis reached for her big brother's hand and she felt safe then. She felt that nothing really terrible could happen to them while he was there.

They were both so sleepy, the trip took on the atmosphere of a dream. Mavis went into a deep sleep and she had no recollection later of being taken out of the van and going into another place. Arthur remembered a house with another woman there, and other children. He remembered crying children and everyone clustered round, and talk of money, and then someone speaking into a telephone. He'd never seen a telephone inside someone's house before.

'She's ready,' said the older man, as he put down the earpiece. 'She's waiting for them.'

And then they were back in the van again. Hardly a moment to breathe between trips. It must have been the middle of the night by now. The streets were silent and deserted and filled with snow. The wheels of the van slid dangerously in the driver's haste to take the bairns to their next destination.

It didn't take too long. Suddenly the engine cut out and the doors were flung open. The cold stole in and Arthur was shivering violently. His sister woke up and reached for him.

When they clambered out, they saw that they were on the driveway of what seemed to them a vast house. It was pale with windows that glowed with golden, welcoming light. All around, the gardens were swathed in undisturbed snow.

It was quiet and it didn't smell. Those were the first things Arthur realised. He held his breath and gradually took in his new surroundings. The two men – one old, one young – laughed at his dumbfounded confusion. But they didn't kick him or belt him anymore. Something was stopping them from meting out any further rough treatment.

'Where are we now, Arthur?' his sister asked. But he didn't have any answers for her.

'Ring the bell,' the older man said, and his driver went to do as he was told.

'Madam, we've brung 'em!'

And then, in the sudden brightness there was a flurry of movement and noise. It was as if a great big feathery angel was swooping out of the doorway to enfold the children in her arms.

Arthur recoiled and pulled Mavis to him defensively, but the angel woman was laughing and crying all at once. 'It's all right! Don't be frightened! Everything's fine!'

The two red-haired men were chuckling at the bairns' fright, too. But their laughter was horrible and mocking. The lady's laughter was light, trilling, delighted.

'You're home now!' she told Arthur and Mavis and put out her arms welcomingly for them to tumble into.

Of course, they didn't do so. They simply stood there, staring at their strange benefactress. Who the hell was she? They'd never clapped eyes on her before in all their short lives. Who did she think she was?

'She's your new mother,' grunted the older of the two men, and he nudged Arthur forward with his elbow so that the boy stumbled on the steps up to the grand house. 'Go on and give her a cuddle! Give your new mum a big kiss!'

The woman drew herself up grandly to her full height and treated the two men to a formidable glare. 'You people have done your part of the bargain now. You have been paid in full. I believe I have everything I need from the pair of you. Now, I'd take it kindly if you left my property at once. My business with you and your family is now concluded.'

The men snickered and doffed their caps sarcastically and clambered back into their battered van. They didn't spare the bairns they had delivered a single backward glance. In an instant the engine was rasping and coughing and off they went, trundling back down the drive and into the darkness.

The children were left alone with the lady of the house. Both stared up at her, shivering.

She really did look like an angel. She was in an ivory white silk dressing gown, feathered round the neck and sleeves. She was large and fleshy and pink. She was all bright colours with her painted eyes and lips. Her voice was light and musical as she cried out, 'Welcome home, my dears. My lovely children! Welcome to your new home, at last!'

Chapter 41

No one had seen the upstairs rooms at Franchino's, and how comfortable and cosy Bella had managed to make them. So far she hadn't invited anyone up to see. This was her own, private place in the world, and though she had friends whom she loved, she still wanted to keep one little corner that was just for her. It was a tiny little flat she could withdraw to in order to hide from the world. From up here her attic windows had a seagull's eye view onto bustling Ocean Road and it was high enough even to afford her a glimpse of the not-too-distant sea.

In just a few months she had created a perfect little boudoir up here, furnished with soft fabrics and warm colours, knick-knacks and books bought from barrows and market stalls. All in all, Bella was proud of what she had accomplished here. But no sooner had she made herself feel at home, she had gone and accepted the hand of Jonas Johnson. Of course, they couldn't both live here in this place when they were wed. It would be far too small. It was a place for a single woman to hide away in, nurture herself and grow strong again and that's what Bella had begun to do. She would have to accept now that it was almost time to move on.

But where would they live together? They hadn't even discussed it properly yet. She wouldn't move in with his brothers and sister, that was for certain. Even if there had been enough room in their house, it was something she wasn't prepared to do. The question of Jonas's income and his day job was a vexing one that she had never quite got to the bottom of. It all had to do with the various shady businesses that the Johnsons were involved in . . .

'Oh, what are you getting into, my girl?' she could hear her papa asking her. He'd be furious about this carrying on of hers! How could she ever dream of hooking all her hopes to a member of such a family!

But Bella found she had no choice. Perhaps Mama might have been more understanding, when she tried to explain to her: it's the man I love, not his flaky family. Yes, Mama would have nodded, her face taking on a far-distant look as she thought about her own past life. 'What? What?' Papa would demand. 'Why are you looking faraway and thoughtful like that? This isn't anything like your life! This isn't like you choosing me! Why, I'm nothing like someone out of the Mad Johnson family! How dare you?'

He would have known for sure what his wife was thinking. Papa had been able to read so much into just the tiniest glance from Bella's mama. That's what marriage really meant, wasn't it? Knowing someone so well you could tell the whole story with just about one look.

And her mama would have worn an ambiguous expression as she considered Bella's situation. Sure, Tonio Franchino had never been a criminal, but back in Naples, as a young man, he had knocked around with funny, disreputable types; he had gambled and cut deals with them. Eventually he had had to flee the country, of course, and poor old Mama had been faced with a choice: flee her home with her husband or never see him again. She had to leave everything behind and perhaps Papa never fully appreciated how it wounded her to leave her town by the sea.

Still, better they did, Bella thought, with a shock of realisation. If we were all still there now, look how different our lives would be. Living under the fascist heel. We'd be on the other side. That's who we'd be!

Maybe one day, when the war was all over – if she could properly even imagine such a time – she would get to visit Naples and see the place her family had set off from. All those legends! About how rough and dangerous it was. Much more so than South Shields. The man in the Panama hat and how he had a vendetta against Papa. How Papa had thrown a dart into a map of the world and how that was the way he chose this cold northern English town to escape to. And how Nonna had upped and started packing at once! The old lady was going with them – there was no way she was letting reckless, hopeless Tonio Franchino take her only daughter away and leave her behind all alone.

As ever, when she was alone in her little flat above the ice-cream parlour, Bella found the presence of her wonderful ghosts swirling around her. Her mama was quietly, cleverly letting her know: 'I recall what it's like to fall in love with a man who'll upend your life and turn everything to chaos. A man who's caught up in nefarious and furtive activity. Despite all of that, you'll still love him. You'll do anything, go anywhere. Like I did with South Shields. I understand, Bella – better than you might think!'

Her papa looked outraged. 'Nefarious? Furtive?'

Old Nonna would be laughing. She liked to fling back her head and screech with laughter. 'This family! This crazy family! It's like we have a thing about gangsters!'

They filled the air with their squabbles and laughter, but they vanished at once, leaving nothing but a faint echo, as Bella received her guest that evening. Her first guest in her little rooms above Franchino's.

'It's like a doll's house up here,' Jonas said, his voice hushed and soft as he stared about in wonder. The shutters were pulled against the dusk and she lit golden lamps, shaded with silk scarves. 'It's beautiful,' he said. 'Like you.'

She let him take her in his arms and kiss her all up and down her neck, nibbling away at the nape where the clasp of her necklace became momentarily caught up in his moustache, making them both giggle. Their laughter broke the mood, which she was relieved about. She had felt herself sliding and giving way under the pressure of his tiny, wonderful kisses. Her whole flesh had thrilled to the touch of his lips on her throat.

She kissed his full, beautiful lips. She lingered on the pink of his birthmark.

I'm going out of control, Bella thought, breaking off and hurrying to make coffee in the metal pot on the stove. Here was a special treat: thick, oily, red-hot espresso from the ancient pot she had found in one of the cupboards up here. It was what her papa used to use before he got that gleaming, modern machine he was so proud of.

Bella set the coffee pot bubbling on the hob and calmed down her breathing. She hoped her beloved ghosts were properly banished and they weren't around to see her entertaining this man. The very thought made her blush.

But what had she brought him up here for? It was a first. He knew full well he was setting foot in her inner sanctum . . .

You have to be honest with yourself, Bella, she told herself firmly. Did you bring him up here in order to do bad things with him? Are you about to risk hell and damnation? Are you going to give yourself up to him?

The coffee frothed and seethed as it boiled up into the top of the silver pot. Why, of course she was! There was no point lying to herself! She knew she was ready by now to throw all caution to the wind. It was ridiculous not to. They were pledged now, weren't they? They were betrothed. Plus, there was a war on. Any wasted time was just criminal, she thought, as the coffee overflowed and sizzled on the hot plate. She turned off the heat with a flourish.

Or am I just full of bravado? Deciding to give this man what he wants, before his interest wanes?

She took the coffee and tiny cups over to the comfy sofa and sat down beside him and they chatted about the film show they had seen tonight. In truth neither of them had taken much of the story in. They had both been too preoccupied by the thought of the other, sitting right beside them in the fuggy, smoky warmth of the cinema. It felt like a constant buzzing headache and fever, this desire they felt for each other. Nothing was going to break it, unless they tackled it face on.

Jonas quelled their vague discussion about Bette Davis's acting talent by saying, 'Bella, can we talk about . . .'

Next thing she knew, she was kissing him. She lurched forward as if someone had pushed her from behind. Jonas made a strange, startled noise in his throat, which he gulped away. He returned her kiss, catching his breath as he did so and ended up coughing and spluttering. She laughed and, without a thought, started to unpin her beautiful black hair. She told him: 'I've decided. I think it's time.'

'Time for what?' Jonas asked her. He was never usually backward at coming forward, she frowned. Is he being deliberately dim? Is he playing games with me?

'Take your shoes off. Make yourself comfortable,' she instructed him.

He pulled a face. 'It's such a faff taking them off. With my injured foot and all. I only take 'em off if I know it's worth it. If . . . if I'm staying somewhere for a while.' He looked up at her and gave a funny kind of smile. 'I mean, if I know I'm staying the night.'

'Ah,' she laughed. 'I see. Well, I guess you'd better take your shoes off then, hadn't you?'

So it became a kind of game, the two of them deciding that he was going to stay all night. This was going to be a night of all kinds of firsts. Bella sipped her scalding coffee and was glad. She watched as he unlaced his heavy work boots and rolled down his thick socks. Her heart gave a tender twinge at the sight of his naked right foot. The gnarled, red flesh. The mangled contusions. The startling absence of three of his toes.

'Oh!' she said.

'It was a stupid accident,' he said, looking ashamed. He drew himself up and faced her. 'Really stupid.'

It was like he was displaying himself to her. Here is my injury. My ugliness. Here is the bit of myself I'm most ashamed of.

Bella was hugely touched by his braveness in showing her. That slight limp of his, which he did what he could to disguise. It was all because of this.

'You poor man,' she told him, and kissed him again. 'Does it hurt?'

'Not now,' he said. 'Just keep kissing me. I'll never feel pain or hurt again . . .'

Chapter 42

'Of course you're very welcome in the mistress's house, and she wants both of you bairns to feel right at home here,' the maid assured them. 'But the pair of you stink to high heaven, pets, and so we've got to get you into that bath.'

It was almost midnight on Christmas Eve on the very night that Arthur and Mavis had moved into Mrs Kendricks' house. They had been swept indoors and embraced by the grand woman in her feathered night gown and the two of them had been dumbstruck with shock.

The cold, unfriendly, dangerous world outside was shut out as the tall front doors swung to and were locked and bolted by the maid.

The children submitted to this woman's embrace and didn't make a single sound. Her white skin was dry with some kind of expensive powder and she smelled of fancy perfume. This woman was like no one they had ever met in their lives before.

Elizabeth Kendricks closed her eyes euphorically as she held her two new children to her breast. This was her moment. It was what she had longed for all her adult life. Now they were here.

And they reeked. The two of them stank to high heaven. An unnameable stench that needed to be eradicated at once.

'Polly!' Elizabeth had called, recoiling from her heart's desire. 'Take these children and get them bathed! Get them into new pyjamas and a nightie. Everything is laid out in their rooms. Dunk them into a big hot bath . . . and burn these filthy rags they're wearing!'

Polly was the sole servant still in residence at the Kendricks house. At one time there had been a staff of six, but times were so much harder. Mrs Kendricks went along as best she could with the muddle-headed aid of Polly, but it wasn't ideal. And what a lot of work there was going to be from now on, with two children to see to!

The bewildered children were whisked up a curving staircase by the skinny and dithery maid. Mavis stared at the girl's prominent front teeth. 'Come along!' Polly urged them. She dragged them along a carpeted hall to the main bathroom, where she started filling the biggest, most ornate bathtub they had ever seen in their lives.

They had thought the house where Mr Alec had installed them was a marvellous place but even there, bath time had meant a tin tub in front of the parlour fire. This was a whole tiled room given over just to bathing!

The air was soon steamy and hot and fragrant with pine scent. Polly sat on the edge of the bath and bossed them about. 'Now children, you must listen to what I say. Mrs Kendricks has taken you into her home out of the goodness of her heart, and so you must do your very best to comply with all her wishes.'

There was a scene, of course, when it came to dragging off all their filthy, tattered clothes. Arthur and Mavis had been living rough for several days and the garments they wore were ruined.

'Don't kick up a fuss, you little monster!' Polly said, as Mavis started wailing. 'These old rags have got to be burned. They're past saving. Washing won't help them. They'll just fall apart. Surely you can see that?'

But Mavis kept on wailing as the serving girl wrestled with her and tried to get her out of the spoiled garments. Arthur intervened, explaining: 'Our mother sewed us these clothes. She always made all our clothes. This is all we have left now . . .'

Polly grunted. 'Well, that's no concern of mine. I've just got to see that you don't bring dirt and vermin into the mistress's house, that's all. You've both got nice new things waiting for you in your bedrooms. You don't need these filthy old– *Ow!*'

Mavis had bitten her on the hand and Polly let go of the girl with a shriek. 'You little bitch!' the serving girl shrieked.

'What's all this?' came a thunderous voice from the bathroom doorway. All three turned to see the mistress of the house looking very displeased. 'I thought I sent you to bathe these children, Polly?'

Polly was examining her bleeding knuckle. 'I was trying to!'

'I'm not getting undressed in front of her!' Arthur spat out, hotly. By his reckoning Polly could only be a handful of years older than he was himself. There was no way he'd strip off and climb into a bath before her very eyes, no matter how wonderfully hot and welcoming that bath was.

Mrs Kendricks was used to people doing exactly as she told them. She glared at the three young people in her beautifully tiled aqua bathroom and took a deep breath. Then she bellowed, 'Get into that bath at once! Do precisely as you are told! Or else there will be no Christmas, no presents and no adoption. I will send both you terrible urchins back to where I got you!'

Her voice was like a blast of arctic air battening them backwards. They stood silently as she turned on her heel and left them to it.

*

'There, now!' said the lady of the house, some time after midnight, in a much sweeter tone. 'Don't you feel better, hm? I must say, the pair of you look absolutely splendid.'

Polly nudged her two reluctant charges into the main living room, where Elizabeth was basking in front of the flames of the log fire. She looked quite regal in her feathers, and very pleased with herself as she surveyed her new children.

'Don't they scrub up well, Polly?' she smiled.

'Aye.' Polly pulled a face, because all the scrubbing had fallen to her, and it had proved to be something of a tussle. It was as if the children had never seen soap before in their lives. They had wriggled and howled at her ministrations. Every second had been an awful ordeal, and if this was going to be how it was every day in this house from now on, Polly was secretly thinking of jacking her job in. She would have to consider her position.

'Aren't they wonderful little children?' Elizabeth sighed. 'Simply perfect additions to our household?'

Polly didn't reply to that, but urged the two of them to go and sit either side of her mistress on the deep and luxurious settee.

They weren't very keen.

'You mustn't be shy of me,' Elizabeth said, patting the cushions and trying to look motherly. 'This is where you belong now.'

'She's your new mam,' Polly explained helpfully, and gave Mavis a small shove.

Mavis was in a frilly nightie made of the most wonderful gossamer stuff. She kept touching the material and marvelling at it. She felt like a fairy, stepping into that room with that old woman sat there and the fire roaring. She couldn't quite get the hang of what was going on, or what was being asked of them. All she could think of was how strange it felt to be wearing lovely clothes that felt lighter than air. And how funny her Arthur looked in his new striped cotton pyjamas. He stood rather stiffly beside his sister, and his face as he stared at their benefactress was all suspicion.

'You really have nothing to fear,' Elizabeth told them. 'God knows what you've been through in your short lives already. The pair of you are probably scarred for life. But you have nothing to worry about now. This is your home, and you will always be comfortable and safe and loved here.'

Mavis glared at Polly. 'She took away the clothes our mammy sewed for us. She said she was going to get rid of them.'

Polly held up her hands. 'You told me to, mistress. Their clothes were putrid!'

Elizabeth nodded and waved her away. Polly's shrill protestations were setting everyone's teeth on edge. 'Fetch us hot chocolate, Polly. That's what children like.'

When it was brought in, it was like nothing the bairns had ever drunk before. Thick and sweet, in large, luxurious bowls. They sat on the settee with Elizabeth and felt like they had died and gone to heaven. Thoughts of her old clothes were suddenly gone from Mavis's mind. She sat there with chocolate round her mouth and called out, 'More!'

'Polly?' Elizabeth instructed Polly to pour a little more from the jug into Mavis's bowl. 'Though not too much, or else you'll get a sore tummy.'

Mavis was beyond reach, though. She was in a trance of sweetness.

Arthur was staring at the tall pine tree in the corner of the room. The scent of it was wonderful. It reminded him of going into Binns the department store with his mammy, when she was trying to teach him how to thieve stuff from counters. In fact, it was probably even taller than the department store tree had been!

'Perhaps you'd like to help Polly decorate the tree?' Elizabeth had noticed his interest. 'It's only got its star on, so far. It needs dressing up properly before Christmas can truly start. Will you help her?'

The boy nodded readily, feeling absurdly shy in the face of Elizabeth's kindness. He couldn't quite bring the words out, but what he wanted to say was: Yes, yes! I'd love to decorate the tree. I'd stay up all night to make it look perfect. And thank you! Thank you, lady. Whoever you are. Thank you for this. For all of this. I think you've probably saved our lives.

He couldn't quite say the words. For once in his life Arthur found himself tongue-tied. But his face was bright with teary gratitude and Elizabeth believed she understood.

Chapter 43

Summer wore on for the newly-weds and Mavis couldn't help herself coming back to life. She longed to get up and about, out of her house and back into the thick of things. She took firm control of herself, and decided that it was past time for wallowing. She had to get out again, amongst life and all that it involved.

Sam was so pleased to see her being much more like her normal self. 'There's a special glow about you,' he told her. 'You look more wonderful than ever!'

'What?' she shouted, dashing round the house at the crack of dawn. She was getting ready for her first day back at the biscuit factory. Her hair was tied up in a great big kerchief and she was hunting through the kitchen for her bait box. 'What's that you're saying?' She was still deaf, though the constant ringing in her ears had faded a bit.

Sam came to take her in his arms. 'I think you're wonderful,' he bellowed at her.

'Oh-hoh! Yes!' she shouted back. 'I know! I am!'

Then she was ready to go, and Sam was proud to be leaving the house with her. The two of them were heading out to work at the factory together on Monday morning, for the very first time. They made a very happy parade of two down the length of Watling Street.

*

She was delighted to be back on duty in the packing room, and submitted to the hugs and cheers of her fellow workers gleefully. Mavis squealed with pleasure as they made a fuss of her, nodding and replying to all their many questions: 'Uh-hoh! Uh-hoh! I'm smashing, yes! I'm feeling champion!'

And the funny thing was, she really did feel fine. It was as if by sheer force of will and the act of flinging herself back into life, she had made herself feel better. She was even glad she couldn't hear the endless grinding of engines and machinery at the factory. The quiet inside her head was almost a boon when it came to being at work.

'We are so glad to see you, Mavis,' cried the supervisor, Mrs Clarke. The older woman came sweeping into the room grandly, her bust thrust out as she made her entrance like a Valkyrie. 'Oh, we've missed your cheery smile, here at Wights!'

Mavis was secretly astonished to find herself so popular. But perhaps everyone really had missed her? Maybe they had found they had taken her for granted up till now? Anyway, the fact was, Mavis was cockahoop to find herself flavour of the month, seemingly everywhere she went.

'What it is, is that you've come back safe and sound,' her friend Plump Mary at the biscuit factory tried to explain.

'Uh-hoh, yes!'

'But so many don't,' Mary went on. 'When people vanish after air raids, they're either dead, or so damaged and injured that you never see them again. But you, Mavis . . . well, here you are!'

'I am!' Mavis shouted. She hadn't quite caught all of Mary's words, but the gist was enough. And that, she realised, had to be her watchword from now on: the gist. So long as she got the gist of what was being said to her, that would just have to be enough.

Those first days back at the biscuit factory went by in a lovely, sugary blur, her legs and back sore from standing so much and her arms and fingers aching with fatigue from their endless activity. But she was sustained by the joyful feeling of being the centre of attention. Her deafened ears burned blissfully for a week or two. And she floated happily on the wonderful aroma of baking biscuits. She hadn't realised just how much she had missed the smell of that place. As she worked, she munched happily on clandestine ginger snaps and all her colleagues were so pleased to see her again, she wasn't reported once.

There was only one real sticking point on those first few days back, and that was to do with her friendship with Irene.

From the very first, Irene had been Mavis's protector at the biscuit factory. Newly arrived from Norfolk, Tom Farley's bride had been appalled at the way Mavis was treated by others. Often she was the butt of their jokes. Irene had been so incensed by the way Megan – her own sister-in-law – had behaved towards Mavis, that Irene had even hit her. She had slapped her at work in front of everyone. Since then, Irene and Mavis had been pretty much inseparable.

Now they were linked by family and the two of them were sisters. They should be closer than ever. But Irene had overstepped the mark. She had gone way too far. While Mavis had been convalescing and out of the picture, Irene had done something terrible.

In all the flurry and kerfuffle of the welcome, and the noise of everyone trying to make themselves understood, Irene at first wasn't aware of how cross Mavis was with her. They had had no quiet chat alone, so she couldn't tell for sure. Mavis was too busy being Queen of the May. She was telling the story again and again – with mimes and actions

– of how she'd been caught in the air raid, and how the coffin containing old Ma Johnson had fallen on her, and how that funeral horse had kicked her in the head.

It was down to the oldest of the Farley sisters-in-law to tell Irene just how offended Mavis was by her meddling.

'What? Why doesn't she just tell me?' Irene gasped.

Beryl shrugged, 'That's what I've heard, anyway.'

It was the Friday of Mavis's first week back at work, and all the lasses had hastened up the hill after the hooter had sounded for a drink at the Robin Hood. Mavis was still basking in all the attention and letting others buy drinks for her. It was as if she had become everyone's mascot or good luck charm. Perhaps, rather superstitiously, they were all thinking that, if they were close to her, then they couldn't be hurt by the falling bombs either?

'Silly girl,' Irene sighed. 'What would she want to turn against me for? What have I done wrong?' Irene was actually rather irked. Who had gone to visit Mavis in her sick bed more than she had? Who had been more concerned for the daft girl's welfare than Irene had?

'Well,' said Beryl, sipping her half of stout and warming to her theme. 'I've only heard this from Lily Johnson, mind.'

'Oh, her.' Irene pulled a face. Lily would be mixing it and causing trouble, of course. Beryl worked with her at the shipyard. The only two lasses on the welding team tended to spend a lot of time together. As they went about their hefty, dangerous work, they shared a lot of confidences, and apparently this had been one of them.

'Lily says that Mavis is upset that you went behind her back,' Beryl told her.

Irene tried to get her head round this. 'Went behind her back to do what?'

'Talking to her adoptive mother,' said Beryl. 'I think it was Sam who told her. And she's not happy. She doesn't think you should be interfering.'

Irene actually felt herself blushing. She pretended it was all down to the frothy beer she was drinking and the warmth inside the pub on a summer's evening. The truth was, she did feel rather awkward about investigating Mavis and Arthur's past lives. Hadn't she been sat there in Mrs Kendricks' fancy conservatory, digging up the past? Hadn't Sam been there with her, just as committed to the idea that it was all to the good that they try to understand their Mavis a little better?

'She doesn't want all her business to be known,' Beryl told Irene. 'That's what I think. She chucked that woman out of the church, didn't she? She must really hate her guts to do that.'

Am I meddling? Irene wondered, watching Mavis with her biscuit factory friends from afar. Maybe I should just let it all alone?

'I've been to see her at her big house,' Irene confided to Beryl. 'I actually went there to talk to her. To try and get more of the story.'

'Eeeh, Irene, you never did!' Beryl gasped. 'Now, I'm surprised at that. That really is interfering, if you ask me. I knew you like to know all the ins and outs of everyone's business, but that's going too far, that is!'

Is it? Irene wondered. 'All I was doing was trying to help. There's a massive rift between them and I think it could be healed.'

'What if Mavis doesn't want it healing? Have you thought about that, hinny?'

'I don't like seeing families at war,' Irene said. 'And this woman – Elizabeth Kendricks – she's so upset. Whatever she did in the past to hurt Mavis and Arthur, she's very keen to make up for it. She wants to be back in their lives.'

Beryl pulled a face and glugged at her half pint. 'I'd keep my neb out, Irene. I really would.'

'Maybe it's too late for that,' Irene said worriedly. 'I've promised Elizabeth I'd ask Mavis to meet her again. I've said I'd talk to her. I'd try to heal the old wounds between them.'

Beryl's eyes widened. 'Rather you than me, pet! When are you gonna ask Mavis this, anyway? She's barely talking to you!'

Irene looked thoughtful. 'Tonight. Mavis is coming over to Ma Ada's for her supper, with Sam. I can come clean and tell her who I've been talking to. I'll ask her then, if she wants to come to Elizabeth's house with me . . . Eeeh, it's a grand house, Beryl. You've never seen anything like it!'

'I hope you know what you're up to, Irene,' Beryl sighed. 'It sounds to me like you've got a whole lot of trouble brewing . . .'

Chapter 44

Elizabeth Kendricks spent the whole of that Christmas doing everything she could to win her new children over.

The pair of them were entranced by the beauty of her home. They were stupefied by the attention they received. It was all a little frightening, and they were much quieter and less obviously grateful than their benefactress would have liked. But the bairns were wary. What did this woman want from them? No one ever gave you something for nothing, did they?

Up in their new bedrooms the maid Polly showed them where everything was kept, and where they must sleep. They actually both had cupboards for clothes! Though all their clothes had been taken off them and were burned by now. 'We'll have to see what Father Christmas brings you!' they were told.

Mavis cried in the night because she remembered that, amongst the filthy rags that had been taken from her, there was the tattered remnant of her mother's woollen shawl. It was the last physical link to their mammy. When she wore it, Mavis sometimes thought she could still catch her scent and even hear her voice.

In the very early hours she went to Arthur's room and wailed at him, explaining her loss. He tried to console her as she sobbed.

They had never slept in different rooms in all their lives. Last night had been the first time they had been separated and they were too tired to argue. 'Girls and boys must have their own rooms,' Polly had told them beadily. 'It's the done thing. You're growing up to be a young lady and gentleman. You're not animals anymore.'

But the separation hurt them, at first. They were so used to being together almost constantly. 'You burned my mammy's shawl,' Mavis snapped at the servant girl, glaring furiously.

'Well, happy Christmas to you an' all!' Polly laughed, bustling about the bright room in the morning. 'Come on. Stop whingeing! It's Christmas and, according to the mistress, Father Christmas has been.'

Downstairs Mrs Kendricks was waiting for them beside the roaring fire again. It was almost as if she hadn't moved all night, except she was wearing a different, beautiful house-coat and her hair was up. She was surrounded by glittering, gaudy packages.

'My dears, come to me,' she said, and seized hold of their hands. 'Now, I don't suppose you children have ever known a proper Christmas before in all your lives, have you?'

Arthur broke in, 'Actually, last year we had—'

'Even if you did have a Christmas last year, I imagine it won't have been anything like today is going to be,' Mrs Kendricks interrupted him smoothly. 'Now, first of all, before you can be allowed to open all of these wonderful gifts from the North Pole, you must help Polly finish deco-rating the tree and, when that is done, Polly will bring in breakfast . . .'

As they worked on the tree, and Polly muttered furiously to herself, Arthur was remembering last Christmas in the little house on . . . what was the street called? Could he even have forgotten it already? Or blocked it out? The house that Mr Alec had got for them – what had that street been called? It didn't matter. Christmas had been wonderful. That man had stayed away all day till evening. Mammy had made them up two little stockings that she put at the bottom of their beds. Stockings so crammed with good things and novelties that they crackled at your touch. It was like magic, last Christmas, with just the three of them . . .

With the tree complete and the old woman applauding their efforts, they were swept off into another opulent room that held a big table laid out with gleaming plates and dishes. They were brought hot, spitting sausages, salty, crispy bacon and glossy fried eggs. Mavis's eyes went wide at the sight of all this food and she started eating mechanically, remorselessly, as if Polly was going to take it all back off her. She folded triangles of buttered bread into her mouth, one after another.

'What do we call her?' she asked her brother, through a mouthful of food. 'What do we have to call that lady?'

The lady had swept upstairs to dress for the day, leaving them to eat in peace. 'I don't know,' Arthur shrugged.

Polly had crept up on them with a jug of foaming, warm milk. 'Her name is Mrs Kendricks. That's what you must call her, same as I do.'

'What does she want from us?' Arthur asked, jutting out his chin.

Polly poured them glasses of milk and sighed. 'You're both hers now. She paid for you fair and square. Now you must be her good and devoted children, just like she's always wanted.'

The rest of the day went by bewilderingly.

Mrs Kendricks reappeared in what looked like an evening gown. She was like one of the women coming out of the theatre in town where the two bairns had begged on the steps before getting shooed away. But she was dressed up for their sake! As she kept saying, everything was all for them.

'And look at the two of you in your new night things! Adorable – like Wendy and one of her brothers, off to Neverland in the night!' She clapped her hands together. 'Yes, that's what you are. The Lost Children, indeed. And now, I have found you!'

It was time to open parcels and packages. They had to be coaxed into ripping the lavish paper and untying the ribbons. Box after box was given to them and they were shy of spoiling them at first. 'But they are all for you,' Mrs Kendricks cried. 'I've been collecting these presents for years and years, all ready for this moment.'

Inside they found perfect little outfits for girls and boys. Clothes that were rich and colourful. Like nothing they had ever seen before. Garments that were even more spectacular than the ones their mammy had sewn for them. Arthur wondered: how could she have been collecting these in preparation for years and years? How did she even know about us so far in advance? How could she ever have known about us previously?

There were mysteries heaped upon mysteries in this place. Just as messy and unfathomable as the wrapping paper and boxes that filled the room. Then it was lunchtime and Polly was dashing about again, dithering between dining room and kitchen. The young woman cursed bitterly as she pushed a golden hostess trolley into the room bearing a glazed and steaming turkey. 'I've had a hell of a time, wrestling with this wretched beast,' she complained.

'Hush now, it's perfect! Isn't it perfect, children?'

Arthur and Mavis had never seen anything like that turkey before.

'Where does she put it all?' Mrs Kendricks laughed, as she watched her new little daughter eating with gusto. 'Look at her go! Ha ha! I think the poor mite must have hollow legs!'

Christmas lunch lasted for quite some time, and the diminutive Mavis out-ate them all. There was a zealous gleam in her eye that Arthur didn't like the look of. She was eating as if this was her last ever meal. She ate everything before her as if she expected someone to whisk it away from her unless she scoffed it up fast.

'Don't you make yourself sick,' Arthur warned her, just before she made herself sick.

She had to be led away by Polly to the nearest downstairs lavatory (a downstairs lavatory!) and spent some time feeling miserably sorry for herself. Mrs Kendricks laughed it off and saw to it that both children were bathed once more and dressed in brand new clothes.

And so the day passed, with Mavis looking slightly pale. Gradually she cheered up, and even started to feel peckish. 'Don't you show me up again,' Arthur told her, as they pretended to play nicely with their new presents. Mavis stared in awe at a perfect china doll she hardly dared touch. Arthur had a paper puppet theatre that drew his attention immediately, more than the other, more expensive items he'd been given. 'I mean it. Don't show us up. We have to be good.'

'Sorry, Arthur,' Mavis whispered.

Mrs Kendricks had flinched only momentarily during the vomiting episode. She had been determined for it not to put a blight on their family Christmas. It was just one of those things! Children being children! Vomiting everywhere!

'Now, children,' she clapped her hands for their attention. 'This evening I have a few friends coming over to the house. Just a few select, beloved friends . . .'

Arthur found himself instantly on the alert. More people! Another new situation to contend with. What would be expected of them?

Mrs Kendricks soon explained: 'I would like you both to show what wonderful, sweet, well-behaved children you are. I'd like to show off the fact that I have adopted the most lovely children in the world.'

That evening the friends appeared. There weren't that many of them, but their noise seemed to fill up the whole house. They were very sure of themselves, piling up their outdoor clothes and coats into the waiting arms of Polly and then surging into the drawing room to be greeted by their hostess.

'Where are they?' a skinny lady with bulging eyes kept asking. 'Did you get them? Are we going to meet them?'

Mrs Kendricks was just about bursting with glee. 'Oh, I did, Cissy. And wait till you see them. They are everything I could have hoped for. They are such angels.'

The woman called Cissy simpered and sighed. 'You are so lucky.'

There were five strange grown-ups standing there in their finery, holding tiny glasses of sherry as the bairns were brought into the room. Polly prodded them from behind, full of impatience. They were shy and awkward, hanging their heads. They felt like strangers, even to themselves, in their stiff new Christmas clothes.

'Oh! What darlings! What sweethearts!' was the general consensus.

Mrs Kendricks glowed with pleasure at the approval of her guests.

'And you say you picked them up out of the gutter?' the woman called Cissy asked. 'You say you rescued them from penury?'

'Let's not go into all of that now,' Mrs Kendricks said, rather sharply. 'What say you we have a little singing? Hm, wouldn't that be lovely? What if our little angels could sing to us? I'm sure they sing divinely. What do you think?'

'Oh, yes!' cried Cissy and her other friends.

Arthur and Mavis held hands, suddenly feeling alarmed. Sing? They were going to have to sing now?

Mrs Kendricks advanced on them. Her pale, beautifully painted face looming as large as the moon. 'What songs do you know, children? Won't you give us a Christmas carol? Will you sing for us all, like the angels you surely are?'

Chapter 45

There wasn't much for supper that night at Number Thirteen. Ma Ada had one of her pearl barley stews bubbling away on the hob and she'd seen to it that there'd be enough for visitors. As she took bread out of the oven and basked in its delicious scent, she thought about how strange it was to think of her Sam – her youngest, most sickly lad – as a visitor to what used to be his own home! How time had moved on!

She ambled into the parlour and set the table ready, rubbing her aching hip and enjoying the quiet before everyone got back from the pub. Both the bairns were in bed and so was their Aunty Megan, who had grumblingly seen to their wants this evening. Eeeh, that lass! Whatever were they going to do with her? Was she ever going to be happy?

Ma Ada settled in her armchair and as the radiogram warmed up, she picked up her knitting and let Lucky hop nimbly into her lap. She frowned as the newscaster's voice faded up and she focused on the details of what he was saying. It was all to do with a bombing raid in Germany. Something about it being a big success. A strategic success. It had been in the planning for months, apparently, and involved a newly invented kind of bomb, one that could be dropped from a low-flying plane and that would hit water at such a speed and angle that it would bounce, several times, before hitting its target. Rather like skimming stones across the surface of a lake . . .

Ma Ada listened, her face creased in consternation. She wasn't sure she liked the sound of this, as the voice continued and explained that not all the Lancaster Bombers had returned from the Ruhr Valley in Germany overnight. Some were still missing. Some had been shot down and others had crashed in the middle of their mission. The death toll was high.

Ada felt her sluggish heart quicken in her breast. This news was coming close to home. She just knew that this news was going to drop a bouncing bomb on top of all their lives . . .

The newsreader went on to explain the vital importance of this secret midnight raid, and how its objective had been to destroy certain dams in Germany. The reservoirs these vast concrete dams held back supplied towns in the great industrial heartlands of the enemy country. This was where the mighty German steel industry created the machinery of war. For months the Air Force had planned this attack on their foe's weakest spot, and they had succeeded brilliantly. The vast valleys were flooded with biblical volumes of water. Whole towns had been swept away. Thousands were killed or made homeless. The flood was still going on into the next day.

What a wonderful success. What a terrible blow to the Nazi war machine. Ma Ada held her breath and waited to hear what the cost had been. Just how many planes had crews who hadn't made it back? And did they have names yet, those lads who would never fly back from their mission abroad?

Ma Ada remembered what Tom had said last time he was home on leave, so briefly. Irene had told her the few snippets he'd let slip, even though she wasn't supposed to.

The two of them had been ensconced in the scullery, huddled and chatting about their beloved Tom as they prepared supper for an evening much like this one. Irene had told her mother-in-law: 'He was talking about them flying close to the ground. Close to the surface of the lakes in Cumbria. They were practising there and in Scotland . . .'

'Lochs,' Ma Ada had said. 'That's what they call them up there.'

Irene hadn't seen that it mattered what they called them. 'He said it's quite tricky. And dangerous, of course. But they have to be at exactly the right height, and at the right speed, and he has to be looking out the front, out of his little window, waiting for the exact right moment . . .' She had shrugged and said, 'Of course, he wouldn't tell me more than that.'

And so the two women had sighed and tried to put it all out of their minds for now. But he had definitely spoken of flying low over stretches of water, Ma Ada thought. Surely that meant he was part of these nineteen crews who had taken off from Lincoln last night? Operation Chastise. Was Tom really a part of it? Surely that meant . . .

There came a clatter at the front door that made her jump. They were home! All the youngsters were home from the pub! And with them came someone with an even louder voice than the rest. Someone who sounded a bit tipsy as they called out, 'Uh-hoh! Eeeh, it's lovely! Lovely to be out! And lovely to be here for me supper, as well! Uh-hoh!'

Ma Ada wiped her face quickly with a tea cloth, blotting the damp from her cheeks and she stood ready to greet the young'uns. There they were, looking worn out, happy, and blurred at the edges by a few drinks. Beryl came in leading the way, flinging her headscarf and coat onto the rack in the hall.

Irene looked less happy than the others. Could she have cottoned on to the news already?

And here, swaying into the back parlour, came Ma Ada's beloved Sam, grinning at his mam and seeming pleased with himself. His arms were around Mavis, who looked – quite frankly – as if she was off her head.

'Eeeh, Ma Ada!' the diminutive girl shouted at the top of her voice. 'It's me, look! I'm back in the land of the living! Uh-hoh! I am! And it's *lovely!*'

They had to try to get Mavis to quieten down somewhat, what with the bairns being upstairs asleep. Her heedless, rasping voice would surely carry up as far as the attic and wake them. There was something indistinct about the way she talked now, and Ma Ada reflected that it must be hard work for the girl, remembering exactly how to say things when she couldn't hear a jot herself. She was tending to gabble in her enthusiasm and it made her hard to follow.

Nevertheless, the Farley matriarch was glad to see this latest addition to the family. They had all been very worried about Mavis since that awful air raid when she was kicked in the head. But it seemed that her injuries had been minimal and she was very nearly back to her normal self.

Beryl helped out with serving up supper and Ma Ada fussed around the young brood, seeing that they had everything they needed. The radio was turned off and the room filled with the noise of them eating with great satisfaction, gossiping about everyday things as they did so.

The news of the operation in the Ruhr Valley weighed heavily on Ma Ada's mind as she watched them. She couldn't eat her supper, and waved Beryl away as she tried to serve her some. None of these youngsters would have heard any news yet today. They had been at work and then at the pub. Surely if they'd heard, they'd be as worried as she was?

Ma Ada was alone with this burden and wondered when would be a good time to tell them what had happened in the wider world overnight?

Their Tom. At the heart of that great venture. It had been an amazing, impossible success. And maybe . . . just maybe . . . it might even turn the tide of the war!

She would take Irene aside. That was the thing to do. That was the right way to go about it. Yes, and maybe Irene already had an inkling that something momentous had transpired? Ma Ada frowned as she studied the Norfolk girl's face. She looked strained, didn't she? She looked as though she was wrestling with something internally, too. Could it be that she had already heard the news from last night?

Irene hadn't heard a thing about Operation Chastise. She was oblivious to everything that was churning through her mother-in-law's mind that evening. She ate her supper mechanically and smiled at the others, but uppermost in her own mind was the business of Mavis and her adopted mother.

Mavis had been wreathed in smiles all evening and had given nothing away about the fact that she was cross about the meddling Irene had done. But neither had she directed much in the way of communication to Irene, either, and that was quite unusual. The two of them were avoiding eye contact and, after twenty minutes of suppertime in Ma Ada's parlour, Irene could stand this tension no longer. She reached for her bag and pulled out her book of flimsy letter-writing paper and a pen.

'Mavis!' she wrote, in bold letters. 'I haven't been meddling, whatever you might think!'

'What's this?' Mavis shouted as the paper was thrust across the table at her.

Sam groaned, seeing the look on Irene's face. 'Not now, Irene,' he said. 'Can't we just enjoy the peace for a while?'

Beryl was alert for signs of fuss. She hated arguments breaking out, especially at home. 'What's going on?' She gave Irene a warning look.

Irene wrote out another page, resenting wasting her precious Basildon Bond. 'Mavis, she's desperate to see you. She wants to make amends. She misses you and your Arthur so much. Surely life is too short for bad blood?'

This lengthier message took Mavis a few moments to digest. When she had taken it all in, she looked up at Irene with a thunderous expression. Then she burst out: 'Elizabeth Kendricks can rot for all I care! She can rot in bloody hell!'

Chapter 46

The little boy had a wonderful voice. That was the opinion held by all the fancy friends Elizabeth Kendricks had invited into her home. They came from as far afield as Newcastle and Morpeth, her well-heeled, music-loving friends, and they all gathered to hear the magic orphans perform. Squinting matrons and whiskered uncles and soulful-looking young women; they perched on well-upholstered chairs and devoted all their attention to the children.

Well, the little girl couldn't sing for toffee, of course, and she wasn't even pretty. She simply stood beside her brother, opening and closing her mouth obediently. What could be heard of her voice was a kind of tuneless rasping noise.

But the boy! He threw back his head and this glorious cascade of notes came out, effortlessly, joyfully. Even he seemed bewildered by the noise he could set free.

He sounded like an angel, they all decided. He sounded like nothing on earth. His voice was high and pure and what gave it that extra shading of pathos was that, surely, it was due to break at any moment as the boy matured? Mrs Kendrick's guests flocked to hastily arranged musical soirees as if they were coming to seize their final chance to see a miracle of nature.

Arthur was bemused by all of this. He learned the new songs that Mrs Kendricks taught him at her piano, and submitted to this new regime of learning, practising and then putting on a show. At first he was nonplussed by the whole thing. So they liked to hear him sing? It made no difference to him. He barely had to try. The long hours of rehearsal were a bit of a pain, but he and his sister had a roof over their heads, so he wasn't about to complain. Perhaps Mavis wasn't so keen on joining in with the songs.

'I think it's best if your sister mimes,' Elizabeth Kendricks decided, after the first few musical evenings.

Polly elaborated later, as she supervised the two of them getting ready for bed. 'She says you're to just open and close your mouth and pretend to sing,' she told Mavis. 'Your voice isn't as nice as your brother's, and people are beginning to remark on it.'

Mavis stared with huge, hurt eyes at the maid, but didn't say anything.

'Her voice is just the same as mine!' Arthur defended his sister, but he knew it wasn't true. He simply hugged her and petted her and went off to his own room to lie awake and think the whole business over.

Arthur lay awake through the night, his mind spinning with possibilities. At first he had thought nothing of his newfound talent – it cost him no effort and he put no value by it. But then he had found himself carefully watching the impact that his voice had on the people who had come to see him. Real people, well-dressed people. People who talked posh, the kind who would have walked past him without a second glance, had he been lying starving in the gutter. Why, now they were sitting up and taking notice. They were hanging on every note he sang and they had funny, soppy looks on their faces – the men as well as the women. All ages. It didn't matter who they were. Arthur had the ability to make them really listen.

Mrs Kendricks taught him – line by line, note by note – funny foreign songs. Schubert, Bach, Beethoven. Names he had never heard before. Then American songs, which he liked a bit more, though he was best at bringing out the darker streaks of melancholy in the songs with the foreign words. He had no idea how he did any of this. He just opened his mouth and let it fly out. And he watched the impact it had on his listeners.

'You have a God-given talent,' Mrs Kendricks told him. 'My goodness, Arthur. It's like magic.'

He just smiled at her, still uncertain about what all of this meant. One thing seemed certain though, and he was glad about that. His singing meant that he had established his and his sister's place here in the grand woman's house. She wasn't going to be letting them go anywhere after this.

It wasn't just in their own, new home that the children sang during those first few weeks and months. Mrs Kendricks ushered the two of them into her beautiful dove grey car and they sat on the back seat, on the shiny red leather, and they were driven to other homes, where they were greeted by kindly people who were clearly expecting them to put on a show.

Polly was their driver for these trips into other nearby towns and she expressed her scepticism about the whole thing every chance she got. 'All these grand houses,' she tutted. 'All these people have got more money than sense or taste. They're just looking to pass their time in idle pursuits. Fancy sitting round, all agog, listening to two ragamuffins like these, warbling away!'

Polly didn't have much faith in the bairns' singing. Oh, she supposed that Arthur could hold a tune right enough, but so what? It was just singing. And anyway, his voice was going to change any day now and then what? Everyone would lose interest in those kids. No one was going to bother with them then, were they? No, as far as Polly could see, it was just raising them up only to dash them down again, sometime in the near future.

Also, that Arthur was starting to put on airs, she had noticed. Polly was the one who had to deal with him day to day, and it was plain to her mind that the lad was becoming downright uppity.

Well, it was the dressing up that had started it . . .

'Hush now, Polly. What would you know?' sighed Mrs Kendricks. 'They have to look the part if they're putting on a show, especially if they're going round other people's homes and standing in drawing rooms, expecting everyone to pay attention. We have to dress them up to seem the part.'

Polly shook her head, tutting, manhandling the wheel of the powerful motor car. All those outfits! Specially made in multi-coloured shades of satin and silk. The bairns were rigged out as maharajas and ranis. Princes and princesses. Ali Baba and Scheherazade. It was ridiculous! But there was no reasoning with the mistress. Her way was the only way and she had decided that her children were going to be the talk of the social season.

'Now remember, dear,' she had to keep telling Mavis, 'you just keep opening and closing your mouth, but don't let a single peep come out.'

Mavis nodded solemnly, but quite often during their little shows she would forget herself, and out would come that disconcerting rasping noise of hers, in complete contrast to her brother's joyful noise.

'It'll end in tears,' Polly kept insisting.

But each performance was a triumph. Arthur's sheer, innate talent held his small audiences rapt. He and his sister became quite used to walking into brand new places. They didn't even gasp or feel cowed by the opulence of these homes anymore. They simply took up their rightful position at the centre of everyone's attention and waited for their new, adoptive mother to cue them in.

Everything went so wonderfully. Even those times when Mavis's voice rose above the volume of her brother's. When her enthusiasm got the better of her, Mavis came close to spoiling the show. Once she had even wet herself as they stood on someone's fancy carpet and Arthur had blushed with shame. Luckily no one seemed to notice, or they were just too polite to mention it. Polly had clocked it, of course.

'You mucky little lass! Fancy doing a wet in front of a roomful of Newcastle folk!'

'I couldn't help it,' Mavis wailed. 'They were looking at us so fiercely.'

Exasperated, Polly was helping the little girl off with her dampened, smelly princess outfit. 'Well, I'll tell you one thing for nothing. It's your brother they're all sitting there to see. Not you, little lass. And don't you ever forget it.'

From the doorway Arthur had heard what Polly was saying. He stood there crossly, still done up as a fairy-tale prince. 'Well, that hardly matters, does it, Polly? Because we're together, we are. And no one's ever gonna separate us. So there's no need to frighten her.'

Polly pulled a face. He was so cocksure these days! Shouting the odds at her! He'd only been here in the Kendricks house for a matter of months. Fancy talking to Polly like that, like he was lord of the flippin' manor!

'Don't get too cocky, Arthur,' Polly warned him. 'Just remember where you come from.'

'And where do I come from, Polly dear?' he laughed.

'Nowhere,' she said. 'You come from nowhere and you're just nothing. You're nowt at all! Never forget that.'

Arthur's eyes blazed back at the maid. 'Aye,' he said, in a quieter voice that made her shiver. 'But I'm gonna be something one day soon, aren't I? I'm not gonna be nowt for ever.'

Chapter 47

The account that Irene got from Ma Ada was somewhat garbled. Apparently the old woman had heard something on the radio that might involve Tom, though she wasn't sure. It might have been an important item, with huge repercussions, but she wasn't quite certain. Ma Ada tried to explain what she had heard, but it didn't make a whole lot of sense.

'There are missions every day, doing this, that and the other,' Irene frowned. 'Why would Tom be on this one in particular?'

In the clear light of day, Ma Ada was less positive than she had been that her son was caught up in this business of bombing the dams. There had been a few more details of planes and crews that weren't coming back, and her heart leapt in fear every time she heard more of the details coming over the wireless.

'If anything had happened to Tom, we'd have heard,' Irene said. 'I'm sure we would have heard by now.' But she was feeling jumpy and scared as the hours went by, waiting to hear the worst.

The one thing in Ma Ada's scrambled message that stood out was the bit about the planes that had dropped the bombs flying low over the reservoir. That's what Tom had told her he'd been doing, wasn't it? That's what he'd been practising. The more Irene thought about it, the more likely it was that he'd flown to Germany that Sunday night, and been a part of this operation. But where was he now? And why hadn't they heard anything?

As Irene left the house for work, Ma Ada was trying to be reassuring for the sake of them both. 'I'm sure he'll get in touch himself. He'll let us know that there's nothing to worry about. Because he'll know we've been listening to the news . . .'

'Yes, of course he will,' said Irene. 'When he gets a chance.' But days had gone by already, and he hadn't got any kind of message to them.

Oh, where are you, Tom? Irene thought, hurrying down Frederick Street on her own. Having half a story was terrible. She was going to be on tenterhooks until she got proper word . . .

Her day at the biscuit factory was a long and annoying one. Because of her nervous state she found that her temper was fraying, and she had no time for the joking and bantering of the girls. The work room seemed extra loud and even more raucous than usual that day.

Mavis's newfound noisiness grated on her nerves. The daft lass kept shouting, 'Uh-hoh! Uh-ho! Lovely! Lovely!' and giving a piercing laugh at everything that was said around her. Irene could tell that she didn't understand half of it, and that she was just chiming in. This should have made Irene feel sorry for the girl, but instead, that day she just felt annoyed.

She worked on the biscuits and tried to lose herself in the rhythm of the work. But really, how pointless it seemed! When all those thousands of miles away, young lads were risking their lives and dropping new-fangled bombs on huge dams and causing massive floods across enemy terrain. They were doing things that might just change the course of the war! And here she was, pressing out biscuits and popping them into little packets . . .

'Are you all right, hinny?' Mavis asked her, not for the first time that day.

Irene nodded dumbly, and tried to smile. At least Mavis was being less frosty with her since that supper at Number Thirteen. She had made her feelings known quite plainly – there was no way she wanted to be reunited with Mrs Kendricks. Irene could stop carrying messages between the two of them. So that was the end of that, then.

That was the last time Irene was ever going to get caught up in the middle of a family drama like that. No one ever thanked you for getting mixed up in their business like that. In fact, quite the opposite. Well, she was more than happy to back away from that mess now.

Still, it was a bit of a shame not to know the full story of Arthur and Mavis and their adoptive mother. But, if Mavis wanted it shushing up, then that was up to her. Irene had bigger things to worry about. This week all she could think about was her Tom.

She walked down Fowler Street with Mavis after their shift at the factory was over. They were both doing a couple of hours together at Franchino's.

The sun was out, lovely and warm, beating down on their heads as they loosened their headscarves and shook out their hair.

The streets of town were busy and it felt like a proper summer's afternoon. It was almost a shame to have to work for the rest of the day, although neither of them really found work at the ice-cream parlour arduous compared with the factory. It was usually a chance to catch up with each other's chatter and news.

Today it was Bella who had the most pressing news. They could tell as soon as they stepped foot in the place. She was bursting to tell them something juicy.

Irene was still tautly wound up with fear, but she was keeping those feelings locked up inside. No reason to unburden herself upon the others. They'd just talk about it endlessly and worry about Tom along with her, and all the talking about him would just make her fretfulness worse. No, best to put it all to one side for now.

She breathed in the wonderful coffee smells and basked in the soothing jazz music Bella always had playing. Then, having changed into her waitress's outfit, she joined Bella at the shining zinc counter.

'Eeeh, listen to this!' Mavis shouted, far too loudly. The customers at the nearby tables and banquettes peered round to see what was to-do.

Bella shushed her. 'It's not for broadcast, pet . . .'

'What's that?' Mavis bellowed, and sighing, Bella fetched out her order pad to scribble down the salient points of her news.

This was going to be it for ever now, Irene sighed. If Mavis's bloomin' hearing never came back, they'd have to be writing down all their gossip in telegrammatical form from now until doomsday.

'He stayed the night upstairs!' Bella wrote, in her distinctive, elegant hand.

Mavis squealed. 'Who did?'

'Who do you think?' Irene snapped. 'Is it true? Did you . . . Did he . . . well, you know?'

Bella laughed at her friends as they stood there all agog, lost for words. She ripped the top page off and wrote again, choosing her words carefully.

'"We didn't do it,"' Mavis read aloud. Too loudly and Bella shrieked at her, laughing.

'Shut up, Mavis man!'

'You didn't do it?' Irene asked.

'No!' Bella frowned. 'But he stayed the night. On the settee.'

'He stayed the night?' Mavis shouted. She was getting better at lip-reading. Now the elderly coffee-drinkers were definitely earwigging and taking an interest. Irene heard someone tutting at all their carry-on.

Bella was writing again now.

Irene was smiling, but this was seeming a bit childish and silly to her. They were behaving a bit like lasses at school, weren't they? With their daft giggling about boys?

Mavis leaned over the counter, reading upside down. '"But I did see him in the wuppy."' She looked puzzled. 'What's the "wuppy"?'

'*Nuddy*, Mavis, *nuddy!*' Bella shouted out, forgetting herself.

Mavis squealed and put both hands over her mouth. 'Eeeh, Bella!' came her muffled cries. 'You shouted nuddy! You saw him in the nuddy!'

Bella looked mortified.

Worried and irritated as she was, Irene couldn't help herself from laughing. 'You've got the whole of Franchino's listening in to your tales of naked men!' For a second, Irene found herself picturing what he might look like, divested of all his workaday, navvy clothes. Jonas Johnson, that red-haired Viking, the most handsome of the Mad Johnson clan. She blinked the picture away. What right had she to go picturing other fellas? In the wuppy or otherwise?

Mavis's voice was still much too loud when she asked, 'Did he take all his things off then? Upstairs here, you mean? Did you both do rude things together?' Mavis's eyes were out on stalks, and she seemed determined to get all the details. Ever since the happy consummation of her own marriage to Sam, Mavis had become quite the expert – and quite a keen one – on all matters sensual.

'Oh hush, Mavis,' Irene warned her. 'Bella doesn't want to shout out all her private doings in public!'

'I can't hear you, Irene. You'll have to write it down!'

Bella agreed with Irene – she wasn't mad keen on giving them chapter and verse right there at the front of Franchino's, what with all the old people's ears pricking up.

But she did tell them something. A little snippet and a detail that had weighed on her heart since Jonas had stayed overnight in her little flat. His injury. She could still picture that gnarled, ruined flesh, and the gap where his toes should have been. Even after seeing the rest of him and glorying in his wonderful masculine form, she was still drawn back to thinking about that damaged foot. It made her insides go chilly with sympathetic pain.

'His foot?' Mavis frowned, not understanding what Bella was trying to explain to them. Why was she describing the bloke's foot to them? It seemed a funny thing to go on about, didn't it?

But Bella wasn't talking about sexy or romantic things now. She was talking about the thing that had moved her to pity. She was talking about the injury that Jonas had shown her, so carefully and shyly. He had offered up the truth of himself to her, and Bella had found this very touching.

'He's missing toes?' Irene asked.

Bella nodded. 'He said it was an accident. With a gun. In the woods. When he first went to war . . .'

Irene let out a cry. 'Oh, an accident, was it?'

Bella was startled by her reaction. 'Yes, that's what he told me, yes. He—'

'I can't hear anything!' Mavis complained. 'What are you saying? Write it all down!'

'He *shot himself* in the bloody foot!' Irene burst out angrily. 'That's what he did! He's one of the Mad Johnsons. It wouldn't surprise me if it was no accident!'

Bella was appalled at her words. 'What are you saying?'

'Don't you see, Bella? He got himself sent back home. That's how he did it! He shot his own bloody foot off! And you're going on like he's some kind of war hero!'

'I–I'm sure he didn't,' Bella stammered. 'I'm sure he was telling me the truth . . .'

'I can't believe you'd give credit to a word he says!' Irene shouted. Next thing, with her face burning, she belted back to the staff room to fetch her coat and bag.

'Where are you going?' Bella cried.

'Home!' Irene shouted, suddenly tearful. 'I'm not hanging around here talking about bloomin' rubbish. I need to see if there's any word about my Tom!'

Chapter 48

They stopped Mavis singing with her brother.

'You simply don't have the talent, dear,' her new mother told her crisply.

Mavis cried for a bit at first. It wasn't fair – she wanted to be with Arthur in everything he did because they belonged together, didn't they? Where one went, the other had to go. And if all the world was looking at one of them, then it had to be looking at both.

Instead, Mavis found herself pushed out of the limelight. When Arthur sang at home for an audience, or they went to other people's houses, Mavis had to go and stand with Polly. Polly wasn't very sympathetic.

'You sound awful, that's why,' the serving girl told her. 'You spoil things.'

Mavis looked up at her with tears brimming in her eyes. 'I do not!'

'Yes, you do,' Polly said. 'I know you're doing your best, but your voice is horrible, Mavis. We've all got things we can do, and singing isn't your strong suit.'

'Well, what is my thing I can do?' the little girl asked her earnestly.

Polly took pity on her. Her toughened heart relented at the hurt look on Mavis's face. She felt bad for her raspy voice, her thin hair, and that occasional whiff of tiddle about her. 'You'll find something you can do, I promise,' Polly said.

'So what can *you* do?' Mavis asked her.

'Me?' Polly laughed. 'What's my gift? Ha! Nowt! There's nothing special that I can do. Cleaning! Fetching and carrying! Going round doing the bidding of my betters!'

'Maybe that's what I'll do, too,' Mavis said.

'Aye, maybe you will,' Polly said sadly.

The best thing about their new home being so close to the sea was being able to clamber over the dunes and the long grass to find a place on the sands for picnics. As the days lengthened and the sun came out, even their new mother would come with them to show them the best places to lay a tartan blanket on the ground and eat outside. They took small parcels of sandwiches, boiled eggs, tomatoes and a flask of pop, all packed up in a wicker hamper by Polly. It was so heavy Mavis had to help her brother lug it over the sand dunes.

They sat for hours in the sun by the sea, dipping the boiled eggs into paper packets of salt, digging and building in the sand, paddling in the cold waters, shrimping and netting in the rock pools. Elizabeth Kendricks watched them with an indulgent eye.

'Are you glad you came here, to live with me?' she asked Arthur outright one day, as he came to sit beside her. He was showing her the strange, whiskery creatures he had put into his bucket. Her question seemed to come out of the blue.

'Yes, we are,' he said automatically, knowing it was what she wanted to hear.

'Your lives couldn't have been anything very much before you came to me.'

Arthur wouldn't be drawn on this point. He tried not to think about their earlier lives. It didn't do any good to think about the dangers and privations they had faced. He did try to summon up a picture of his mammy's face each night before he went to sleep, and he tried to hear her voice again. It was getting harder to do so, as his new life crowded in and took up all of his attention. Only in his dreams did he seem to see and hear her with any clarity anymore.

Mavis was still by the shoreline, poking clumsily at the damp sand with her wooden spade. As they watched she dislodged a tangle of black weed and showered herself in wet sand. She squealed and Arthur laughed.

'You know,' Mrs Kendricks said. 'I feel I can tell you this, Arthur, because you're such a mature and grown up boy for your age. I feel like you'll understand.'

He was hardly listening really. Sometimes he found the things that Mrs Kendricks said made him feel uneasy somehow.

She went on, 'But this is all I ever wanted. This, here. Sitting out here today with my children in the sun. Something as simple and as straightforward as this. Not really much to ask for, is it?'

He shrugged. 'No,' he said, not sure what she was meaning. To him it seemed like a very great deal. This whole wonderful beach! This empty, bright blue sky and all that sea! All theirs, all day long!

'Children of my own to share my life with,' his adoptive mother sighed. 'Of course, I never anticipated taking on two of you. Oh, no. That was just how it worked out. Needs must. Really, I'd have been happy with one child. One little boy, who I could mould and shape into a proper little gentleman. A talented little boy whom I could lift out of his life of deprivation and hopelessness. And I could give him everything. Every chance at becoming something rather special.'

Arthur kept very quiet and tense. He felt like he was ready to spring and run away. What was she saying about Mavis? What did she mean? She never wanted the two of them? Mavis was just a kind of accidental extra?

'We must all make the best of the hand we are dealt, young Arthur,' Mrs Kendricks told him loftily. 'That is what life is all about. And so I took you both on. You are both my children now, and I am glad.'

Here came Mavis, trailing her liberated rope of slimy seaweed after her, a grin on her tanned face like Arthur had never seen before. 'Look at what I've got!' she cried, waving it about her head as she approached.

'Very nice, dear,' Mrs Kendricks sighed. 'Mind you don't ruin your nice new sun dress.'

Perhaps Mavis became aware that her new mammy didn't think as much of her as she did Arthur. Perhaps it was just obvious in the way that Arthur was treated, with his special dress-up outfits and his being put in front of everyone to warble for them. Small wonder that Mavis felt left out.

Polly thought there was rather more to it than that. The youngest child had had her nose pushed out, right enough, but she also seemed to pick up on the fact that she was merely being tolerated in the Kendricks household. She knew she wasn't really wanted there.

The way to be wanted and needed was to have a talent of your own, Mavis reasoned out, in her slow and deliberate way. To that end she started practising the one thing she knew she could do. It was the thing that only Arthur had any inkling that she could do.

It was her talent for listening in.

Like when she used to touch that long-gone shawl of her mammy's, and still pick up her scent and, if she tuned in very carefully, she could still hear the sound of her voice. Not just memories. Her mammy had been telling her new things. She could hear her quite distinctly. And it was a talent that Mavis knew was very special.

So she practised, in secret. When the others were busy and when they had forgotten all about her. She went round the vast rooms of the Kendricks house and touched things. The grandfather clock in the hall. She felt its wooden sides quiver with the weight of the gears inside. The fat, elaborate ginger jars displayed on the side table. The silver-framed pictures on the piano. She went round putting mucky fingerprints on everything. Curtains. Cushions. Pictures on the walls.

Polly, whose job it was to eradicate smudges and smears left by mucky-handed children, soon caught on to what she was doing. All those tiny fingerprints! 'What do you reckon you're doing, Missy?' she shouted, grabbing her by the elbow one day. She had caught Mavis clutching a pewter tankard in the drawing room.

Mavis squealed, shocked at being touched. She hadn't seen the maid creeping up on her. She wrapped both her hands around the dull silver mug and hugged it close to her chest. 'He's talking,' she said.

Polly frowned. 'Put that down at once. You're muckying everything up!'

'He says that *she* needs to watch out,' Mavis went on, in a voice that was strangely calm, and quite unlike her own. 'He says she needs to be kind to both the strays. She has longed for this all her life, Edward knows. But she must not spoil it. She must be fair or else she'll lose everything.'

Then Mavis stopped and put the tankard back on the credenza table.

'What did you say?' Polly asked her, seizing hold of her again and shaking her. 'What was all that about?'

'I don't know!' Mavis was starting to cry. 'I don't know what I was saying!'

*

296

Polly took her mistress aside after supper, after both children had been put to bed.

'Childish imaginings, Polly,' Elizabeth admonished her. 'That's all it is.'

'You wouldn't have said that if you'd seen the look on her face. All screwed up with the effort it was, and her voice went deeper, like a man's. Gruff . . . and the things she was saying . . . it weren't like things a kid would say . . .'

Elizabeth didn't have much patience with this kind of thing. 'Tell me again what she said.'

'It was about looking after the strays. Looking after both of them and being kind. And being careful not to lose it all.'

'Rubbish,' the older woman sneered. 'What drivel! That girl is having you on!'

Polly was red and flustered by now. 'But she said his name! She said it was Edward who was doing the talking . . .'

Now Mrs Kendricks was looking annoyed and even upset. 'Then she has heard me say the name. Or she read it on the tankard itself.'

Polly knew that Mavis was no good with reading, however. Plus, she also knew that Elizabeth Kendricks only rarely mentioned the name of her deceased husband. It would have been unlikely for the little girl to have picked it up.

'I think it was real,' Polly told her mistress. 'I think she was doing something weird.'

'Nonsense!' Elizabeth laughed. 'Remember, they said their grandmother lived in a caravan on Gypsy Green! She's just picked up some superstitious nonsense from her silly relations . . .'

Polly shook her head. 'No, I think there's something in this. If you'd only seen her face! Oh, it went so strange. I think there's devilment in this, Mrs Kendricks!'

Chapter 49

Of course, Irene felt terrible for telling Bella that her intended was a deserter who had shot himself in the foot in order to avoid active service. She regretted bursting out with this almost straight away. It was typical Irene, to come out with something when it was still a half-formed thought, and then to spend almost a week cursing her own spikiness and her quick tongue.

She even avoided going into Franchino's for her next couple of shifts. She sent a feeble message via Mavis that she wasn't feeling well, knowing all the while that Bella would know she was simply avoiding her.

'Bella's the last person you want to fall out with,' Beryl told her sensibly as they shared an early morning cup of tea. Irene had her daughter on her lap, and Marlene was steadfastly refusing to eat her porridge. Her red-faced temper summed up exactly how Irene was feeling, too.

'I know, I was daft to lash out at her like that,' Irene sighed. 'But when I think about those Mad Johnsons and all the bother they cause . . . and him – that Jonas – doing that! Damaging himself like that, just to come home. When our lads are . . . are . . .' Irene was close to tears, stumbling over her words.

Her sister-in-law eyed her solemnly. She had never seen Irene as highly strung as this. She was usually the one who managed to keep her cool head in times of uncertainty and fear.

Ma Ada came shuffling into the room wearing her dressing gown and hairnet, clutching Lucky under her arm like a hot water bottle. 'What are you two lasses whispering like thieves about, eh?'

'Oh, it's nothing,' Irene waved it away. She hadn't told Ma Ada about Bella's fiancé and his foot. She didn't need to hear anything else bad about that young man to confirm her opinion of him.

'We'd best be getting to work,' Beryl necked the rest of her tea and stood hurriedly buttoning her overcoat while Irene passed Marlene to the old woman.

'I've got both bairns all day,' Ma Ada grinned. 'What a treat!'

Irene couldn't tell whether she was sincere or not. Just lately Marlene had become something of a handful . . .

At the biscuit factory, Irene was hectored in a very loud voice by Mavis. 'You've made Bella feel horrible about her love life! Uh-hoh! Aye, it's true!'

'Oh, do hush, Mavis.'

'Eeeh, but she feels terrible. She was just on the point of giving her all to that young fella, but now you've gone and made her think he's a yella-belly! A deserter! Now she's saying she's gonna call it all off! Uh-hoh!'

Of course, everyone else in the work room was agog and listening in. Plump Mary shuffled over. 'Who's been calling who a yella belly, then?' she wanted to know. 'You've never been saying that about one of the Mad Johnsons, have you, hinny?' She stared at Irene in appalled dismay. There was almost a hint of admiration in her voice when she said, 'You have to be very careful. Accusing any of the Johnsons of this and that. Especially that!'

But Irene didn't care much for the stranglehold of fear they seemed to have over everyone else in town. She merely pulled a face at Plump Mary and told her, 'This is a private conversation.'

The big girl laughed raucously. 'Nothing's private when you're talking with Foghorn Mavis over there!'

'Aye!' Mavis chimed in, seeing that she'd been mentioned, but not sure how, exactly. 'Uh-hoh! That's right!'

'I'll say what I think,' Irene said, gritting her teeth. 'And no one's going to frighten me out of speaking my mind.'

'But you can't go round saying fellas are yella,' Plump Mary said. 'He could be a war hero for all you know.'

War hero my foot, Irene thought, returning to her biscuits. Or rather, *his* foot. But she knew that she was in the wrong. She had leapt to conclusions and shouted her mouth off. But she saw no reason to go explaining herself to the likes of Plump Mary. It was Bella she ought to be talking to . . .

There came a kerfuffle after the lunch-break hooter sounded, and Irene had an unexpected visitor on the factory floor. Three unexpected visitors, as Ma Ada came bustling in with both Johnny and Marlene tagging alongside her. The old woman was flustered and out of puff from steaming down the great hill of Frederick Street. She hadn't been inside the biscuit factory for years, ever since she had worked there herself as a much younger woman in a more carefree era. But she still knew her way to the packaging room. She came storming in like a locomotive, oblivious to the cries and queries from Mrs Clarke, the supervisor, who came hurrying in after her.

'Irene! Irene!' Ma Ada cried lustily, bellowing over the noise of the conveyor belts.

Everyone stopped what they were doing, shocked and alarmed by the intrusion. Oh, what was it now? Surely only bad news. Ma Ada was a well-known face in the Sixteen Streets and her advent here at Wights could only bode something momentous. And bringing those two startled bairns with her, too! What could it all mean, the lasses were wondering.

Irene stood very still at her work station, feeling all the blood draining out of her face. It was like going into some kind of terrible dream as she watched the old woman lumber heavily into the room, clap eyes on her, and then make her way towards her.

Oh God, Irene thought. It's happened, hasn't it? This is the news that I've been dreading.

And, indeed, Ma Ada was clutching a flimsy piece of paper and waving it aloft. 'Irene!'

Mavis was on her feet, getting herself between them and looking panicked, too. 'Eeeh, what's going on now?' Little Johnny was so confused by the noise he was starting to blub. Marlene stood there in her coat and looked crossly at her mother, as if outraged by the disruption to her day.

There was nothing for it but courage. That's what Irene needed now, perhaps more than ever before. This could be the worst news that she would ever receive in her whole life. In the next few moments everything could change.

Ma Ada waved the telegram in the air. Her face was red and glowing. She hadn't even put her teeth in before flying down the hill to see Irene.

'A-Ada?' Irene said, aware that every pair of eyes in the place was on them both.

Ma Ada stopped in her tracks, right in front of her daughter-in-law.

'He's alive! He sent us a telegram to say he's alive! Tom's all right, Irene! And he's coming home!'

'What?' Irene was sobbing and laughing in shock at the same time. She plucked the telegram from Ma Ada, but she could barely focus on the tickertape words. 'What does it mean?'

'He's been in sick bay since his last mission,' Ma Ada gabbled. 'Some problem with his lungs. He couldn't contact us before. Couldn't let us know – he's been out of it. But now – now he's all right! They're letting him out! He's coming home to us!'

'But . . .' Irene shook her head, trying to take it all in. Now Johnny was wailing loudly, and the women around her had picked up on her good news. They were cheering and clapping. Mavis had only managed to get the vague gist and she was yelling, 'What is it? What is it that's happened? Is our Tom all right, then?'

His lungs? Irene thought. He's been in hospital because of his lungs?

Ma Ada threw her hefty arms wide to hug the girl with relief. 'Let's not worry about all the details just yet, bonny lass! Let's just be thankful! Let's be as grateful as we can! Our lovely Tom's coming back to us and he's all in one piece!'

Irene found that she was crying as she bent lower to be enfolded in the matriarch's arms. The blessed telegram was crumpled between them and she felt like she had swallowed something huge. Something like a hot Christmas pudding was wedged inside her chest and it was choking her. She couldn't laugh or cry properly. She could hardly even breathe. Every emotion she had ever felt was welling up inside her and threatening to suffocate the life from her.

As the others cheered and cried out with joy, Irene simply closed her eyes, hugged Ada hard and tried to control her breathing.

It was all fine. Everything was all right. Tom was alive.

She looked up and hooked an arm around their daughter. Marlene submitted stiffly to the hug with a frown. 'Your daddy's alive, Marlene! He's coming home again! What do you think about that?'

Before Marlene could say anything at all, Mrs Clarke intruded on their family drama. 'Much as we are all delighted to hear your wonderful news, Mrs Farley, do you think we could save all this for later? For when the working day is over, perhaps?'

'Of course,' Irene said hastily. 'Ada, would you take the bairns back home. I'll be out in just over an hour . . .' She wiped her damp face with her hanky and folded the precious telegram safely inside her pinny.

Ma Ada was furious at being interrupted in the middle of this most important scene. She glared up at Mrs Clarke with great hauteur. 'There are some things in life more important than bloody custard creams, you know!' Then, seizing both children by the arms, she turned on her heel and marched stoutly out of the packing room.

Chapter 50

Devilment it may have been, perhaps, but Elizabeth Kendricks knew a good, intriguing thing when she saw it. And so did her friends from Sunderland and Newcastle and farther afield. Just when nearly everyone had heard Arthur singing once or twice, and had exclaimed fulsomely over his undeniable talent, suddenly there was another new novelty to take his place.

'You've never had so many parties and visitors for years,' Polly told her employer. The girl was in two minds about this. She liked the excitement and the glamour of all those people turning up in their fancy clothes, and she liked, in turn, driving Elizabeth's car to park outside other, even more elegant homes. But there was a lot of work to do to prepare for one of Mrs Kendricks' soirees. A great many canapes to prepare, and a lot of smudgy glasses to polish.

'It's all down to my orphans,' Elizabeth kept saying. 'Who'd have thought that doing a charitable good deed would improve my social standing by this much?' She laughed and gave an ironical toss of her head. 'People I've never seen for years are suddenly keen as mustard to get an invite to one of my evenings.'

It had all started with the boy. Arthur's frankly astonishing voice had been the initial draw and for several months it had been enough for them all to sit there, ramrod-straight and attentive, heads cocked appreciatively as they listened to his magical outpourings. Such golden, heavenly sounds from one apparently untrained! From one who had been scooped up from the dung heap by Elizabeth Kendricks in her munificence. Through the spring and summer, this had been enough to send ripples of enchantment through the beau monde of Tyneside.

But come the autumn, Arthur was being superseded. His own star wasn't dimming exactly, but there was another sparkling talent in the firmament – and it was his own sister. She who had had to be dissuaded from croaking along with his songs because she was spoiling them! She had uncovered an incredible gift of her own.

It had begun with Bernard Davis's golden watch. Then it had been Erica Beesley's hair comb. At the next party, someone's ancient mother had proffered a pearl brooch, and someone else – jokingly – their shoe. Week after week guests offered up new objects. Soon they were bringing ones they had brought especially, after digging around in cupboards and trunks at home. 'Tell me about this!' they would say, presenting their offering ceremonially, with a sidelong glance at everyone else sitting in Elizabeth's drawing room, as if to say: 'This one'll stump her! I bet she won't get anything from this!'

And it was true that sometimes, the little girl didn't hear anything at all. She took delicate hold of whatever it was they had brought for her – whether it be a brooch or a comb or a lady's shoe – and she would clutch it to her chest. Mavis would close her eyes and mutter to herself in her strange, rasping voice. This could go on for several minutes and the whole room had its attention trained on her, completely rapt.

Sometimes she might open her eyes and shake her headful of pale curls – no, nothing. Everyone's shoulders would sag back down, disappointed.

But other times!

The air went electric. There was a very strange ambience in the place.

Mavis would deliver one of her messages from beyond.

They were never very long. Sometimes just a few sentences. Other times just a word or two. But they were always quite convincing. She almost always said something that meant something very precise to the owner of the object in Mavis's hand. People were startled by the messages they received.

'He never loved you! You knew it, too and you both never said.'

'The money is in the alcove under the stairs in a brown package inside a boot! It's never been found!'

'She was never dead when you thought she was. She ran away! She just let you think she'd died!'

'He's not your dad. You always thought he was, but your mother kept it from you. And that's why he hated you!'

Her dry little voice – which always sounded like she needed to cough – would call out and quite often someone would gasp at the secrets she brought out. Then there would be murmuring excitement as the ramifications struck home. These really were long-held secrets bound up in the very substance of the objects that had been given to her. Many scandals and folderols were brought back to the surface and this was part of the fun of these soirees held by Elizabeth Kendricks. Who dare have their darkest, untold family secrets aired in front of their society friends? After the initial shock of Mavis's success rate, it became quite a fashionable thing to do.

'Of course, it can't all be true,' Polly said breezily, many times over during that autumn. 'The little monster is making everything up. She has to be.'

'I'm not so sure about that,' Elizabeth Kendricks said. 'The things she's coming out with are way above a child's understanding, surely? All those tales of indiscretions and crimes of . . . well, passion, and so on . . . What can she know, at her age, of adult matters like this?'

Polly pulled a face. 'They've seen a lot of life, them kids. The lives they lived before they come here; I reckon they're old before their years . . .'

Arthur didn't much mind having his limelight stolen by his younger sister, or so it seemed at first. In fact, at first he was proud of the attention she was garnering with her special abilities, though he worried about her at times. She went quite thick-headed and dreamy for almost a full day after one of their new mother's events. To him it seemed as if she was communing with another world and it was leeching away her energy. Perhaps one day that spirit world would snatch her away completely?

One morning, a few weeks into her sudden fame, he found her playing with brand new dollies that Mrs Kendricks had gifted her as a special reward for her psychic shows. The dolls came from the wonderful toy shop Rippons on Fowler Street, and they were almost taller than Mavis was herself. She was delighted with her presents and, to Arthur's eyes, was seeming just a little bit smug and full of herself.

'You know,' he told her, 'you don't have to do that thing for Mrs Kendricks' friends if you don't want to.'

'I like doing it,' she said.

'But, don't feel like you have to do it. She brought us here before she even knew we had talents. She was going to be our new mammy anyway, even before.'

Mavis looked up at him and her face was red. Her eyes blazed with an anger he'd only rarely seen. 'She's not our new mammy. She says she is, but she's not. She never will be. Our own mammy is still here. She's right by us. She's watching over us all the time. She's right here now, listening to every word you're saying.'

Arthur gulped. 'Mavis, you don't have to put the act on for me. I don't need to hear ghosts . . .'

'She's here! She's here!' Mavis raised her voice at him like she never had before. 'I'm close to her now. I can hear her now. When I do my listenings, it means I can hear her every day. She helps me!'

Her brother was worried for her. She was getting worked up about this whole business. It was like she was really starting to believe all this stuff too much. 'Mavis, Mavis, stop it now . . .' He went to take hold of her and hug her, but she thrashed around, lashing out at him, kicking him in the shins. She shrieked like a banshee, and brought Mrs Kendricks running from her drawing room.

'What on earth is going on here?' she demanded. 'You two never fight. You're always so good to each other. Whatever's the matter?'

Arthur was about to explain, and to tell their new mother that he thought his sister was doing too many of what she called her 'listenings'. It was turning out to be too much of a strain on her. All that attention from anxious, excited grown-ups. Not to mention the dabbling in unseen forces . . . Arthur was on the point of telling Mrs Kendricks that he thought that Mavis ought to give her newfound gift a rest.

'He's jealous of me,' Mavis said. 'He saw my pretty dolls from Rippons and he's jealous because he didn't get anything. Arthur likes dolls too and he hasn't got a single one.'

Mavis glared at him and Mrs Kendricks burst into laughter. 'Oh, Arthur! Say it's not true! Surely you aren't jealous of your dear little sister?'

He was appalled at Mavis. 'No! That's not it at all!'

'I think the pair of you might be becoming rather spoiled . . .' Elizabeth Kendricks said musingly, before leaving them to their devices and calling for Polly to sort out their squabbling. 'Perhaps I've been indulging you both too much . . .'

Polly came dashing in at the tinkling of the little bell. 'Yes?' She looked flustered and her hands were covered in sticky pastry dough. 'What's going on?'

'These two are fighting,' her mistress sighed. 'I suppose it's inevitable. But I don't need all this noise and aggravation in my home, Polly. See to it that they quieten down, would you?'

Just before Mrs Kendricks left the room, Mavis called out in a voice that was bolder and clearer than her usual one: 'Edward says you're doing a fine job. He says he wished you and he could have had children of your own. They'd have been better ones that these little urchins! You deserved the very best, Elizabeth. And he's so sorry that you have had to make do.'

When they all swirled round to stare at her, they saw that Mavis had gone into one of her queer trances again, though no one had asked her to. She was clutching a small framed photo from the piano to her chest and her eyes were shut dramatically. When she opened them, she found Mrs Kendricks' face only inches from her own.

'You spoiled little witch,' her new mammy shouted. Then she slapped her hard in the face.

Chapter 51

There was much excitement at Number Thirteen, once it was known that Tom was coming home. As yet, there was no further information on his injury or how long he was on leave for, but those details would just have to wait. The women of Frederick Street swept into action, preparing to welcome their wounded hero.

Ma Ada beamed from ear to ear as she mixed together vital supplies of flour and sugar to make a cake for her son. 'I was right, wasn't I? When I heard the news? That was him in the middle of that deadly mission! Bombing the German dams!'

Irene had to admit that it certainly seemed that way. Fancy their Tom being involved in something that had made the international news! But it didn't do her any good to try and imagine the particulars. The danger he'd been in filled her with terror. It would be better to let Tom describe it all himself, when he eventually made his way home.

The knowledge that he was on his way made her feel lighter and happier than she had for weeks. Even Megan's usual surliness and nasty comments couldn't touch her. 'I wonder if he'll be getting a big medal for what he's done,' Megan sneered.

This was over tea one afternoon. Beryl burst out, 'Well, if they do, it'll be no less than he deserves, our Megan. And you can stop it with your snide comments, thanks very much.'

Megan's eyes opened wide. She was used to Beryl being a walkover and never criticising her.

'Ha!' laughed Ma Ada. 'That'll teach you, Megan.' The old matriarch was quite used to refereeing between her daughters-in-law by now. She helped herself to bread and butter and enjoyed the spectacle of them glaring at each other. 'Wait till our Tom's back home! He won't put up with you lasses bitching at each other. He'll tell you all to behave yourselves. Men don't like all that cat-fighting!'

'We were hardly cat-fighting,' Megan muttered.

'Well, that would make a change, Megan Farley,' Ma Ada snapped. 'You could cause a fight in an empty wardrobe, you could. You're a saucy minx.'

This made Megan laugh bitterly. 'Aye, well maybe you won't have to put up with me for much longer, will you?' Then she was up on her feet and fetching her coat from the hall. As she belted it up she said, 'I'll try and nick some corned beef. I'll see what I can do.' She was heading off for her afternoon shift at the butchers on Fowler Street.

When she was gone, Irene frowned. 'What was all that about?'

'She often slips a couple of slices into her pocket,' Ma Ada sighed. 'I keep warning her: she'll be in bother if they catch her!'

'No, I mean that stuff about putting up with her for much longer. Where's she planning on going?'

'God knows,' shrugged the old lady. 'But it's the kind of thing she says all the time. Just to remind us that she's here.'

Irene bit her lip. 'I'm not so sure. She looked to me like she's planning something . . .'

That afternoon, Irene was back at Franchino's. After a few days off, letting things settle down between Bella and herself, the two friends were back to normal again. 'I'm so sorry for saying too much,' Irene hung her head in shame.

'You speak as you find,' Bella said, accepting her apology. 'And that's good. My papa would have approved of that.'

Irene knew that this was quite right and, as she changed into her waitress's smock, she wondered what Bella's papa would have had to say about his beloved girl running around with Jonas Johnson! She was absolutely sure he wouldn't have been very impressed.

But Bella had to go her own way. Just like they all had to. People had to be allowed to make their own mistakes . . .

'Coffee?' Bella asked her, as she joined her at the gleaming bar.

'Oh yes, please,' Irene sighed. 'We've only got that horrid chicory stuff at home and it gets right on my clack.'

'Your friend's back, look,' Bella said as she fetched down the heavy white coffee cups and saucers.

'Who's that?' Irene asked, and glanced over to see Elizabeth Kendricks swinging open the glass door. Today she was in an immaculate dark suit with boxy Hollywood-style shoulders and a chic little hat. She fixed a smile on Irene immediately.

Irene was ashamed to find her heart sinking at the sight of the woman. Well, at least Mavis wasn't in work this afternoon. That might well have turned disastrous. Irene experienced a small flicker of irritation – why did this woman keep chancing a terrible scene? Why did she keep coming here and demanding Irene's attention? She'd never asked to be drawn into this unfortunate tale.

'If you want to have coffee with her, go and sit and I'll bring it over,' said Bella.

Irene felt like saying, 'I don't really . . .' but it was too late. Elizabeth was clopping over in her fancy heels and greeting her friend and ally very brightly. Soon they were sitting over steaming cups of coffee and Elizabeth was telling Irene how wonderful it had been to have her visit her at home.

'You have no idea how empty and lonely that place of mine has been,' she smiled. 'To actually have guests and to spend a civilised hour or so in their company – well, it did my heart some good, I must tell you. It reminded me almost of the old days. When my little home was filled with lots of lovely friends, and wonderful music and laughter . . .'

Irene smiled awkwardly, remembering how stiff and uncomfortable both she and Sam had felt during their visit to Elizabeth's house. It had been a huge relief to be out of there and wait for the trolley bus home. And yet she indulged the older woman, smiling tightly and saying, 'We'll have to come again soon.' Sam would kill her for promising such a thing! 'Though Sam is rather busy, with his new job . . .'

'Ah, yes. At the biscuit factory, alongside both you and dear Mavis,' Elizabeth nodded. 'How cosy! Working close by each other like that.'

Irene smiled, and was about to launch into an explanation of her own restricted free time – especially now, with the news of her Tom's imminent return – but Elizabeth Kendricks' hand shot out and grasped her wrist. Irene was so surprised she gasped out loud.

'I'm sorry, my dear. But I find I must be brave. I must tell you the truth.'

Dread filled Irene. Oh help. What was coming next? 'What is it?'

'I haven't been quite open and honest with you.'

'What do you mean?'

'I mean, about my reasons . . . for all this alacrity . . . the very reason that I must insist on seeing my daughter and her brother . . . as soon as I can.'

Her face was very flushed and earnest-looking. Irene's heart was thudding fearfully as she tried to imagine what was coming next.

'I haven't lied to you about anything,' Elizabeth reassured her. 'But I haven't told you the whole truth, either.'

'And what is the whole truth, then?'

The grand woman took a deep breath and said: 'The fact is, my dear, I am dying. I've a matter of months left here on this earth. And I must – I simply must – make peace with my loved ones, before it is too late.'

Trying her hardest not to earwig on the clearly dramatic conversation Irene was having with her visitor, Bella carried on with her work. Mechanically she cleaned surfaces and cabinets and polished the nozzles and pipes of the coffee machine. Her thoughts returned to the plans she'd been brewing for weeks, for the expansion of her papa's precious business.

'When life gets back to normal,' was how she had put it, when she was discussing the matter with Jonas. 'When all this madness of the war is over.'

'Aye,' he'd nodded soberly. 'And when all that's behind us, and we can all get back on with our lives, I'll be right beside you – to make Franchino's ice-cream empire the greatest there's ever been!'

His enthusiasm for being involved in her business had struck her as rather touching at first. She had been glad to imagine a future of being married to a man who could help shoulder the burden and the responsibility of her family's precious legacy. And yet . . . and yet . . . suspicions had soon come stealing in. Irene's tart words about the reliability of the Johnsons – about them being criminals and gangsters – those words had lodged in her mind and they wouldn't leave her alone. With them came the awful thought: was the prospect of this marriage just a takeover deal, as far as Jonas was concerned? Was his engagement to Bella simply a way for his notorious clan to get access to the Franchino franchise?

Oh, surely not, she tried to reassure herself. And she thought about the love in his eyes when he was with her. Those bright green eyes, so full of clarity and honesty. Surely they were honest eyes? He had offered his whole self to her, so openly and readily. She thought about that birthmark, so bold and unashamed. There was no subtext nor subterfuge in Jonas. Surely not. And surely she was wicked for even suspecting that there was?

However, there was one thing she wanted to ask him to explain. Irene had sown a seed of doubt in her mind recently and it was going to flourish pretty soon if Bella didn't have it out with him. To that end, she had planned on leaving work early today and letting Irene shut up shop without her. She was going to see Jonas at home.

'Are you all right?' she asked Irene, shortly after that woman in the big shoulder pads had bid her farewell and hurried out of the front door.

Irene looked stricken. 'I'm fine. It's just . . .'

'Bad news?'

'Yes, very,' she nodded. 'Awful news.'

'Have you been sworn to secrecy?'

Irene nodded, biting her lip. 'I really wish I'd stayed out of this business.' She pictured herself on Mavis's wedding day, all those weeks ago. How she'd so blithely run after that Kendricks woman through the graveyard. Her own nosiness had led to this! She had no one to blame but herself.

'Well, I shan't probe,' Bella said. 'I'm sure I'll hear all the ins and outs in the end. In the meantime, I've got my own worries to see to . . .'

'Oh?' asked Irene, but there wasn't time to go into it. Bella was due at the Johnson household.

It didn't go very well.

Jonas was acting off with her. He wouldn't look her in the eye. He was monosyllabic. There was a bridling tension in the air and Bella didn't understand why. Surely it was her with the problem? She was the one feeling awkward and cross. What was the matter with him, then?

Eventually she had to ask him what the matter was.

Jonas looked at her and his face was pale with anger. The blemish on his cheek stood out starkly and his green eyes flared.

'I've learned what you and your friends really think of me,' he said, and his voice was trembling.

'What?' Bella couldn't understand what he meant. They were standing in the messy kitchen of the Johnson house on Tudor Road and the atmosphere was thick like there was about to be a thunderstorm.

'How dare you, Bella?' he said, in a low, dangerous voice.

Beside them the table was laid for a little tea that Lily had prepared. Tiny sandwiches and home-baked biscuits. The old mother's best china was out and ready to be used. All of this had been for Bella's sake, and now it was ruined.

'I'm sorry,' she said. 'I don't know what you mean . . .'

'I heard you. The other day. You and that Irene. Talking about me. When you didn't know I was there.'

'What?' she gasped. 'What were you doing? Eavesdropping?'

His eyes were cold and bright, boring into her furiously. 'Of course not. I'd slipped into the bloody ice-cream parlour, quiet like. Thinking I'd creep up and surprise you. Thinking it'd be a laugh.' He swallowed thickly. 'But then, while I was out of sight I heard you. The two of you. Talking about me.'

All at once Bella was filled with dread. 'What did you hear, Jonas?'

'I heard what you think about me,' he snapped bitterly. 'I heard you saying stuff you've never said to me. About my injury. About my foot.'

Bella's blood ran cold. Oh god, he'd heard. And she'd had no idea he was there. Which time was he even talking about? Bella and Irene had discussed the matter several times recently.

'You think I'm a yella belly. You think I shot myself to get home from the war.' His voice was hollow with anger.

'I never thought that. I never thought any of that. Not for myself,' Bella said. 'It was Irene. It was Irene who was saying all of that,' she protested, and couldn't believe how willing she was to spill the beans on her friend. Did she have no shame? 'Irene was the one who put the suspicion into my head. It was her who said it!'

Jonas listened to her with scepticism writ large on his handsome, imperfect face.

Then they were joined suddenly by Lily rushing down the stairs in a new print frock, eager to get their little tea started. But she perceived the nasty tension in the air at once. 'What's the matter?' she asked warily, from the doorway.

'Tell her!' Jonas growled at Bella. 'Tell her what you and that Irene were saying about me!'

Bella drew herself up and tried to regain her dignity. 'It doesn't matter. We should never have discussed it.'

'What?' Lily frowned darkly. 'What's going on?' She was furious that her special plans for a nice tea had been scuppered. What the devil had this girl been saying?

'Tell her!' Jonas thundered.

Bella gritted her teeth and said, 'It was just . . . me and Irene were talking about . . . whether his accident . . . really had been an accident.'

Lily narrowed her eyes. 'You what?'

'His foot.'

Lily pursed her lips. 'What about his foot?'

Jonas said, 'They were talking and I overheard them. Just the other day. Talking about whether I'd shot my own bloody foot off. In order to get out of the war.'

There was a dreadful silence then. Bella opened her mouth to defend herself but nothing came out. Jonas's summary had been pretty near the mark, after all. That was precisely what she had asked.

The diminutive Lily was glaring at her with green, hostile eyes. 'Get out of our house.'

'W-what...?' Bella asked, startled, as Jonas's sister advanced on her.

'I mean it,' Lily said. Her hand flashed out and she picked up the bread knife. 'Get out! And don't you dare come back!'

Bella gaped at her for a second, watching her brandish the bread knife. She realised: this girl could murder me, quick as a flash. There was nothing she'd put past the Mad Johnsons.

Bella told Jonas, 'I'm sorry . . .' before hurrying out of the room.

He stood there impassively by the tea table until he heard the front door slamming on her heels.

Lily was furious. 'That cheeky, stuck-up cow!' she shouted. 'Who does she think she is? Well, that's your wedding off, then!'

Lily looked at her brother. His face was like marble, and just as pale.

'Isn't it?' she demanded of him, sounding – if only she knew – just like her querulous and dominating mother always had.

'I guess it is,' Jonas said, and turned to limp heavily up to his room.

Chapter 52

Arthur went cold inside. When he looked at his new mother, Elizabeth, all he could see was her raising her hand to strike Mavis in the face. He recoiled, again and again, as he pictured his tiny sister's face receiving that shocking blow.

Who could hit Mavis? Who could ever bring themselves to? She looked so fragile and small. It would be like trampling on a little flower.

Mavis herself became very closed in and quiet after Elizabeth hit her. She withdrew into herself. She was shocked, but she was also determined to avoid doing anything else that would get her into trouble. There would be no more laying her hands on objects and telling their tales to people. That business had only caused trouble for her.

Arthur hated to see his little sister become so quiet and timid. She skulked around that house they were supposed to feel at home in, never speaking until she was spoken to, and meekly doing exactly what she was told.

'That lass is scared,' was Polly's opinion on the matter. She put her hands on her hips and shook her head sorrowfully at the thought of it. 'She was just coming out of herself before. She was even starting to blossom, that poor, plain little thing. And now she's been set right back.'

Elizabeth Kendricks was in no mood for any of Polly's nonsense. That maid of hers loved to mix up trouble, and she often took the orphans' side just to rile the mistress.

'Enough of that now, Polly. I want you to help me make some alterations this afternoon. I've not got time to send this dress back to the shop.'

Polly was all fingers and thumbs when it came to needlework, however. From downstairs Arthur could hear Elizabeth berating her for her cack-handedness. He was never sure what guided him that afternoon – perhaps some instinctive, unconscious need to prove something, or to make his new mother grateful and beholden to him – but he slipped upstairs and stood in the doorway of Elizabeth's bedroom. 'I can sew. My mother taught me.'

Elizabeth was over at the window, holding Polly's shoddy workmanship up to the searing daylight. 'What's that?'

Something in the boy's earnest tone made her take him seriously, and the next thing, Arthur was sitting on a stool in her room, bent very closely over the filmy peach chiffon of a dress even he could see was too young for Elizabeth. He was wholly absorbed in the task of unpicking clumsy stitches, working with a practised rhythm that Elizabeth found fascinating to watch. 'Your mother taught you this?'

He simply nodded and kept on with his work. He made alterations with ease, his mouth full of pins and his dancing fingers hardly ever pausing. He made that dress fit his new mother like a second skin and, when she wore it in front of her cheval mirror she could have swooned. 'This is miraculous. Nothing has ever fit me like this. Everything always hitches or bulges or twists around me awkwardly. They always tell me I'm an awkward shape to dress . . .'

Arthur shook his head. 'My mother taught me.'

Elizabeth beamed at him and flew to her closetful of expensively made but always unsatisfying dresses. Many of them had been bought for her by her late husband and she'd never had the heart to throw them out. They were unfashionable now, and all of them fitted her badly, but she would never have got rid of them. 'Could you . . . Could you make all of these fit me better? Could you alter them so that they look more up to date?'

Elizabeth Kendricks could have laughed at herself. How ridiculous! Talking to this child as if he could work miracles! And yet . . . yet there was something so intense and expert in his expression as he peered into her wardrobes at the softly hanging ghosts that had been there for so many years. 'Can you?' she asked.

He nodded, and she set him to work at once.

The boy was going to start earning his keep! she thought happily. He was going to bring her entire wardrobe back to life! All those disappointing garments were going to suddenly look marvellous on her . . . and Elizabeth was thrilled as she watched the boy work.

'I'm amazed,' Polly kept saying. 'What a worker he is! He barely stops to eat. He's working from first thing in the morning till it gets dark. He'll ruin his eyes.'

But Elizabeth thought it was worth the risk to his eyes. 'He's young. He can work as hard as he likes. And look, Polly! Look at what he's done!'

And then the pale carpet of her bedroom became a catwalk in a Parisian salon, with Elizabeth Kendricks swishing up and down in Arthur's latest repair job. 'You look beautiful,' Polly had to admit.

Mavis watched all of this going on with wary, hooded eyes. She stood leaning against the doorway of Elizabeth's bedroom. She stared at her brother, working away at yards of stiff tulle, cursing as the material snagged.

'Why are you being so nice to her?' she asked her brother at last.

322

It was an afternoon when Elizabeth had left them in the house with Polly. She had swanned off in one of her favourite new outfits to have lunch with friends.

Arthur shrugged, barely pausing in his work. 'She took us in and she feeds us. We're very lucky.'

'Mammy taught you to sew like that.'

'I know.'

'Our mammy would hate Mrs Kendricks.'

'You don't know that.'

'I do.' Mavis felt sure. 'She would say she's horrible, and she is.'

'She's all right,' Arthur said, though he didn't mean it. All he knew was that he was making the woman grateful, by fixing up all her clothes so that they looked nice on her. So that for once she actually felt good about herself and as confident as she pretended to be. He felt like he was casting a spell over her.

'You never play anymore,' Mavis complained. 'All you ever do is sew.'

This made him look up and smile at his little sister. She was quite right. He set down the fabric that was so tough and unworkable it was bringing up blisters on even his tough fingers. 'Hey, I know what we should do,' he grinned.

Next thing, to Mavis's delight, he was across the room, and opening each of the tall doors of their pretend mother's wardrobes. Mavis crept over to watch him unhooking long gowns and holding them up for display. He was behaving as if he was familiar with all of them. He was carrying on like he owned everything here.

Mavis giggled as he held them up to himself, one after another. 'Look! How's this? How do I look?' Something slinky from twenty years before, in cream silk. Arthur wiggled and sashayed across the carpet until he had his sister shrieking with laughter.

'Let's dress up,' he said. 'While she's gone!'

Then he was fetching out long evening gloves and stoles and beautifully patterned scarves and draping them around Mavis's neck. He darted into Elizabeth's dressing room with a black beaded cocktail dress and emerged, moments later, utterly transformed.

'Arthur!' Mavis gasped, appalled by this new version of her brother. He strutted into the room like no creature she had ever seen before. He moved with such instinctive grace, trailing one of those delicate scarves in his wake. 'Oh, Arthur! You mustn't!'

But all of a sudden he felt as if he must. He was seized by a manic devilment, completing a circuit of the luxurious room and gazing at himself in each of Elizabeth's many mirrors. He was marvelling at himself.

Then he seized other items of vintage apparel in every colour imaginable, grasping them to his thin, flat chest, and diving back into that dressing room. As he stripped them off each time and slipped into something new, he found he was trembling with excitement and anticipation. He had never felt like this before.

Mavis sat on the end of Elizabeth's bed, waiting for each new emergence he made through that mirrored door. She clapped and cheered, louder and louder at each transformation. When Arthur pinned on a dark wig and made himself look even more unfamiliar and glamorous, she howled with mirth and delight.

Arthur whirled about the room in a joyous cascade of fabric and a wild dance of disguised selves.

'More! More!' Mavis roared, stamping her feet. She hadn't sounded so happy for weeks.

Everything was wonderful until Polly came hurtling up the stairs to see what all the hullabaloo was about. She'd

324

been left in charge of the bairns and had spent the whole time in the kitchen, not paying heed and listening to her serial on the wireless. Now she was red-faced in the doorway of Elizabeth's room, surveying the scene of disaster.

There were dresses and precious items of the mistress's everywhere. On the floor, on chair backs, slung any old how. That little girl was rolling about on the satin bed coverlet, gurgling with joy. And Arthur! There was Arthur, standing in his underpants, with a backless, strapless frock sliding down his shoulders. He was standing quite still, staring back at Polly. He was frozen as if he was caught in a game of statues.

'You awful, selfish little buggers!' Polly wailed at last. 'What's she going to say when she gets back and sees all this lot?'

Polly's panicked words brought both bairns back to their senses. All at once they could see what an awful mess they had made. Wigs and hats flung just anywhere. Ivory, lilac and apricot lingerie ground into the carpet under Arthur's dancing, stamping feet. What on earth had they both been thinking of?

'You've got to help me tidy it all up,' Polly gasped. 'Before she gets back.'

So the three of them swung busily into action. They were united by their fear of what Elizabeth might say or do if she found out what had been going on. They worked busily to make the place shipshape. So concentrated on the task were they, that they didn't hear the front door opening downstairs, or the friend's car that had dropped her off pulling out through the gates. They didn't even notice Elizabeth hurrying up the carpeted staircase and they had no idea she was even there until she cried out: 'What's been going on here?'

Polly and the children were only halfway through making the room look as normal. There were still clothes strewn about the place. Arthur himself was still wearing that strapless gown. He stood there with bare, shaking limbs, staring back at his adopted mother.

'Would one of you care to explain yourselves?' Elizabeth asked, in a quiet, frightening tone.

Chapter 53

Mavis had company when Arthur came home.

If she had known he was about to turn up, she would have made sure the place was ready for him. She would be all prepared with a proper welcome. She'd have put the flags out for her hero!

But as it was, he came sauntering down Watling Street completely out of the blue and just about gave her a heart attack. The back door flew open and, even though she was still stone deaf, she could feel that someone had stepped into the house. Someone known and beloved.

'Arthur!' she squealed at the top of her voice. 'Eeeh, man!'

He stood there grinning in his long army coat. His hair was shorter than she'd ever seen it. He looked tanned and dark and delighted to be back. 'Hello, there, Mavis,' he mouthed.

That evening had already been a busy one, with Mavis and Sam sharing a light, early supper of spam and bread and some onions, from the allotment, which Sam had tried to pickle. They had come out a bit of a disappointment. Sam had announced he needed an early night for work tomorrow and was about to suggest that Mavis join him when they had their first sudden visitor of the evening.

Bella was upset and required a drink and an understanding ear. Sam made his excuses and slipped upstairs. Mavis took out her latest notepad and slipped it across the table so that Bella could explain what the matter was.

'So the engagement is off then, is it?' Mavis asked, once Bella had told her the highlights of her awful evening.

The Italian girl nodded miserably. 'He was furious with me,' she scribbled. 'And who can blame him?'

Mavis was still trying to understand it all. 'Do you still think he shot his own toes off?'

Bella pushed her hair out her face and rubbed her eyes with both hands. Then she wrote: 'I don't even know what to think anymore.'

'Hmm,' said Mavis. She had thought it was funny, right from the start, that the youngest Johnson fella had managed to get sent back home from the war.

'I really love him, too,' Bella wrote.

Mavis grasped her hand. 'If he loves you back, hinny, he'll come running and wanting to make peace with you. You'll see.'

'But what if he doesn't, Mavis?' Bella sobbed, forgetting to write it down. 'I'll just be on my own again. I thought I had someone. I thought I didn't have to be lonely anymore . . .'

Mavis squinched up her face, trying to read Bella's lips, and that was when the back door rattled and flew open in the kitchen behind them. Perhaps it was Bella's changed expression that alerted Mavis first, rather than some sibling sixth sense.

'What is it?'

'There's someone in your kitchen!'

And that was when Arthur came stepping into the parlour, large as life and mucky after a week's travel. Mavis flew to him squealing and wouldn't let him go.

Bella hurriedly dried her tears with a napkin and put on a brave face. It was hardly right to be bawling her eyes out in

328

front of a proper war hero. Because that's what Arthur was, true enough. He'd been right around the world, returning from the Far East. Facing Lord knows what kind of horrors in the jungle.

'What are you doing back already?' Mavis shouted at him at last. 'You've only been gone six months!'

He winced at the loudness of her voice. 'I'm allowed leave, aren't I? Besides, I read all about how you'd done yourself a mischief and had a dead body drop on you, and a horse, during an air raid and I simply begged them to let me come home. This is compassionate leave and I'm here to see what a palaver there's been without me.'

Mavis was glaring up at him in puzzlement as he gabbled away. Bella handed him the same pad that she'd been using up until a few moments ago, spilling her heart onto. 'You have to write it all down, Arthur,' she told him.

'What?' Then he stared at Mavis and his tanned face softened with pity. 'Oh, of course. You really have gone completely deaf, haven't you?'

Mavis got the gist of that. 'Uh-hoh! I have! Completely! Aye!'

Arthur sighed. 'This is going to be a faff, writing everything down.'

'We've all had to get used to it,' Bella said. 'We're just happy to see her back up on her feet again. She was quite ill you know, and it took her a while to get back to relatively normal.'

'Aye, that's why I came back as soon as I could,' said Arthur. 'ENSA aren't very happy with me, as it happens. They said, "It's not like there's been a death." And then I told them, "Then there's the other business, too. The other letter I got. That's another reason I have to go back." And to their credit, they let me travel all the way across the world again, all for a couple of weeks' leave.'

Mavis was staring at him uncomprehendingly and Bella poured him some of the brandy she'd been having for her shock. 'I don't understand. What was the second letter?'

'Well, I got letters from lots of folk, as it turned out, telling me everything that's been going on here. I've not really felt out of the loop. But then I got letters from a most unexpected source. I've no idea how she found me nor how she was able to start pulling strings with the army to make sure I got leave. But somehow she did, the old dame.' He slung back his brandy and sighed.

Bella said, 'You mean Mrs Kendricks!'

Arthur's eyes widened in surprise. 'So you know her?'

'She's been coming to Franchino's and sitting with Irene. Giving her all kinds of sob stories about the past . . .'

'Irene's always a soft touch for a sob story,' Arthur rolled his eyes.

Now Mavis was getting impatient. She burst out, 'Stop talking between yourselves! Write it all down so I can see!'

Bella mouthed to Arthur, 'Mavis will have nothing to do with this Mrs Kendricks one. She gets in a tizzy whenever her name is mentioned.'

Arthur frowned at this and started writing on Mavis's pad, 'I'm here for two weeks, pet. Can I stay here with you?'

Tears stood out in her pale eyes when she saw what he'd written. 'Of course you can! Uh-hoh! Uh-hoh! This will always be your home, Arthur!'

She hugged him hard and gave in to tears again and it was at this moment that Sam came downstairs blearily. He'd been woken by all the raised voices and had assumed, hearing Arthur's, that he was having some bizarre dream.

But Sam stepped into the messy parlour and, lo and behold, there Arthur was. Still in his army great coat. 'Eeeh, lad,' Sam said, 'you're looking well.'

Arthur met his gaze and grinned. 'Thanks, Sam.' He reached out and they shook hands. Perhaps shyly? Perhaps in a strangely formal way, for two men who had known each other practically all their lives? Bella wondered, watching them, what it was that put such a distance between two blokes? Men were strange, though. She couldn't even pretend to understand their ways.

'Two weeks you're back for?' Sam asked.

'That's right. It's ridiculous. All this way for just two weeks. But I've had special dispensation.' He wrote those words down for Mavis.

'Special dispensation?' she cried. 'Eeeh, you bugger! What's that? Have you got yourself in bother, Arthur?'

This made her brother laugh. 'Why, no!' he said. 'It's because I'm a star, that's what! It's because I'm the star of the whole bloody show!' And then he roared with laughter and seized his little sister by the waist to dance her around the room. 'Remember when we used to dance in here together? Practising and practising every dance we could think of? And then the singing, eh? My God, all the songs we learned to sing and how we belted them out in here! Well, it's all coming true, Mavis. Those hours are all paying off!'

'What? What?' she laughed, not following a word as he whirled her about. The other two were laughing at the pair of them.

'I'm a star!' Arthur told them all. 'They love me! All of them! I sing my heart out for all the boys and I've got them howling. They're begging on their knees just to touch the hem of my frock. They say I make it all worthwhile, my little troupe and me turning up in their corner of the godforsaken jungle . . .'

'Arthur man, slow down,' Sam begged him. 'Mavis isn't getting a word of this and you're joggling her around too much. She'll bring her spam back up. I'm dizzy just watching you.'

Reluctantly Arthur set his breathless, laughing sister back down on her chair and he fell into his. 'I am having the most fabulous war,' he grinned. 'I don't know why I didn't start it earlier.'

His sister's face was aglow as Bella pushed a hasty note under her nose. 'He says his shows entertaining the troops have been a big success. He says he's like a star!'

'Uh-hoh! Uh-huh!' Mavis beamed at her older brother. 'Why, I always knew he'd be a star! Aye! Aye! Of course, he is!'

But then as Arthur turned to smile at her words, her face suddenly crumpled. She looked stricken. Something terrible had occurred to her, in just that instant. 'Eeeh, but Arthur love. I'll never hear you sing a song, I'll never hear your beautiful voice . . . ever again!'

Chapter 54

Elizabeth Kendricks found that her own star was rising in the firmament of Tyneside society. It was all down to her two gifted children.

'You must bring these discoveries of yours to entertain my lot on Sunday,' she was told. 'We've heard so much about your prodigies! The boy's voice and the girl's peculiar talent for speaking with the dead.'

'She doesn't speak with the dead, exactly,' Elizabeth protested. 'She has an insight, nothing more, when she lays her hands on certain objects.'

'Nevertheless, you must bring them both, on Sunday.'

Whole evenings were planned in grand homes so that Arthur and Mavis could demonstrate their talents. Doors opened to Elizabeth that had never been open before. She had been known far and wide as a witty, wealthy woman. Somewhat acidulous in her manner, possibly as a result of her young widowhood and childlessness. Not everyone's cup of tea perhaps. Slightly vulgar, even, in that house standing ostentatiously by the sea.

But now everyone wanted to invite her. She should have been glad. But it irked her that it was only for her children that people wanted to see her.

She confided, as ever, in Polly. 'I wish I'd never started this,' she sighed heavily. Polly was fixing her hair for her in old-fashioned ringlets using twists of paper and a scalding iron. They'd had the same hairdressing ritual for years.

'What's that?' Polly asked, wrinkling her nose at the whiff of scorching.

'His singing. Her strange spells. I wish we'd never set them before anyone. I wish we'd kept it quiet. Now everyone wants a piece of them, and it's giving them ideas above their station.'

'Aye, it's true,' Polly nodded sagely. Arthur was forever boasting about his marvellous voice and he could be heard practising round the house at all hours. He went out to stand on the sand dunes under the vast empty skies, to sing snatches of Italian arias he'd memorised from old '78s, and he'd set off all the gulls that were nesting in the long grass. How they'd shriek!

And Mavis was becoming creepier by the day. Everything she touched – chairs, curtains, cutlery – could send her into a fluttery, eye-rolling trance. In Polly's opinion the two of them had become quite wearing. 'They'll be getting big heads,' was Polly's opinion.

Something important had shifted in their house, a profound alteration in the power dynamic. It had happened just after that day the mistress had been furious to find all her clothes strewn everywhere about her room and those children looking so guilty. Arthur half naked in one of her gowns. Spots of rouge on his cheeks. There had been a scene at the time and the two had been suitably punished, but their popularity in Elizabeth's social circle was such that she simply had to relent. She had to keep them sweet. And now, it seemed to Polly, it was the children who were calling the shots.

'And to think, only a few months ago, no one wanted them at all! They were starving on the streets!'

'What do you think, Polly,' asked Elizabeth in a troubled tone, as her maid yanked irritably at her thinning hair.

334

'What do you make of this business of Arthur dressing up in order to sing? Is it healthy, do you suppose?'

'Oh, but he looks so beautiful,' Polly gushed. 'Is there any harm in it really, do you suppose?'

Elizabeth pursed her lips so much she had lines radiating out at the sides of her mouth, almost like cats' whiskers. 'I'm not sure. It was all his own idea, you know, after I discovered him parading around in my things. He apologised and wept and made a scene, but then he came to me, a little later and said wouldn't it be wonderful if, when he was singing these songs that were, after all, written for girls and girls' voices, he could dress up like one?'

'He's a funny lad,' Polly sighed.

'He wants to start putting on a proper show when we go to people's houses. Dressing in my old things. Beads and bangles and what-have-you. He's had all my old wigs out. Tell me, Polly, am I right to indulge him? Will he turn us both into a laughing stock?'

Polly didn't really have an answer for that. The truth was, Arthur made a bonnier lass than his sister did and, when he dressed as a lady, it somehow seemed that his voice sounded better than ever.

'It's like watching someone special on the stage,' Polly said later that night when Arthur treated them to a dress rehearsal. 'He's like the real thing. A proper star.'

Arthur heard her and was tempted to grin. He just held his pose and took his bows. His face felt funny, all covered in make-up he'd borrowed from Elizabeth. It was the first time he'd worn it and let others apart from Mavis see. He curtsied and basked in their applause and waited to hear if his adopted mother would let him sing for her fancy friends on Sunday all dressed up, or whether her nerve would fail her. Maybe she'd be ashamed of him. His heart was beating anxiously under the thin beaded dress.

'You must dress how you wish when you perform,' she told him then. 'What do I know? You must follow your own instincts.'

The boy squealed with joy at this and ran to her. He clutched Elizabeth in the first genuinely warm and spontaneous hug she had ever had from either of the two children. She froze in surprise as he kept hold of her and she felt her heart melting, sadly, hopelessly, as both Mavis and Polly watched on.

'You're a brave lad,' Polly told him.

He looked at her strangely. 'It's just what I have to do.'

Then Mavis piped up, 'Will they still want me to do my readings?'

'Oh yes,' said Elizabeth, repressing a shudder. 'I'm sure they'll want to hear what you've got to say.' She couldn't help it. She felt repulsed by the girl's macabre gift. She didn't doubt the truth of what she did. It all seemed true enough. But it was wrong, somehow, and the girl didn't seem to understand that.

What have I done, bringing this strange pair into my home? Elizabeth wondered. Why couldn't I have rescued normal children? Simple, uncomplicated, loving, grateful children?

Sunday night came and Polly drove them to a house north of Newcastle. It was the furthest afield they had ever been. Even Elizabeth hadn't been to this particular home before. They were friends of friends. She had been recommended by word of mouth and, as the car accelerated on the winding country roads, she felt herself moving up the social scale. She sat back and wondered woozily how far it was possible for her to ascend into the Empyrean, riding on the coat-tails of her children's strange talents?

Ah, and weren't they loved by all and sundry? Even in this most grand and bohemian of homes. How the guests cooed and sighed over Arthur, already dressed up as Elizabeth herself, back in the twenties, with a little cap and a shoulderless dress, shimmering with gold embroidery. Beside him marched the solemn little figure of his sister in a black dress and shawl she had insisted on wearing. She had dressed herself up as a tiny Romany fortune teller, and all the Morpeth people were enchanted by her.

'How very unusual!' Elizabeth was told. 'How utterly charming! What very novel orphans you have brought us!'

And something inside Elizabeth reacted furiously at these words, though she would never let that show upon her face. As she was welcomed, and she and her children were ushered into this stately hall, and met these fancy and rather louche people, Elizabeth felt that she was being patronised. It was a new feeling altogether for her. These people were talking down to her. They were treating her as as much of a novelty as they were her children.

She took a drink – a lurid green cocktail – and observed as they assembled for the show.

Arthur and Mavis didn't let her down.

Arthur sang more finely, more thrillingly, than ever before and they all swooned.

Mavis went among them, eyes fluttering, tiny hands reaching out, her rasping voice changing with every mumbled message that she passed on. And they all shivered at everything she said.

And soon enough the little show was over and thunderous applause filled the room. Elizabeth found herself doused in congratulations and goodwill. It should have been making her happy. This was precisely what she had sought for years: acceptance in places like this, acknowledgement by people like this. But it all felt somewhat hollow.

As the evening ended and the guests waved Arthur and Mavis goodbye and the little family trooped back outside to Polly and the waiting car, Elizabeth examined her feelings.

I feel jealous, she realised. I'm feeling jealous of my own children. Yes, my star is on the rise in these rarefied circles. Just like I always wanted. But it's only because of them. I'm only following in their wake . . .

'I heard it went well tonight?' Polly asked, jauntily revving up the engine as they settled on the backseat, still in their stage outfits and worn out with all the attention. 'I stood in the hallway with the other servants and we could see and hear a little of the show . . . They seemed to love you! You brought that whole grand house down!'

'Just drive us home, Polly,' Elizabeth snapped. 'The children are very tired. They don't want all your chatter just now.'

'Arthur, you mustn't go too far . . .' Mavis was worried at how he was getting too big for his boots.

'I just want to see what else she's got tucked away in here.'

'She'll go mad, Arthur. You know you're not supposed to . . .'

'She loves it!' he laughed. 'She's getting as much attention as we are. And look at these old frocks of hers. They're all stashed away here out of sight. In bags! They're hanging in the dark. Well, will she ever get back into any of these? I don't reckon so. She must be twice the size as she was back then. It's such a waste, Mavis. I should be wearing these when I do my turn . . .'

'But Arthur . . .'

338

'Stop mithering, Mavis!' he snapped at her eventually, and plunged completely into the darkness of the wardrobe.

Mavis stood quite still, very careful not to touch anything. She didn't want to damage any of these precious gowns and accoutrements, but neither did she want any voices coming to her unbidden.

'Ooh!' Arthur's voice came muffled from the recesses of the closet. 'I think this could be her wedding dress . . .'

'We don't know what time she's getting back home, Arthur. Come out, won't you? I think I can hear Polly coming up the stairs . . .'

Arthur emerged with a look of triumph on his face. He held a buttercream dress up to the startling light. It looked very fragile and old-fashioned with its delicate lace neck and cuffs. It almost looked Edwardian. 'I think this really must be her wedding dress . . .' he said, lowering his voice reverentially. 'Mavis, take hold of it. See if you can tell.'

She snatched her hands back. 'No!'

Arthur licked his lips. He held the dress this way and that. Elizabeth must have been tiny back in those days. She must have been an altogether different woman. Why, it looked like it might even be too small for Arthur himself.

'Watch the door,' he said, with sudden steely determination in his voice.

'What? Arthur, no! You can't!'

But he could. And he was going to. While the coast was clear. His heart was thudding loudly in his chest as he threw off his sweater and his vest. 'Mavis! Watch the door!' he thundered. Then he flung off the rest of his things.

Mavis backed away, shaking her head. She didn't need her special talents to sense that something terrible was going to go wrong. And she really had heard Polly on the

339

stairs. It was laundry day and she'd be lugging baskets up and down. 'Arthur . . .' Mavis fretted.

But Arthur was in a world of his own. Holding the dress up to himself. Unhooking the pearl buttons. Were they real pearls?

The fabric felt so soft and delicate. Like a spider's web. Like gossamer.

He took a deep breath and stepped into the tiny dress.

'Arthur!' Mavis hissed. 'I can hear . . . someone's coming down the hall!'

And in that instant, the wedding dress tore from end to end. With barely a whisper of sound it simply fell apart at the seams and the gorgeous pieces slid onto the floor.

'Oh, Arthur . . .' said Mavis, just as Polly burst into the room.

Chapter 55

Those first few days after Arthur's return from Asia were like a whirlwind, visiting everyone he knew and all his old haunts, with Mavis tagging along after him whenever she could spare the time from work. He had never been so popular in all his life and had never felt as welcome in the place that was supposed to be home.

Arthur was a star now. Just as Mavis had always known he would be. In those few months he had been away – less than half a year – something fundamental had changed about him. Something had clicked into place, and he had become the person he had always been meant to be. Now he seemed fearless. Now there was nothing that could knock him off his stride.

'Well, to be honest,' he said, 'once you get used to slogging through the jungle, expecting to be attacked at any moment and hacked to death, then nothing can faze you. And once you've faced three hundred hairy-arsed soldiers on a Friday night, waiting to be entertained and reminded of home, then you'll never feel stage fright ever again!'

He told his same stories again and again, in Franchino's, at the Robin Hood, at all the little pubs by the docks. Wherever he went, groups of old cronies and familiar faces gathered to hear him, and Mavis basked quietly in the glow of his celebrity. Of course, she couldn't really hear what he was saying, but she'd had all his stories written down by hand, so she got the gist. She just loved to watch his expansive gestures and his wonderful malleable face as he acted out the roles of his various superiors and his gruff sergeant major and the men he had to perform with, and the Malaysians they had working to keep their show on the road.

In the Robin Hood he got up and sang for them all. Mavis had to hide her tears, pretending that it was just her pride and joy leaking out. Really, though, she was gutted that she couldn't hear a note.

Arthur stood by the battered piano and messed around with old Aunt Martha, who sat poised ready to accompany him, and he drew all the drinkers into his confidence. 'They love me because I'm the only man who can do both Gracie Fields and Marlene Dietrich!' he laughed. 'I can stretch – oh, yes I can! – from the sublime to the ridiculous!' Then he performed 'Lily Marlene' followed by 'Sing As We Go', the dour melancholy of the first song complemented wonderfully by the jauntiness of the second. The whole pub erupted with the voices of everyone warbling along. Everyone but Mavis, that is.

Sam hugged her. 'Ah, pet. You look sad,' he wrote.

'Aye, I just wish I could hear him! Uh-hoh!' she bellowed.

After drinking their fill and accepting a free drink from the landlady, Cathy Sturrock, Arthur, Mavis and Sam were about to wend their way back across town to Watling Street, but before they could leave they were caught at the door by Ma Ada, who gazed up at them challengingly.

'Hey you, funny fella!' It was what she had always called Arthur, from the first time she had met him. 'Why don't you come over to Number Thirteen for tea at ours tomorrow, eh? Sam will bring you. You'll be very welcome to sit in my parlour.'

Arthur smiled, almost speechless with surprise. 'I'll be glad to,' he told the matriarch, and said to the others, as they set off into the night, 'I suppose that's really acceptance round here, isn't it? Being invited to sit at Ma Ada's table!'

Sam couldn't help but agree. 'It certainly is, bonny lad.'

Arthur turned to give him a strange look under the moonlight, as Mavis walked between them. Bonny lad? It was a long time since Sam had called him anything like that.

'Eeeh! The stars are bright tonight, aren't they?' Mavis shouted. 'That's the best thing about the blackout, isn't it? Aye! Uh-hoh!'

She was too loud and a nearby sash window shot up in its casement. 'Shut your flamin' gob, woman!' came a voice from a bedroom window, and they scurried away.

'The most important moment, I have to say, was this,' said Arthur. Once again he was gathering all the attention to himself and knowing that everyone in the room was hanging on his every word. But today the crowd was smaller. He was sitting in Ma Ada's parlour and his audience was just the old woman and her daughters-in-law, plus Sam. 'This was the moment that I realised I was in the right place, doing the right thing, and doing my bit. It was after a show. Not an especially big show. It hadn't even gone all that well. The loudspeakers kept shorting out and I'd had to perform some of my act without a mike. And there was I, all dolled up as Rita Hayworth in this heavy, ginger wig made out of wool. And there was this lad, see. Still sitting there in his seat, after the others were all getting up to leave. And he was sobbing into his hands. He was crying like he couldn't stop.'

Ma Ada said, 'And you talked to him, did you?'

'I couldn't leave him sat there. No one could have. I thought, he's gonna get himself into bother, too, if he doesn't leave with the others. So I crouched beside him. All in my drag, you know. Well, you can imagine, can't you? I bet Rita Hayworth never smelled as sweaty as I did, after that show. I was absolutely dripping! And I asked him what the matter was. And do you know, he couldn't even put it into words. He just cried like a bairn. It was like he had to let it all out. Everything he'd been feeling for months. God knows what he'd seen out there in the jungle. God knows what he'd been through. So I just cuddled him. I crouched there awkwardly and cuddled him like his mammy would.'

Ma Ada took a hanky out of her cardy pocket and blotted her eyes. 'Eeeh, lad. That's a good thing you did.'

'Well, his mates were laughing and jeering. Some of them came by and took a look and shouted awful stuff. "You do know he's a fella, don't you!" Stuff like that. But I didn't move. And I let this boy have his whole cry out. He was shaking, Ada. Shaking in my arms and he was a skinny little thing. I had more muscles than he had, and I was the one dressed up as Miss Hayworth. When his crying died down, I told him, 'Now look, lad. You have to think about home. You have to think about everything you're looking forward to seeing again. One day you'll be back there and you'll be safe again, with them all. Think about your mam! Think how much she'll love seeing you again. And don't you go giving up!' Arthur shook his head and plucked up his packet of cocktail cigarettes: a pale purple one, this time. 'So that's what I left him with, and I hope it did some good.'

'I'm sure it did,' said Beryl.

'It's a lovely story,' Irene smiled, hugging Marlene on her lap.

'I bet his mates had his life after that!' Megan smirked. 'Seeing him cuddling another fella!'

Ma Ada shot her a look. 'He was being Rita Hayworth! It doesn't count!'

'Funny business, if you ask me,' Megan said. 'Dressing up in women's clothes in the jungle. Funny way to fight a war.'

'No one is asking you, lovey,' Arthur snapped at her, forgetting that he was supposed to be at a genteel tea party. 'Shall I go out back to smoke this tab, Ma Ada?'

'If you don't mind, pet,' the old woman smiled, delighted by his manners. 'It's the cat, you see. The bairns don't mind, but the cat starts sneezing, and it's pathetic to see.'

'I'm glad old Lucky is still going strong,' Arthur said, heading out to the scullery.

Irene followed him out to the back yard. 'There hasn't been a moment for us to have a word together yet,' she smiled, as she watched him lean against the mildewed red-brick wall and smoke so elegantly. He sent plumes of lilac smoke up into the air.

'It's good to see you again, Irene. And you say your Tom's coming home?'

'Day after tomorrow,' she grinned, looking excited. 'But we don't know what state he's going to be in. I mean, he's travelling up under his own steam, so he's not an invalid or anything . . .'

'But he was part of the squadron that bombed those dams!' Arthur shook his head, amazed. 'That'll be in history that. It'll be one of the things, maybe, that turns this whole war in our favour. He's part of history, Irene!'

'I just want him home,' she said, hugging herself.

Arthur was gazing at her levelly. 'Come on, hinny. Out with it. What is it you followed me out here to say? I know that look on your face. Ulterior motive, it says.'

She smiled ruefully. 'Can you really read me like a book?'

'A book! Stop flattering yourself, pet. I can read you like a four-page pamphlet in big type. What is it?'

Irene sighed. 'I don't think you're going to like this any more than Mavis did . . .'

He narrowed his eyes. 'Go on.'

'It's Elizabeth Kendricks.'

'Back on the scene, isn't she?' he mused. 'I heard about her, turning up unwanted at Mavis and Sam's nuptials. The silly cow. Of course Mavis went doolally at the sight of her! And then, of course, Elizabeth wrote to me, didn't she? She interfered with my superiors, pulling strings . . .' He took a long drag on his cigarette.

'She's been coming to see me,' Irene said. 'Because I was the only one who talked to her when she was chucked out of the wedding, she thinks of me as an ally.'

'Ally!' Arthur smiled. 'You're just a nosy parker. That's you, Irene Farley.'

'It is not!' she protested.

'You love knowing everyone's business, and being in the thick of it all,' he prodded at her. 'Just look at all the secrets you know about me, lady.'

'Yes, well,' she said, glancing at him, up and down. 'At least I'm discreet about what I know. Anyway, the point of all this is – it's bad news, I'm afraid, Arthur. She's very ill. She says she's only got a matter of months, or even weeks, to live. And she's desperate to see you and Mavis before the end. She's got things she wants to say to you.'

'Desperately ill, is she?' Arthur said, colourlessly. He scraped his golden cigarette butt on the wall, carefully putting out every ember. 'Well, I suppose the only proper thing is for us to pay a visit. Isn't it? Will you come with us, Irene?'

Chapter 56

'It was me!' Mavis kept protesting. 'It wasn't Arthur. It was me who fetched out your wedding frock, Mrs Kendricks. It was me who ruined that dress!'

Everyone was startled by the vehemence in her voice and the way she stared dead straight at her adopted mother as she said these words. Even Arthur was startled by her.

The girl was still holding tatters of the creamy satin and lace as she bravely faced her fate.

Both Polly and Arthur were wondering, why is she so set on taking the blame for this?

The little girl's eyes were blazing and Elizabeth Kendricks was startled. The three of them had stormed into her breakfast room and now they were kicking up an awful ruckus. And her dress! The dress that she had tucked away so long ago. What were they doing with it out? Why were they taunting her like this?

Arthur was about to step forward and do the correct thing. He was standing there in his vest and pants. Of course it had been he who'd been messing with the frocks again. But before he could intercede on her behalf, Mavis had gone rigid. She made a strange noise in her throat and all three could see that she was about to go into one of her routines.

Oh, not now, Mavis, Arthur thought. You know the old dame doesn't like it . . .

To everyone's surprise, Mavis's voice became quite light and refined. 'He doesn't really want me,' she said, clutching the panels of frayed silk to her skinny chest. Her eyes flicked back in her head, revealing the whites. 'He pretends, but I can see it in his face. It's too late for him to back out of it . . . Now he feels he must go through with it, or my father will shoot him through the heart . . .'

Elizabeth had gone pale. 'Stop! Stop it at once, girl! What the devil are you talking about?'

'But he doesn't really want me. He wishes he had never let it get so far . . . But he must do the honourable thing . . . Oh, Edward . . .'

Polly was standing with her mouth open. 'What's the girl on about? Who does she think she's being now?'

Elizabeth shook her head firmly. 'No, no. I'm not having this. I'm not being mocked in my own home. Not by a child. Not by an urchin.'

Arthur was worried by the anger in Elizabeth's voice. He reached out to shake his sister by the shoulder. 'Snap out of it, Mavis! No one wants to hear your trance today.'

But Mavis couldn't help herself. Her eyes flickered and she felt as if her vocal chords were working themselves. That's how it felt to her. 'Oh, Edward! Edward, forgive me! For trapping you. For being a wicked girl. I should never have tempted you . . . Will you forgive me? Can you be happy here, with me?'

Mavis was flinging out her arms and doing beseeching gestures like she was on the stage. Her adoptive mother looked like she recognised the melodramatic play she was putting on. 'Stop this at once, girl. Stop it!' She rose up and put her hands over her face. 'How dare you!'

Polly took hold of the little girl. 'She doesn't mean nothing by it. She's just got carried away . . .'

'Making things up! Making up evil stories. Well, I won't have it!' Elizabeth lowered her hands and took a deep, shuddering breath. 'I knew that one was trouble. I knew I should never have agreed to take both. But I let them talk me round. I let the Johnsons dictate to me. Well, she can go back! I can send her back! I'm not having this demon in my home!'

Arthur and Polly stared at her in shock as she hurried from the breakfast room. 'But . . .' Polly began.

Mavis was surfacing out of her trance. The sudden noise and all the shouting was scaring her. 'Arthur, what's going on?'

It seemed that Elizabeth wouldn't be deterred. Polly tried to reason with her. Arthur went up to her room and begged with her. Mavis sat where she was and felt scared. She knew what was going on all around her but didn't quite know what it meant.

'It's all right,' her brother told her. 'I won't let her separate us. No one can separate us.'

That felt like a knife going into her heart. Separate them? Whoever had said such a thing? Surely that could never happen? It must be impossible.

'I've tried. I've tried my best,' Elizabeth Kendricks said. 'For the good of us all I've given it my best shot.' She was brushing out her own hair in front of her dressing table with long, savage strokes.

'Oh, Elizabeth,' Polly said, taking a risk by using her name. Her employer hated that, but out it slipped. 'It would be cruelty, separating them.'

'I know. I know it would. But . . .' And here the older woman almost broke down. Her resolution was slipping, Polly thought. Perhaps her anger was losing its hold over

349

her. 'But you know . . . I've even thought about getting the Johnson people on the telephone, Polly. I thought about talking to Mother Johnson herself. I thought, God help me, that she could take this girl back. Find her somewhere else to go.'

Arthur was on the landing, listening to every word.

'But you won't, will you?' Polly said. 'You would never separate the bairns, surely?'

There was murmuring and quiet after that. Arthur couldn't be sure what was being said. His head was pounding as he listened at the door and his heart was racing.

What had Mavis done that was so bad? Only what she thought the adults had wanted her to do. And she'd lied about that wedding dress, in order to protect him. He couldn't imagine life without her. It was his job in life, wasn't it? His mammy had always told him so. His job was to look after his little sister, come hell or high water.

He couldn't stand for this.

'If you send her away, then I'm going, too,' he warned Elizabeth.

'Now, now, Arthur, you must listen to me,' she said, her voice suddenly sweet. 'You know that whatever I decide for you and your sister is surely for the best. Now, when you get older you will understand. Everyone has their place in this world. The right place to be. We all find our level. And sometimes all the shifting about and the adjusting can be quite painful. And our families can sometimes break our heart.'

The two of them were taking a walk along the sands towards Marsden Bay. The sun was out and it might have been a perfect day. From afar, what would they look like? The elegant and well-to-do mother. A slightly older mother, perhaps, but still glamorous. Blessed in later life by the arrival of this beautiful boy. Look how devotedly he walks alongside her. How neatly he's dressed. How attentive he is to her every word. What a wonderful picture they would have made to anyone watching.

Arthur's heart was seething with rage and frustration, though. He did everything to hide it from this woman who, he was now coming to realise, was his enemy.

She was still talking. Trying to explain. Wheedling and trying to twist him around her little finger. 'Surely you can see that your sister has caused some problems? She doesn't fit in quite as easily as you do. Not like you, my darling boy. Why, you took to our lifestyle so easily and naturally. Like a prince! But Mavis, I've wondered whether she might not really belong elsewhere. Somewhere more suitable. With people who are more like herself . . .' Elizabeth was musing and thinking aloud as they strolled along. She couldn't see Arthur's face. Of course she had no intention by now of separating the children. She thought she was merely explaining to him her thought process; talking to him as a little adult. Surely he could understand? She was telling him that he would have to help Mavis to change, to better fit in . . .

But Arthur was taking her words very seriously. He was taking them to heart. The boy was horrified. His heart was racing. The sound of the rushing surf and the crashing of the waves were smothering his thoughts. I can't let her get away with this. I can't let this happen . . . She can't send my sister away.

But what could he do? He was just a little lad. Elizabeth had all the money, all the power. She had bought the pair of them. It was up to her and her alone what became of them . . .

One thing he knew. He had to keep his counsel. He couldn't let her know what he was thinking or feeling. By now Arthur knew enough about being powerless to know that he should never show his true feelings. Not to those who had more power than him.

Instead he took a deep sigh and said, 'I understand, Mother. I didn't at first. But now I do. You have made me see sense.'

Elizabeth stopped walking and turned to him. Her face was all lit up with joy. 'Oh, I knew you would! I knew you'd listen . . . to your mother.'

'I will always listen to you . . . Mother,' he said.

Elizabeth's heart glowed. All she wanted was for Arthur to help Mavis fit in more. No one was going to be sent away. Not now all the anger had passed.

But Arthur's anger was only just beginning, and he was secretly hardening his young heart against Elizabeth Kendricks.

'Mavis?'

'What time is it?'

'Doesn't matter. It's time we went.'

'Went where?'

There was no moon on the night they snuck out of Mrs Kendricks' house. They knew that on moony nights the whole long smooth run of the beach was exposed and figures could be seen for miles, just as clear as in daylight. But it was three in the morning and no one was awake anyway. No one except the children.

'We can only take one bag between us,' Arthur said.

Mavis shrugged. She didn't want anything much. She looked at the dolls she'd been given at Christmas. Cumbersome, lifeless things with eyes like black jet. 'Where are we going?'

'I don't know,' he said. 'Just away.'

And it was remarkably easy to slip out of that house at night. Nobody stirred. It really wasn't like escaping from an enchanted castle at all. It was just a simple matter of finding the keys and slipping the bolts. Then dashing over the lawn and through the hedge, onto the soft sugary sand and away.

'But Arthur, Arthur . . .' Mavis kept saying.

'Shush! Shush!' He squeezed her hand till he knew it must have hurt.

'Won't she cry? Won't she be upset? Won't she be angry when she wakes up tomorrow?'

They ran across the sands and through the tangled grass. Everything was deep blue and pale gold in the faint light from the horizon and the smouldering smudgy light from the distant docks.

'Aye, she'll cry,' said Arthur. 'I reckon she'll cry.'

'Where are we going?'

'Back to South Shields,' he said. 'Back to the streets of our own town. Ha'way, pet. Don't cry. We'll find somewhere. You'll see. We'll find people who want us.'

Then they ran together, back to their town.

Chapter 57

They were halfway to Elizabeth's on the trolley bus before Mavis even realised where they were going. One minute they were sitting happily, staring at the clifftops and the bright, wide-open skies and then she was on her feet.

'No way! Nuh-hoh! I'm not going back there! You can't make me!'

All at once she was struggling down the gangway as the bus lurched along. She was heading for the open door at the back.

Arthur hurried after her. 'What are you doing? You can't jump off a moving trolley bus, Mavis man!'

The conductor was looking alarmed because that's exactly what Mavis seemed about to do. Arthur grabbed her by the arm. 'Mavis, listen to me!'

'I can't hear a word you're saying!' she shouted mockingly. She looked stricken as she stared at her brother.

'You look really frightened,' he said as she shook her head and tried to get away from him.

Irene was on her feet too by now and trying to coax Mavis away from the open door. 'Come and sit down, pet. We can't talk to you here . . .'

Relenting, Mavis flung herself back down in her seat. 'What did you bring me here for?' she moaned loudly. 'I know what you're doing! I know who we're going to see!'

Arthur patted and rubbed her hands. 'There's nothing to be frightened of,' he said. He wished the bus wasn't bouncing around so much, or else he'd have written the words down for her. 'She's just a lonely old woman who wants to see us.'

The conductor came to hover over them, looking worried. 'Is that lass all right? She was going crackers just then . . .'

Arthur glared at him. 'Mind your own beeswax.'

Soon they were deposited on the long, lonely road by the cliffs, with the prospect of the pale house belonging to Elizabeth Kendricks ahead of them.

'Maybe we've been daft for bringing her, and not warning her,' Irene worried. She glanced at Mavis and saw that she was rigid, expressionless, like a sleepwalker.

'I think you're right,' said Arthur. 'But I didn't think she'd react as strongly as this. I mean, when we left here, we were only little kids. Mavis was tiny. I'm surprised she can even remember it . . .' But even as he said this, he knew it was false. Of course Mavis would remember every single thing that had happened to them. Especially here.

Irene could remember the look on Mavis's face on her wedding day. The moment the radiant bride had clapped eyes on her adoptive mother she had transformed into a helpless, raging child. She had been filled with anguish, screaming until the woman had turned and fled.

'Well, mistaken or not, we're here now,' Arthur said firmly. 'We don't have to stay long. We'll just hear what she's got to say to us and then we can go. She doesn't have any kind of a hold over us.' Then he turned to squeeze his sister's shoulder. 'Are you all right, hinny?'

Mavis had a curious look on her face. It reminded Arthur of how she looked when she used to go into a trance. She was clutching her hand to her chest and, unbeknownst to the others, she was holding a certain locket tightly in her palm. The feel of the locket was welcomingly smooth and warm against her skin. It seemed to remind her of the insights she once had access to. She could almost sense those powers coming back to her. But the locket was tainted with a feeling of guilt, too. Whenever she touched it, Mavis remembered where she had taken it from. She shook her head as she stashed it away and her scrambled thoughts came back to the present moment again – to this awful predicament she was in. She shuddered at the very thought of once more meeting her adoptive mother. 'What does she want with us?'

The garden was tangled and overgrown. The windows were blacked out. Mildew and vines had encroached across the pale walls of the house. Close to, it looked as if the Kendricks place was going to rack and ruin. To Irene's eyes it looked even more neglected than it had the last time she had visited.

Elizabeth answered the door herself. She looked nervously excited, in a worsted suit with a pale blue trim. Her hair and make-up were immaculate, just as if she were greeting guests of great importance.

'You came,' she beamed, ushering them into her home. 'You came back to me.' She gave Irene an especially grateful look. 'I can't thank you enough for this, my dear.'

Arthur strode into the house, ahead of the other two. He took a deep breath and put everything into his performance. He was going to be brave and confident. He was going to use every ounce of the star quality he knew he had learned to exude. 'Well, here we are, in the old homestead!' he said grandly. He sounded falsely bright, he knew.

Mavis just looked glum and wary.

'Come and sit with me in the breakfast room,' Elizabeth urged them. 'I've made some tea. And I've even managed to get some walnut cake. That was your favourite, do you remember? I remembered that it was, so I did everything I could to get hold of some.'

They allowed themselves to be ushered into the familiar room, and seated themselves at the polished table, under the watchful eyes of all those Kendricks family portraits. Arthur watched her cutting the small slab of cake and was puzzled. Surely she meant ginger cake? It had been ginger cake both children had loved so much. She had remembered it wrong!

Once she'd served them, and poured out dainty cups of milkless tea and lemon, Elizabeth produced a rather smart pad of writing paper. 'I understand that I must write everything down,' she wrote to Mavis in beautiful, flowing script.

'Aye, I've gone stone deaf. Uh-huh,' shouted Mavis. She was still glaring at Elizabeth like she didn't trust her an inch.

Irene sipped her tea and wondered if she should somehow make conversation. She could ease things along. There was such an awkwardness in the air. Such a weight of unspoken things. She longed to fill that silence with happy chatter. 'Arthur's doing a smashing job of entertaining the troops,' she said, all of a sudden.

Elizabeth nodded and smiled. 'Well, naturally he is. I remember what he was like when he was here! And who encouraged you to explore your talent, Arthur, dear? Who put you in front of your very first audiences?'

He gave a wan smile. 'Why, you did, Mother Kendricks.'

She blushed and a breath caught in her throat when he called her this. 'A-are you still dressing up in ladies' clothing?' she asked.

'The men seem to like it so much,' he nodded, stirring his tea. 'I do Gracie Fields, Marlene Dietrich and Rita Hayworth. It's quite a faff on.'

'All those changes!' Elizabeth allowed herself a smile of amusement. 'What a lot of work you must put into it. And the boys out there must love it, though. I bet you're quite splendid. You always were. I'm so proud, Arthur.'

Irene watched Arthur smile tightly. He was trying to hide his pleasure and pride for Mavis's sake, but Irene knew that he was chuffed by Elizabeth's praise. He drank in any praise gladly, wherever it came from. Praise, attention and applause were the things that kept Arthur going. But praise from Elizabeth was especially well received, she noticed. So he was still that little boy, at heart. He was still that strange little lad who had found himself at home here, in Elizabeth's big house.

'Honestly, Irene. If you could have seen him,' Elizabeth was saying. 'I caught him, more than once, going through my wardrobes. Digging out all my frocks from my youth. Dressing up as soon as my back was turned! My maid, Polly, she used to come running to me, "Ma'am! He's at it again!"'

Arthur asked, 'Where is Polly? Is she not with you still?'

A shadow of regret passed over the older woman's face. 'She's with her people, in Darlington. Soon as war was declared she went back to them. Now she's working in her father's grocery shop, I believe, and looking after her mother. That's why this place is looking so dowdy. I have to do all of Polly's work myself, and I no longer have the energy I used to . . .'

Irene thought: she does look much less vital and healthy than she did when I first met her, just a few months ago. She looks as if years of misery have sapped her life away. And yet today, just having Arthur sitting here with her, talking to her . . . it seemed to be restoring her somewhat.

'You need to write down what you're saying,' Mavis reminded them loudly, through a mouthful of cake.

'Oh, yes. Of course,' Elizabeth said, hands fluttering over her notebook. 'We were just discussing Arthur's successes abroad.'

'Oh, aye,' said Mavis.

Elizabeth carried on writing. 'And what of your special talent, Mavis? Do you still use that?'

All eyes were on Mavis, then. Mavis looked surprised even to be asked. She remembered the fear and hatred in Elizabeth's eyes when she had channelled those voices out of the air. 'All that faded away years ago,' she shouted. 'I stopped being able to do that when I grew up.'

'Ah,' said Elizabeth, nodding.

Mavis didn't say anything about her recent feeling that her abilities were – perhaps – starting to return. She'd had some odd intimations since her accident, as if her secret senses were rising up again to compensate for the loss of her hearing. But she wasn't going into any of that today. Why give her secrets away to this old woman? Mavis found herself growing irked and impatient. 'What are we here for anyway? Why did you ask us to come, after all this time?'

Elizabeth let out a long sigh. 'If you recall, I've asked you many times over the years, to come and see me.' She paused while Mavis read her words. 'But you never did. It had to be enough for me to know that you were both well and healthy and living in your little house. You at least let me buy you that. So you'd have somewhere safe to live.'

Ah, thought Irene. So that clears up that little mystery. The mystery of the house on Watling Street. Elizabeth had bought it for her two little runaways and let them live there even though they never went to see her again. Not until now. She was amazed that neither of them said anything just then. Neither of them thanked her. They didn't say anything at all.

'I'd have loved to see you in your little house,' Elizabeth wrote. 'I had hopes that, when enough years had passed, we could all be friends again. When you were grown-ups.

When everything was forgiven. I thought maybe we could see each other.'

Mavis croaked with laughter. 'Friends! Are you joking?'

'Mavis . . .' Arthur touched her arm. He gave her a warning glance.

'You wanted rid of me,' Mavis said in a loud, accusing voice. The louder she spoke, the more blurred her words became.

Elizabeth shook her head sorrowfully. 'No, you're wrong. I spoke too harshly, and I never meant it, I . . .'

'You need to write it down,' Irene reminded her.

Elizabeth seized her slender, silver pen once more. 'I tried to take it back. Make amends. I never meant it. I loved you both. You must believe me . . .'

'No,' Mavis said. 'I don't believe you. Nuh-huh. You wanted Arthur. Not me. You didn't want me. I just got in the way.'

Elizabeth scribbled faster, her writing growing messier. 'But I loved you both. And you were my daughter. I thought I'd have you both here for ever. But you ran away. You left me.'

'You were going to give me back where I came from,' Mavis said. 'That's what you warned me.'

'It was never true. It never was. I'd never give you back to the Johnsons.'

Mavis read those words and instantly turned white. 'The Johnsons?'

Elizabeth stopped breathing. She nodded.

'You got us from the Johnsons?' Mavis turned to Arthur. 'Did you know this?'

'I . . . I *might* have . . . I don't know . . . it was so long ago . . .'

Mavis's face screwed up with confusion. 'What are you saying?'

360

Elizabeth wrote, 'It was old Ma Johnson. She took my money. Her boys brought you here to me. That was one of their businesses in those days.'

Mavis looked sick. 'The Johnsons? *They sold us . . .*'

'But you belonged to me,' Elizabeth wrote hurriedly. 'You came to me and I loved you both equally. Whatever was said in the heat of the moment, I'd never have let you go . . .'

Now Mavis was standing up. She was moving away from the table, muttering to herself. 'Does Lily know? Would Lily know anything about this?'

'Mavis man,' Arthur shouted at her. 'Come and sit back down. Does it matter? After all these years? Does it even matter where we came from?'

Irene tried to help. 'Come and sit with Elizabeth. She's got things she wants to tell you . . .'

Elizabeth wrote, deliberately controlling her emotions and making herself legible. 'I want us to make peace. I want to ask you for forgiveness. I don't have long on this earth . . .'

Mavis barely paused to read her message in full. She swung round to Arthur and said, 'But don't you see? If the Johnsons were the ones who brought us here, maybe they know what happened to our mammy? Perhaps they know what became of her?'

Her ragged words hung in the air. She stared at both her brother and sister-in-law beseechingly, desperately.

'Oh, Mavis,' Arthur said, and felt like his heart was breaking. 'Are you still hoping to find out, after all these years?'

'What?' frowned Mavis, trying to follow his lips.

Elizabeth hurriedly wrote out another message, even as all three young people were getting to their feet, leaving the dregs of their afternoon tea behind. 'Won't you listen to me? Won't you forgive me?' Elizabeth wanted to know.

Mavis was heading for the door. 'I don't want to stay here.'

Arthur said to his adoptive mother, 'Yes, yes, it's fine. Everything is fine. We both forgive you. It doesn't matter now. It was all such a long time ago. Mavis isn't herself lately. Her mind is on other things . . .'

Elizabeth could see her guests were leaving her. In another few moments they would be gone from her home for good. The reunion hadn't worked out the way she had dreamed. 'Oh, please will you come back? To see me again?'

It was Irene who, before she hurried after her friends, tried to reassure Elizabeth: 'I'm sure they will. I'll talk to them. We'll come again soon.'

Then the young people were gone. The front door crashed on their heels. They had hurried back outside into the surging tide of life. And once more Elizabeth Kendricks found herself alone in her big house by the sea.

Chapter 58

Ma Ada listened almost in complete silence as Irene told her the tale.

'And you all just walked out together and left that poor old biddy alone?' she said at the end of it. 'Her being ill and all alone in the world?'

Irene felt ashamed. 'I went hurrying after the others. What with Mavis being upset and all . . .'

'That girl's always upset.' Ada pulled a face.

It was the next morning and, just before work began at the biscuit factory, Irene was chatting over tea with her mother-in-law.

'Those poor bairns,' Beryl said, thinking of Arthur and Mavis, out on the streets when they were so young.

'According to Arthur,' Irene said, 'they went straight back to this woman their mother knew – Old Beattie – who worked at the fish market. She took them in again and let them work with her, but the next thing was, there were people looking for them. They thought Elizabeth Kendricks was getting people to hunt for them, so they ran away and lived on the streets for a while.'

'They'd have been better off going back to the Kendricks woman,' said Ma Ada. 'I've never heard the like! Kids running around, going feral.'

'I suppose Arthur thought that he had to protect his sister,' said Irene. 'They both really thought that Elizabeth was going to separate them.'

'I bet she never would have done,' Beryl said. 'Not really.' She tied on her headscarf thoughtfully, readying herself for work.

'Well, that's what she reckons now, that she never meant it at all. It was just an idle threat about separating the bairns. She would never have done it. The pair of them got the wrong end of the stick as to her intentions for them,' Irene shrugged. 'That's what she said yesterday, but who's to know what really went on in the past?'

'Aye, who's to know,' murmured Ma Ada gloomily, swirling the last of her tea around in her cup. 'And then she bought them their own house, you say?'

'Apparently,' Irene went on, 'she got a message to this Old Beattie at the fish quay. A solicitor went to see her and the woman was terrified that she was in trouble. Mavis says that there was a letter from Elizabeth addressed to the two bairns telling them that she wanted them both to come back to her, with all her heart. She wanted the two of them in her life. She would always see to it that there was a place for them to live in. And if they didn't want to return to her home to be with her, then she would find them something else. Nothing too fancy, but all their own. If they didn't want to come back to her, then she had made arrangements to make sure that they didn't have to live on the streets anymore.'

Ma Ada could hardly credit it. 'Is that even legal? Letting kids have their own way like that? Giving them their own house?'

'When you've got money, you can do what you want, I reckon,' Beryl shrugged. 'Right, are we off then, Irene? We're running late, what with all your gossiping.'

'It's not gossip!' Irene protested. 'It's important stuff this! I think it explains why Mavis and Arthur are the way they are. You know, a bit peculiar.'

'You can say that again,' said Beryl.

'Mmm,' said Ma Ada. 'I think I might just drop a line to this Elizabeth Kendricks. We're both connected by family in a way, now. I'm not quite happy about her being left out in the cold like this. Especially if she's not well . . .'

'You do what you think is best,' Irene told her. 'Right, come on, Beryl! Or else that hooter will be sounding!'

Across town on Watling Street, Mavis was already late for work and she didn't even care.

'Come on, love,' Sam urged his despondent wife. She sat at the breakfast table and she hadn't touched a thing. She stared blankly at Sam like she didn't even recognise him.

Arthur appeared, ready for coffee and cigarettes, already dressed and ready for the day. He seized Mavis's writing pad and pressed on firmly, 'I'm not having you turn all sad and mopey over visiting there yesterday.'

Sam was annoyed at the pair of them. 'What were you doing, taking her to see Mrs Kendricks? And why didn't you tell me first?'

'You were at work,' Arthur shrugged. 'And it seemed like a good idea at the time. A bit of forgive and forget . . .'

'But it's just stirred up even more bother!' Sam burst out. 'Now Mavis is just thinking about your real mother again and this business about the Mad Johnsons. What was it Elizabeth even said to her? And what right did that old woman have to go stirring up the past again?'

The past, as far as Mavis was concerned, was well and truly stirred up again now. It never really went away, did it? A few hasty, misplaced words from a sick, regretful, dying woman like Elizabeth Kendricks – that's all it took to bring the past rushing back like floodwaters. Like someone

365

had gone and set off bouncing bombs and blown up the bloody dam.

But the secrets of the past were always there, as Mavis knew. Yesterday was so close she could almost taste it. Those wonderful and terrible days when she was just a helpless kid, tagging along after her brave and brilliant brother. They were only a few breaths away. She was still haunted by them, every day of her life.

That morning after breakfast, she took out the locket she had stolen from the dressing table of old Ma Hendricks. Just before her accident. Before her bang on the head and this bloody, infernal deafness of hers. Back then, this worthless, cheap little locket had called out to her, from the tangle of jewellery and chains. She had laid hands on it, as she stood there in the middle of the old dragon's treasure hoard, and she had stowed it away. She had stolen it, knowing that it was somehow meant for her.

It had spoken to her in words too quiet to hear. It was like those powers of hers, which had been dormant for so many years, had started to wake up again . . .

'Arthur, look at this,' she told her brother. This was in the kitchen after breakfast, after Sam had gulped down his tea and hastened out for the biscuit factory. ('Tell them I'm sick,' Mavis said. 'Tell them I don't care.' Actually, the truth was, she did feel rather sick. She had thrown up once this morning, after a single bite of dry toast. Same as she had yesterday.)

'Look at what?' Arthur said, and took the locket from her.

'Have a look at the picture inside,' she shouted. 'Is that her? Is that our mammy's face?'

He frowned. The photo was so tiny and smudgy and old-fashioned. It was just a smear of old ink, really. And in his memory his mammy was so much more than that.

366

She was everything. A scent, the sound of her laughter, the feel of her hugging him. He looked at this tiny face, all these years later, and he just couldn't know. 'Where did you get this?' he mouthed, right into Mavis's face so she could follow his words.

Mavis told him. She was upset and her words ran together, but Arthur could follow most of them and got the gist. 'That old mother of the Johnsons, she had a heap of gold and chains and jewellery in her room. And I thought when I was up there, helping Lily to lay her body out, I bet it's all nicked. That's what those brothers and sons of hers have been doing for years. Pinching stuff from the dead. And now we know it's even worse than that, don't we? They were nicking and selling helpless bairns, as well . . .'

Then Mavis was sobbing into Arthur's shoulder and hugging him hard. 'What did they do to her, Arthur?' she cried out, muffled against his shirt. 'What happened to her?'

He closed his fist around the locket and he could feel his anger rising. Why couldn't he properly remember his mam's face? It seemed like the cruellest thing, the worst thing yet. Was it that long ago? Was she really that lost to them?

'Let's go round there,' he said.

'What?' Mavis could only feel the vibration of his voice in his chest. She looked up and asked him what he was saying.

'We're going to go round the Johnsons' house and we're going to ask them,' he said.

They were lucky to find Lily at home that day. It was her day off and she already had her hands full dealing with her brother, Jonas. 'He's been in a right state since he fell out with that Bella from the ice-cream parlour.'

'What?' Mavis frowned, following her friend inside the dark, cluttered confines of the Johnson home. The place had become even less inviting in the weeks since the old mother's death. It was like a dusty mausoleum, in fact.

'We've got something to ask you, Lily Johnson,' said Arthur, with a clipped formality that he seemed to have picked up in the army.

'Oh, have you indeed?' she smirked at him. She wasn't scared of Arthur. She had that one's number. 'And what's that?'

Mavis brought out the locket. 'This,' she said simply.

'Where did you get it?' Lily frowned. 'What's it got to do with me?'

'Mavis . . . uh, found it, amongst your mother's stuff when she died. She was drawn to it, somehow and the picture inside . . .'

Lily let out a squawk of fury. 'She found it? In my mother's stuff?'

'Apparently when she was helping you with doing the laying out . . .'

Lily was scandalised. 'You nicked it! You nicked this from my mother's room! Mavis!' And suddenly the wiry girl had seized hold of Mavis by both arms and was shaking her hard. 'I trusted you! I thought you were my friend . . .'

'Hey! Hey!' Arthur yelled, trying to get himself between the two of them, to protect his sister. 'Leave her alone!'

'You thieving little cow!' Lily cried, and shook Mavis so hard that she dropped the locket at once. Mavis was moaning in misery as Lily shook her and all three of them were suddenly embroiled in a tussle in the middle of the living room.

'What the hell's going on here?' came a loud, commanding male voice.

They stopped fighting at once. Arthur took a step away from the furious women and felt something go crunch underneath his boot.

It was Jonas Johnson who was staring at them from the bottom of the stairs. 'I was trying to get some bloody peace. What's all this screeching in here? It's like flamin' alley cats!'

'Jonas Johnson,' Arthur glanced him up and down. 'Well, well. I hear you've been upsetting my good friend Bella Franchino.'

Jonas had the good grace to look abashed for a moment or two, then he growled at Arthur, 'It's got bugger all to do with you, Shirley Temple.' Then he shouted at the two women, 'Stop fighting and tell me what's going on here. I'm not having daft lasses grappling and screaming in our front room.'

'This one nicked something from our mother on her deathbed!' Lily panted furiously.

Mavis shouted bluntly, 'Your family sold us! Your old mother sold us to that rich woman in the big house like we were slaves!'

Jonas's eyes widened. 'Sold you?' It was like the wind had been knocked out of him. He stared at Mavis in utter disbelief. 'Are you joking?'

Mavis clamped her mouth shut and her eyes blazed furiously.

Lily knew that it was down to her to explain to her brother. It was time to unpack one of the family's dreadful secrets. Just another long-held secret. It wasn't fair that she was the one who had to know these things. It was stuff like this that weighed heavily on Lily's shoulders. Now she looked at her brave, handsome brother and had to tell him the plain truth. She sighed deeply and said: 'No, Jonas, she's not joking.' Lily's shoulders slumped and she had to rally, to stand up straight and explain. 'What this daft deaf cow's saying is actually right, Jonas. You're too young to know about this. But it's true. Our mother – she did indeed sell young bairns. She took in strays and she sold them on. These two were among them.'

Arthur gasped at her. His tone was incredulous. 'So you admit it then?'

'Aye, I do,' Lily said. 'I was only a bairn myself but I was there, and I know. I saw what went on round here. She took possession of both you and your sister and she sold you on to Elizabeth Kendricks.'

'What's she saying?' Mavis frowned.

'It's all right, Maeve,' Arthur said. Then he looked down to see what had crunched under his boot in all the kerfuffle. Of course, it was the locket. The tiny sliver of glass had shattered. The locket dangled from its slender chain and the tiny photo dropped into his palm.

'It's all folded up, this,' he realised and very carefully he picked it open.

The woman on the photograph was beautiful. She wore a blouse with ruffles, like someone from a different age. When the creased old paper opened out like a flower it revealed that she had her arms around two little bairns. Two happy-looking bairns. A little boy and a younger girl.

Arthur's breath just about stopped. 'It really is our mammy. Mavis, you picked this up because it really was hers. It spoke to you, Mavis. It really spoke to you.' He handed the picture over to Mavis, who looked at him uncomprehendingly. Then she stared at the picture of her mammy and cried again.

'What happened to her, Lily?' she begged her friend. 'What happened to our mammy?'

Jonas didn't like the sound of any of this. 'Do you know?' he asked his sister.

'I do,' she said. 'And we'd better have a drink before I tell the tale.'

Chapter 59

Lily took charge. Just as her mother would have done before her, she suddenly rose up and started telling everyone else what to do.

She began with her brother, Jonas. The tall Viking stared down at her, utterly perplexed. Where did she get all this ferocity from? Who gave her all the answers? He stroked his moustache crossly as she told him: 'Now first of all, you get yourself down that bloody ice-cream parlour and you just tell that girl.'

'Tell her what?'

'That she belongs to you. That all this nonsense about your bloody foot has got to stop. She thinks you're a yellow belly who blew his own toes off to get out of the war, and now you've got to tell her that you're not.'

'She won't believe me,' he said, and he knew he sounded just like a surly child.

'Is it not true then?' Arthur piped up, very interested. 'Were you really shot in the foot by a German?'

Jonas glared at him. 'For all it's got to do with you, yes, as it happens.'

Arthur studied him carefully. 'Then your sister is quite right. Get yourself down that bloody ice-cream parlour and you just convince Bella. That's what you've got to do.'

Jonas stared at them. 'Will she listen to me, do you think?'

'From what I hear, you made her happy,' Arthur said. 'I like seeing friends of mine being happy. Just you make sure that you make her happy again. She's a good lass.'

'She's a wonderful lass,' Jonas said.

'Get yourself gone, then,' Lily told him. 'And then I can get on with telling these two everything I know about their mammy.'

Jonas hunted for his boots and put them on hastily. He was clumsy with his damaged foot and Arthur's heart went out to him. Imagine having everyone think you were a coward when you weren't. Imagine having the person you loved starting to think awful things about you! He smiled at the tall redhead when he straightened up and dragged his jacket on. 'Good luck,' Arthur told him.

'Aye,' said Jonas. 'Thanks.' And then he darted out of the front door.

'Now,' Arthur turned to Lily. 'What have you got to tell us?'

Lily took a deep breath. 'Follow me.'

It was harder, telling all of the story she knew, what with Mavis being deaf. She had to write some of it down and tell other parts slowly, very clearly, mouthing words as plainly as she could. Mavis was frustrated and annoyed, trying to follow everything that was said. Arthur held her hand throughout in that shrouded, funereal house.

Lily led them upstairs, where the old mother's bedroom was still set out as it had been on the day of her death. Nothing had been touched. The dressing table and its glittering freight of valuables still lay in a heap. 'It's a proper magpie hoard,' Arthur observed.

'That was my ma,' Lily sighed. 'She was a thief. All our family are thieves and liars and bullies and thugs. They'd hate me to say it, but that's what we are. That's what I come from. And believe me, I'm ashamed. I burn with shame. I've tried to make the best of myself and live honestly. But everything we've got – it's all built on generations of shame.'

Arthur eyed the pale-haired girl with a strange expression. He felt himself starting to look at her with a new respect. 'I'm surprised to hear you bad-mouth your own people like that.'

Lily laughed. 'They all knew what they were. And the whole of South Shields knew what they were. What my older brothers still are. They're gangsters. They're rotten to the core.'

Mavis was getting impatient. 'What are you two saying? Write it down! Write it all down for me!' She was pushing her notebook into Lily's hands.

Lily took out a pen and wrote: 'I had an uncle called Alec when I was a little girl.'

When he read this over her shoulder, Arthur felt a cold rush go through him.

'Eeeh, we did as well,' Mavis burst out. 'Aye, we did, didn't we Arthur?'

Arthur nodded.

Lily wrote more: 'He was a horrible pig of a man. He's in America now. He ran away. He went off on a ship to New York years ago. Ma gave him his fare.'

Uncle Alec, Arthur thought. It's the same horrible pig of a man. 'Go on, Lily.'

Lily wrote, 'He had to run away to America because of something that he'd done. Something terribly bad. I don't know what it was, but it must have been awful, for him to take off like that. The Uncle Alec I remember was fearless and loud-mouthed and heedless . . . But then he got scared at something he'd done. And he had to run away.'

373

The room was starting to whirl around Arthur's head. That dimly lit, unaired room was suddenly making him feel confined and sick. He had to sit down. The only place was the bed that the old woman had died on.

Mavis was frowning, reading Lily's words slowly. 'Uncle Alec? Our Uncle Alec?'

Lily had to think for a moment before continuing. 'He's probably dead by now. He was a horrible man. I bet he's come a cropper. Got what he deserved.'

Arthur said thickly, 'Did you have no clue about what he'd done, that was so bad?'

Lily looked upset. 'He said there was a girl who kept coming after him, begging. Saying she needed this and she needed that. Saying he owed her. Well, he never thought he owed her anything. But she wouldn't leave him alone. But she kept on showing him up. She came banging on the door here. I remember the scenes. I remember my ma getting furious about it. "Get her away from here, Alec. Another of your girls! Another one with bastards hanging off her skirts."'

Arthur asked, 'So what did he do?'

Lily said, 'I-I remember him crying here, sitting on the floor with his head on my ma's lap. All the story came out. My other uncles were all stood round, disgusted with him. Not cause of what he'd done, but because he was crying. I remember my ma saying, "And where is she now? What did you do, Alec?" And then he said, "She won't bother anyone now."'

'Write it down!' Mavis complained. 'Write down so I know what you's are saying!'

But neither Lily nor Arthur thought that Mavis was up to hearing all of this.

Arthur's voice was low. 'I knew it. I knew it was down to that bastard.'

'What?' Mavis cried. 'Tell me!'

Arthur took the pen. 'Mavis, you were right. All that time. Remember when you thought you'd seen what happened to our mammy?'

His sister went very still and white. 'Uh-hoh,' she said. 'I remember, Arthur. I saw our mammy falling down into the black water and the mud. And the man had pushed her in there. And she never came out again.'

Arthur wrote: 'It was Alec. Our Uncle Alec. It was him who did it.'

Lily didn't know what to say. 'I'm sorry. I . . . I knew all about this. All these years. And I couldn't say. I don't even know why.'

Arthur stared at her. 'You knew all of this? You kept it secret?'

'What good would it do?' Lily said bitterly. 'My ma would have killed me if I'd told anyone our family secrets. That's what it's like, being one of the Mad Johnsons.'

Mavis came to sit on the hard, cold bed beside her brother. She took the creased, brittle photo out of his hands and studied it. 'Poor Mammy,' she said. 'Our poor, poor mammy.'

'Look,' Lily said. 'Alec is probably long gone. This was so many years ago. It's best just to forget about it all . . .'

The room was still spinning inside of Arthur's skull. What a mess. What a horrible, violent mess. 'And you people – your family – were waiting to grab us. Me and Mavis. You grabbed us and sold us to the woman with the most money.'

Lily looked defeated. 'Yes. That's exactly what happened. But, Arthur . . . all those people who are responsible for all that misery . . . they're all dead now. They're all of them dead. There's only us. We're younger. We can make amends, can't we? We can go on with our lives?'

He snorted. 'Well, we have to, don't we? What choice do we have?'

Lily said, 'I've kept an eye on her, on your Mavis. All these years. Because I knew. I remembered. I knew that one of us had to make amends someday.'

The three of them sat still in the gloom of the dead woman's bedroom for a few moments. Then Mavis held up the photograph. 'I want to keep this. Can I keep this?'

Arthur said, 'Christ, does that mean Alec took it from her? He took that cheap gold chain and locket from her neck before he threw her in the water?'

Lily nodded. 'And brought it back here for his ma. For her treasure box.'

'Jesus,' said Arthur, and wept at last, for his mammy and everything they'd all been through, together and apart.

Mavis spoke up again, 'You can keep the locket I stole, Lily. But I'm keeping the picture. That's of me mam and me brother and me. And it's mine, do you hear me? Aye, it's mine. Uh-hoh. It's the most important thing I own!'

'One day,' Arthur said, once they were downstairs and Lily was fetching them another stiff drink, 'one day I'm gonna be a star on Broadway. Aye, you can smirk, Lily Johnson. But I can make it happen. I know where I'm going.' He wrote it down for Mavis's benefit. 'I'm gonna be a star in New York, on the stage.'

'Aye, you will be, uh-hoh!' Mavis tried to smile at him.

'And when I am, I'll bring you over the sea, Mavis. You'll be on a big ocean liner, travelling in style to New York City, to see your big brother on the stage.'

'Can I come as well?' Lily asked, testing the waters. She had told them awful things, but she wanted to make peace. She wanted things to be all right between them.

Arthur simply tutted at her. 'Well, maybe. You can look after Mavis on the voyage. This will be after the war is over and all the world will be wonderful again, and we can go

376

anywhere, do anything. And I'll be rich and everyone will know my name.'

'Aye, aye!' Mavis said, her face lighting up just a little, as she sipped medicinal brandy and sat on the old mother's armchair.

'And when we're in New York we'll look in all the phone books,' said Arthur. 'Why, I'll have enough money to hire a private detective, I should think.'

'What for?' asked Lily warily.

'Why, then we'll find out if old Uncle Alec is still in the land of the living,' said Arthur. 'And whether he's living like a prince or in a rotten slum or whatever. If he's still alive, it hardly matters to me. But do you know what, when I find him, I'm gonna go round there. And I'm gonna take him by surprise.'

'Aye, aye!' Mavis said, though she was no longer sure what Arthur was saying.

'And then I'll cut his filthy heart out,' Arthur added softly. 'Just like he cut out mine.' Arthur slugged back the last of his brandy. He held his hand out for Mavis to take. 'Ha'way, pet. We're due at the Robin Hood tonight, remember? Tom's coming home.'

Mavis stood up, feeling a little unsteady after her drink. She held out her hand to Lily.

'Lily?'

Eeeh, Arthur thought. After everything and all. That's how pure a heart my sister has. The daft little cow. Look at her. Holding her hand out to Lily Johnson.

'Lily, are you coming out as well? It'll be a grand do tonight. Tom's getting home.'

Lily smiled at her. 'Will I be welcome?'

'Ah, come on, pet. It's not your fault,' Mavis said. 'You've never been anything but kind to me. And that's what really counts in the end, isn't it. That's all that really counts.'

Chapter 60

Irene kept glancing at the clock above the coffee machine. She could fly out of Franchino's with only minutes to spare. It was only five minutes across the town centre to the railway station. She could set off at the very last minute and make it just in time. She had to be there. But she couldn't be late. No way could she leave Tom waiting for her when he stepped off that train.

The trouble was, Bella was upstairs. Irene was manning the counter all on her own during the busiest part of the day. It really wasn't like Bella to be neglectful, but today she had vanished up to her flat above the ice-cream parlour and she had been there for quite some time.

She was with him. Her fella. Of course she was. She was with the man who she had recently fallen out with. Jonas Johnson.

'I'd like to talk to you.' He had stepped up to the counter while Bella was working and given her a shock. 'Will you talk to me?'

Wordlessly Bella had stared at him. 'I'm not sure.' She had turned back to her coffee machine and the screech of the steam had filled the air.

'I've been walking around all afternoon, thinking about it,' Jonas shouted over the noise. He really didn't care that all the other customers were listening in. 'I've been thinking about us.'

378

Bella was pouring coffee and slamming cups and saucers down on the zinc counter. 'Is there still an "us"?'

'I think so, yes,' he nodded. 'I hope so.'

They sounded so deadly serious! Irene thought, listening to every beat.

'You let your sister chuck me out of your house,' Bella said.

'She's fierce,' he shrugged. 'She'd defend me to the last. And she knew you were wrong. You had the wrong idea about me.'

'I did, did I?' Bella asked.

Then Jonas started to grow conscious of all the old ladies standing nearby with their ears cocked. It was better than the pictures, this! Here was this tall, red-haired fella, beseeching the beautiful Bella for her love. Gruff as he sounded, he was begging her, they all knew. And she was proud and bruised, going about her mundane tasks very deliberately. Looking so pale and solemn with that ivory complexion and that mass of raven black hair. All her customers were waiting to see if Bella's heart would soften and relent and if she would look this proud man straight in the eye and see his honest feelings plainly.

'Talk to me,' he told her.

She nodded, and then she looked at him. 'Come upstairs.'

And that had been an hour ago. Slightly more than an hour.

Scribbling yet another order for coffees and ice creams in her pad, Irene found that she was losing patience. This was cutting it fine. Too fine. Irene would have to run out of here in her waitress's pinny with no time to change, no time to spare.

What on earth were they doing up there?

She hoped they weren't arguing. After everything she had been through, Bella deserved to be happy. She didn't need any more upset. Was Jonas really the man who could do that for her?

379

The teatime crowd of coffee drinkers and gossiping old people was showing no sign of abating. Irene glanced past the queue at the door opening once more to let in two more customers. Their smiling faces gave her a shock.

'Ma Ada! And . . . *Elizabeth!*

Ma Ada was in her nicest summer coat and hat, and she was looking very pleased with herself. Beside her stood the elegant, beaming Elizabeth Kendricks and together, the two of them looked like they had been best friends for years.

'I nipped up to her house on the trolley bus,' Ma Ada explained, with a careless shrug. 'Didn't I say I was going to? Anyway, I explained who I was – Mavis's new mother-in-law – and suggested that we really ought to get to know each other.'

'And I said we ought to come here,' Elizabeth smiled. 'Because your coffee here is second to none.'

Irene stared at them both in amazement. The last time she had seen Elizabeth she had looked so bereft and distraught. Today she was back to her immaculate, indomitable self.

Ma Ada said, 'I've told Elizabeth not to worry about Mavis and Arthur. I said, Mavis couldn't be cruel if she tried. She'll come round in the end. She'll accept Elizabeth back in her life again.'

'Oh . . .' Irene smiled. She wasn't quite so sure herself, but as ever, she admired Ada's optimism and her powers of persuasion.

'And so here we are,' smiled Elizabeth. 'And I've even been asked by your splendid mother-in-law to attend your welcoming party in the pub this evening . . . for your husband. That's all right, isn't it, dear?'

Irene was about to tell her yes, that was fine. She glanced at the clock. 'Oh, no! It's time! I'm going to be late!'

At this exact moment it seemed that Bella had suddenly remembered her duties at the counter. The private door flew open and she and Jonas appeared in a flurry. 'Irene!' she cried. 'I'm sorry!'

Irene couldn't help noticing that both she and Jonas both looked a bit flustered and red. But at least they were smiling. At least they weren't fighting anymore.

Ma Ada said, 'Isn't Tom's train due in about now?' She frowned. 'You've left it a bit late, Irene hinny.'

Irene was flinging off her apron and scooting out from behind the counter. 'I know! I know! I'm on my way!'

And then she left them. The whole lot of them. Ada and Elizabeth. Bella and Jonas. And everyone in the queue for the best frothy coffee in all of South Shields. She left them all standing there while she hared out of the ice-cream parlour and up Ocean Road, all the way to the railway station.

When she hurtled onto the platform she was fighting against the tide of people exiting the busy train. Only just in time, Irene ploughed through a jumbled mass of bodies, keeping her eyes peeled for her beloved Tom. She was feeling anxious right down in her belly; she wasn't even really sure why. There was something different this time. There was going to be something quite different about this leave of his.

The train doors were slamming closed again, one after another as the carriages emptied and already the station master was tooting his whistle. The frantic noise all about her only made her increasingly edgy.

Where was he? Oh, say he was here. Say he hadn't failed to get on his train. 'T-Tom?' she called, but it was hopeless with all the noise.

What if hadn't made it? What if he'd been taken ill? What if he was still down in Grantham, or in a hospital somewhere? Maybe they'd not been able to get a message to her. Maybe something terrible had happened to him and she didn't even know it yet?

'Hoy, you,' came a voice, softly at her shoulder, making her jump. Irene whirled around to come face to face with him. With the most familiar, beloved face in all the world.

Tom dropped his kit bag to the floor and his arms went about her. They kissed tenderly and everything in their little bubble in the world went completely still. The crowd streamed past them and the engines roared as the train shunted back out of the small station. The two of them stayed locked there together in their precious embrace.

'How long are you back for? You never said.'

'A little longer this time. Longer than usual.'

'Oh! I'm so glad, Tom . . .'

He smiled and she pulled back to look at him. He was different somehow. Hesitant, perhaps. Stooped, slightly. When he looked at her there was pain there. There was something complicated and unreadable in his clear blue eyes. Was he feeling pain now? Her heart was racing.

'Are you all right?'

'Just a bit short of breath. Just worn out from travelling. I'll be all right when we get home . . .'

She shouldered his heavy, lumpy bag for him. It was mucky and grease-stained from all his days of travelling. 'Let's get you back home. They all can't wait to see you. Marlene's talked about nothing else for days.'

She put her arm around his shoulders and was surprised to find him trembling and leaning into her.

'I can't wait to see them all,' he said.

Her heart roused fiercely in her breast for him. This man was leaning on her. She could feel him drawing strength

382

from her as they carefully trod the tiled steps down from the platform, out of the emptying station.

It was as if something had weakened him profoundly. He was home to recuperate and she would see that he did. She would somehow bring all his strength back for him. She knew that she would do anything to see him come back to his normal self.

Because he wasn't quite his normal self, was he? Irene knew that, as she led him through town, back towards the Sixteen Streets and the place where he belonged.

Chapter 61

'Ha'way in, pet! Your first drink's on the house!'

Cathy Sturrock gave them a huge, warm welcome as they stepped into the familiar, smoky confines of the Robin Hood. Almost at once Tom's eyes were smarting and he started to cough. 'You can't keep giving us free drinks every time I come back,' he laughed, through his wheezing.

'It's my pub, and I can do what I want,' she replied lustily, filling up his tankard. Like all of her prized regulars, he had a tankard of his own kept on a high shelf. 'And if I want to welcome back one of our local heroes with a pint, then it's the least I can do.'

Tom ducked his head, looking grateful and abashed. He hadn't actually said much about the mission he had been on, yet. Not to Irene, nor to anyone. There hadn't been time yet. But the way he smiled and looked away when Cathy praised him made his wife suspect that it might be a little while before he spoke openly about any of it.

'I'm just lucky to be back,' was all he had told her, on that walk back from the railway station to the Sixteen Streets. 'Lots of us didn't fly back the next morning. The most heartbreaking thing was the empty places at the breakfast tables, set out for the ones who were never coming back.'

He had been invalided out for a little while. He was recovering from some kind of infection on his lungs. He had his strength to build back up. He was thin and drawn,

Irene had seen that at first glance. That cough of his that had always disturbed her was even worse. It sounded almost like a hoarse barking. But she would see to it that he got rested and recovered, here in the bosom of his loving family. Their brave, wonderful airman would be back to rights before he even knew it. She was determined about that.

'Eeeh, I bet it's good to have him back with you,' Cathy smiled at her, pouring her a glass of stout. 'Where you can keep an eye on him.'

'It's wonderful,' Irene agreed. She felt like she was smiling through a worried frown, and fighting away her tears, though. Tom looked older and there were lines on his face she could swear had never been there before. There was something tight about his grin as he gazed around that busy bar at all the familiar faces. He disappeared into the crowd for a while, surrendering to their cries and embraces.

'I hope Bob gets home soon, too,' Cathy said. 'It's been a little while.'

'Have you heard much from him?'

'He's not one for writing, as you know,' Cathy smiled. 'But I know he's out there somewhere, thinking of me and looking forward to coming home. And that's enough for me on the long, lonely nights.'

Beryl appeared in the snug then, with Marlene holding her hand and baby Johnny in her arms. She had become the Farleys' number one baby sitter, even though she was the only one besides Mavis without any bairns of her own. She looked frazzled and unkempt, as if she'd had no time after work to get herself ready for an evening at the pub to welcome Tom.

'Ah, me bairn!' Tom cried, appearing out of nowhere to grasp Marlene up in his arms. She beamed at him delight-edly, transforming herself from sullen monster into angel child in a single instant.

'Me, me, me an' all!' Johnny kicked and wriggled in Beryl's arms, wanting the same attention.

'He's not your daddy,' Marlene glared at her cousin.

'Eeeh, listen to her!' Beryl laughed.

Tom hugged both babies as if they were his own. 'You don't mind the kiddas being in the bar, do you, Cathy?' he shouted at the landlady.

'Not seeing as it's a special night!'

Little Johnny's mother, Megan, had managed to find the time to doll herself up in a new frock that she'd bought at a rummage sale and taken several nights to alter to fit her perfect hourglass shape. She enjoyed making her entrance into the Robin Hood with all eyes upon her. It was rare that she ever made an appearance in that pub, given that the landlady had stolen her man, only the previous year. True, she herself had had no further use for him, but it was a matter of pride, wasn't it? Anyhow, she had broken her own embargo to be here tonight. It was a special night in the pub at the top end of Frederick Street, and Megan was damned if she was going to miss it. There might even be a few new fellas in the place . . .

'Mammy! Mammy!' Baby Johnny yelled at the sight of her, his hands reaching out across the crowd to be taken up in her arms.

'I'm surprised the bairn even recognises her,' Beryl muttered to the person standing closest to her, who happened to be Ma Ada. The Farley matriarch had arrived in the pub, all flustered and hot in her old-fashioned fur-trimmed jacket. She had raided her wardrobe for a special outfit to wear and was already regretting her choice. 'I'm far too hot in this,' she muttered. 'And I reek of mothballs, don't I?' She shouted at Megan, 'Megan Farley, take your bairn off Beryl, will you, hinny? She's not your paid nanny!'

'Mam!' Tom shouted and appeared in front of his tiny mother.

She gazed up at her son and opened her mouth to say a word of welcome, but nothing sensible came out. Just a kind of anguished squawk. She put out both arms, stiff in the old, uncomfortable jacket, and he gathered her up in his dark uniform. She felt her teary face pressed into his silver buttons and sobbed her heart out, not caring who saw them showing all their feelings in public. 'Eeeh, Tom,' she choked out. She looked up at him and didn't know where to begin. 'Eeeh, pet. Where have you been? What have you been up to?'

'I'm home for now,' he told her. 'You won't have to worry about me for a while.'

Ma Ada rested her head against the stiff material of his jacket and sighed. Yes, here was one of her lads she could relax about. For now, at least. One that she didn't have to pray for and picture and imagine what he was up to. Here was one that she could keep within her sights for a little while longer.

Aunty Martha was at the piano, clattering at the yellowed keys and thundering the pedals, and that got the place a bit livelier and noisier, as second and third drinks were consumed and she ran through her usual raucous repertoire of songs they could all get singing along to. Before long, all the houses of Frederick Street and the next two streets along were represented by delegations of happy faces come by to welcome Tom.

'Surely there's not a do like this every time someone is back from the front?' he smiled at Irene.

'They all know what you did,' his wife told him. 'They all know what you were part of. Operation Chastise. We've all listened to the radio and read about it. They won't ask you about it. But everyone knows what you did.'

He nodded. 'I'll tell you all about it . . . when I'm ready, Irene. I'll tell you the whole lot.'

'I can wait,' she said.

'But at the moment, if I think about it, all I can hear is the drone of the engines, filling up my ears. It's too loud to even think about talking. Let alone describing the whole thing to someone who wasn't there. It's just bloody deafening. That's how it feels to me . . .'

'I understand,' she said. 'You can talk about it in your own time. I'm just glad you're back in one piece. I'm just glad you're back here at home with all of us again.'

There was a whooping cry then, from the door of the saloon bar as newcomers made an excited entrance. Irene couldn't quite see who it was, but she saw Arthur coming in after them, bringing with him Mavis and Sam. Mavis was looking brighter and fresher than she had for weeks, in a new frock sprigged with spring flowers and her hair freshly set.

'You look lovely,' Irene told her, when she hurried over to kiss her hello.

'What?' Mavis bellowed. She looked at little Marlene, who glared suspiciously up at the deaf woman. 'What's that, pet?'

'I said, you look as if you're feeling a lot better?'

'Huh? Oh! Aye! Uh-huh!' Mavis nodded quickly. 'Aye, I've been busy, I have!'

For the first time Irene noticed that the little gang from Watling Street had brought Lily Johnson with them. The little blonde was in one of her showy gowns that she wore when she got up on the stage. Irene winced, supposing that that meant they'd be getting treated to one of her dreadful performances this evening. Well, at least other people seemed to get a kick out of them. 'I hope Ma Ada doesn't mind one of the Johnsons crashing the party . . .'

Sam appeared suddenly, still in his work clothes from the factory. His hair was awry and full of wood shavings from the despatch room, and his billowing shirt was damp with sweat. He was a blur of motion as he swept in to hug his older brother. They barely said a word. They just clung on to each other for a moment. For once in their lives there was no awkwardness between them. Just the simple joy and relief of being back together and seeing the other one safe. Things had changed, in the past year, since the loss of their Tony at sea. The Farley boys had learned – perhaps a little late in the day – how to express their love for each other.

Lily Johnson had muscled her way through the crowd to the piano, and was issuing instructions to Aunty Martha. Now she was clearing her throat and starting to sing.

'Christ Almighty,' Ma Ada was heard to mutter. A rare example of blasphemy from the old lady. 'I can't listen to that warbling all night. Arthur, will you get up there and shunt her aside? Give us a few of your numbers?'

'I'm not dressed right,' he frowned and pouted.

'I'm not asking for a full glamour show, you silly fool,' Ada laughed. 'Just bloomin' well get up there and sing! Knock that daft little tart off her perch.'

'Well, I quite like her voice, to be honest,' Arthur said, and it was actually true. There was something gutsy and honest in Lily's performances that touched his heart. She seemed to him like a girl who'd had to shout up, as loudly as she could all her life, in a noisy house full of boys and rogues and bullies, simply to be heard at all. 'But don't you fret, Ma Ada,' he grinned cheekily. 'I'll make sure I get top billing and put on a show for you!'

'Calling me Ma, indeed!' Ada cried. 'I'm not your bloomin' Ma!'

Arthur leaned forward and did the unthinkable. He took hold of the old woman's wizened, crab apple face, squashing it tenderly between both palms and then he kissed her warmly on the nose. 'You know what I think? I reckon that you're Ma to all of us. Every single one of us! Whether you want to be or not.'

Then he whirled away dramatically, leaving Ma Ada feeling rather flushed, silenced for once, and oddly pleased with herself.

Irene ducked across the room to welcome two more newcomers. They seemed delighted to be there. 'You're very welcome,' Irene told Bella and Jonas. 'Even you, matey. Even if you did put a brick through Ma Ada's window last time.'

'That wasn't me!' he protested. 'That was me brother!'

Irene mock-punched him. 'I believe you. And I'm glad to see you both here together. Does that mean the wedding's back on?'

'Well, we haven't got that far, yet!' Bella looked alarmed.

'Why not?' Jonas laughed. 'Why don't we just say yes? Why should we wait any longer?'

He was drowned out then by the shrill voice of his sister, Lily. The girl was sitting on top of the battered upright piano and she was waving her arms in the air, getting everyone to sing along with her. It was the old, old song, 'Cushie Butterfield'.

> *'When I axed her te marry us she started te laugh*
> *Noo, none of your monkey tricks for I like nae such chaff*
> *Then she started a–bubbling and roared like a bull*
> *And the chaps on the Quay says I's nowt but a fool*
>
> *'She's a big lass and a bonnie lass*
> *And she likes her beer*
> *And they call her Cushie Butterfield*
> *And I wish she was here.'*

'Oh, look,' Beryl nudged Irene. 'Here comes trouble.'

Rather nervously, and wearing a hat that made her look like she was attending a society wedding, Elizabeth Kendricks stepped cautiously into the saloon bar.

Luckily the music kept on playing. Everyone carried on singing and laughing and drinking. She didn't feel a roomful of hostile eyes were suddenly trained on her. The woman from the fancy house on the coast wasn't made to feel unwelcome.

She spied Ma Ada first. 'I came,' she smiled nervously. 'Thank you for the invite. You have made me feel brave.'

Ma Ada clapped her on the back. 'I'll buy you a drink, pet!'

'No, let me treat you,' Elizabeth said. She glanced round at the raucous, heaving-full bar. She hadn't been in such a place for a very long time. The curious thing was, though, she didn't feel as if she was out of her element. There was nothing off-putting about the Robin Hood or the people here tonight.

In fact, it was all rather cheery. It was lovely, actually, to be among people being so happy and excited and looking delighted to be together.

You'll oft see her doon at Sandgate when the fresh herring
   comes in
She's like a bag full of sawdust tied roon' with a string
She wears big galoshes tae, and her stockin's once was white
And her bedgoon it's lilac and her hat's never straight

'She's a big lass and a bonnie lass
And she likes her beer
And they call her Cushie Butterfield
And I wish she was here.'

'What will you drink?' Elizabeth asked the matriarch of the Farley clan.

'I'll partake in a little sherry,' Ma Ada beamed.

Then Mavis was standing there, between them. She had appeared out of nowhere. Her expression was unreadable as she stared at her adoptive mother.

Oh help, Irene thought. I hope we're not going to have a scene. I do hope Mavis isn't going to throw the poor biddy out.

'Mavis,' Elizabeth Kendricks began. 'I hope that—'

But whatever words the older woman had prepared in order to ease the way and to make peace between them were lost right then.

Mavis interrupted her, loudly.

'I'm going to have a baby! Aye! I'm going to have a bairn of my own! Uh-hoh!'

Elizabeth stared at her in shock. This was the last thing she'd expected. '*What?*'

Ma Ada almost choked. 'What did she say?'

Mavis yelled again, so that the whole bar could hear her announcement: 'It's my wonderful secret! I'm going to have a bairn! Uh-hoh! Aye!'

Sam appeared at her side. '*What?!*'

'No more fighting,' Mavis said. 'No more tears and crying about the past.' She eyed her adoptive mother and then slowly, haltingly, held up her arms to embrace her. 'No more secrets and upset. Let's just get on with life, eh? Shall we? Aye! Uh-hoh! That's what we all have to do!'

'Ts a broken-hearted keel-man whats ower heed in love
With a young lass from Gateshead and I call her my dove
Her name's Cushie Butterfield and she sells yellow clay
And her cousin's a muck-man and they call him Tom Grey

'She's a big lass and a bonnie lass
And she likes her beer
And they call her Cushie Butterfield
And I wish she was here.'

Chapter 62

Tom and Irene ducked out of the party as it was getting noisier and the room was getting smokier. They helped Beryl get the two bairns home and saw them to their beds. Then they wondered whether to have a twilight walk around the streets, just to take the air before settling down for the night.

'Ah, you two go and take a romantic stroll,' Beryl smiled, getting settled with her cocoa and a novel. 'I'll listen for the bairns.'

So off they went, back into the balmy evening.

'I've missed the sight of the docks,' Tom chuckled, as they ambled up the steep, cobbled street. 'Can you believe that? How could I miss the sight of girders and cranes and chimneys?'

'Because it's the sights of home,' Irene said. 'You grew up looking at this horizon, and all this view of the town. All the docks and the ships. It's majestic! It's wonderful! And the skies up here on nights like this. They're so dramatic . . .' The heavens were lilac and gold tonight, darkening into plum. Stars were coming out and it might have been Irene's imagination because she was happy and relieved tonight, but they looked more brilliant than usual.

'I can still hear the singing from the Robin Hood!' Tom laughed.

'That's Arthur singing now,' said Irene.

'His voice certainly carries . . .' Tom shook his head. 'He's singing Cushie Butterfield again. Is that Lily singing with him?'

'Eeeh, I wish we'd stayed to see the two of them singing together,' said Irene. 'That'd be a sight to see.'

'We can go back in there,' Tom offered. 'If you want?'

'No! I'm happy out here. Walking with you.'

'I thought so.'

They carried on stretching their legs, up to the top of the town.

From here they could see the harbour and all the way round to the sea. They could see the ships in the harbour and almost all the way to North Shields.

'I can smell the biscuit factory!' Tom said. 'That smell! I never thought I'd miss it, but I did. When we flew on missions I'd take a penny packet with me, just so I could open it and take in that smell. Like it was good luck or something. The others thought I was daft. Or greedy! Eating biscuits even when I was terrified. But I wasn't even eating them. It was just that smell. Like a little breath of home, sealed up inside that packet. I was inhaling it. To bring me luck.'

Irene clutched his hands and felt so much love for him just then that she couldn't say anything at all. She wanted to tell him: the penny packets were mine! I've been on with making them ever since I first started working at the biscuit factory. Every little breath you inhaled was like a kiss from me!

'Eeeh, Irene,' he sighed happily, squeezing both her hands and facing her. 'I think it's going to be all right. I just have a feeling about it.'

'About what, love?'

'About the future and everything. This war will be over and we'll all be all right. We'll be safe again. And life will get back to normal.'

'It'll never be normal again, pet,' she said. 'Too much has changed and moved about. It'll be new and different . . .'

'But it'll be ours, Irene,' he said. 'The future will be ours. When I get home for good, and we can get our own house. Somewhere closer to the sea, maybe. And we can have more bairns and be happy. Growing old together at last.'

'Growing old!' she laughed. 'I'm not sure I like the sound of that.'

'Oh, I love the sound of it,' he smiled. 'Growing old with each other in a home of our own, with everyone we love all around us. To me, that would feel like conquering the world.'

Irene told him, 'You're a funny 'un, Tom Farley.'

'I am, am I?' He took hold of her in both arms and whispered into her ear. 'Hey, do you remember that first time you came here? When we arrived in South Shields and the Sixteen Streets?'

'How can I forget?' she said. 'There were bombs falling all around our ears. I thought we were goners.'

'And we were fighting with each other, as well,' he reminded her solemnly. 'I thought you were foolish for wanting to be here. And I felt like an idiot for going along with what you wanted and bringing you north. I thought bringing you here was a huge mistake . . .'

'Aye, you did,' she said softly. It seemed hard for Irene to imagine now – a time when all this was new to her. The Sixteen Streets. Ma Ada and the whole Farley clan. Franchino's. The biscuit factory. Marlene hadn't even made her appearance back then. It was only a couple of years ago, but look how much had happened.

To Irene, tonight, it felt like her whole life. Everything that came before seemed so distant and long-gone.

'It was the right thing to do,' she told Tom now. 'This is my place in the world. It's where we both belong.'

'Yes, I think you're right,' he said. 'When I see you with my family, and with all our friends. When I see you in the centre of everything, at Number Thirteen or in the middle of that daft jamboree down there at the Robin Hood, I think you fit in here more than anyone, Irene Farley. You belong here more than most.'

'It's my home,' she said. 'It's always felt like that to me. But most of all, it feels like home when you're with me, Tom.'

They kissed.

The ragged, noisy music was still drifting up from the pub, as twilight deepened into a soft and peaceful night.

And back in the middle of that daft jamboree – as Tom had described the party at the Robin Hood – Sam was hugging Mavis. They stood in the midst of all the dancers and all the hullabaloo around them and cuddled each other as hard as they could.

'You're really having a bairn?' he grinned at her. 'Is it true?'

'Aye!' she shouted. 'I am, Sam Farley! And what do you think of that?'

'I reckon we'll muddle through,' he said happily.

'Oh-hoh!' laughed Mavis. 'I reckon we will, an' all!'

The End

Acknowledgements

Thank you to my agent and editor and all at Orion.

Credits

Elsie Mason and Orion Fiction would like to thank everyone at Orion who worked on the publication of *A Wedding for the Biscuit Factory Girls* in the UK.

Editorial
Rhea Kurien
Sanah Ahmed

Copyeditor
Clare Wallis

Proofreader
Francine Brody

Audio
Paul Stark
Jake Alderson

Contracts
Anne Goddard
Humayra Ahmed
Ellie Bowker

Design
Tomás Almeida

Joanna Ridley
Nick May

Editorial Management
Charlie Panayiotou
Jane Hughes
Bartley Shaw
Tamara Morriss

Finance
Jasdip Nandra
Afeera Ahmed
Elizabeth Beaumont
Sue Baker

Production
Ruth Sharvell

Sales
Jen Wilson
Esther Waters

Victoria Laws
Rachael Hum
Anna Egelstaff
Frances Doyle
Georgina Cutler

Operations
Jo Jacobs
Sharon Willis

Also by Elsie Mason

The Biscuit Factory Girls

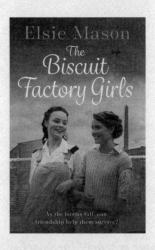

Can Irene find a new home by the docks?

Newly married to dashing RAF officer, Tom, Irene
Farley leaves behind her safe countryside life to move
in with his family by the docks in South Shields. Little
prepares her for the devastation the Jerry bombers have
wreaked on the Sixteen Streets or the fact that they
would be living under her mother-in-law's roof, alongside
Tom's three brothers and two wives!

Irene's only escape is her job at the local Wright's Biscuit
factory packing up a little taste of home for the brave
boys fighting for King and country across the channel. As
the threat of war creeps ever closer to the Sixteen Streets,
the biscuit factory girls bond together, because no one
can get through this war alone . . .

The Biscuit Factory Girls at War

Home is where the heart is . . .

Beryl was the first Farley clan bride, finding a home in the arms of loving, attentive, elder son Tony. Yet even now, wrapped in Tony's embrace, Beryl has never quite been able to forget the past she ran away from, nor the shocking family secret she tried to bury.

With Tony away fighting the Jerries alongside his brothers, it's up to Beryl and her sisters-in-law to keep the family afloat. Hard, gruelling work doesn't faze her, but the sudden arrival of a devastating letter does . . .

Will Beryl be able to hold her family together and face up to her past? Or will the war take away the one thing she holds most dear - the one person she never thought she deserved?